The Realm of Pain

The Hars Ticlarim was an empire built on the suffering of others. Its builders wanted it that way. They didn't want to take responsibility for their own spells; they didn't want to limit what they could do merely to defense. More magic use meant that they could expand the empire, or keep in line the parts of it already acquired. But what wizard would use magic if he had to take the cost of the spell from his own flesh and blood and bones and life? Why would he do that, when he could channel both the power to fuel his spell and the rebound from it into caged creatures that he had convinced himself were not truly human? Who was going to overturn three thousand years of "this is the way we do things"?

Praise for Holly Lisle's The Secret Texts

"A grand adventure."

—*Locus*

"Tension-filled . . . a worthy successor to the works of Tolkien. . . . The pacing is fast, the dialogue believable. The writing is poetic and lyrical, celebrating all the joys of living."

—*VOYA*

"Rousing."

—*Science Fiction Chronicle*

"Carefully crafted and well thought out . . . wonderful."

—*SF Site*

BOOKS BY HOLLY LISLE

The Secret Texts Trilogy
Diplomacy of Wolves
Vengeance of Dragons
Courage of Falcons

Available from Warner Aspect

VINCALIS
THE AGITATOR

HOLLY LISLE

ASPECT®

WARNER BOOKS

An AOL Time Warner Company

Aspect® name and logo are registered trademarks of Warner Books, Inc.

Warner Books, Inc., 1271 Avenue of the Americas, New York, NY 10020
Visit our Web site at www.twbookmark.com.

An AOL Time Warner Company

Printed in the United States of America

First Printing: March 2002

10 9 8 7 6 5 4 3 2 1

Library of Congress Cataloging-in-Publication Data

Lisle, Holly.
    Vincalis the agitator / Holly Lisle.
        p. cm.
    ISBN 0-446-67899-6
    I. Title

PS3562.I775 V66 2001
813'.54—dc21   2001046675

For Matthew

And to
Betsy Mitchell
with thanks

Book One

✤

Wraith the Challenger

We were friends in a place that had no friendship, in a hell born of forced mindlessness and subterranean despair; and because we found our impossible friendship in the Warrens, we brought forth revolution. Thus a world died, and its death bore a new world.

VINCALIS THE AGITATOR
THE SECRET TEXTS—OF THE FALCONS

Chapter 1

Down below, in the cages where they'd been born, Wraith's only two friends in the world starved and waited. So the boy crouched in the shadows, heart racing in his throat. Without food, he couldn't go home. Without food soon, he would have no reason to go home. The strangeness of this place frightened him, and he yearned for the familiar back ways he'd left behind. But some instinct had drawn him to this rich and impossible place, and he promised himself he would not leave empty-handed.

This city in the sky terrified him, though. To his right, a fountain erupted from nothing, spraying streams of crystalline liquid and gemlike shards of red and blue and green into the air. No solid structure supported this delicate miracle, but the many people who strolled past seemed not to even notice it. All around Wraith, buildings spun of smoke and light rose from foundations equally ephemeral, yet within them people moved easily from floor to floor, visible through lovely archways and on broad balconies. Below his feet, through roads like ribbons of stained glass, lay the other, lesser city—his city—so far away that streets looked like silken threads and buildings like beads sewn on fine cloth.

Wraith did not belong in these fine streets, in this city above the city, in this realm of men who would be gods. But because he *could* come here—because the city itself let him enter—no one looked at him with suspicion or with doubt. No one questioned the shabby nature of his clothes, the rough cut of his hair, his shoeless feet, or his gaunt child's body. If he was here, they seemed to think, then it could only be because he belonged here—for magic barred those who did not belong from the secrets of Oel Artis Travia—the Aboves.

And here, where he knew he had no business, he found the thing he had so desperately sought. In the Belows, no one would think of displaying food in the open air, where anyone might walk up to it, touch it—steal it. But here it lay, in vast and wondrous quantities and unimaginable varieties. Wraith routinely stole thrown-away food from the containers behind stores and homes in the Belows, but this was new food, right where he could get it.

His stomach rumbled; the fruits and vegetables, breads and cheeses, pastries and beverages spread like a banquet before him, and he wanted so much to eat something. Anything. He had eaten scraps of bread soaked in some sort of gravy the previous day, picking tiny maggots off before taking bites. Aside from water, he'd had nothing else.

Any bite of food at all would have been wonderful—but none of the other people wandering through the aisles ate anything while they walked. He'd watched carefully; after years of scavenging, the knowledge that calling attention to himself would cause him trouble had become so deeply ingrained he didn't even need to think about it. The shoppers all around him carried baskets that they picked up from one corner of this odd open-air market, and they wandered through the aisles, sorting through the offered produce and putting their chosen items into their baskets. When they finished, they simply took the baskets with them and left. They never paid, as people in the Belows paid. Wraith had seen money many times, and understood that it could be traded for food; what he had never been able to discover was where he might get money of his own.

Here, however, no money appeared to be necessary.

So he took a basket, and like the other people, he began putting food into it. In one basket, he would have enough food for Jess and Smoke and himself to live on for several days—and to live well. He mainly chose breads, dried meats, and pastries, because these, from his experience, would last longest. However, he couldn't resist just a few of the beautiful, brightly colored fruits and vegetables. He could imagine the expressions on the faces of his friends when he returned with such a bounty.

When he finished collecting the food he wanted—not letting himself be as greedy as he desperately wished to be, but still with a nice haul—he headed for the exit, following the precise route those before him had followed. But whereas no one paid any attention when those others left, when he left someone said, "Hey, that boy didn't pay!"

And then someone else said, "But he didn't set off the alarm."

And a woman shouted, "Master! A thief!"

A man of young middle age rose from the edge of the market, where he had been sitting, apparently doing nothing more important than watching the water falling in the fountain. He turned, and stared at Wraith with eyes as cold as death, and pointed a finger. "You. Stop."

His voice had an odd echo to it. Wraith didn't waste time contemplating what that echo might mean; he simply clutched the basket of food to his belly and fled.

The man, strangely, laughed. In the next instant, blinding white light surrounded Wraith, making the air around him crackle and sing, and scaring him so badly that he dropped the food. He didn't dare stop to pick it up; the man hadn't hurt him, but the wizard's next attack might be more than fancy lights and noises.

Racing for the nearest of the little side streets that fed the square, Wraith ventured a glance over his shoulder, and got a bad shock. The square had been full of people. In just an instant, impossibly, they were gone, and only five remained: the man, the woman who had called out that he was a thief, and three gray-suited guards. The wizard's oily voice carried clearly as Wraith darted down his chosen street. "That's the one. When you catch him . . . bring him to me. I want to take him apart and see what he's made of."

Something in the wizard's voice told Wraith that if the wizard caught Wraith, he would kill him. But over a basketful of food? In this place of such plenty, where people chose what they wanted and took it freely?

"We will, Master," one of the guards said in a voice that sounded as frightened as Wraith suddenly felt.

He heard the hiss and whisper of the guards' skimmers behind him, and he looked for cover. They could fly faster than he could ever hope to run, and with three of them after him, he probably didn't have much chance.

His feet pounded over the translucent pavement, and he did not let himself look down to the ground far below. They could throw him off the road and he would die of terror long before he smashed into the pavement in the Belows.

He wished as he ran that he had not dared to chance the gate that led upward on the spiraling, spun-glass road. He wished he had stayed firmly on the ground where he belonged. There, at least, he might have found food that would keep Jess and Smoke alive a little longer. He would have managed, somehow, to provide for his friends the things they could not provide for themselves. But if he died here, the two of

them would be lost; they would either starve to death or return to the
hell of Sleep, from which he would never dare awaken them again.

He had to live. He had to.

The street down which he ran was a neighborhood thoroughfare. Behind the glass wall that edged the thoroughfare, houses built on clouds
stood inside secondary walls blocked off by high, gracefully deadly gates.
The translucent white walls of the houses gleamed with inset stones and
metals, and the light that shone through them made them look as
evanescent as soap bubbles, and as lovely. The inhabitants had spun
their gardens of diamonds and stars that glittered and gleamed in stunning configurations. And singing fountains and streams that ran burbling and chuckling between invisible banks served as destinations for
the gossamer paths that led from the gates to the houses.

Wraith thought it all very lovely, and all horrifying. He saw no place
to hide, for even if he could climb a wall, he could not hide in a yard
made of air and decorated by floating lights. He would be visible from
any of the paths. And he didn't see an alley, an open gate, something that
would let him escape from that whine that came closer and closer to
him.

Tears clogged his throat, and the air that fought its way through the
narrowed passage burned in his lungs. He thought his heart might stop
on its own before the guards behind him could touch him. Everything
was closed. Locked. Impenetrable. And the next intersection was so far
away, it might as well have been on the moon.

Then, as he bolted toward one great house, he saw that its owners
had not worried about a physical gate with bars and spikes. Instead, the
archway lay open. No doubt the invisible gate would be as formidable to
most people as one of the tangible ones—but not to Wraith. He put on
a burst of speed and threw himself through the opening. Cool fires of a
hundred hues played across him, as they had earlier when he'd entered
the gate that led to the Aboves—but those fires did nothing to him.

A boy of about his own age—stocky, blond, elaborately dressed—
had been entertaining himself in that yard, sitting in a comfortable chair
with his feet propped up, making three gold balls and a bit of rope spin
through the air. The boy jumped at the flashing lights, and stared as
Wraith lunged at him and said, "Hide me."

The boy gave one startled glance at the gate. But then he nodded and
pointed Wraith to a tiny house with its own cloud-spun path that hung
in the air almost against the wall.

Wraith didn't ask questions. He didn't let himself look down. He just ran.

The little house had, thank all the gods, a real floor. It held a table and four chairs, shelves full of books and jars and paraphernalia that Wraith couldn't begin to identify, and on the floor dozens of dolls and brightly colored blocks and wheels and balls. It consisted of one room, a door, and four small round windows set a little lower than Wraith's eye level. He crouched, and through the window that faced back the way he had come, he watched the boy, pointedly not looking at the little house, return to his activity of making all three balls hover in the air while the string braided itself between them.

The guards stopped outside the gate. Two of them stared at the little house. The third glowered at Wraith's unexpected ally. "Where is the little bastard?" the head guard asked.

The boy rose, not yet acknowledging any of the guards, and pointed to the translucent yard. All three balls spun neatly downward and settled into a line there. When he had summoned the rope to himself and it had wound itself around his arm as if it were a living thing, he turned and slowly walked to the gate. "Perfann, do you know to whom you are speaking?"

The guard ignored the question. "Master Faregan told me to catch that little thief and—"

"My name is Solander Artis," the boy interrupted. "Son of Rone Artis. *Artis,* perfann—which should have some meaning even to one of Faregan's men. And this is *Artis* House. So . . . now that you know to whom you are speaking, would you like to reconsider your . . . presence?"

The guard's ruddy face bleached the color of bone. He said, "My apologies. I would not bother you. But a thief escaped from the market, and Master Faregan has demanded that we . . . ." He paused, considering his words. "That we capture him and remand him over to Master Faregan for questioning."

"A worthy thing, no doubt," the boy Solander said. "And had he come into my yard, I would without hesitation turn him over to you. But no one has come through the gate. It's armed, and since I did not wish to be disturbed at my studies, I did not unarm it. Did you notice anyone trying to cross an armed gate? That's a fairly obvious thing."

"Well, we saw the gate light up . . . but we saw the boy on the other side."

"You saw the gate light up." The boy smiled coldly. "And the gate is armed, and there is no boy. I can only reach one conclusion from that, perfann. I suggest you tell Master Faregan that the thief died trying to escape; in a fashion, perhaps justice has been served."

The three guards stared from the little house in which Wraith hid to the boy who faced them at the gate, then back to the little house.

"I saw the gate light up," one of them said.

The other two both nodded and agreed.

"So he couldn't be alive."

"But I swear I saw him running on the other side."

The one in charge shook his head. "Can't have. He cooked in the gate."

The three of them stood there staring at each other, and Wraith sensed that they had come to an agreement before the other two spoke. When at last they said, "Yes," and "There's no other possibility," it was merely formality. The head guard nodded to the boy Solander and said, "Then we thank you for your time, and we apologize for the disturbance. We will be on our way."

And they left. Solander stood at the gate for a moment, watching them get on their skimmers and leave. Then, a thoughtful expression on his face, he turned and strolled down the path to the playhouse.

He came in and sat down, and for a moment said nothing.

"Thank you," Wraith said. "You saved my life. Those three had orders to give me to the market wizard—he said he wanted to take me apart to see what I was made of."

"Really?"

Wraith nodded.

"What did you do?"

"I'm not sure. I went through the market like the other people in the square, and put food into a basket, and left out the same gate through which they all left, but when I left, someone shouted that I was stealing food."

"Did you lose your credit amulet?"

"My what?"

The boy reached into his shirt and from beneath it pulled out a small white disk on a gold chain. "This. What happened to yours?"

"I don't have one of those. What does it do?"

"Takes money from your family account to pay for whatever you purchase. The shields around each business are spelled to read your amulet and . . ." He shook his head. "You should know this. Why don't you?"

Wraith shrugged. "We have no credit amulets in the Warrens. No open markets. And what are shields?"

The boy sat down and rested his elbows on the table and his chin on his fists. "Why would you have been in the Warrens? No one goes there."

"I live there."

"With the riots and the murders and the mind-drugs and the crime lords and the prostitutes and . . . I've seen the nightlies. None but criminals live there."

Wraith tried to figure out what Solander was talking about. "You must have heard of a different place. That's nothing like where I live— the Warrens are the quietest place in the city."

"If you lived in the Warrens, you wouldn't be here," the boy said. "Because the Warrens are gated to keep the criminals in; you couldn't have gotten out. And you certainly couldn't have come to Oel Artis Travia."

"I just walked here. Walked out of the Warrens, too."

"How?"

"The same way I ran into your yard."

"The gates in the Warrens are malfunctioning, too? My father will have a fit. He's going to be upset enough that something's wrong with our gate. Lucky for you those guards didn't try it."

"The Warren gate worked the same way all gates work for me. I can walk through any of them that don't have real locks on them."

The boy shook his head. "Nonsense. I saw you go through the gate. It lit up, but it didn't do it right."

"They always look like that when I go through them."

Solander thought about this for a moment, staring down at the floor and frowning. "You mean our gate might be working? If I'd told the guard the gate was malfunctioning and he'd tried to cross, he might have been killed? Oh, hells, I would have gotten into trouble for that." The boy gave Wraith a speculative look, and then a tentative smile. "My name is Solander Artis," he said.

"I know. I heard you tell the guards."

"Now you're supposed to tell me your name."

"It's Wraith."

"Wraith what?"

"Just Wraith."

"That's a funny sort of name."

Wraith shrugged. "I liked it. That's why I picked it."

"You picked your own name?"

"Yes."

"Well, that's different. Wraith, I want you to show me how you got through our gate."

"All right." The two of them rose, walked out into the yard together, and after Solander checked to see that no one who mattered was looking, Wraith walked through the gate. The lights played over him—and then he was on the other side. So he turned around and walked back.

The boy frowned. "That can't be. It looks like it's working, but . . . Wait right here. I have to go get something. Don't go *anywhere,*" he said, and raced to the big house.

Wraith waited, and waited, and at long last the boy came racing back, carrying a small bag full of greenish lumpy balls.

"You took long enough."

"It's a big house," the boy said, "and I had to get the testers out from under the watchman's nose without him catching me."

"Testers?"

"Gates only attack living human beings. Otherwise, they would have to be constantly raised and lowered for deliveries of supplies and other things that come via mage-carts. Pets and birds and other wildlife wouldn't be able to pass through them, either, and the families do love their deer and peacocks and griffonelles. They'd be most upset to find their expensive pets roasted by a gate. So it used to be that the only way to test a gate was to shove a prisoner through it. Only now prisoners are used in work gangs, and they're too valuable to just roast; so the wizards had to develop gate testers. You throw one through, and the gate thinks it's a person who isn't supposed to be there, and . . ." He pulled one out of the bag. "Here. I'll show you."

He tossed the ball through the gate. The lights erupted again, but this time, along with the light, Wraith heard an eerie hum, and the ball stopped dead in midair, turned a brilliant glowing red, and exploded into dust with a crack so loud and sudden and emphatic it made both boys jump.

Wraith closed his eyes. He'd seen the gates work on something other than testers before, and all because of his stupidity in thinking that if he could walk through them, anyone could.

"It's working," the boy whispered.

Wraith nodded. "They always are, I think. Gates just don't work on *me.* The man in the market who sent his guards after me pointed his finger at me first, and the same sort of light came out of it. But that didn't do anything, either, though I'm pretty sure he expected it to."

Solander leaned against a wall and closed his eyes. "Oh, dorfing hell-dogs! Master Faregan took a shot at you and it didn't do anything? *Drowning* dorfing hell-dogs! No wonder he wanted his guards to grab you." He stared at Wraith, his expression an eloquent testimony to awe. Without another word, he traced a short series of loops in the air. To Wraith's amazement, a line of light glowed in the air in the wake of the boy's finger. "Cover," the boy said.

The loops coalesced into a thin, wavering sphere of light that bobbled through the air to Wraith, touched him . . . and popped like a soap bubble, disappearing without a trace.

"How did you *do* that?" Solander asked.

Wraith said, "I didn't do anything. I don't do anything when I go through the gates, I didn't do anything when that man pointed his finger at me and hit me with light. I don't *ever* do anything."

"Would you walk through it for me one more time? I want you to carry a tester with you and see what happens."

Wraith nodded. Solander handed him a tester, and Wraith walked through the gate. Lights crackled and hummed around him, the tester exploded in his hand with a heat and a force that scared the breath out of him, but as before he remained unscathed. He turned around and stepped back through the gate again.

The boy looked pale. He said, "Let's go back in the playhouse to talk. I'm not due for lessons for a bit, and none of the juniors will be out in the yard until after midmeal. Once they get out here, the place will be hell, but for at least a while we have it to ourselves."

They both returned to the little house and drew up chairs, and Solander leaned his elbows on the table and said, "I'm the only child of Rone Artis, who is one of the top Dragons in the world, and Torra Field Artis, who is the daughter of one of the great wizards of all time. Qater Field—you've heard of him?"

"No."

"Of course not." Another exasperated sigh. "No matter. According to my parents—hells-all, according to everyone—I'll become a powerful wizard when I grow up, because I already show incredible talent and aptitude, and have remarkable visual-spatial memory, and . . . I don't even remember all the things they say. But if they're right, I have a good chance of ruling Matrin. I can already build minor gates of my own. But *I* can't walk through a gate untouched. Neither can my father. If wizards could cross armed gates, the gates would be worthless. You have something special going on with you. And I want to find out what it is, because it has to be important."

Wraith said, "All I want to do is find food for my friends and go back home. They have to be getting scared by now—I couldn't return there yesterday."

Solander considered that in silence for a long while. "Your parents didn't look for you when you weren't there?"

"My parents don't know who I am."

Solander's face went blank. "I don't understand—but you'll have plenty of time to tell me. If your parents don't know who you are, they won't miss you, right? So just stay here. You can live in my house."

"I can't. If I don't go back, my friends will starve to death."

"Well, are their parents as terrible as yours?"

Wraith considered that for a moment. "My parents aren't terrible. They're just . . . Sleeping."

"Doesn't matter. Are your friends' parents like yours? They must be, or they'd see to it that all of you had food."

"They're all the same."

"Fine. Then bring your friends with you. More than a thousand family members and friends live in our winterhouse here, and about twice that many staff. I won't have any trouble moving you and your friends in and creating a story for you. How many friends do you have?"

"Two. Jess and Smoke."

"That's no problem. We'll just pretend you're distant relatives from somewhere, here on the career exchange program. No one ever checks the paperwork on that very carefully." Solander shrugged.

Wraith, whose hard life had taught him that the time to be most suspicious was when anything looked too good, asked, "Why would you have us come here? Why offer rooms or food to people you don't know?"

"I could use some friends. My cousins are creeps or dullards, and if you can walk through gates, you can do things they could never do. Your friends will have a good place to live, and you can take classes with me, and I can figure out why gates don't work on you. I'm going to specialize in magical research," he added. "You'd make a perfect case study."

Wraith stared through the door of the little house up to the big house, and tried to imagine walking through those grand front doors as if he belonged there. He tried to imagine never going back to the hollow, chilling silence of the Warrens. All of his life so far had been a dare—a strange, lonely challenge. This next step made an odd sort of sense to him. He'd been leaving the Warrens a little at a time since he was born.

"We'll do it," he said.

"Bring them with you tomorrow, then," Solander said, but Wraith was already shaking his head in disagreement. "No? You won't bring your friends?"

"*I* can go through the gates. *They* can't."

Solander looked startled. "Oh. I forgot about that." He frowned thoughtfully and said, "And you and your two friends live in the Warrens."

"Yes."

"Then I have to figure out some way to get an aircar with universal clearance into the Warrens. That might take a day or two. Going through gates like that—well, that isn't the sort of thing you want to make a mistake about."

Solander thought for another minute, then said, "I'll figure something out. In the meantime, we're going to steal some food for you and your friends."

Wraith and Solander stood in one of the pantries of the house's enormous kitchen, loading food into a box. Wraith had a hard time believing his eyes—he could not begin to guess the purpose of all the equipment in the huge outer room, nor what most of the many people out there were doing. Cooking, obviously—the smells alone whispered every wonderful promise possible about the food being prepared—but none of them did anything that looked like drawing Way-fare out of the wall-tube. Wraith knew of no other method of food preparation, so he kept peeking over his shoulder to see just what they did.

That was how Wraith saw a hard-faced older boy coming toward the pantry where he and Solander picked out supplies for him, Smoke, and Jess. "Solander," he said, keeping his voice low, "someone's coming."

Solander looked toward the door and groaned. "Luercas—he's a distant cousin." Solander hid the box in with other boxes on the floor behind him and turned quickly, several small pies in hand. He passed one to Wraith and started chewing on the other one. "He's . . . awful."

Wraith said, "Oh," and then took a bite of the pie. It tasted so impossibly good, tears started in the corners of his eyes—and at that moment Luercas sauntered into the pantry.

"You," he said, looking past Wraith to Solander. "What are you doing in here, you little rodent? Your parents should keep a tighter leash on you."

"I have as much right to be in the pantry as you do." He muttered something the tone of which sounded insulting to Wraith, though he couldn't make out the words.

Apparently neither could Luercas, because he glared at Solander. "Not if I tell you that you don't, worm." Luercas then looked at Wraith, and his eyes narrowed. "And what in all the hells is this thing?"

"A . . . distant cousin from . . . Ynjarval," Wraith lied. "Here on temporaries."

"Looks like something you found in the street. You, street-dirt. Disgusting black-haired stick. All by yourself in the real city, eh? Let me see you bow to your superiors." He smiled at Wraith, a most unpleasant smile.

Wraith felt sick to his stomach. But he looked Luercas in the eyes and said, "I don't think so."

"Don't you, street-dirt? With Mama and Papa back in Ynjarval, they're not going to be able to do much to help you. Better get used to bowing if you're planning on transferring here."

"No," Wraith said, shaking his head. He felt pretty certain if he'd had more than that single bite of pie in his stomach over the last day, he would have thrown up right there, but he tried not to let it show in his face or in his voice.

Luercas pointed at Wraith, and Wraith heard Solander gasp. "I said bow," Luercas said, and a pale line of fire sketched itself from Luercas to Wraith . . . and promptly died.

Wraith crossed his arms over his chest and tried to look confident. He said nothing. His heart was racing, and his knees were so weak he could feel them trembling. He leaned back against the shelving for support, but it apparently had the effect of making him look self-assured.

"I said *bow!*" Luercas snarled. The second bolt of radiance that leaped toward Wraith looked big.

"No, Luercas!" Solander said, but he need not have protested. This attack, too, died before it reached Wraith.

Luercas's face went red. "Think you're clever, do you? Think your little trick is amusing. Let's see how funny you think real magic is. *BOW,* you filthy bastard!" Luercas bellowed, as outside Wraith heard running feet. Two adults burst into the pantry just as Luercas's third—huge—attack blasted toward Wraith and died.

Both adults grabbed Luercas and dragged him out, and Wraith heard them shouting about him bothering children, about using magic attacks large enough to set off alarms all over the house to try to hurt children— about how he was suspended from his sessions and how this incident was going before the reviewers and certainly going to go on his records, and how he'd find it difficult to get any sort of good posting with the Dragons after demonstrating such poor judgment and poor self-control. The adults, dragging Luercas with them, moved out of earshot then, and Wraith turned to Solander.

"I think I'm going to be sick."

"He's going to hate you forever for that," Solander said, awed. "I can't believe you didn't just . . . bow."

"I looked in his eyes. If I'd given him what he wanted that time, the next time we met, he would have tried to make me do something worse. He's . . . I don't like him at all."

Solander dragged the box out from under the shelves and sighed. "I don't think anybody likes him. Most people don't manage to get so completely on his bad side so fast, though." He handed the box to Wraith. "You'd better get out of here. I'll walk you to the gate. Will you be all right getting home?"

"I'll be fine. Nobody ever pays me much attention. I'm good at not being noticed."

Solander looked at him sadly. "Not good enough, apparently. When we move you back here, we're going to have to make sure you look different."

Wraith took the box of food, and followed Solander out the door and out of the house. *Maybe I should have bowed,* he thought. *Maybe it would have worked out better that way.*

But he didn't think so. He'd seen something in Luercas's eyes that hunted for weakness, that took pleasure in pain.

Wraith decided to make avoiding Luercas one of his big objectives in the future.

Solander sat in his room after Wraith left, idly balancing the three gold balls in the air, and wondered what his father would make of the boy. Wraith showed every sign of being impervious to magic. Yet Solander's father had told him many times that magic affected everyone—that magic was the sixth force of physics, and that one might as well look for a man who wasn't affected by gravity as a man who wasn't affected by magic.

The balls spun in a neat little circle before Solander, swimming through the air like trained fish. Light from the window gleamed off of them. They were solid gold and terribly heavy; without magic, Solander wasn't strong enough to lift one of them off the floor. But, as he'd told

Wraith, he had a remarkable aptitude for magic. And, he thought, a remarkable aptitude for spotting what might be the biggest flaw in theoretical magic in the last two thousand years when it presented itself to him.

I probably should tell my father about Wraith, Solander thought. He'd want to know that such a person could exist.

But visions of unveiling Wraith on his own—and with him a new theory of magic that included proofs for Laws of Exclusion, those heretofore mythical and much yearned-after laws that would permit wizards to create spells without any rebound effects, or *rewhah*—sang to him like the Temptresses of Calare. He wanted to earn his place in the Academy. No. He wanted to earn the *highest* place in the Academy, and he only had four more years to do something that would place him above all the other applicants. His father had said Solander was on his own in gaining admission—that the elder Artis would not use his influence or his position on the Council of Dragons to gain a place for his son. And his reasons seemed valid—that if Solander did not earn his way into the Academy without parental assistance, men who stood against him in later years would question his qualifications for any worthwhile position on the Council of Dragons, or for any worthwhile appointment within the sphere of influence of the Empire of the Hars Ticlarim.

If Solander could disprove one of the central tenets of current magical theory, though, and take not just a stack of papers into the exam room but physical demonstrations of his theory, no one would ever be able to question his right to stand among the Masters—to lead the Empire—to become head of the Dragons and eventually Landimyn of the Hars. He balanced the three gold balls in the air and smiled, imagining himself carried through the underwater streets of Oel Maritias, dressed in glorious robes of state, cheered on by the thousands who lined the Triumph Road beneath the glittering arch of the ocean above. He would smile slightly. Wave his hand just . . . so . . . to let the people know that he had once been like them. One of them. Once—but not anymore.

He sent the balls spiraling to the floor, then pulled his knees up to his chest and stared out the window by his bedside, which overlooked one of the many hidden courtyards in the grand old house. In that courtyard, three young girls played a game of skippers, laughing at the patterns the skipper-stones created in the floating fountain. Watching them, Solander was reminded that he would have to create identities for Wraith and his friends if they were to be successfully hidden in plain sight within the household. He might, he thought, create them as the children of distant relatives from across the Bregian Ocean. He liked Ynjarval. It was distant and poor, and adults seemed to mostly ignore anyone from there.

Better than Benedicta—relatives there were always sending their children to Oel Artis to get a real education and to meet the right people to further their careers. But they were the sort of relatives who called their children home for holidays and made surprise visits, which wouldn't work well for Solander's needs. Or Wraith's.

Solander would have to create a couple letters of introduction and forge necessary identification papers. He'd heard Luercas bragging about doing that so that he could get into adults-only taverns and theaters down in the Belows. If Luercas could find a way, then Solander thought he could find a way, too. But any chance Solander had of asking Luercas how he did it was now gone. If Luercas were to get wind of Solander's searching after forged papers, he would find out why and Solander would spend the rest of his natural life paying blackmail to the bastard. And Wraith . . . Solander didn't even want to think about what would happen to Wraith.

He flopped back on the bed and closed his eyes. Letters. Forged papers. A means of transporting three people from the Warrens to the Aboves, and some sort of excuse for going into the Warrens that wouldn't raise suspicion. A foolproof, questionproof reason for three Warreners to be in Oel Artis and staying in Artis House more or less permanently. A good change of appearance for Wraith, so that Luercas wouldn't recognize him.

Rone Artis cleared his throat—evidently he'd been standing in the doorway for some time.

"Are you ready?" his father asked, and Solander, guilty of all sorts of disobedience in his heart, nearly jumped out of his skin.

"Sorry," he said, scrambling to his feet. Solander gathered all three balls and the cord with a single mental swoop. He began spinning the balls in the air, concentrating on their differing weights and masses, and the very different composition of the cord. "This is what I've been working on most." The balls swam like fish through the air, forming the test patterns perfectly; the cord played counterpoint, weaving its way through each of the prescribed forms.

Out of the corner of his eye, he finally saw a small smile on his father's face—the first one in a long time.

Chapter 2

Vincalis Gate—a lesser gate, unfrequented, unimportant, mostly unnoticed—led to a place no one wanted to go. Its broad arch sat next to a narrow, rarely used thoroughfare, providing a comfortable, hidden perch for anyone agile enough to clamber up to it and slender enough to lie across it without sticking up above the little parapet. It was Jess's favorite perch. Jess, tiny for her age and whisper-thin, could lie along its gentle curve and watch the wondrous traffic that traversed the cloud road to the Aboves, and the occasional pedestrians who passed on the walkway beside her from mysterious points of origin to mysterious destinations, and wonder at the world outside of the gates . . . a world denied to her by tradition, by law—and by the murderous gate that only Wraith could pass at will.

Wraith, who dared challenge the gate, told her about what lay beyond her narrow view, and she loved to hear his stories. More than anything, she yearned to move from the dreary, dead confines of the Warrens into the living world beyond.

And where was Wraith?

Jess dreaded giving him her bad news—and at the same time, she feared that this time something had happened to him, and that he would not come back. That she would have to face—alone—the choice between Sleep and death.

She'd lain across the arch, watching and waiting, all of the previous day and most of this one. She'd returned to the basement the night before only after dark, when she felt safe on the streets, and resumed her perch along the arch at first light. The guards who patrolled the Warrens never paid much attention to anything around them, but in daylight accidents were much more likely to happen, so she only moved in darkness.

Now, thirsty, hungry, and worried, and with the sun dropping toward the horizon for the second day—with still no sign of Wraith—she contemplated her choices. She tried to imagine stepping into one of the homes, taking a bowl from the dispenser, pouring in the Way-fare, and eating herself into oblivion. Her memories of her time in Sleep were vague—little flashes of conscious desire to move, to breathe, to act, to escape, that lay in the middle of vast, deep, ugly pools of nothing. The Sleep terrified her. But she didn't know if she had the courage to choose death. Already, she felt the burning in her gut that the few bites she'd allowed herself from the last crusts of old bread, doled out over two days, did nothing to assuage. How much worse would the pain be in four days, or in ten? How long would she take to die?

And then, movement down the narrow road. In the twilight, she could not at first be sure the boy was Wraith, though he was thin enough. His way of moving was right, but his clothes were all wrong. And he carried an enormous box with him. She wondered what it was— he had never brought anything with him that he could not hide beneath his shirt. This he carried openly.

But it was Wraith. She checked on the street behind to make sure the Warren guards were nowhere nearby, then shinnied down the arch, dropped to the low roof of the guards' shed, then lightly to the ground.

Wraith came through the gate, heralded by the usual explosion of light, and said, "Quick. We need to get out of sight. I have wonderful news."

And I have terrible news, Jess thought, but she kept her silence and ran beside him. Her news would become obvious all by itself, and if she did not need to crush his apparent joy right away, she would not. She loved him, and she loved this new smile he wore on his face, and this air of excitement that he carried in his step.

They ran down their street, ducked into their stairwell, and squeezed through the broken window into their hideaway.

Boxes and crates stacked along all the walls and in the middle of the floor, a dirt floor with a little nest of rags for sleeping on, and darkness, always, because they did not dare any light to call the guards' attention to their presence—this was the home that was, to Jess, freedom and life.

"Where's Smoke?" Wraith asked, putting his box on one of the crates. "He has to be here to hear this, too." And without waiting for an answer, he handed her something beautiful, and cool, and smooth, and round, and said, "Take a bite. It's the best thing I've ever tasted in my life."

She took a bite and almost cried. It crunched, and its juice burst on her tongue, and its sweetness seemed to her to have not just smell and flavor, but color and sound as well. She took another bite, and the sweetness began to mix with the salt of her tears. Smoke would have loved this thing, whatever it was.

"Great, isn't it?" Wraith asked, grinning.

She swallowed around the growing lump in her throat and put the round thing aside. "Smoke is gone," she said.

Wraith's smile vanished. "Gone? The guards found him?"

"He . . . he gave up. He said you couldn't provide for two of us anymore—that we ate too much and that trying to keep us both fed was killing you. And he said I was the smallest and I ate the least, so I had to stay, and he would go back. He ran out of the door. I chased him, but he runs faster than me, and I don't even know which of the homes he went into."

"When?" Wraith whispered.

"Right after you left."

"Then he's been asleep for two full days, and then some."

Jess nodded.

"Too long. And he's too old now. If we tried to take him away from the Way-fare again, this time it would probably kill him."

"If we even knew where to look for him."

"Yes. That, too. He would still be easy to pick out—he won't start actually looking like them for months. But where would we start looking?"

"He didn't want you to find him. He didn't want to be a burden anymore."

Wraith's face wore anguish. "But I found us a way out. All of us—you, me, and him. I found us a home, a place where the three of us can live, where they serve food this good and better several times a day, every day, and where they walk in the streets whenever they want, and wear different clothes every day." He buried his head in his hands. "Why couldn't he have just waited?"

"He's been talking about this for a while now," Jess said. "He made me swear to keep silent; he worried for you, that something bad would happen to you because of us. I've worried, too, but I was too much of a coward to do what he did and go back. If I weren't so weak, I would have just gone to Sleep one day, too—and then you wouldn't have had to risk the gates anymore. You could have stayed out there, where it's wonderful." She whispered, "But I miss him."

Wraith had his knees pulled tight to his chest and his face pressed into them. He sobbed. Jess sat beside him for a long time, patting his back and stroking his hair. "He wouldn't have gone if he'd thought you would ever find a way out of here for us. He only gave up because he could see us getting you killed, and for nothing."

"Never for nothing," Wraith said between sobs. "What I do for you is never for nothing. You're my friends. You're my family. You're all I have in the world."

"That's why he went back," Jess said softly. "Because he loved you."

He looked up at her. In the dark, she saw the gleam of his tear-filled eyes and the pale blur that was the rest of his face. He looked haunted, haggard. Despairing. "I can't go to get him, Jess. After my brother, I swore I would never chance killing anyone else. He's already had the Way-fare in him for too long. I can't get him back. And I won't try. I won't kill him, too."

"He knew that. He knew when he went."

"But we're going to get out of here, Jess. And someday, I'm going to come back, and I'm going to find a way to free everyone who's in here. Every single one."

She held his hand and nodded. "You will. I know you will. You can do anything, Wraith." And then she hugged him, and prayed that once they were free of this place, he would never look at the Warrens again. She would miss Smoke; her heart ached for him, and for the knowledge that only two days had stood between him and hope.

But the Warrens had a poison to them, a creeping, insidious evil that she could feel hanging in the air, leaching the life out of her day by day by day, and she feared that if Wraith didn't get away and stay away, he would at last fall victim to that poison.

"Grath Faregan, bound and blindfolded you come into this chamber to take an oath—to swear fealty not to magic, and not to the government of lesser men, but to the Secret and Honorable Society of the Silent Inquest. We hold the reins of the world in our hands, and you have, by word and action, proven that you deserve to be one among us. Before you passed through the final doorway, you were told that you could only pass through it again in one of two ways—either as our friend or as a corpse. Do you acknowledge that you came here of your own free will?"

"I do," the bound man said.

"Will you take the test of loyalty?"

"I will," he said.

"Know that if you fail, you will die—and your death will be terrible. You still have the option of a quick and merciful death, should you so choose."

"I'll take the test."

"Very well." Two men removed the bonds from Faregan's hands and the hood from his head. Shackles still held his ankles to the dais in the center of the floor.

He could see nothing beyond a brilliant light that poured at him from all directions. He lifted his chin, and took a deep breath, and waited.

From all sides, then, spells attacked him. He knew that under no circumstances could he defend himself in any way or resist or reverse what was done to him. He proved his loyalty by proving he acceded to the will of those above him, whoever they might be. But when his body caught fire, he needed every bit of his control to let himself burn. He screamed, he fell to the ground—but he did not use the power at his disposal to put the fire out.

He smelled his own flesh burning, and he wept, and he pissed himself from fear and pain—and then, suddenly, the ordeal ended. Though he still had pain in his right leg, in every other way he was fine.

"Stand," one of the voices from the darkness said.

He stood. The right leg screamed, but he bore it without a whimper. No signs of piss, no signs of fire, no smell of smoke or roasting skin.

"Repeat after me: I am a friend of the Inquest, a brother of the Secret Masters of Matrin, and I acknowledge no power save that of the Master of the Inquest. . . ."

Faregan repeated the words.

"No god, no vowmate, no child shall come before the needs of the Inquest. . . .

"No life shall be sacred, if I am ordered to end it. . . .

"No law shall be sacred if I am ordered to disobey it. . . .

"From this day until death, the Secret and Honorable Society of the Silent Inquest is my first family, my first love, and my sole master, even to death."

As he finished repeating the oath, a voice said, "The brand on your leg is your mark—the mark that you are chosen. Your life is bound to it—if you deface it or remove it, you shall in that instant die. You are ours, and we are yours. And together we rule the world. Welcome."

The bright lights went down, and a cluster of old men moved around him, and hugged him, and gave him the clasp of family—right hand to right hand, third and fourth fingers curled tight to the palm.

Faregan wept with the joy of it. He was one of the Masters of the Inquest at last. As low in the order as a Master could be, but still a Secret Master. Time and good fortune would carry him higher, he thought. And if it did not, still he stood among the only men in the world he had ever cared to join.

Wraith sat in the basement, listening to Jess breathe. For a while he sat next to her, watching her curled on her little pile of rags. In the next few days her life would change, and he couldn't know whether he was taking her into a disaster or rescuing her from hell. Trusting, she slept.

Wraith couldn't sleep, though.

He moved to the top of the stairs and opened the door just a bit and stared up at the sky above, and at the dark spots that blotted out some of the stars—blots that were the grand homes of the Aboves floating overhead. Solander waited up there at that very moment.

Solander had said he thought he might be able to move them in as little as three days.

Wraith listened to the silence around him. The Warrens were always quiet at night—people went to bed soon after the sun set and got up just as it rose—mindlessly obedient to the dictates of the gods, the lessons, the prayers, and the distribution of the Way-fare.

He had created Jess and Smoke—had stolen them away from their worlds of prayers and lessons and Way-fare because he had been lonely. A lost, lonely little boy, surrounded from the moment of his birth by people who could not see him—who fed him and changed him by rote and dictates, but who did not understand when he cried, and did not respond to his pleas for someone to play with him. Wraith was in his world but not a part of it, and he had discovered early that in his world, he could do almost anything without reprimand, censure, or even notice. He could skip lessons, could skip prayers, could go out the doors after dark—and contrary to the endless droning teachings, the gods never struck him down for his blasphemy.

But he could not get his mother to see him. Nor his brothers, nor his sisters. He went to his daily lessons because he could think of nothing better to do—and when he was there, he began to notice children whose eyes wandered from the teacher-screen. They did not speak to him when he spoke to them, but sometimes they looked his way for a moment—

and for the first time since his birth, he thought he might not have to spend his life alone.

So he'd led the children whose attention wandered away from lessons, only to find that they would not stay with him. They fought him stubbornly, returning to the nearest homes and prayer-lights as soon as they could break away from him, and going the next day to their lessons and the teacher-screen as if nothing had happened. They did not recognize him. They did not seem to remember anything. But when he spoke to them, they sometimes briefly glanced his way.

A girl he'd called Shina had been his first success. She'd been closer to the surface all along than the rest of his classmates, and when he spoke to her one day, she'd managed to make an actual sound. She had not made any words, but just the sound had been so exciting to Wraith that he had wept. He pulled her to his little hideout, and this time he locked the door with both of them inside. He'd stolen food from beyond the gates, for even then he suspected that the food was part of what was wrong with everyone in the Warrens—that something about the Wayfare, the manna of the beneficent gods, held a deadly bite within it.

He'd ventured out of the Warrens before, startled but unscathed by the flashing gate light, to find a wonderland beyond. He kept in his hideout a little stash of foods he'd found or stolen—wonderful foods, with flavors and textures and colors—and when his still-nameless captive stopped trying to get out the locked door, he'd shared with her.

It had been a hard night. She would sleep, and in her sleep rise and try to leave, and Wraith had worried that she would hurt herself on the stairs or the crates. Finally he'd taken off his shirt and used it to tie her feet together.

When morning came, she was . . . herself. She looked around her— the first person in the Warrens that Wraith had ever seen do that except for himself—and then looked right at him.

And her first words were the first words each of his subsequent rescues had asked, in one way or another. "Are you one of the gods?"

He did not know what to say. He'd once thought he might be one of the gods. So he told her his name was Wraith—the Unseen One. That seemed right to him. And he told her she was Shina. The Mother Goddess. He'd liked the name, and the image of lovely, dark-eyed Shina (one of the few benevolent gods of the Warreners' pantheon) speaking from the prayer-lights reminded Wraith of the girl who sat before him.

"Am I a god, then?" she had asked. And because she had not been struck down by the gods for the heresy of not praying the night prayers or going that morning to lessons, he told her that he thought she might be.

Three days later, never suspecting that the gate would do more than shine light on anyone who dared trespass it, he tried to take her out to see the city beyond the Warrens' walls. He'd been holding her hand when they started across, had been staring into her eyes with a delight and a joy that he had not imagined possible in his pale, lonely existence. And in the moment of crossing, the gates that could not touch him devoured her utterly. She did not have time to cry out. Did not have time to blink. He was staring into her eyes, and then staring into nothing. Nothing remained of her except the rags she'd been wearing.

Shina. He tried not to think of her, but every time he lost another friend, he found himself staring into her lovely brown eyes in that single last instant they shared, and wondering what his life might have been like had she lived to share it with him.

That had been long ago, with its brutal lesson not lost on Wraith. Never again had he let anyone try to cross the gate. Never again had he tried to make one of his made friends into a true equal, a true partner.

Wraith, sitting in the doorway staring up at the sky, thought of the ones he'd rescued after. Red-haired, freckled Smoke. A boy he'd named Trev, lost to guards perhaps a year ago. Jess. His own older brother—the first and last member of his true family that he'd tried to save—who had won his way to awareness, had wept his thanks for the freedom of mind and body, and then had died in wracking, horrible pain because he was too old to escape the poisons of the Way-fare.

Those who lived had kept the names Wraith gave them because those names were gifts. To have a name at all was a gift. To be aware of names, to see the world, to do things by choice and understand that the choice existed—all gifts. Of all of them, only Wraith had been born free. The rest of them had come to freedom through him, and they held him in a place of honor for that.

But he had never let himself care for or love them the way he had cared for and loved Shina. They were his friends . . . but fragile friends, held always at a slight remove, so that if he lost them—the way he had now lost Smoke, second-born of the free—he would still be able to sleep at night, at least a little. Would still be able to rise to face the new day. Would still be able to go on, sneaking out the gate, gathering food for his . . . companions? Associates? Pets?

Wraith leaned back against the doorframe and felt the movement of air against his cheek, and smelled the night smells of the city, and wondered what mistake had created him free in this city-within-a-city of helpless slaves. Solander said that magic couldn't touch him. But why? Why was he different? Why had he been so long alone, so long hungry for simple acknowledgment from another human being?

Wraith ran a finger over one of the pieces of fruit Solander had sent. He'd lost so many people. With each one he lost, he lost another part of himself, because when he alone remembered the things that happened, it was as if they had not happened. Only when he had someone to talk to and to remember with did he feel that he had really existed at all.

He took a bite of the fruit, marveling at its sweetness and the way it quenched both his thirst and his hunger at the same time. To him it represented wealth—more than the grand houses of the Aboves, more than the streets built on air, that single piece of fresh fruit, intact, unbruised, and free from maggots and flies, spoke of a life that he wanted to have, and wanted to share. With Shina—the dark-haired, dark-eyed girl he still loved and still cried out for in his nightmares. It was the best of the world he had wanted to give her. Of everything that he had fought for, of everyone he had tried to save, only Jess remained—the youngest. The one who had shared the least with him. He would have traded her for any of the rest.

But he tried to be grateful that at least she survived, and that he did not go to his new life alone.

Solander sat in his room working on the distance viewing kit his father had brought for him from the research base in Benedicta, when the doorman rang his room. Solander snapped his fingers to activate the speaking spell and said, "I'm here, Enry. What do you need?"

"There's a boy here for you, *Ris* Solander. He says his name is . . . er, Wraith. Were you expecting him?"

"He's a friend of mine," Solander said. "Bring him in, will you? I can't get the pieces on this *dorfing* kit to go together, but I don't want to leave it right now. I think I almost see where I'm going wrong."

"Yes, ris. I'll bring him straightaway."

He must have taken Wraith by the long way, though, for Solander already had the lens fitted against the spell-projector and was connecting them when Wraith finally tapped at his door.

Solander watched Wraith as the Warrener nodded polite thanks to Enry. Nothing the boy did would have told Solander that he was from the lowest of the lower classes. A chadri like the merchant who imported silks and brought samples to the house would duck his head to any stolti. A mufere like Enry kept his head down and averted his eyes unless spoken to directly, and never spoke uninvited or about something not within the realm of his duty as houseman. A parvoi would have hidden himself from the presence of a stolti. And Wraith was a Warrener, even lower—if not by much—than a parvoi. Considering that, Wraith's complete lack of awe or respect seemed to Solander astonishing, if fortunate. Just as well Solander had given the boy some of his own clothing, though; the questions Wraith's old clothes would have raised with the houseman might have found their way to Solander's father—and who needed that? Not Solander. He was simply grateful to have come through his father's last test without making an ass of himself again.

The houseman gave Wraith the same bow he would have given Solander and said, "*Ris* Wraith, when you need to leave you may call on me. I have greatly enjoyed our talk." Wraith nodded politely and smiled at Enry, and met his eye; the houseman was first to look away.

This pleased Solander. Wraith had none of the subservient characteristics of the lower classes. He acted exactly like the highest of the stolti—like Solander or any of his cousins. When Solander brought Wraith and his friends into the house and presented them to his father as relatives from someplace far away, Wraith would have to look Solander's father in the eye—Solander's father, who made everyone nervous—lie about where he came from and who he was, and exhibit no fear of the great man. And then Wraith would have to live that lie for gods-only-knew-how-many months or years. Maybe forever. And his friends would, too.

Solander had a brief, niggling sense that perhaps this plan of his was not the best—that if he enlisted his father in it as an ally, he might hope to at least gain some of the credit for the discovery of the magical rules that Wraith broke simply by existing. Solander would still further his career, would still get an appointment into the Academy, would still be able to become a researcher.

But he wouldn't have the discovery under his name alone. He would be a minor footnote to the single greatest proof ever presented that the Dragons' view of the magical universe was incomplete, when what he wanted was to be that theory's sole author. The difference would be one of degree, but at fifteen he was sensitive to how great a degree that would be.

And his father might decide not to share at all. Rone might decide that the secrets to be found on Wraith's person were far too important to be entrusted to a child; he might classify Wraith "Secret—With Prejudice," as he did anything that he thought might be of real interest to his competitors, and if he did that, Solander wouldn't even be able to find out what was happening.

Wraith might not like becoming a classified study object, either, Solander thought.

Wraith came over and looked at the equipment Solander was putting together and said, "That looks complicated. What is it going to do?"

"It's a distance viewer—one of the really good new models with focusable sound. My father told me he wouldn't buy the completed model for me because it was much more expensive and had more features than I could justify, but he told me that he would get the kit for me if I'd do all the preliminary studies so that I could put it together when I got it. He tested me, too. When I had the theory down, he got me the kit."

Wraith nodded. "Well. That's . . . very good of him, I suppose. But what does it do?"

Solander stared at him. "You've never seen . . ." But perhaps they didn't have distance viewers in the Warrens. "Once it's all together, I'll be able to look at the screen on the base—right here—and turn these knobs—they adjust for altitude, longitude, and latitude, you see, based on true north. This one has gross controls and a switch—right over here, you see?—that changes the knobs over to fine controls, so that you have basically room-to-room capability anywhere within the viewer's range. And here—this is your sound capability, so that you can hear what people are saying. Getting the spells for simultaneous sound-and-view transmission into place has been almost as hard as doing the gross-to-fine coupling link-up to the switch."

Wraith sighed, and Solander, who'd become absorbed in the explanation of his new piece of equipment, looked over to find that the Warrener looked exasperated.

"What?"

"What can you *do* with it?" Wraith asked. "What's it good for?"

"Oh." Solander felt just a bit stupid. "You can watch people with it. This one has a range of about fifteen furlongs—pretty good, really. You can get amplifiers that let you see farther away than that, but a lot of them ruin the purity of your main signal—" He caught himself and said, "You can turn the viewer to anyplace you'd like to watch, and if that place isn't shielded by magic, you can see what the people there are doing—and with this model, you can also hear what they're saying."

"When they're outside?" Wraith asked.

"It wouldn't be much good if it only worked when they were outside. No, you can see inside, too. No place like here, of course—my father has shields on top of shields around this place. All the Dragons do. And a lot of the other people who live in the Aboves, too—the ones who know about things like the distance viewers. They aren't too happy about the idea that someone might be watching them at any time."

"I can understand that," Wraith said.

"But it's a lot of fun," Solander told him. "And you can learn some interesting things by focusing on places that aren't shielded."

Wraith gave Solander a doubtful look. "I bet."

"You don't sound like you like the idea much."

"I don't. The fact that someone might have been watching me at any time—"

Solander stopped him. "Not a chance. The Warrens are shielded."

Wraith looked startled. "They are?"

Solander nodded.

"Just like the houses of the richest and most powerful people in the world?"

Solander nodded again.

"Why?"

Solander, dumbfounded, couldn't come up with an answer to that. He had never even considered the strangeness of the fact that an entire section of the city had a shield around it as solid as the shield his father had cast around their house. "I . . . that's a really good question," he said. "Once you and your friends have moved in, we'll find out."

"Me and my *friend*," Wraith corrected. "I lost one right after I left to get food the last time."

Solander didn't catch his meaning. "Lost? Lost how?"

"He gave up. He went back to the houses, and he went back to Sleep."

"That doesn't sound so bad. When will he be back with you?"

Wraith said, "Never. He's too old. If Jess and I tried to wake him up now, he'd die. Just like my brother."

Solander considered that and tried to understand what Wraith might mean. "That doesn't make sense. What kind of sleep don't people wake up from?"

Wraith said, "The food in the Warrens makes people Sleep their whole lives away. They have their eyes open, they can follow the instructions of the prayer-lights and the dictates of the gods, but when they aren't being told what to do, they don't do anything. They sit. They stare ahead of them. For their entire lives, they just sit and stare ahead of them."

Solander shuddered. "How many people does this happen to?"

"All of them. Mothers give their babies Way-fare as soon as they're born, and the babies don't cry. They sleep, they wake, the mothers give them Way-fare just like the prayer-lights tell them to, and the babies grow up to be children who walk in lines to classes where they learn command words, and how to bathe, and how to move while they're sitting so they don't get sores on their bodies, and how to use a toilet, and how to flush it when they're done. And how to take their own disposable bowls, and get their own Way-fare from the taps."

Wraith closed his eyes, remembering the endless, repetitious droning of the gods who spoke through the prayer-lights: "Time now to get out of bed. Walk in place. Walk. Walk. Walk. Go to piss and move your bowels now, each in turn. Form a line, and wait patiently until the door opens in front of you. Wait. Wait. Wait. Eat your Way-fare now. Two bowls each for people this tall, and one bowl for people *this* tall," with the lights flashing the correct heights, "and in a disposable bottle mixed with water for those no taller than this. Remember to feed littles who cannot feed themselves. Don't forget the littles. Don't forget. Don't forget. Don't forget."

He shook off the memory. He and Jess needed papers that said they belonged in the Aboves. They needed a story that would allow them to blend in with Solander's enormous extended family. They needed a way out of the Warrens, and the person who got them out would first have to get in—no easy task.

Solander sat there shaking his head. He said nothing—he had no words that could comfort someone who had lived in such a hell. All he could do was keep Wraith and his friend from having to go back. He was fifteen years old, and he had no illusions about his ability to find the person he needed on his own. He lived a sheltered life of privilege, far from the sort of people he was going to need. He spent his time in study and practice of the things his parents felt would give him the world when he became old enough to take it—his father's magic, his mother's philosophy. Even within his own family, he had few friends.

But he did have one person he thought could help him: a distant cousin a few years older than he, whose secret interests had taken her out of the Aboves and introduced her to the sort of people Solander figured he would never meet on his own. She and he got along well enough—he impressed her with his ambition and his talents for magic; they both enjoyed a good debate over the importance of the *Ruminations of Chedrai* and the *Tosophi Feschippi Tagottgoth*. Most importantly for his needs at the moment, however, he had recently caught this cousin, named Velyn Artis-Tanquin, with a boy from the Belows doing things that would have cost her any hope of making a permanent alliance among the right families, and that would have, most likely, forced her parents to cut her off and find placement for her among one of the cadet branches of their line overseas. He had not only looked the other way, but had supplied an excellent alibi for her when her parents had heard a rumor that she had broken family law.

She owed him. A lot. Enough, he thought, that he could trust her to help him out and keep the secrets that he needed to have her keep.

He sent word via one of the servants that the friend he'd wanted her to meet had arrived, and not long after, she tapped at his door.

Velyn, tall and lithe and golden-skinned, with a silken curtain of copper hair that hung far below her waist and copper eyes flecked with gold, sauntered into the room and Wraith fell silent in midsyllable, his mouth open and his eyes wide. Solander wanted to laugh—Velyn had that effect on a lot of men, both young and old.

"Dear cousin," she said, "you interrupted me as I was winning at dice. Another roll and I should have had all of Drumonn's weekly allotment."

"And Drumonn's mother would have cried foul and made you give it back," Solander said. "This is my friend Wraith—the one I told you needed help. Wraith, this is my cousin Velyn. Don't play cards or dice with her. She cheats terribly."

"Untrue," Velyn said, smiling at Wraith. "I cheat very well—that's why I win so often. I'm delighted to meet you."

Solander watched Wraith's pale face go vivid red. "I'm . . . yes," he said, and faltered to a stop.

Velyn tipped her head and her smile grew broader. "You should remember how you did that," she said after a moment. "It makes a woman feel like she's the most beautiful creature in the world."

The red of Wraith's face grew even redder, to Solander's amazement and amusement, but he did find his words at last. "That's only because you are." He was looking her straight in the eye when he said that, and to Solander he sounded completely sincere.

Velyn blushed. This stunned Solander; Velyn hadn't even blushed when he'd caught her and her young man wearing little pieces of next to nothing and doing things that Solander doubted were legal even when both participants belonged to the Registry of Names. She stood there staring at Wraith, and Solander saw something pass between them: some spark, some understanding. He wondered what Velyn would do when she discovered that Wraith wasn't even Second Registry, but was from the Warrens—so far below her that she should never have even been able to lay eyes on him.

"Wraith and I and a friend of his need your help," Solander said when it became apparent that both Wraith and Velyn would be content to stand in his room looking at each other like the long-lost lovers in a bad play. "You have access passes to the aircars, and you know people. Wraith and his friend Jess need Registry papers. Good ones. Good enough that both of them could move in here. And Jess is going to need transport, too—and from someplace even you might have a hard time getting into."

Velyn at last looked away from Wraith. "What sort of story do you want to provide with the papers?"

"Both of them sent over here by their parents from Glismirg or the Cath Colony in Ynjarval or someplace in Tartura or Benedicta. They're on hardship grants because of their families, and they're to take general training and make contacts to better their family lines, and then move to advanced training in whatever they show aptitude for."

"Cadet branches all right with you?"

"Better than first lines, I would think," Solander said. "After all, Uncle Non is more likely to check their papers if they're first lines—try to keep in touch with their parents, make sure they're getting all the attention they need. If they're cadet branches, he'll just check to make sure their parents actually exist."

"They won't get top-tier rooms."

"We want them to be as close to invisible as we can make them while still giving them the privileges of the place. If they were top tier, too many people would want to know them."

Velyn nodded. She didn't ask Solander why he'd chosen her for this enormous favor—she already knew that. She did not question his reasons for wanting to do this thing; she seemed completely incurious about his reasons, in fact, whereas had he been asked a similar favor, he would have been dying to know the story behind it. She simply leaned against the doorframe, stared off at nothing, and gnawed on the middle knuckle of her index finger. "I don't know anyone right off who does false papers," she said, "but I know a few people who probably do know the right people. I'll need a day or two, probably—and this will be expensive."

"I'll pay. I haven't spent any of my last few months' allotment."

"Good." She frowned. "As for transport, where do I have to get his friend from?"

Solander hesitated for a moment. If she was going to refuse him, it would be over this. Then he shrugged. He could only ask. "The Warrens."

She laughed. "Right. Seriously, where? I'll need to get an aircar with the right clearances, so I'll have to know in advance."

"The Warrens," Solander repeated.

"I can't get a car that will go into the Warrens. That's absolutely off limits. That would be like trying to fly into the Dragons' Experimental Station airspace. You simply cannot go there."

"That's where we have to go."

"You're mad. Even if we could get there, we'd be killed. They have riots, murders, mobs in the streets, people who rip the arms and legs off of anyone who isn't from there, criminal squads, every imaginable form of vice. . . ."

"I watch the nightlies," Solander said. "But that's where we have to go."

He glanced over at Wraith, who looked bewildered. "Mobs in the streets? Riots? What are you talking about?"

"The Warrens," Solander said. "All the killings, the rapes, the . . . Why are you shaking your head like that?"

"The only people who walk on the streets are the guards—and children who are going to or from lessons. Killings? Rapes? Riots? The Warrens are so quiet, if you stood at one wall and shouted, you could be heard by someone standing down the same road at the other wall. Sometimes people from outside sneak in, but then they can't get back out, and they end up eating the Way-fare and watching the daily prayers and lessons, and they turn into Sleepers, too."

Velyn smiled at him—the smile of an older person to a younger one who is sadly misinformed about something of common knowledge. "I cannot imagine where you got such silly information—" she started to say, but Solander cut her off.

"He's from the Warrens."

"He can't be. Warreners would never be allowed up here. He'd be stopped by the gates."

"The gates don't work on him," Solander admitted, and Velyn now stared as if told that the world around here was all merely a figment of her imagination.

"What are you talking about?"

"He can walk right through them. They go off, but the wards don't touch him."

"Does your father know? Do any of the Dragons know?"

"No," Solander said, "and I don't want them to. Wraith is going to let me try to figure out how he does what he does, which is going to get me into the Academy in a top slot. In exchange, he and his friend are going to live here. But you have to help me." Solander leaned forward and stared into her eyes, willing her to realize how desperately he needed her help. "This is important, Velyn. Maybe the most important thing I'll ever have a chance to do in my life."

She nodded. "Yes. Yes." She closed her eyes, rubbed her temples, frowned. "I could get an aircar with a universal pass from one of Keer Perald's subalterns, perhaps, or one of your father's—but for that I'd have to get into the restricted lot, and I'd owe . . ." Her voice faded, and Solander saw her lower her lashes and angle her glance toward Wraith for just an instant. She glanced away so quickly Solander could almost have thought he imagined the look; he did think he imagined the context of it. Could his wild, rebellious cousin be looking at Wraith, at that scrawny Warrener *boy*, with interest? Attraction? Surely not.

And Velyn straightened, and rubbed her hands together, and said, "Yes. I can, I think, get the necessary aircar after all. And we can get the papers, but you're going to have to have someplace down in the Belows to hide the two of them for a few days while all the papers are made. I know absolutely that they're going to have to be present before any of the real work is done. They'll have to give some of their blood, and have their images spelled into the disks, and there's no way to do that in advance."

Solander glanced at Wraith. "We can wait a few days to get you up here."

"We can," Wraith agreed. "But we can't wait at all to get Jess out of the Warrens. The guards could inspect the basement where we hide at any time—or just do a house-to-house sweep and take people away, and get her when they get the Sleepers."

"A house-to-house sweep?" Solander felt a little sick to his stomach. "What are you talking about?"

"A couple of times a month, the guards bring a truck, go into one of the buildings, and take away most of the people who live there." Wraith shrugged. "Then, a few days later, they bring in people who aren't Sleepers, and lock them in the house until the Way-fare has had time to work."

Solander could not believe Wraith was describing reality when he spoke of this; in no way could taking people from their homes be something that happened under the watchful eyes of the Dragons, in the benevolent world to which the Hars Ticlarim had given birth. Wraith's friend had seen something that he hadn't understood, or . . .

Solander shuddered. The little hairs on the back of his neck kept trying to stand up, and his belly tightened of its own accord, as if he were facing an examination from his father for which he had neither read his texts nor studied his practicals. Wraith couldn't be right. But if for some reason there was some truth in what he was saying, then Solander could lose the one person whose very existence flew in the face of everything he'd learned about the workings and applications of magic; the one person who promised a look into a universe with a different set of rules, or into facets of his own universe which no one before him had ever suspected.

He turned to Velyn and said, "Could you get that aircar today?"

Velyn bit her lip and avoided looking at Wraith at all. "If I'm to be the one to drive it, I'm going to have to do a great deal of convincing. But I know a subaltern I think might be . . . willing to be convinced." Her voice dropped to almost a whisper for those last few words. She turned away from both of them. "I'll go now. If I have any luck, I'll be back with you as soon as I can. Wait here, though—I don't want to have to do anything to find you that might call attention to any of us."

Both boys nodded their agreement, and Velyn vanished down the hall.

Solander sat on one of his chairs and watched Wraith, who had gone to the door and was staring after her.

"What's she like?" Wraith said, his back still to Solander.

Solander tried to figure out what to tell this strange boy. "She likes men," he said after long thought. "I've never seen her show any interest in boys. She's very smart, and talented in her own way, but a lot of her talent seems to be in getting herself into trouble and then evading the consequences of it—at least that's what my father told my mother. Her own parents have considered sending her to Berolis Undersea—that's a finishing school for young stolti women—for a year or two to calm her down. Her mother and my mother are from the same great house and are either second or third cousins—I can never quite keep it straight— but they're also very good friends."

Wraith seemed uninterested in any of that. "What does she like to do?"

Solander thought about the only things he had any real proof that she liked to do—one of which she was probably on her way to do again in order to secure Wraith's friend an aircar—and decided that he had better stick to the less inflammatory facts, and leave the more hurtful ones for Wraith to discover on his own once his puppyish adoration had found the time to dim. "She likes to gamble. She likes to discuss philosophy. She likes to read and to dance. And she's very fond of running, for some reason—I cannot imagine why, but she asked that a track be laid for her through the stargarden, and every morning she goes out there and races around it in circles as if she were being pursued by the Lost Gods."

"She runs. . . ." Wraith smiled when he said it.

"You sound like you think that's a good thing."

Wraith finally turned away from the door and looked at him. "*I* run."

Solander laughed a little. "Don't get your heart set on her. I like her—she's a friend, and a good person, I think. At least mostly. But . . ." He stood up and headed back to his still-in-pieces distance viewer. "Just don't get your heart set on her. She's going to end up taking oaths with a Dragon, I'd wager."

Wraith said nothing, but in his eyes Solander could see the stirrings of defiance.

Velyn came back a very long time later—the sun had moved to the middle of the sky, Solander had completed his kit, and both boys had eaten a large meal brought to them by Enry.

She erupted through the door and wasted no time on pleasantries. "Now, if you want to go—both of you after me, and try to keep up. We have almost no time, and I swear it's our heads—mine as well as both of yours—if we get caught."

Velyn bolted back out and took off at a run down one corridor and then another. Wraith kept pace with her without any trouble, but poor Solander kept getting left behind.

"Keep up," she called back, and the red-faced, gasping Solander would lift his hands from his knees, straighten out, and start after them again.

Velyn took them to a place she referred to as the "private drive deck." The vehicle waiting for them was huge, and of a black so dark it seemed to surround itself with a cloak of night in the middle of the day, and marked on each door with a circle of gold and green. Solander hobbled onto the drive, leaned over and gripped his knees, and stood gasping while Velyn got in and started the spells that made the aircar float just above the ground. Wraith tried to figure out the mechanism that opened the back door; Solander saw that he was having trouble and, still gasping, opened it for him. Wraith climbed in, and Solander flopped onto the seat behind him, clutching his left side and groaning, "I'm dying. I'm dying."

"You're not dying," Velyn snapped. "You're just lazy."

Solander managed to sit up straight. "I may be lazy, but you're simply mad. Do you realize that this is my father's carriage-of-state? If we take this and he finds out, he'll kill us. All of us."

"Shut up. This cost me more than you can imagine. And this is the *only* one that we can count on to make it into the Warrens no matter what, without us getting stopped or searched or shot down when we come back out." She glared at Solander with murderous eyes, and Wraith watched Solander shrink in on himself. The doors shut, and the windows instantly darkened. Wraith suspected that outside, no one would be able to see anything of the people inside.

All to the good. He held no illusions about how well two boys and a girl, none of them old enough to be people in positions of authority, would fare taking a car designed to draw attention to itself into the Warrens, and then back out. Best that no one could tell who hid inside the vehicle.

Wraith gave Velyn instructions on which roads she should take to get to the Vincalis Gate of the Warrens. He noticed, too, how tightly her hands gripped the steering posts, how tense she sat, with her back rigid and her jaw clenched, how she would not speak a word to either of them, except when she needed to know where next she had to turn. Wraith sensed both anger and fear in her, and he ached that it was for his cause that she should feel either of those things.

The great black aircar cruised up to Vincalis Gate, and the gate peeled back as if afraid. They slipped behind the walls, and Wraith noticed that now both Velyn and Solander stared around them as if unable to believe their eyes. They had wanted screaming mobs, painted women, fighting and madness and violence to fulfill their lifetime expectations of the place, and instead they got empty streets and silence. He was shocked, too, but for a different reason. On every corner two guards stood, and at every fourth corner a huge windowless ground vehicle sat, back doors flung open so that he could see people—Warreners—already sitting passively in the back. Accepting their fate, unquestioning because they were unable to question, or to fight.

As he pointed Velyn down a street toward his hideout, two guards came out of a building with an entire family of Warreners between them— mother, father, and a dozen children from near-adult to passive, blank-eyed infant. Velyn stopped and watched and waited as the whole troop crossed the street in front of her, and Wraith saw her face lose its color.

"They're . . . so fat. So pale. And why are they just . . . going with those men? They aren't fighting. They aren't even arguing. . . ."

Wraith, who had never seen adults from the Warrens outside of their tiny homes, had to agree. The adults and older children, all dressed in simple, sleeveless white shifts that fell about to their knees, all shoeless and hatless, carried so much fat on their frames that their feet disappeared beneath rolls of it, so that they looked like they walked on huge, quivering pillars. Their arms stuck out at near-right angles from their sides, their eyes nearly disappeared in rolls of fat, their heads sat on massive rounded shoulders, necks reduced to nothing but rolled tubes of fat stacked one on top of another. Outside of the Warrens, he had never seen anyone who looked even remotely like them.

"Those are the Sleepers. They can't argue," Wraith said. "They can't fight. They don't really know where they are or what is happening to them. They spend their lives in a walking Sleep—the food they eat makes them fat, and it keeps them in the haze they live in. If the daily lessons didn't tell them to feed their children and wash themselves, or sleep at night and use the toilet to relieve themselves, they would do nothing but suck Way-fare from their little dishes all day until they exploded."

Velyn watched the mother carrying the baby—how she seemed almost unaware of it, and how it seemed uncaring of her oblivion. "Are they even human?"

"You'll meet Jess soon," Wraith said. He was watching for Smoke, praying that Smoke wouldn't be among those who marched toward . . . vanishment. "She was once like those people. I got other food for her, and kept her away from the teaching screens and the house altars. Eventually, she got better. I freed other friends, too. . . ." His voice trailed off.

Solander said, "Then someone is doing this to them. This isn't what we see in the nightlies. This isn't anything like the Warrens that everyone talks about. This is . . ." He sat in his seat, transfixed, leaning a little toward the guards and their captives. "This is worse."

"It's the worst place in the world," Wraith said. "If I could save everyone here, I would."

"How could we? Cut off the food they eat? Bring in better food?"

Wraith shook his head. "Most of them would die without their Way-fare. I tried to save older people, but they don't last without their Way-fare three or four times a day. They start tearing their eyes out and screaming and beating their heads against the walls, and if you don't get them back on the Way-fare fast enough, they die. Some children do, too, and there's really no way of knowing which ones will, or when it's safe to try to save them, or when it's too late."

He tried not to think about that. Not now. Not with some new horror being unleashed on the people of the Warrens, people who were being dragged from their homes helpless and uncomprehending and led off to unknown horrors. These were more people he could not save.

The car started moving forward again as Velyn got her nerve back, and Wraith guided her through the broad, clean white streets to the place where Jess huddled in near-darkness, waiting.

Guards were working their way down this street, too.

"We should wait," Velyn said. "Until they've moved past. Once they're past, we can open the doors and get your friend out."

"We can't wait," Wraith said. "The guards are going into basement apartments, too, and they might open the one Jess is hiding in. And then we'll sit here and watch as they shoot her with their stop-sticks and drag her into the back of one of their trucks. And we'll have to watch as they drive off with her. And we'll never know where they go, or what has happened to her, or anything."

Velyn said, "Shit," under her breath, and pulled the car up onto the walkway, angling it so that it blocked access to the basement door from the street.

"Get her fast," she said. "The second a monitor comes up to this aircar and wants to see my identification or to know what I'm doing here, I'm leaving. And if you're not in the car, I'll leave without you. Either one of you, or both of you. Your father, Solander, will just have to guess what happened to you."

"You can't leave me," Solander said.

"I'm not going to spend time in Refinement for you," she said, eyes locked straight forward, resolutely not looking at either Solander or Wraith. "So get this person and let's get out of here."

Wraith took a deep breath and opened the door nearest the basement.

olander had no difficulty imagining a disastrous outcome for this whole exercise. He wanted to stay in the aircar. Hells, he wanted to tell Velyn to forget the whole thing, leave Wraith with Jess, and get out of the Warrens before something horrible happened. But he wasn't going to find another Wraith out there somewhere, just waiting to make him famous. Wraith was a miracle, and Solander knew it—and above all, he had to protect him, as he would protect any other investment in his future.

So—unasked—he followed.

Across the narrow strip of walk at a crouch, down the stairs, through the already opened door into—

Gloom. A stink that rolled over him with horrific potency; filth and sweat and food gone bad, things he couldn't pin down and didn't want to. His eyes adjusted, and he saw a pile of dirty blankets, and a stick-thin person in white rags gathering up blankets and little boxes and turning to look in terror at him. He flattened himself against the wall, thinking with horror, *That stinking stick is going to sit its filthy body in my father's state aircar?*

And then Wraith was dragging the girl and her things and the box of food he'd given them the day before up the stairs, and grabbing Solander by the shirt and dragging him along behind, and Solander, finding himself flung back into the aircar, could only think, *Wraith didn't need me along after all.*

"Go," he heard Wraith tell Velyn, and he sat up in time to see guards moving toward the car from two different directions, their stop-sticks drawn and suspicious expressions on their faces. Did they not see the insignia on the sides of the car? This aircar couldn't be stopped; Solander knew neither he nor Velyn could offer adequate registration for the state carriage they were in—and they certainly couldn't provide documentation for the two scruffy children hiding in the back.

"I'm going," Velyn said. She veered the vehicle out onto the street and accelerated it almost straight up. In the backseat, Jess screamed.

"Rooming house first," Velyn said, looking back at Solander. "We'll drop her and Wraith off to let them shower, and then I will get rid of this aircar, and then you and I will go out and buy them some clothing. Something loose and casual and expensive—maybe a little out of fashion. After all, they are supposed to be from the backwaters. You have your cards with you, don't you?"

Solander nodded. He was going to buy both of them expensive clothing? Well . . . yes, he was. The price of fame, he told himself. The price of immortality, of making his mark in the science of magic, of changing the way the masters in the field understood the workings of their universe. Stolti clothing for two Warreners versus the whole of a world in his hand, to create and reshape in his vision . . . yes. He would buy them clothes. Rent them a couple of rooms for a few days. Pay for their false documents. His parents gave him a generous allowance, and he never really spent it on much except for research books and gadgets. He had money saved away that he would never miss.

Velyn took them not through but over the gate—they went sailing through an arc shield that sputtered and played light across the surface of the aircar as they blasted through it—but the car did have clearances for every place in the city. It passed through without damage, and Velyn headed them directly for a good neighborhood in the Belows.

"Rainsbury Park has some excellent little rooming houses," she told Solander. "I've been to a few of them."

Solander noticed that the back of her neck turned bright pink when she said that, and he wondered if Wraith had noticed.

She brought the aircar to a stop at the side of an attractive house artistically hidden beneath a canopy of ancient oaks. "Wait here, all of you," she said, and then glared when Solander didn't move. "Not you. You have to go in and pay."

The manager of the house, a bored young man with his attention focused on a triphase display of the ongoing Oel Artis/Chamilleri phaeton races, barely even looked at either of them as they took keys and signed in for two rooms at the back of the house.

"He gets paid extra not to pay too much attention," Velyn told Solander as they hurried to the aircar.

They moved Wraith and Jess into their rooms, made sure the dividing door between the two rooms was working, then they took the aircar straight back to the house car pool. Velyn hurried over to a young man in uniform, who gave her a smarmy smile that Solander didn't like.

Velyn, in a foul mood, came back and led Solander to another vehicle—a little red all-terrain sportster with water wings and a bubble hood. "Let's go," she said, and refused to speak to him for most of the rest of the trip.

The pounding water of the shower soothed Jess. Apartments in the Warrens had showers, but none with warm or hot water, none with any real water pressure, none with the glorious array of perfumes and soaps that sprayed from the nozzle when different buttons on the console were pushed. Jess had a hard time forcing herself out from beneath the clean-scented spray, and only Wraith's worried voice finally moved her to try one of the thick towels. When she was done, she wrapped the towel around herself and headed out to the main room; she couldn't bear to put on the stinking Warrener rags.

Then she waited, sitting on the edge of one of the two enormous, wondrously soft beds in the room. Wraith sat with her. Neither of them moved; they weren't sure what they were permitted to touch and what was forbidden. Jess tried to realize that she was out of the Warrens, that this beautiful room—with so many colors that her eyes had a hard time seeing them all—was her room alone, not even to be shared with Wraith. But none of it seemed real. The guards loading Warreners by the hundreds into the back of trucks—yes. That seemed real. But this felt like an impossible dream.

Then Wraith opened a large copper box that sat against one wall of his room and said, "Jess, there's food in here!"

Jess walked over to take a look. Cold air washed over her, air that smelled deliciously of winter and snow. She saw all sorts of foods and drinks she didn't recognize, with perfect fresh fruits, delicious sweets wrapped in lovely colored papers, and things she couldn't begin to recognize by their look or their smell.

"Can we eat them?" she asked.

"Just a few bites, perhaps," Wraith said.

Tentatively, he unwrapped one of the bright papers and took a little bite of the brown sphere inside. "Oh," he whispered, and handed the rest to her.

She took a bite, and the flavor hit her like a shock. She closed her eyes and let the sweetness and the richness and the faint bitterness all melt into her mouth at the same time.

"What is it?"

"I don't know."

"Is there more?"

Wraith unwrapped another of the colored papers. "This one looks a little different. You want to try it first?"

She nodded and took a bite. It was different. The same rich brown stuff, but this time with a fruit-flavored filling. "Oh. Wraith." She handed him the other half. "We've died and gone to the God-home."

The knock at the door froze them—it wasn't the right tap. Not two quick, soft knocks and a finger scratched from the left of the door to the right. Just a flurry of loud raps. They looked at each other, wild-eyed with terror, and Jess grabbed Wraith and fled for the bathroom in her suite. She'd seen a lock on that door.

But Solander walked into the room carrying a stack of boxes almost as tall as himself. "Wraith? Jess? Where are you?"

"You didn't use the knock I showed you," Wraith said. He looked a little pale still.

Solander shrugged. "I forgot. And my hands were full."

They edged out of the bathroom and looked at Solander and his stack of boxes. Jess's heart continued to pound in her chest; this place was too different, too alien for her to feel safe. She wondered if she would ever be able to feel safe.

"We brought clothes and food," Solander was saying, and behind him, the golden-skinned girl with the copper eyes came through the door, studied them, and shook her head.

"Oh, gods! They look even thinner wrapped in towels," she said. "We'll have to hide them here until they put on a bit of weight."

Jess looked from that girl's sleek, rounded body to her own sharp angles, and felt her cheeks go hot with shame. Her thighs were thinner than her knees, her upper arms thinner than her elbows. She could clearly make out every bone in her own ribcage, and could clearly see both the bones and the tendons outlined on the backs of her hands. Wraith was the same. But the white Warrener robes hid a lot of that— not even she had noticed how very thin they were until she compared them to Solander's cousin Velyn.

"We got food," Solander told Velyn. "They'll look a little better soon."

"They'll have to. I don't think we can pass two starvelings off as the children of colonists—not even colonists from Ynjarval."

Wraith sighed.

Velyn said, "Don't worry about it. We'll manage. In the meantime, Solander and I found the two of you some clothes. These are guaranteed to fit—they're spelled, so that no matter which of you wears them, they'll look like they were tailored just for you.

"Tomorrow," she continued, "I'll come back here and take you to different salons to get your hair cut and styled, your skin colored, and your hands manicured." She turned to Solander. "You can find your own way home unless you're coming with me now. I have things I have to do."

Solander and Wraith conferred for a moment, and then, with a slight nod of the head to all of them, Solander and Velyn left.

Jess was relieved when they were gone. She'd liked Solander well enough, but she hadn't liked Velyn at all. She'd seen the way Wraith looked at the other girl—with his eyes all wide and wondering. That was the way she wanted him to look at her. But he didn't. She was too scrawny, she thought. To skinny, too plain, too young—and he had saved her from the Way-fare twilight, from being a horrible fat lifeless slug. How could he ever see her as anyone but someone he had rescued?

Velyn would never look like that to him. He would see her perfect, as she was the first time he met her, and not hideous, helpless, someone who needed to be saved.

Jess, in that moment, decided that she hated Velyn—for everything Velyn was, for everything that Jess could never be.

A week of searching for someone to make papers for them. A month beyond that to learn to speak with a bit of the accent of the colony from whence they supposedly came—one carefully obscure, with few ties to Oel Artis, a colony clear across the Bregian Ocean, in the southern hemisphere, on the Strithian continent, in lands only held with difficulty by the Hars. Beyond that, another two months for the Warreners to fill out to a point that Velyn announced was acceptable.

And then the move; the day Wraith and Jess had come to both yearn for and dread, when, carrying their false Letter of Presentation sealed with the signet of a real, if very minor, Dragon from the far city of Cachrim, they appeared on the front porch of the great house in the Aboves at Oel Artis. They brought carefully collected bags filled with clothes meant to look like styles from a colony behind the times—a bit shabby around the edges but still respectable; and they offered their papers to the Master of the House, an old patriarch who still maintained his Dragon ties, even though he had for all purposes given over all responsibility except for the greeting of newcomers to the house and the verification of their status to younger and stronger men.

Solander greeted Wraith and Jess as cousins whom he had met and was expecting, with an enthusiasm greater than he usually displayed, and the old patriarch, who knew Solander as the son of a major Dragon of the Council, gave their papers a polite, perfunctory glance and filed them, giving them not another moment's thought.

We shed lives the way snakes shed skins, Wraith thought, remembering the nest of snakes he'd discovered in one of his early hiding places. We peel away old people, and emerge with new ones. New names. New faces.

He stood just inside the door, a heavier boy now, though still thin, with his dark hair neatly cropped and the beginnings of a fashionable braid down his back. He had a new name—Gellas Tomersin—a good story about a family far away who cared about him, a friend who had been born into freedom and who knew the joys of comfort and the pleasures of wealth and security. He had a chance to live a wonderful life.

Why should we ever go back and pick up those dead skins? he wondered. When we're free of them, can't we simply put them behind us and forget they ever existed? Can't we simply be happy and beautiful in our new skins?

He'd thought he wanted to free the Warreners. But now, standing at the beginning of his new life, he discovered that more than anything, he wanted to be sure that he stayed free himself.

Rone Artis held the paper in front of him and sighed. "Ten years of research, and all we have to show for our work is . . . well, simply more of the same."

His assistant shrugged. "Everyone has followed every lead. Just because we can't find a way to pump enough magic out of the sun right now to keep the Empire running doesn't mean that we'll never find the key. The same with the sea, and with the world-heart. Sometime soon, someone will figure out how to make those power sources work. This is just a temporary measure."

Rone laughed. "Do you really believe that?"

"Of course. The Empire would never accept this as a permanent solution."

"Do you know how long this temporary solution has gone on so far?"

"Not long, certainly. Five years, perhaps. Or maybe . . . ten?"

Rone Artis, Master of Energy for the city of Oel Artis, smiled at her slowly. "In its current form, more than a thousand years."

She paled and looked sick. "That can't be."

"It is. And before that, we were doing the same thing, but in a less organized fashion."

"But . . . that's not right."

"No," he agreed, and took out his official pen, and checked the tip on a plain piece of paper to make sure it was working. "It isn't right at all. But what are our options? Let Oel Artis Travia fall into the Belows? Let the citizens starve and live without light and heat? Let the seas crush Oel Maritias and the other undersea cities? Give up flight? Give up magic?"

"Well . . . no . . . not that."

He nodded. "No. Not that. We maintain a magnificent civilization, but men pay a price for civilization. We do the best we can. Sometimes our best is . . ." He slowly signed his name across the bottom of the paper that permitted the Research Department of the Dragons to take an additional five hundred units a month from the Warrens for energy experimentation. "Sometimes our best is very, very bad."

Book Two

❖

Master Gellas

I stood with one foot in three worlds—which is one foot too many. The Warreners, the stolti, and the Kaan all owned a piece of me: I loved the beauty, the grace, and the luxury of the stolti world, which I knew to be fed by unthinkable evil; I could see the impracticality of the Kaan world, which worked well enough for a few people, but which would leave Matrin a stinking ruin were it the only option; and my heart cried out for the Warreners, dying body and soul for a life they could never experience, while remembering that the price of the Warreners' freedom would be the lives of innocents.

I knew the costs and the benefits, had discovered and listed for myself the favorables and the unfavorables. The only thing I could not find was an answer.

VINCALIS THE AGITATOR
THE SECRET TEXTS—OF THE FALCONS

Chapter 4

In the last days of spring, when the sun in Oel Artis begins to roll across the land like an invading army and the heat turns everything green to brown, the rich and powerful of the Aboves begin their annual migration to their city beneath the sea, Oel Maritias.

In the spring of the year that Solander turned twenty, and that Wraith, still known by all but Solander, Jess, and Velyn as Gellas, guessed that he must have turned nineteen or twenty, the household took itself down to the cool blue depths of the summerhouse yet again, down to the world of perpetual twilight where the sun was merely a promise of light that lay, painted and flat and dull, on the top of the blue-black liquid sky.

To celebrate their arrival, they and the other families who summered there held each year a First Week Festival, and for the first time, both Wraith and Solander were deemed old enough to attend the adult celebration, instead of being kept with the children.

"What do you suppose is the difference between the adult celebration and the children's festival?" Wraith asked.

Solander, stretched out on his bed with his feet propped on the wall, said, "No one will ever really say. They serve distilled wines and set up vision chambers, I know. And sometimes the adults go into the festival chambers and don't come out again until the end of the week. I know my parents used to leave me with the house staff when I was younger. I wouldn't even see them for days, and when they did come back, they looked tired."

Wraith laughed. "That sounds promising." He draped himself over one of Solander's overstuffed chairs, head on one arm and legs across the other, and sighed. "Jess is furious that we're going and she can't."

Solander let his head hang off the side of the bed so that he was looking at Wraith upside down. "I'd take her with me if I could. I wish she
would go places with me."

"I wish she would, too. She's about to drive me mad."

"How can you not be in love with her?" Solander asked. Wraith
guessed that his expression was meant to be mournful, but upside down
it wasn't coming across. "She's beautiful, she's clever—"

"She's moderately clever. She plays zith and metachord well enough
not to offend, but she'd never be able to play for anyone but us. She has
no skill with numbers, is only moderately successful at getting off a spell
correctly, can't find her way from one part of Oel Artis to another without getting lost, and is useless at history, science, and literature. She
doesn't even like to read. Beyond that, she's bothersome and domineer-
ing and vexing and always certain that she's right and that she knows
best."

"She adores you."

"Mmmm. I'm glad to have her for a friend, but I truly wish she
adored you. Every time she sees me talking to a girl, her eyes go all daggers at me."

Solander flopped over and rested his chin on his hands. "We'll get
back to research after the festival."

Wraith said, "You only have another two months before you have to
present your research before the Board of Advisors, and you still don't
have anything."

"I have a lot. It's all work that I got as spin-offs from trying to figure
out why you are the way you are, but if nothing else, I can present that.
I have a refinement for a spell's energy transport mechanism that's rather
elegant, and a few applications for the self-powered magic system that
I'm developing—those are completely original. And I have my theory on
you. I simply don't have any real-world proofs yet, and I can't drag you
in with me, for obvious reasons."

"No, you can't. I don't want to be a caged exhibit, or a study case for
the entire Division of Theoretical Magics."

"Have you given thought to what you will be doing?"

"I've had offers from some of the covils. I scored so highly on history
that the Ancients and Devoteds of the Fen Han Covil have been at me to
join them right after the festival. One of the literary covils offered me a
seat, too."

"Which one?"

"The one that thinks all of Premish's work is excrement."

"Oh. The Clickers."

Wraith nodded. "But those are covils. They don't . . . matter. And the fact that my roll of tutelage lists nothing but theoretical magics makes anything worthwhile off limits. *No one* needs a stolti with theoretical but no practical magical skills. Which takes us back to you and what you're doing." Wraith shrugged. "I would help you with more than the theory if I could."

Solander nodded. "I know. But if you could, you would be just like everyone else. The fact that you can't do any of the basic prep work or *anything* magical is part of what makes you unique."

Wraith considered the frightening truth of that for a while. His uniqueness was the only thing that had let him be a human in the prison of the Warrens, that had given him a ticket out and allowed him to bring Jess with him, that had moved him into the highest circles of Harsian society and had given him access to science, history, philosophy, magic—he knew the theories well, even if his uniqueness prevented him from gaining any practical experience—literature, music, art, and government.

Why? Why had he been born different? It was the question he and Solander had spent the last five years trying to answer, without success. But why did the Warrens exist in the first place? He once had a family somewhere in the Warrens. He might still have, if they hadn't been rounded up and put into trucks and hauled away; they might at that minute be sitting in a tiny, stinking apartment, growing older and fatter, oblivious to their lives and yet chained to those appalling lives by the very food that sustained them. If they still lived, his parents and brothers and sisters lived out their days in a prison and a hell. What purpose did that hell and its inhabitants serve?

He'd spent years avoiding that question—until he began having nightmares.

In those dreams, a great golden bird of prey caught him up in its talons and carried him off, depositing him at last back in the little basement where he and Jess—and, once, others—had hidden. On waking, he remembered the bird, and with a bit of research, he'd identified it as a falcon. Gold-crested fish-falcon, to be specific, but since he'd never seen any other sort, he was happy enough to think of it simply as a falcon. He would have been happier not to think of it at all, but it wouldn't leave him alone. When he slept, it haunted him with memories of the Warrens, and guilt and a vague uneasiness that there was something that he was supposed to be doing.

So recently, on his own, he'd tried to locate the truth about the War-rens—to find any sort of information about the area and its people in public records, to find some sort of history of how one section of society had been locked behind high walls and drugged and then forgotten—but there were no true records of the Warrens available anywhere. None. Only the false reports of riots and prostitution and crime rings and mur-ders and rapes and mob rule, complete with recorded "live" images.

"When do you think your father is going to let you use his work-room?" Wraith asked.

Solander said, "Never. Why?"

"Never?"

"No. I don't know of a Dragon anywhere who permits anyone in his workroom. Ever. When a Dragon dies, the spells he has that shield it usually weaken enough that another Dragon can force his way through, but prior to that, the workshops are impregnable. . . ." He sat up and looked at Wraith.

"They wouldn't be to me, would they?"

"If my father found you in his workroom, he would kill you. I mean—quite literally—he would kill you. No one is permitted into a Dragon's workroom. They keep all the government's secret documents and defense-project plans and things like that in there. I've overheard my father talking to other Dragons about what he's working on and . . ." He shook his head vehemently. "If you went in, you would be committing treason against the whole Empire of the Hars Ticlarim."

"I want to find out the truth about the Warrens. I want to find out about why my family was . . . the way they were. Maybe still are, if they aren't all dead. I've looked through the public records, I've scoured the archives, I've read up on history, and I haven't found *anything*."

Solander said, "You're out. You're free of the place, and so is Jess. Why are you suddenly going back to that?"

"Nightmares," Wraith said. "And . . . I don't know. I think once I un-derstand the reason why the Warrens exist, I'll be able to let it go, but I . . . I have to know. Why is this being done? Who are the Warreners? What did they—we—do that was so terrible?"

Solander stared down at his hands. "When I'm accepted into the Academy, I'll get a workroom of my own, and I'll start getting the Dragon references that my father uses, and then you won't have to take any chances going into his office."

Wraith said, "By the time you've finished your first degree in the Academy, that will be five years—"

"I'm thinking I'll be able to do it in three," Solander interrupted, but Wraith shook his head.

"Or maybe you can do it in three, but that's still three more years before I find out the truth. If I do then. You might not get the truth even when you become a first-level Dragon. Maybe what's going on in the Warrens is some sort of government secret, and no one but the people at the very top know the truth."

Solander laughed. "That's ridiculous. What kind of government secret would involve slums?"

"If it isn't important, why is it that the only things we can find out about the Warrens are lies? Why are the Warrens shielded so tightly that your best viewer has never been able to so much as peek over the walls?"

Solander shrugged. "What difference does it make, Wraith? Really? You know what I think? I think that the Warrens really were as awful as the reports show. I think the images of riots and other things shown on the nightlies are from the Warrens, only before the Dragons started a program to settle things down. They . . ." He shrugged. "They put the walls up first, but the walls didn't take care of the problem. So the Dragons created a food distribution system, and put something into the food to calm the criminals down. And now they keep the stuff in the food so that the troubles won't start up again."

Wraith sat up and put his feet on the floor. Carefully. He felt his hands curling into fists and forced himself to relax them. "So the people in the Warrens are natural criminals—if they weren't drugged, they would be rioting and murdering and raping and robbing."

"Well . . . yes. I guess so."

"Like me. Like my friends who never managed to escape." He paused. "Like Jess."

Solander's face flushed deep red, and he averted his eyes. "Well . . . you got out of there. If you'd had to live there your whole lives—"

"We are who we are. The Warreners live behind walls and gates that would kill them if they tried to cross. And those same gates would kill anyone who tried to get in without authorization. So how are the Warreners supposed to improve their lives or do something to make themselves better? Even if they weren't drugged into a stupor, they wouldn't have any chance for a better life."

"Maybe it is a prison, and everyone in it has been sentenced to be there."

"You mean like me? And Jess? We were born there, and both of us have older brothers and sisters who were born there—people who are old enough that they'll have their own children by now . . . if they're still alive. People aren't born with criminal records, Sol."

Now Solander sat up, too. "Look, you're suggesting that the Dragons are doing something wrong. Something big, and secret, and bad."

"Yes."

"That's treason."

"No—it's just looking at the situation and seeing how the pieces fit."

Solander leaned forward. "And what do you want to do about this conspiracy you're alleging? This awful thing you're hinting that my father and other great men in the Hars are responsible for?"

"I want to find out the truth. That's all."

"What if there is no 'truth'? What if there is a good, simple, reasonable explanation?"

Wraith said, "If your brother died because you tried to set him free, if your parents and brothers and sisters were in a cage they could never escape, what sort of good, simple, reasonable explanation would satisfy you?"

"You're obsessed."

"More like haunted. I haven't had a real night's sleep in a month."

"I don't want to have anything to do with this."

"Then I'll leave and find another way to help my family."

Solander rose and paced across the floor. Outside his window, a school of fish flashed into range of the lights that ringed the mansion, and for a moment their black shapes erupted into a riot of reds and yellows and silvers and blues. And then they were gone again.

"Why now?" Solander asked at last. "Why are you pushing this now?"

"Because I'm not a child anymore. And I owe *something* to the people who gave me life and to the world I came from—even if it's nothing more than finding out why that world exists."

"All you want is answers? Once you get your answers, you'll be satisfied with them, and that will be the end of any interest in the Warrens?"

Wraith thought about that for a moment. "If we find a good reason for the existence of the Warrens, I'll let it go."

"Which means if the Dragons are involved in something you don't agree with, you're going to insist on getting yourself into trouble?"

"If you're right, there's no conspiracy related to the Warrens. You're convinced that the Dragons' motives in broadcasting their propaganda and keeping the Warrens beneath a tight shield are completely innocent. So put your convictions where your mouth is. Help me find the truth."

Solander closed his eyes, covered his face with his arms, and groaned. "You want to get both of us killed."

"I won't get you killed, Sol. I swear it."

Solander moved one arm just enough that he could give Wraith a one-eyed glare from underneath it. "All right, then. I'll help you. My parents will be at the festival a lot of the time. Everyone will expect us to stay for the entire week—most of the people our age will. But we won't. We'll go, we'll make sure people see us there, and then we'll leave separately and meet back here. You'll go into my father's workroom, and I'll stand guard to make sure that you don't get caught. You'll look for anything you can find on the Warrens, and then you'll get out of there. And that will be it. Agreed? If you find something, good. If you don't find anything, we still aren't going back. This will be the only time we do this."

Wraith nodded. "I don't want to spy on your father. It's just that he's the only one I could think of who might have access to the answers I need."

Solander said, "I understand, I guess. If I had escaped from that place, I would want to know why it was there, too."

Rone Artis met with the rest of the Dragon Council in secret, in the tower that was the true—if unsuspected—heart of Oel Maritias.

He settled into his seat at due north on the round table and said, "We're called to order. What crisis have you found so great that it has to disrupt my preparations for the festival?"

Tare Desttor-fator, Master of Cities, an old man who had always loved his work, looked grimmer and unhappier than Rone had ever seen him. He said, "There's some cracking at the periphery of the city. Spell-shields there have been suffering from fluctuating energy levels, and a few of us have added braces. But we're going to have to increase our base power level."

Rone tried not to show any expression, but he feared his colleagues might have seen some hint of his dismay in his eyes. "Cracks?"

"The Polyphony Center has severe weakening along the second-tier dome. Several of the houses along Sea Cliff Corridor have minor compression damage. Almost all of the buildings right up against the Upwelling have some shear damage. Nothing has started leaking yet, but you know that most of the year-rounders, myself included, stay in the city core—the scenic peripheral properties are mostly occupied by those of you who aren't here for half the year. A lot of damage can happen during half a year."

"But fluctuations should have been noticeable to everyone," Jonn Dart, Master of the Air, said.

"They've apparently been quite small but also quite persistent," Tare told everyone. "I've been doing some checking—the spellshields are running at a constant underpower of .00125 percent—not enough to show unless you're looking for it, but enough to allow the pressure to work constant, tiny damage."

Around the circle of Dragons, heads shook, faces paled, knuckles whitened.

"I thought we had surplus power," the Master of Transports, Kenyan Inmaris, said softly.

Rone, the Master of Energy, said, "We've been running tight Upstairs for the last year. A number of new projects have put a drain on the supply, and we haven't been pouring in resources as quickly as we need. No wars, empty prisons, and a declining birthrate in the Warrens due to several centuries of serious inbreeding have kept us behind the curve. I'd like to say that this is an easy fix, but it isn't. We're going to have to find a new energy source, and we're going to have to do it fast. Research—you've had people working on alternative energy for the past twenty years. I know we've been funneling whole breeder pods out of the Oel Artis Warrens on a regular basis for you to use as research subjects. I've heard that you've had some breakthroughs, but none of them have ever come as far as Council."

Chrissa Falkes, Master of Research, a stunning, young-looking woman who was in fact several years Rone's senior, said, "I don't like the direction some of our research has taken. Yes, we have some possible alternatives. But our current energy sources were supposed to be temporary—until we found non-human alternatives. And my alternatives are simply going to increase our dependence on human-based energy."

Rone sighed. This again. Every time they tried to make changes, to expand services or improve the city, it came back to the complaint about human-based energy as the fuel that fed the Hars Ticlarim. "Stolta Falkes, solar-driven magic is weak. Core-driven magic is weak. Elemental magic is weak. Even sea-driven magic is weak. Every attempt at amplification has failed to produce anything that would even come close to meeting the needs of the Empire. We have eight billion people pulling off of just eighteen main centers and one hundred fifteen secondary buffer sources. We're an absolute marvel of economy—but the only source that will allow us to support eight billion energy-using citizens at even our current level of civilization—never mind making things better—is human-based." Rone looked directly at Chrissa. "Unless you've found something outside of flesh and bone and blood and life that will fuel spells of the magnitude and multitude we have to work with."

Chrissa bit her lip and looked down at her hands. "How bad is the shortage?"

The Master of Cities said, "I predict a collapse along the outer rim within the year unless we shore up the spellshields and repair the damage. And a collapse anywhere in the city will put extra pressure on the buildings closest to the one that goes: If we lose something sufficiently big in the first blow—like Polyphony, for example—the whole of the city could explode around us in a matter of minutes. We aren't likely to have any more warning than what we already have."

"Oh, gods." The stolta buried her face in her arms and sat there for a long time. Everyone watched her, silent, waiting. At last she lifted her head. "The greater good," she whispered, then said, "We've developed something that gives spell energy at an order of magnitude greater than the *combined* energies of flesh, bone, blood, and life. But it's a dirty source. Dirtier than all of those together."

Dirty meant that anyone using it was at risk of serious magical rebound effects, or *rewhah*. *Rewhah* was the bane of all magical research— it could turn a man into a smoking pile of twitching tissue in an instant if not properly handled—and life energy was so dirty and so dangerous that Dragons only dared operate with it from a distance, and through mechanical devices that diverted the *rewhah* and spread the effects over the entire population. Rone couldn't imagine a source of energy dirtier than life energy.

"A whole order of magnitude?" the Master of Cities said with wonder in his eyes. "A hundred thousand luns per unit instead of ten thousand. You're sure?"

"I'm sure. And it's constant per unit—no factoring for size, age, or health."

"Good gods," Rone said. "We're only getting ten thousand LPU in controlled settings right now. With a constant, we could stop worrying about undersized units throwing off our power estimates. We would be able to tell exactly how much available power we had at any time."

"There's a downside," Chrissa said. "It's a big one."

"Bigger than the *rewhah* factor?"

Chrissa nodded. "We'd be burning souls."

The debate ran a long time. They needed the energy, needed it badly. And their two options were to use more people, which meant rewriting laws that made into capital crimes things that were currently minor infractions, so that they could fill up the Warrens with fresh prisoners; or to use the people they already had more completely.

Kenyan finally said, "It isn't like the Warreners are real people—they don't think from the moment they're born until the moment they die—we've seen to that. They're nothing but caged and cared-for animals—no feelings, no ideas, no dreams. That they have souls at all is a wonder, but that we can use those souls to provide a better life for real people is a gift. A true gift."

Chrissa wasn't appeased. "And what about the prisoners that we put into the Warrens? They were real people once."

"We only send in the life-criminals. I've always thought the comfortable oblivion of the Warrens was too kind a treatment for the horrors they perpetrate on citizens. Look at what they've done and tell me—what kind of souls could they have, anyway? Evil souls. If we can feed the good of the city with the loss of evil souls, then we are in effect turning evil into good."

"You'll find a way to justify anything, won't you," Chrissa asked.

Rone held up a hand. "In this instance, I have to agree with Kenyan. We have to find energy to protect and maintain the Empire. Our other alternative is to put more people into the Warrens, enlarge the Warrens, use people who aren't nightmare criminals or the animals we've been breeding for this purpose for the last thousand-plus years. If we broaden our spectrum of people we're willing to have in the Warrens, where will our broadening stop? Our energy needs will grow. They must. We can keep moving our breeders around to prevent inbreeding and keep our reproductive rates high. We can move more criminals who have done less to deserve punishment into the Warrens. We can take the rebels and the traitors out of the mines and factories and feed them into the Warrens. But even so, our need for energy is expanding, and our space for new Warrens is not. This alternative you've given allows us to make incredible use of limited resources. It isn't pretty. We'll certainly have to design specialized facilities to handle this new form of energy. But I think it's the best alternative we're going to get."

Chrissa slumped back in her seat, disgusted and defeated. "Fine. Rone—I'll have the specifications and incantations couriered to your workroom as soon as I leave here. I want you to look over our research, see what I've seen and noted on this in the past twenty years of development, and then decide if you still think it's a good idea. With the power-to-*rewhah* curves in front of you, you might just change your mind. If you don't, you and your people should be able to put together a quick patch in the next day or two—I'm sure you'll have long-term facilities set up in no time." She closed her eyes and exhaled slowly. Then she stood. "And as soon as you've received the information, you'll receive my formal resignation. I've considered going into private practice—I think I've just reached the point where I can't do this job anymore. I'll send along my recommendations for successors from within the Research Department, some of whom are quite excited about the possibilities of this project. I'm sure you'll each have favorites of your own you would like to consider, too."

"You're quitting?" Rone asked, stunned. Chrissa was second in line for Grand Mastership of the Dragons of the Hars—no one who held the second spot had ever quit. It would be like being one step from godhood and turning down the job.

"I'm quitting. This isn't something I can keep on my conscience. We've pursued this line of research against my personal recommendations, because influential researchers below me outvoted me; I presented the option hoping against hope that one of you would offer some alternative—a way of reducing energy consumption, of conserving the resources we currently have, of doing something sensible. But you are set on expansion, and you will have your added power. I just won't be a part of it."

"Chrissa . . ." Jonn Dart, as Master of Air, specialized in developing and improving the special spells that kept the floating cities and the aircars aloft. His unit always had energy expenditures far above those in other units, and though he and his people had become quite good at economizing, their work was a massive energy drain. "Are you going to leave Oel Maritias? Or Oel Artis? Are you going to confine yourself to the dirt, to ground transport and ground housing, and turn your back on the wonders and the artistry and the beauty we have wrought in true civilization?"

Chrissa rose, gathered up her things, and looked at him with pain in her eyes. "I don't know what I'm going to do. I just know that we shouldn't be doing this."

"It isn't voted on yet," offered the Master of Cities.

"No. Shall I wait for the vote to be counted to see who among you are secret advocates for the poor and the defenseless?"

"There are no poor and no defenseless involved in this," Rone protested. "Only lab animals who wear almost-human skins—though you have seen them in the flesh, and you know how little they resemble real people—and criminals who have caused so much suffering that they have been exiled from humanity." He rose so that he stood facing Chrissa and, with a voice carefully controlled but edged with anger, said, "The Hars is the most humanitarian government this world has ever seen. No one starves in our Empire. No one goes without food, without clothing, without a solid roof or a place to sleep. No one is without an education. For the poorest people, we pay for everything. Even the Warreners, whose ancestors were gathered from the gutters and the madhouses and the prisons, have food and water, beds and shelter, clothing and protection, supplied by us from cradle to grave. They want for nothing, and they want nothing, and they live long lives."

"And you burn them as fuel in payment for your 'generosity.' And now you will be burning not just what is mortal about them, but what is immortal, too. Do not be too quick to applaud yourselves for your generosity—for your humanitarianism. Not everyone in this world is equal, Rone."

"Equality is a myth. A fantasy of dreamers and revolutionaries. We do the best we can. There are always costs. But I think we have done well in keeping our costs within reason, and offering good to the most people for the least price."

"If you and yours were the ones who had to pay the price, I suspect that you would think it a little less reasonable." She gave a formal bow to all of them—coldly precise, almost insulting in its perfection—and said, "I won't wait for the results of your vote. I'll simply go and ready the information you will need. And will, in the meantime, come up with a suitable story for my sudden resignation."

She left, and in the wake of the slamming of the door, the Dragon Masters of the Hars sat in quiet contemplation.

Finally, however, the Grand Master of the Dragon Council, who until this time had been silent, rose and said, "A vote must be called. We have a quorum present, and due to the severity of the situation we face, and the way that history will judge what we do here, I hereby declare that we require not a simple majority but a two-thirds majority in the question we must now answer. Before we bring the question before this body, you have heard discussion both for and against the use of this new form of energy. Does anyone among you have anything further you wish to add?"

No one spoke. No one moved. To Rone's eyes, it seemed they barely breathed.

The Grand Master nodded. "Then I ask that one of you present the question to this body for consideration and vote."

The Grand Master stood and waited. A few of the Dragons cleared their throats uncomfortably. Finally the Master of Air and the Master of Cities both started to rise at the same time, and the Master of Air, junior in both age and seniority, bowed slightly to the Master of Cities and sat back down. Tare Desttor-fator straightened his shoulders and took a deep breath. "I bring before the Master Dragons of the Council of Dragons of the Empire of the Hars Ticlarim the following Question of Merit, requiring a two-thirds vote of approval of a quorum of this body: I move that we—with all haste and yet all caution—bring into use soul-energy drawn from current fuel units. Furthermore, I move that Oel Maritias and such other undersea cities as are found to have low-energy damage be immediately given access to the first energy drawn from this new resource, in order to effect emergency repairs and prevent unnecessary loss of life. Finally, I move that no new fuel units be acquired or placed at this time, but that we make all efforts to efficiently use those units already in place."

"Second," a couple of voices from around the table said.

"Duly moved and seconded," the Grand Master said. "At this time we will entertain discussion either for or against the merits of this motion— each speaker has three minutes."

No one rose to defend either the pro or con views. Rone watched, already quite sure of how he would vote. Everyone else seemed certain, too. The Grand Master waited long enough to be sure that no one would leap to his feet at the last moment for one impassioned plea, then said, "Very well. We have a motion on the floor to make more efficient use of our current energy units by adding soul-energy usage to their current utility. This motion specifically excludes the possibility of adding new units to our energy production, and requires first fruits of the new technology go to undersea cities to effect emergency repairs. A two-thirds vote of quorum is necessary to pass this motion. Twenty-five of twenty-eight active members of the Council are present—a two-thirds majority of that number is seventeen. Since no tie is possible, I will not vote."

Rone had a sudden sense that there were things the Grand Master was leaving unsaid. He raised a finger. "Rone?" the Grand Master asked.

"Might I ask how you would vote if you were voting?"

"No." The Grand Master's voice was neutral. His expression betrayed nothing. Rone could not tell if the acknowledged leader of the Dragons thought the idea wonderful or terrible, or if he was not even thinking about it at all, but was instead considering the state of his sterrits game, and how he might improve his opening moves. "And that question answered," the Grand Master said gently, "I now put before you for vote the question on the floor, reminding you only that you speak not just for this day, but for the future."

The members of the Council each withdrew from the drawer in the table directly in front of their seat three balls—one white, one red, and one purple. White, the absence of color, stood for abstention with prejudice—a comment that the proposal put before the Council was in itself flawed, and that while neither a yea vote nor a nay vote suited the voter, a restatement of the question might. Red—the color of blood, war, and loss—signified a negative. And purple—the color of the Council's flags and pennants, the color of power and wealth, the color of abundance—signified a positive vote.

Each member of the Council took all three balls, so that no one might take a dissenting vote that he had left behind and throw it into the black jar, thus throwing the results of the vote into doubt and requiring a revote.

A councilor could vote four ways: yea; simple abstention, in which the voter dropped all three balls into the discard container; abstention with prejudice; and nay.

Rone palmed the purple ball in his right hand and the other two in his left, and moved into the line behind his fellows. He heard the familiar shuffling of feet, sighing, the clicks as the balls dropped into the voting jar and the discard jar. No one talked—discussion while the actual vote was in progress was absolutely forbidden. No one looked around much, either. Everyone seemed nervous. Because of the makeup of the Council, Rone expected the vote would be close. He wished the Grand Master had not excused himself—Rone could think of more than eight Council members who had in the past exhibited the same lack of logic and foresight that had suddenly erupted from Chrissa, though they rarely had the courage or the integrity to make their preferences clear in the way that Chrissa made hers clear. They were cowards, to his way of thinking—people who voted against progress but would never have the backbone to stand up and *say* they had voted against progress.

Rone dropped his purple ball in the vote container, discarded the red and white ones, and then returned to his seat.

He waited. A few councilors stood over the vote jar, pondering even in the instants before they dropped their votes, and he could just see it. A handful of whites that would invalidate the current question, but might bring up some alternative to the question, a handful of purples from people like him who understood expedient need, who knew that emergencies and disasters could only be prevented by taking whatever steps were required, but in a timely manner—*not* when the city was ready to implode around them all—and a handful of reds from the idiots who had never seen one of those Warren monstrosities, who insisted on thinking of them as people, and who would refuse to acknowledge their debt as councilors to the real humans of the Empire and their needs.

He glanced at each councilor as he or she sat down. Most of them would not meet his eyes. Most of them, in fact, sat with their heads down, guilty expressions on their faces.

Cowards.

All was not lost, though. Chrissa had left before the vote. If she had already couriered the necessary information to him, and if it had been delivered safely to the house, he could do what needed to be done to put the new measure into practice in spite of the vote.

And then the last of the councilors sat, and the Grand Master picked up the black jar that held the votes, and the clear jar into which they would be counted, and took his place at the table. Before all of them, he carefully poured the contents of the black jar into the clear jar, careful not to touch any of the balls that passed between the jars—for even in this stage, he might be accused of tampering with the vote if he was not careful.

And the mass of councilors gasped. The vote was unanimous. Every single ball that fell from the black jar into the clear jar was purple.

Shocked, Rone leaned back in his chair and stared at his fellow councilors, who—wide-eyed—were staring at each other.

The Grand Master looked at the balls. He rolled them from the clear jar into the voting groove carved into the table. Each ball rolled to a numbered slot. The vote lay clear before everyone. Twenty-five votes in favor of adopting the measure. No abstentions except for that of the Grand Master. No abstentions with prejudice. No nays.

"Please record the vote," the Grand Master said, looking at the Master of Histories. The Master of Histories nodded and wrote the vote into the meeting log.

"The vote has been recorded," the Master of Histories said.

"Then record this, also. 'Following the unanimous vote by the membership of the Council of Dragons in favor of the question of the use of human souls as fuel to run the Empire, the 872nd Grand Master of the

Council of Dragons submitted notice of his resignation from the Grand Mastership, from the Council, and from the Dragons, and announced both his retirement and his decision to emigrate from the Empire of the Hars Ticlarim to the outlands—effective immediately." He looked around the table at all of them, his eyes meeting each of theirs in turn, and when he looked into Rone's eyes, Rone felt the Grand Master's disgust with him, his distaste for this heinous thing they had all done—and in that one moment, Rone doubted that expediency was the best course to follow.

But the Grand Master picked up his belongings and said, "I am ashamed that this iniquitous thing has happened on my watch," and turned to Rone and said, "You were third after Chrissa, and I do not doubt that she meant her resignation as deeply and as sincerely as I mean mine. Which makes you acting Grand Master for the rest of my term, and obviously leaves the wolves in charge of the sheep; I hope this nightmare that you and all your fellows have enacted does not soon turn and devour you." And he left.

And with the old Grand Master gone, and Rone placed abruptly and solidly in the Chair, he realized that all of his doubts about the rightness of his vote were erased. His conscience eased. He was among men and women who understood what was best for the Empire of the Hars Ticlarim, and who would do what had to be done to lead it to new heights of greatness.

Chapter 5

In the warm summer currents, festival globes spun the sea into rainbows, and the many-colored streamers brought forth fish by the tens of thousands, so that they became like living stars dancing in the liquid sky.

Music swept out into the currents—the sweet strains of romantic ballads, the cheerful lilt of dance music, the martial strains of the military bands that were the only public remnant of the Hars Ticlarim's warrior past. Mingling in the water, the many strains produced not discord but a magnificent upwelling, a wondrous and stirring symphony that summoned up visions of life and hope and passion, and that seemed to struggle to define the frailty and yet the magic that was humanity.

Through the crystalline arcs of the corridors of the city, thousands thronged, dressed in finery created especially for this day, this moment, this place. Women painted like the fish that swam just beyond their reach and men masked and jeweled like the primitive gods of the sea that they represented moved toward the Polyphony Center for the opening ceremonies of the First Week Festival.

And Jess, wearing on her left wrist the bracelet that attested that she was indeed eligible to attend the festival, a bracelet given to her by the Artis cousin who had attended the year before and who swore she would never go again, moved in the throng with those who truly had the right to pass beneath the golden arch. She wore a simple green sequined mask that covered her eyes, a headpiece that trailed a delicate line of feathers from her forehead over the top of her head and down her back, and a green one-piece suit covered with iridescent scales and meant to mimic body paint. No one spoke to her, but then, she realized no one spoke to anyone else, either. How strange, this crowd that murmured not a syllable, not a whisper, nor cracked a joke, nor spoke in anger at an elbow carelessly jabbed or toes clumsily trampled. In all her years since the Warrens, Jess could not remember any people who moved with such silence.

But she remembered well people who moved so silently within the Warrens, and she tasted a sharp, bitter burst of fear on her tongue as the tide of people moved her ever forward.

She had hoped to find Wraith and, disguised, to watch him. She did not want him to know that she had gone to the festival to spy on him; she was ashamed of her jealousy, ashamed of her need for him, ashamed of the painful hunger that she felt but hid because he never looked at her with anything but friendship and a kind of amused tolerance—and sometimes with regret. She was ashamed—but she feared that at the festival he would meet someone who caught his fancy. That he would dance with some woman who would see in him all the wonderful things Jess had seen in him first, and that Wraith, his head turned by a new face, a clever turn of phrase, a mind that challenged him in a way he found·attractive, would leave, never to return. She did not know what she planned to do if she saw him dancing or talking with a stranger—but if she did not go she would be helpless to do anything.

She had not anticipated the number of people who would be attending the festival, though. Children's festivals were small by comparison, though they had always felt quite large and busy to her—several hundred children gathered in one place, mostly free of adult supervision, had seemed to her a veritable throng. But each house held its own separate festival for children. There was only one for adults, and it was for every adult in the city, and from all appearances almost every adult in the city was attending.

How, in this impossible mass of humanity, could she hope to find Wraith?

She became aware of the steady, soft chiming of a bell from somewhere ahead of her. Then she saw a lovely golden arch above a doorway, and she realized that she neared her destination. As she moved toward the sound, the chiming became slightly louder, but remained pleasant. Abruptly, the cluster of people in front of her each lifted one arm, and she saw a tiny flicker of light dance around the bracelets that each wore on the wrists they presented to the arch. She did as she had seen them do, and felt a faint tickling along her skin. And then she was beyond the arch.

The crowd thinned out. The Polyphony Center, layered like a hive and sprawling for half a dozen furlongs in all directions, swallowed the people thronging in from the many corridors and channeled them in a hundred directions, and seemed always to have room for more. She found a place along the railing of a balcony, and stopped and simply stared. Though she had been to Polyphony, she had never entered the immense Hall of Triumphs, which was used only for the festival, and sometimes for the affairs of state.

She felt like she was standing inside the radiant heart of a faceted gemstone. The distant walls of the center, clear and seamless, spread before her the panorama of the illuminated sea, in which swam both the angels and the demons of the aquatic universe. All of them, drawn by the twisting, dancing sheets of colored lights, arced and curvetted, sometimes hidden in darkness only to be revealed again as the light spiraled around and caressed them. Hunter and hunted moved in weightless beauty—and if that vast domed wall had been the only decoration for the festival, Jess would have thought it enough. But nearer, fountains glittered and danced in the air, lit from within by fires of red or gold or green or silver or blue. The floor, worked in a rich stone mosaic of undersea designs, seemed in scale with the space in which she found herself—but it made the people moving across its lovely surface appear as inconsequential as insects. Perfumes of summer flowers, of meadows and leaves and rushing streams, filled a breeze that brushed against her skin. Between the mosaicked lanes, glades of grass surrounded by flowering trees held benches and tented pavilions, and formal gardens displayed flowers and shrubs and trees, and provided privacy within their mazy twists and turns for couples and groups, and swimming pools let humans dive and float and play as if they were denizens of the sea. She saw floating floors for dancing, and courts for eating, and things she could not identify.

"First time?" A hand brushed lightly across the little tail of feathers that she wore and settled on the bare skin of her back. She turned and looked up. The masked man who looked down at her had a pleasant smile and very pale, silvery eyes.

"I feel . . . rather lost," she said.

He nodded and smiled again, encouragingly.

"I'm . . . well, not really sure what I'm supposed to be doing here. This doesn't look anything like the . . ." She felt her cheeks heat up. "Like the children's festivals I've been to."

"Of course not. Adult activities would hardly be appropriate—or even enjoyable—for children. But . . ." He smiled again, broadly this time, and said, "I had friends meeting me, but I remember how confused I was my first festival. Why don't you let me show you around a bit?"

"Is there any way to find someone specific?" she asked as they left the balcony and started down the spiraling ramp to the main floor.

"Sometimes. If the person you're looking for has not requested privacy, you can locate him or her by asking your bracelet. Friends can find you in the same manner."

"Really?" She was startled.

"Certainly. Your bracelet was spelled with information about you before it was sent to you. It isn't merely a bracelet, or your ticket to the event. It also tells anyone who cares to look that you are safe and well— and, if you don't mind being found, where to find you."

Which meant that she was parading around as Sharawn Artis, a deception that was going to get her into real trouble if someone came looking for the real Sharawn Artis.

"How do you keep people from finding you?"

The corner of her companion's mouth twitched just a bit, and through his mask she could see his eyes narrow. "You simply tell the bracelet, 'Give me privacy.' When you don't want to be private anymore, you tell it, 'Make me public.' It will do what you want. The instructions did come in the package," he added.

"I don't remember seeing them there."

"All first-year attendees get them."

Which explained it. Sharawn wouldn't have been coming for her first year, but for her second. "I didn't see them," she murmured.

They reached the main floor, and her guide said, "So what would you like to do first? Dance? Have something to eat? Try out one of the vision booths? Go to a park?"

"I don't know. Aren't you going to tell me your name?" she asked. To her right, a booth selling sparkling festival necklaces and headdresses glittered at her so temptingly that she looked away from her guide for a moment. And then, to the left of the path they'd taken, a pair of tadaka dancers returned from their break and they erupted into incredible, heel-pounding, sword-swinging gyrations as a trio of decalyre players bowed out music that sounded to Jess like standing in the middle of war itself.

Her guide hurried her forward, shaking his head. "Too loud to think," he said, and aimed her away from the booths and demonstrations, down a quieter path. "Did you read *any* of the information that came with your bracelet?"

"Nothing came in my package but the bracelet," she said.

"They get sloppier every year." He looked a bit exasperated. "Here are the rules, little feathered fish. You don't ask names. You don't try to find out names. If you want to find your friends you can, but you cannot find out the identity of a stranger unless the stranger gives it to you, or unless a crime is committed. Anonymity is a part of the joy of the festival. Here you can be anyone, do anything within the bounds of law, experience pleasures forbidden elsewhere without the repercussions of public censure, and for one week be free from consequences, free from burdens, free from everything except the thrill of the moment. If you have fantasies, here you can act them out with one partner or a dozen; anything you have ever dreamed you can make real for this small span of days. Anything you want, here you can have."

Jess looked at the stranger, startled. She had fantasies of taking vows with Wraith someday, of becoming a brilliant, acclaimed metachord player for one of the symphonic interpretation packagers, of having a grand house in Oel Artis Travia that she could call her own, of having children . . . but somehow those did not sound like the sort of fantasies this man was talking about.

Then they reached the end of the narrow path they'd been following, and her guide gave her a gentle push to the left, through a pretty gate of shimmering magical vines and ruby flowers, and into a writhing cluster of naked and half-naked bodies that made her gorge rise. Men and women, men and men, women and women, in pairs, in clusters—her hands knotted into fists and she twisted away from the hand her guide rested on her bare back.

She had envisioned a grand showplace for the arts and sciences, a refined and magnificent display of all the highest and best of human achievement. After all, this was . . . And instead she was entering into a parade of magic-drunk debauchery. Magic-drunk debauchery that her guide—who, from the lines at the corners of his mouth and the coarseness of the skin on the back of his hands, was old enough to have fathered her *and* a whole raft of older siblings—apparently intended to partake in it with her.

She wanted to scream. She wanted to run. But more than anything, she wanted to find Wraith.

"I think I'll be on my way," she said, and her erstwhile companion frowned.

"It's customary to spend time with the people you talk to."

"I did spend time with you," she said. "But my friends will be waiting on me."

"I don't know how they could be, since you had not even the beginning of an idea of how to find them when you came here."

"No doubt they will be looking for me, too—and this isn't their first year. But"—she bowed with polite and distant formality—"as I have already made plans for this festival, I will thank you for your time and let you be getting on to yours." She turned her back on him and walked resolutely away, holding her breath the whole time and praying that he would not follow.

She moved at a fast pace, in and out of the little side lanes, through big pavilions, and across artificial glades that would have been quite lovely if they had not also been filled with squirming, moaning, gasping humans engaged in activities she did not wish to see.

Finally, near a busy food court, she stopped and caught her breath. That pervert had given her a scare. She realized she was not protected by being a child, because here she had disguised herself as an adult, and she carried identification that proclaimed her an adult. Things she did not want could happen to her here, and she would have no one to whom to run for help. Wraith didn't know she was here. Solander didn't know she was here. No one would be looking for her, and even if someone did look for her, she couldn't be found because her identification proclaimed that she was someone other than who she said she was.

But if this was no place for her, it was no place for Wraith, either. He didn't belong here. She didn't want him going off with some masked woman to do . . .

Her mind balked at the images it conjured, and in desperation she turned to her bracelet. "Help me find Wraith," she said.

The bracelet did nothing.

She frowned. "Help me find Gellas Tomersin," she whispered to it, thinking perhaps it could not understand what she wanted and had to go strictly by what she said. Wraith always went by the name Gellas with anyone who didn't know who he really was. So perhaps the bracelet had been spelled to recognize just his name.

But it still did nothing.

"Help me find Solander Artis."

Again, nothing. Maybe, she thought, the bracelet would only work for its rightful owner. Or maybe he had already found a woman, or several, and had requested privacy. Her stomach churned at the thought.

She turned in a single slow circle, looking at the massed humanity all around her—humanity still pouring in through the gates all around the center in steady streams—and her eyes filled with tears. How could she ever hope to find Wraith in the middle of all of this without any help? She would never approach someone, never make herself beholden for a favor, never voluntarily speak to anyone in this place again. The lesson taught to her by the predatory stranger had not been wasted.

She closed her eyes, took one deep, steadying breath, and chose a direction at random. She might not find him. But she didn't intend to just give up and go home without a fight.

"He told my mother he only had one thing to finish and then the two of them would be on their way," Solander said.

He and Wraith had found the library—unoccupied by anyone because the festival was in progress—to be a perfect spot for keeping watch on Rone Artis's workroom door. He was still in there—they couldn't hear anything, but no one ever could. They had, however, seen him go in, and they had not yet seen him come out, and they had sworn they would not move until he was gone and they had taken their chance to look at what he had in there.

"How long have we been sitting here?" Solander said after a while.

Wraith pulled out his little pocket clock, a gift from Jess some months earlier, and said, "Four hours, twenty-three minutes. Some odd seconds. The time is naught-twenty by Work."

"That all? It feels later."

"I wish we'd brought food with us."

"Yes. Or at least we could have eaten something before we hid in here. Who knew he was going to camp in his workroom today of all days?" Solander leaned heavily against the wall and rubbed his eyes. "We're missing the festival for this. I'm dying to know what goes on at one."

"Your parents haven't told you anything?"

"Of course they told me something. They told me the same damned thing every adult tells every child who asks. 'The joy of festival is discovering each one on your own. I wouldn't think of taking that joy away from you.'" He sighed. "We could do this tomorrow, Wraith. Go to the festival now, leave when we're sure both my parents are there, and come back here to do this."

Wraith just looked at him.

"No, eh?"

"No. We were *going* to go to the festival first, but you suggested that we take care of this instead, so that it wouldn't be hanging over our heads during the festival. You didn't want to worry about it. So I'll find out whatever I can, and then we'll go have some fun."

"I was afraid you were going to—" Solander froze, shoved a finger to his lips in warning, and flattened himself back from the fractionally opened door. Wraith, watching him, froze, too. He could hear a voice murmuring something, and then a door opening, and then the door closing. A long pause. More murmuring. And then footsteps striking the floor briskly, sharply, moving away toward the living quarters of the house.

Solander held his frozen pose even after neither of them could hear the footsteps anymore.

Wraith, in fact, was the first to move. He took a step toward the door, and Solander winced.

Wraith shrugged in question.

"I don't want to go through with this," Solander whispered.

"All you have to do is stand in front of the door and tap on it if you hear anyone coming."

"I know—but we could get in such trouble. . . ."

"I have to know."

Solander looked almost defeated. "Fine," he said at last. "You're determined to do this. I think there may be other ways . . . but it's your skin if you get caught."

"I know that."

They crossed the hall. Wraith would never admit to Solander how scared he was. He knew—or at least was almost certain—that whatever magic Rone Artis had left in place would have no effect on him. But he couldn't be sure that it would fail entirely. What if a spell were set not just to destroy anyone who tried to enter uninvited, but also to let Rone know who the unauthorized intruder had been? He might go in, find whatever he needed, and come out to discover Wraith's father and a whole crew of guards standing over him in the middle of the night, ready to ship him off to work in the mines for the rest of his natural existence. He dreaded getting caught—but he had to understand where he came from. He had to understand the meaning of the Warrens, for he was sure they had a meaning, and he was equally sure it was not trivial.

His hand hovered over the door's handle, and Solander whispered, "Still not too late to change your mind."

Wraith grasped the handle firmly and opened the door. He could see, in the dimly lit interior, one long table covered with an unimaginable tangle of books and papers and magical paraphernalia, a couple of chairs scattered around, a desk, and shelves that lined the room from floor to ceiling and from wall to wall, all so full of books and manuscripts that they sagged in the middle like swaybacked horses. In spite of the size of the room—and it was quite large—it managed to give the impression of being cluttered and overcrowded and tended by frenzied rats.

From all the way across the hall, Solander said, "That is the messiest place I have ever seen in my life." Wraith could tell that was as close as Solander was going to go, too, by the way he stood—as if at any second he might simply turn and flee.

"Finding anything in there is going to be a real trick." Wraith didn't wait for Solander to suggest yet again that they just go on to the festival and skip this spying attempt; instead he clenched his hands into fists, straightened his back, and stepped into the workroom.

Lights came on all around him—but this was nothing he had not expected. Lights came on by themselves everywhere in the city of Oel Maritias. And they went out on their own the instant the last person had left a room. Rone had once described this bit of spellwork to Solander and him as a neat bit of energy conservation. He was always suggesting that Solander do his research for his Academy entrance presentation in spellcasting energy conservation. He seemed to think that was the most important issue in magic.

But then, he was Master of Energy.

Wraith looked around. How, in this vast, muddled rat's nest of a workroom, was he supposed to find what he was looking for? Should he look at the books? The papers? Read correspondence on the desk? Try to figure out what the multitude of apparatuses scattered around were meant to do?

Well . . . people kept their most pertinent projects on their desks, didn't they? If Rone Artis followed any form of organizational scheme at all—and Wraith, looking around the workroom thought this might be hoping for too much—current things should be on the top layers of stuff. Older things would be deeper in the piles. Maybe books might be filed by topic, or alphabetically.

Maybe. But maybe not.

"How could he find anything in this mess?" Wraith muttered.

"The Master uses my locator-spell function to rapidly acquire necessary background research. By simply asking for the data he wishes to acquire, he summons this portion of me, and I, in turn, illuminate all relevant materials."

Wraith went flat to the floor, his heart pounding at his ribs like it was trying to dig its way to safer quarters.

Nothing happened. No follow-up comments from the mysterious voice, no queries, no alarms. After several minutes of lying on the floor feeling increasingly silly, Wraith cautiously sat up. "Who are you?"

"I am not a who. I am a what. I am the workroom ward—a nonsentient collection of spells created and collated to provide protection, filing, and organizing capabilities to this room, while logging all movement within the room."

That didn't sound good. "Well, then . . . who am I?"

"You do not exist."

Wraith considered that for a moment. "I'm talking to you, therefore I must exist."

"Speech is immaterial. You do not present a profile within the parameters given me for those things which exist. Therefore, you do not exist."

Good enough. His inexplicable invisibility to magic continued to stand him in good stead. "I want information on the Warrens."

"Do you wish to have it presented in order of most recent date, volume of research done, subject of research, or other?"

"What is the date of the most recent research on the Warrens?"

"Today."

Wraith shivered. "Give me the most recent research. If that doesn't tell me what I need to know, we'll try something else."

Around the room, various papers and objects began to glow. Some were much brighter than others, a few so brilliant he had to squint to look at them. He guessed that the brightest objects were those most recently used, and went to the very brightest he could see. It was a sheaf of paper as thick as his thumb, fastened into a binder. The second he touched it, the light died away so that he could look at it without difficulty.

The binder title was imposing.

Methodology for Extracting Energy from Human Souls,
With Comparisons to Current Energy Extraction Methods
With Suggested Applications
Plus All Cost-to-Benefit Rations and Energy-to-Rewhah Data

Wraith frowned and opened the binder. Pages and pages of spell-equations, comments in margins, notations on possible refinements written all over facing pages, lists of figures and graphs with curves drawn in various colors that overlapped, crossed, and crawled across the pages like nests of snakes.

And stuck in between those, a neatly written section labeled *Suggested Applications* that noted that by using this new series of spells, the amount of energy harvested from each unit in the Warrens would more than cover the needs of the Empire, not just for the next decade, but well into the next century, without a necessary increase in unit numbers.

It took Wraith a few minutes of scanning to realize that the units the paper kept referring to were people.

When he realized that, everything else fell into place. He wanted to throw up.

But Solander would never believe him if he claimed the Dragons were using Warreners to fuel the Empire. Never. He had to get this through the door—but he was willing to bet that, even though the warding spell didn't recognize him as a threat, it would notice secret papers leaving the security of the workroom, apparently unaccompanied. Much of the purpose of the warding spell would be to make sure that things didn't walk out on their own—and in a city where those who might have an interest in the subject matter of a wizard's private workroom would also have the talent to give wings to inanimate boxes or build cities in the sky, papers suddenly getting up and walking out on their own would be a real threat.

"What would happen to this document if it left the room?" Wraith asked.

"It would immediately disintegrate. Not even dust would remain."

"I thought so." Wraith clutched the document, which demonstrated not only how magic would be drawn from the sacrifice of Warreners' souls in the future, but how it had been drawn from their flesh, their bone, their blood, and their life force for the last thousand years. Solander had to see it.

"Damnall," Wraith muttered. "How can I get a copy of this that can leave the room?"

"Request it."

Wraith stared around the workroom, stunned by the obviousness of that. Master Rone would have to have removable copies of his work for many purposes; he was, after all, Master of Energy for the city of Oel Artis and its sister city of Oel Maritias, and rumors attached him as a close personal advisor to none other than the Landimyn of the Hars herself. People speculated that the Landimyn was old and becoming reclusive, and that Rone stood well placed—with only a few others in serious contention—to receive her appointment to the post when she stepped down.

He would have to present copies of his work to colleagues, to subordinates, to the Landimyn.

"Make a duplicate of this document that can be removed from the room without its destruction," Wraith said. "And keep no record of the existence of the copy."

"Done," the voice that surrounded him said. In his hand, an identical copy appeared. Wraith carefully put the original back where he'd found it and walked to the door clutching the copy. "No one has been here from the time Master Rone left until he returns again," Wraith said. "And nothing has left or will leave the room." He felt that he might be pushing his luck; still, he didn't want to leave any chance that Rone might discover his intrusion accidentally.

"Correct."

He glanced through the copy quickly to make sure that all the pages had writing on them and that the writing matched what he had already seen. He didn't trust magic. It had too many loopholes to it, and because he lived within its loopholes, he always checked for failures that might affect him.

The copy looked perfect. He stuffed it inside his shirt, tucking an edge of it beneath his belt so that it would not slide around and betray its presence to anyone looking at him. Then he took a breath, stepped back through the door, and closed it behind him. He heard the magical locks hum to life.

He could see Solander peeking at him from across the hall; he nodded and started toward his room. Solander trotted out of the library carrying two thick reference volumes—their cover story for being where they were—and caught up with him.

"Well?"

"If we had wagered, you would owe me now," Wraith said under his breath. "But we have to talk about this in my room. Not here."

Solander said nothing else until they entered Wraith's room. Then, however, he turned and said, "All right. You're going to make this into a big, dramatic presentation, aren't you? Just get it over with. Tell me—what's going on in the Warrens that's such a big gods'-damned secret?"

"The Warreners have been the only effective magical fuel source of the Empire of the Hars Ticlarim for at least a thousand years. Maybe longer."

All the color drained from Solander's face. Almost instantly, though, he regained his composure. He shook his head and laughed. "Damn, you're good at that. I almost believed you. Wraith, the Empire draws power from a complex combination of earth energy, star energy, elemental energy, and a few special secret things that are still under development, and that will be announced when the Research Department can assure their safety."

"So you're told."

"I've seen the plants that draw the magic from the sun and the sea and convert it."

"No, you haven't. You've seen the plants that draw energy from human 'units' in the Warrens and run it through some pretty coils and lights to make it look like it's from the sun and the sea. The Dragons don't want the citizens of the Empire to know they are burning human beings to keep their floating mansions in the air or their lights lit or any of the other millions of things that now depend on Warrener fuel. According to the paper I found, humans are an excellent source of renewable energy. Way-fare keeps them as fat as they can be and still survive because when they die, they then provide huge amounts of flesh-and-bone energy, which has always been some of the strongest available. Their food is spelled to be both addictive and toxic so that if somehow someone manages to get free of the addiction, he'll die of the poison—can't have the truth getting out, after all."

Solander's smile went away. "This isn't funny. You're suggesting corruption of the government at a level and of a degree that would, if it were discovered, lead to the destruction of the Empire. Such a government would have pulled itself apart—or would have been torn apart by its people—long before this. Any government that survives more than three thousand years can only do so when standing upon a foundation of righteousness and purity."

"Really? Who told you that? The Godlet of Governments?"

"I've studied government, Wraith! One of the things we discussed in great detail was how corrupt governments die and pure governments succeed."

"The person who taught you that ever hold a position in government?"

"Well . . . of course. Who else could be expected to understand the workings of the Empire?"

Wraith smiled a little. "I'm only saying that your idealistic view of the Hars Ticlarim might not be based on the most unbiased of opinions."

"People would riot and hang the Dragons in protest if they thought the Hars was using human-based magic for its fuel."

"Maybe," Wraith said. "Maybe not. Maybe all the people who live in cities in the sky or under the sea won't think the lives of Warreners will matter much when compared to the survival of their cities. But it gets worse."

"No, it doesn't. I don't know what you think you've found, but—"

Wraith held up a hand. "*It gets worse,*" he repeated. "Now they've found a way to burn human souls. I have proof."

He pulled the bound copy of the research paper out of his shirt and handed it to Solander.

"Oh, gods. You stole something from the workroom. Are you insane? That's treason."

"It's a copy," Wraith said. "A legal copy, for which no tracking will be done, and of which no record has been made."

"You can't—"

"Just read it. Please. You can tell me what a terrible thing I've done after you've read it."

Solander studied the title, opened the first page, and began to read. After a few minutes, he got out stylus and scribe and began working out equations. He was quiet for a very long time.

Wraith watched him. He thought about his family, trapped in the prison of the Warrens, chained there by walls, poisons, magic, and the indifference of the world outside, and now robbed not just of their lives, but of eternity as well. He sat on the corner of his bed. He tried to push the memories of all of them out of his mind—tried to tell himself that they didn't feel anything. That at least they would suffer no pain for the horrors that they were living through and would die from. And in spite of his best attempts to get control of himself, he started to cry.

Chapter 6

Master Grath Faregan watched the tracking device he'd placed on the back of his little fish the first time he touched her. The girl's simulacrum moved through the maze of the festival in frantic, wandering worm-trails. Fast, never stopping, never moving off the path into any of the amusements. Faregan smiled. So she hadn't found her friends yet. She was underage—he was sure of it. If he could get her while she was still in the festival, he could have her without repercussions; after all, disguised as an adult, she gave up the protections of childhood. And he couldn't be expected to know that she had no business being at the festival, could he? She wore the necessary identifiers, after all.

No doubt the bracelet didn't belong to her, but that wouldn't be his fault:

He decided it was time to bump into her again. Perhaps get her very drunk on one of the aerosol intoxicants in a floating pavilion, take her right there . . .

. . . Or maybe he would delay his gratification. Drunk and pliable, she would offer no real resistance and no credible protest. He could pretend to be anyone, get her out the gate, destroy her bracelet, and take her home to add to his collection. And there, he could enjoy her repeatedly and at his leisure.

No one would ever know—with the wrong bracelet on, the girl she really was would never show up on festival records. And the girl who did show up would be found safe wherever she'd decided to stay.

Faregan took his bearings, shut down his tracker, and headed on an intercept course. A genuine stolti girl would be the centerpiece of his already superb girl-menagerie.

*　*　*

Jess caught a glimpse of the man she'd met just inside the festival entrance. He was smiling and walking toward her. She didn't want to meet him—she didn't know why, but he frightened her. So she bolted back the way she'd come, doubled back around him, and headed out of the festival.

She'd been pawed, grabbed, groped, and fondled in her search for Wraith, and she couldn't take any more. She reached the arch, saw that same man heading toward her *again,* and bolted outside the festival. With her body trembling so badly she almost couldn't stand up, she ripped the mask from her face and threw it to the floor. She tore off the bracelet and flung it back through the arch, so that she could never be tempted to go in there again. If Wraith was in there, he had his privacy guarded—he could be anywhere, doing anything with anyone. She didn't know how she could ever look him in the eyes again.

She felt sick. Men and women, singly and in groups, had pursued her, caught at her, tried to drag her into chambers and pavilions and onto floating beds, all of them clamoring to convince her that this would be good for her, that she would like it, that it was all a part of growing up.

This was not what being stolti—being free of the Warrens and free of all restrictions on the lower classes—had meant to her. She'd dreamed of creating beauty, of rising above her beginnings to bring her vision of art and wonder to the world. She'd hoped in this way to pay penance for her years of deception, to somehow validate her worth to people she saw as inherently more deserving of the privileges they enjoyed than she could ever be, because they had been born to them.

She did not—would not—embrace this facet of the stolti. She did not think she could look at these people she had known and ever see herself as part of them again.

It didn't matter, she told herself, that no one knew who you were. What you did when you were hidden mattered just as much as what you did when everyone knew you—because you were still the person doing it.

In that moment she realized that the future she'd planned for herself as a stolti—vow-bonded to a stolti man, with a great house and beautiful things all around her, creating things of beauty as the covil-ossets did—was dead.

And she had no idea what would replace it.

Rone Artis left the festival as quickly as he could—as soon as Torra found a group that interested her, he told her that he was going to go private and find a party for himself. She'd been pleased by that; this one time of the year, she preferred that he didn't stay too close.

He had a temporary patch-up—he'd cast a small version of the new soul-spell in his workroom, and had done the necessary diversions and buffering from there—but he didn't want to leave such a volatile spell running in his own home. He planned to pick up the complete spell schematics from his workroom, gather his supplies, and move his work to the Department of Energy in the City Center, which had a reliable, full-time buffer running. He didn't need to deal with a spell backlash and all its attendant problems now; he'd finally achieved his goal of becoming the Grand Master of the sister cities of Oel Artis and Oel Maritias; with time and some good luck and a demonstration of his ability to manage the current crisis, he could find himself sitting in the Dossmere Chair—the throne occupied by the Landimyn of the Hars Ticlarim. From there, he could finally effect all of the changes that the Empire needed. He had his platform worked out; hells-all, he'd been working on that platform for the last twenty years, though he would never admit as much to anyone else.

Pity Solander wasn't a bit older, with at least a few years of Academy behind him. Rone had to move someone into the Master of Energy seat, and he would have loved to have put his son there. Solander would learn a lot from the post, and one guaranteed friendly vote would always be good.

In a few years, he'd make sure the boy got a good post. Solander was shaping up beautifully—had a deft hand at spellcraft; a keen, questioning mind that had finally developed some focus; absolute dedication to his goal; and even a good way with people—something that Rone wished he had more talent with. Solander had friends, but managed to have all of them working on his projects with him. Free labor, a devoted little triad of followers—and if they were cousins from a minor sub-branch, no matter. Gellas and Jess were distant cousins to whom the Artis family owed nothing more than room and board in their home, and Velyn would make a decent pairing with a Dragon soon enough and provide Solander with excellent connections via a lateral line of attachment; Solander would not turn around in later years to find that his friendships had cost him debts in distant cities.

Rone smiled. The boy was no doubt enjoying his first real festival at that very moment. First Festivals were wondrous things—a young man full of drives and hungers found spread before him an endless and eager banquet, and had no more responsibility for the whole of the week than to sate his appetite in a hundred different ways. Rone had actually helped his son design his first costume, and had brought in the finest tailor in the city to make sure it fit perfectly. Solander would be a Dragon— as the son of a Dragon and a young man on his way to the Academy, Solander could legally wear the mask, spined headdress, and winged cloak that set the Dragon costume apart from all others.

The women would be standing in line for his boy, Rone thought, and walked into Artis House whistling under his breath. Life gave of itself to those who deserved good things. It gave of itself to him.

Then he reached his workroom, and shoved all pleasant thoughts behind him. For the next hours—perhaps days—his focus had to be on the preservation of Oel Maritias, and beyond that, the energy needs of the Empire.

He set the temporary spell he'd created to link itself to the Department of Energy in the City Center building. He put a contingency in its basic run order. The instant he successfully summoned soul-energy in the Department of Energy, it would shut itself down. With that bit of housekeeping out of the way, he created travel copies of all the important documents he needed, put them inside a case that would turn itself and everything within it into dust if anyone but him attempted to open it, and left, making sure, as he always did, that the door closed completely and the locks reset as soon as it did. As an added precaution, he reset the spells—he had changed them just the day before, but considering what his workroom held right then, he thought extra caution only made sense.

Satisfied, he headed for the center of the city.

Jess didn't bother to knock—she was sure Wraith's room would be empty. So the presence and the panicked reactions of not just Wraith, but Solander and Velyn, too, as she burst through the door scared a shriek from her.

Velyn. She *would* be with Wraith, wouldn't she?

Wraith's festival costume hung untouched in his opened closet. He and Solander looked like they were working; further, from their harried expressions and the amount of paper scattered around the room, and from the sheets of paper pinned in rows on the wall, all of them covered with formulas, they'd been at work for quite some time. They acted for all the world like people who didn't even know such a thing as a festival existed.

"Missing the festival?" Jess asked, her voice sharp and her eyes on Velyn.

Wraith said, "About time you got here," as if she'd been summoned and expected.

And Solander flushed and said, "I tried to find you as soon as we realized we needed you, but you weren't in your room and you weren't at the . . . er . . . children's festival."

"No. I wasn't," she agreed. She didn't elaborate. Better neither of them knew what a fool she'd made of herself. Their response soothed her, though. They'd wanted her. They'd been looking for her.

Solander's expression of bone-weary dismay washed away, and he smiled at her as if she were the first light of morning, and he a man condemned to die unless he stayed awake to see it.

That smile always unnerved her. Solander liked her, and while she liked him well enough as a friend, she couldn't imagine ever feeling about him the way she felt about Wraith.

But he was on his feet and coming toward her, saying, "You couldn't have picked a better time to get here—we found out some things tonight that have just . . . have just . . ." and his face bleached out again, and he wrapped his arms around her and pulled her close.

Wraith stood, too; he'd been crouched over a line of equations that Jess vaguely identified as defining a spell in spatial and differential magic. But he simply smiled weakly at her, stretched, and rubbed his thumbs over his eyes in tight, tired circles. "You and I are lucky to be out of the Warrens," he said. "We never knew how lucky until tonight. But now that we do know . . ." He glanced at Solander and Velyn and said, "The three of us have been trying to figure out just how this spell works, so that maybe Solander can develop something to counter it. It's the scariest thing any of us has ever seen."

"Wait. Just wait. What are you talking about?"

Solander finally let go of Jess. "You'd better sit down," he told her. When she took a good look at him, she could see the streaking of tears down his cheeks and how red and swollen his eyes were. She felt a chill working its way from her shoulders and back all the way down her arms and legs. She shivered in spite of herself and sat.

And between them, Wraith and Solander introduced her to a real and present hell.

When they finished, she stood up. Crossed her arms tightly over her chest—her heart felt like it was going to explode out of her body, it hammered so hard at her ribs. "Leave it alone," she said.

Solander and Wraith stared at each other as if they couldn't have heard her correctly.

"What?" Wraith said. "You can't mean that. You have family there. So do I. Smoke is still in there—somewhere—"

"Smoke is dead." She cut him off and glared at him. "Our families are dead. They were born dead, and if they stay dead, so what? *You're* my family, Wraith. You. Solander. That's it. And if the two of you get involved in this, something terrible will happen, and I'll lose both of you. I can feel it. I just know it."

"Smoke is *in there*," Wraith repeated.

Tears welled up in Jess's eyes. "You think I don't know that? You think I don't remember that he went back to Sleep so that you could be free? You *can't* help him, Wraith. You can't save him, you can't set him free—so don't waste the sacrifice he made for you. He *died* for you, Wraith—he died so that you could be free of that hell." She balled her hands into fists and through clenched teeth said, "So live for him. Stay free of that place, and live, and make your life something wonderful. And never look back."

The door chime rang, and all four of the room's occupants turned toward it. Wraith and Solander quickly threw evidence of their foray into the magic workroom under the bed; Velyn sprawled on the floor in front of the bed with a viewsphere, and pretended that she was watching one of Wraith's collection of ancient dance re-creations.

And Jess, blinking away tears that she refused to let the other three see her shed, went to see who was at the door.

A short, dark-haired man in a Security uniform that fit so badly he seemed to have shrunk inside of it looked at her and said, "We have a missing girl from one of the children's festivals. I need your name, miss—and . . ." He shook his head, looking at the other three. "It looks like your name will do."

Jess flushed. "Jess Covitach-Artis," she said.

He looked at the little board in his hand and said, "Not the one. Thank you." And left.

Jess closed the door and turned back to her friends and Velyn.

"We're going to have to find someplace safe to work on this," Solander said to Wraith.

And Wraith nodded.

Neither of them had listened to a word she'd said.

*　　*　　*

Grath Faregan took back the Security uniform he'd borrowed from the Silent Inquest's costume room and tucked it away in a bag. "Jess Covitach-Artis?"

"Yes, Master Faregan."

"I see."

"Shall I watch her? Or remove her?"

"No. I'll find out about her. I'm in no hurry. She's a lovely little thing, and she'll still be a lovely little thing when I . . . ." He looked at his servant, who knew the details of Faregan's private hobby, and smiled.

The servant, who sometimes got to play with discards from Faregan's collection when they broke—before Faregan disposed of them—returned the smile. "Of course, Master Faregan."

By the time Wraith finally got everyone out of his room, the night was half over; Oel Maritias would be getting ready to light the sun-lights soon. He fell into bed, so tired the mattress seemed to roll and slide beneath him—and someone knocked on his door.

"You cannot mean to bother me at this hour," he muttered, but he rose and made his way through the dark room without doing too much damage to his shins, and opened it to find Velyn there again.

Wraith leaned against the door and managed a weak smile. "Forgot something?"

"Yes," she said, and brushed past him, pulled the door closed, and took his face in her hands. She kissed him—kissed him with such passion and such hunger that his knees turned liquid and his spine tingled and every part of his body woke up. "You were supposed to go to the festival today. This was to be your initiation into adulthood, and I was going to make sure that I met you there, so that I could be the one who . . . initiated you. And then"—her thumb started moving in circles on his chest, each circle a little lower than the one before—"you didn't go to the festival, and when I checked for your bracelet, I found that you hadn't even put it on yet. It was still in your room. So I came here to find you"—the hand had moved much lower, and Wraith discovered that he was having a hard time following what she was saying—"and you were here, but so was Solander, and then along came Jess. And I couldn't very well interrupt this work to . . . well. But this is the festival. And if you can't go—and I understand why you can't—at least the two of us can celebrate here."

To Wraith's amazement, his sleep pants slipped free of his waist and slithered down his legs to pile around his ankles as if they had a life of their own.

"I've waited, Wraith," Velyn was saying, as she undid the laces of his sleep shirt. "I've waited for you for a very long time, when I didn't want to wait a day, because I knew you were special, and because this needed to be . . . right. You had to be a man, not a child. And now you're a man, and so help me, I don't want to wait another instant."

Wraith found himself standing naked in his room, with Velyn running her hands all over him, and the lump in his throat almost kept him from breathing, much less from speaking. "Ah," he said. That didn't seem like the right thing to say, but he couldn't think of anything better.

Velyn decided that sufficed, though, because she started kissing him again, and taking off her clothes at the same time.

He reached for her arms, slid his hands to her wrists, and stopped her from removing anything else. Finally, finally, he found coherent words.

"Let me," he said, and led her over to his bed.

He moved the blind over his window into the side wall so that he and Velyn could see the glorious festival lights. The lights served a second purpose, too—they illuminated the soft curves and long, smooth lines of Velyn's body, one bit at a time, as he undressed her.

"Beautiful," he whispered.

She shivered at his touch and said, "You, too."

And when they were both undressed, she said, "I wanted this to happen a long time ago. But now . . . now . . . now I don't have any reason why I shouldn't be here, and I want you. I love you. I've wanted to touch you, to feel you and taste you and hold you, for the longest time."

Her hands never stopped moving, and Wraith lay back on his bed and watched as she moved above him, outlined now in silhouette. She touched his face, his shoulders, and then put her hands to either side of him and shifted until she held her body along his length but just above him, so that he could feel the heat of her skin but no touch except for the points of her breasts brushing against his chest.

"I . . ." he started, then stopped. He tried again—and tried not to get so lost in the sensation of that twin-pointed touch that he forgot what he wanted to say. "I fell in love with you the first time I saw you—when you came into Solander's room that first day. But you never gave any sign that you . . . that you considered me anything special."

"I did. I always have—but women who take advantage of boys don't fare well in Oel Artis. Same goes for men who set their sights on girls. Instead, we have the festival—and anyone old enough to go to the festival is old enough to be acceptable, and anyone younger than that will get the adult sent to the mines for a few years. I had no wish to be a miner, Wraith. I had to wait. For you, for me—for any chance of a future for the two of us, if even you wanted one, I had to wait."

Wraith wrapped his arms and legs around her and pulled her tight against him. "You don't have to wait anymore," he said.

"No. I don't." She moved just a bit, and without warning he was inside of her—and equally without warning, he lost control, and everything exploded in a thundering rush in his ears and a warmth that rushed from his loins outward and left him limp and panting and sweating beneath her.

"Oh, god," he whispered. "It wasn't supposed to go like that, was it? I'm . . . I'm sorry. I'm so sorry."

"Don't be," she said, and nipped lightly along his neck. "We're just getting started."

The second time went better. The third time went better still—and by the time they got to the fifth time, after some hours, one shower, and having to have food brought to the room once, Wraith no longer felt embarrassed about that first time.

"We should probably sleep," Velyn said at last.

"We should. But Solander and Jess will no doubt be showing up at the door soon. Far too soon."

"We could pack a bag and go to my suite for a few hours—and just sleep, I promise. No one will look for you there, and I have a feeling that one of your friends won't be too happy to find me here with you."

Wraith frowned at her. "Who wouldn't want me to be happy?"

"I think Solander and Jess both want you to be happy. I just suspect that Jess would rather you weren't happy with *me*." When he gave her a puzzled look, she said, "I think she would take my place here with you if you asked her."

Wraith sighed. "Jess is . . . Jess. She'll get over it when she grows up and finds the right man. I've known her since the moment she first woke up. She and I have always been good friends; when she sees how right you and I are for each other, she won't resent my happiness." But as the words were coming out of his mouth, he really thought about them. Thought about Jess watching him out of the corner of her eye, of the way she would bring things to him that she thought he would like, of the special smile that she reserved for just him. In fact, Jess probably would resent Velyn.

Well, she would just have to, then—because Wraith had decided that if Velyn was willing to be seen with him, he would not hide his feelings for her, nor would he hide the relationship they shared. He wanted everyone to know that he was in love with her, and that she was his.

Velyn. Beautiful, mysterious Velyn.

He desperately needed to get some sleep before he got back to work on trying to understand the soul-fuel equations and how they might be countered. He wanted to be with Velyn, too—to go to sleep with her at his side, and to wake with her in his arms. Solander and Jess would be able to work for a few hours without any help from him. He decided going with Velyn to her suite would be his best course of action.

"We'd best hurry, then," she said. "You won't need much—just a change of clothes for when we wake up—maybe two, just in case—and your personal kit. I probably have everything else, and if I don't, we'll just send one of the servants to get it for us."

Wraith kissed her, and ran the palm of his hand down the long curve of her spine. "We ought to get dressed." But he knew what he was doing wouldn't lead to getting dressed.

She stood up and turned around and said, "We *will* get dressed. You haven't seen my bed yet, and you should."

She started pulling on clothes.

Intrigued, he followed her.

Rone had spent the whole of the night and most of the morning prepping the spells that would bring the new soul-energy on-line. He'd developed a massive buffering system that split the *rewhah* into two streams—one that poured back into the Oel Maritias Warrens, and one that drained straight into the sea. He was a bit concerned about the effect that the *rewhah* would have on undersea life—the ecology of the shelf was delicate, and he and other Dragons had spent a great deal of time making sure that the presence of the city of Oel Maritias wouldn't disrupt it. But if he had to choose between fish with two heads and wings or the implosion of the city, he wouldn't have to think twice.

But the spell wasn't ready yet. The little setup he'd linked from his workroom kept a thin but steady trickle of the new energy pouring into the city's magic grid, but that trickle only buffered the little bit of energy that had been short over the past months. It helped, but it didn't cover new expenditures—and someone had badly misfigured the energy consumption of the festival. He could see the power usage patterns on the flowsheet that shimmered in the air in front of him—and Polyphony Center had dipped out of clear, reassuring purple and started fading toward white.

Too many people in there, too much magic being used—and he had no doubt figuring what some of that magic was, either. Trivia. Gods'-damned trivia. Sex spells, seduction spells, compulsion spells, perverse glamours—all utterly unnecessary in the grand scheme, but within the tiny lives of the fools casting them, essential. Add to that the planned magic—the vision centers with their spells that would put a couple or a group into the heart of a shared and jointly concocted illusion, and the multiple float bases for dance floors and beds, and the magic necessary to sustain the bracelets and the privacy spells and the contact tracing, and beyond that, the lights, the water, the air purification, the pressure control—and it wouldn't be long until the whole Center dropped straight through the white zone and into the red.

And Polyphony Center already had some of the worst damage of any building in the city.

He rubbed his temples and frowned. Should he cancel the festival and evacuate everyone? As Grand Master of the Dragon Council of the sister cities, he had the power to do it—but it would cost him tremendous goodwill. And not just among the citizens, but also among the Council and his staff. He could afford to have some people angry with him, but he could not afford to have *everyone* angry with him. No leader whose power often depended upon consensus could.

Rone wished he could pass this all off on the new Master of Energy, but he had yet to appoint one—he had to admit that he hated the feeling of giving up control of the office. Energy ran everything directly—and though he was now Grand Master of the Council and in theory had control over every aspect of the cities, he discovered in fact that he would be at one remove from the thing he knew best and cared most about.

He did not want to put the design of the new buffers or the new spellchannels in the hands of any of his assistants, either. Talented though they were—and there were some among them who had created some amazing practical applications for the Department of Energy—he could not think of one who would be able to handle the delicate mechanisms of buffering as well as he could. He *did* wish that a few of his closest assistants had decided not to go to the festival—he would have been happy to have the extra hands. But again, he stood to lose more than he gained by recalling them from their all-too-brief holiday.

He looked around the Department of Energy. The skeleton crew running things were almost all low-level employees of the department: simple spell-readers, gauge-watchers, knob-turners. He checked the sign-in board and saw two on the list who might be of some use to him: Maidan Quay, who stood for a promotion to associate spellcaster in the next few months if she passed her final Level Fours in the Academy, and Luercas tal Jernas, a genuine young star of the department, though with some negative marks on his citizen record that were standing in the way of his achieving his full potential. The rest were worthless.

He called Maidan and Luercas in.

"We have a problem," he said. "Polyphony Center is draining us." He pointed to the flowsheet and watched both of them pale.

"I'll go switch down the nonessential areas of the city to minimum power," Maidan said.

"Do that," Rone told her, "and then come back. We have another alternative that we're going to take. We can't leave any part of the city underpowered for long." Maidan nodded and ran off. Rone turned to Luercas. "You've finished your Level Fives already, haven't you? Got your security clearances?"

Luercas, his eyes still on the pale cycle bars on the flowsheet, just nodded.

"And your security level is . . . ?"

"Nine."

Nine was good enough. Rone said, "There's more to the problem than I told Maidan. She can't know how serious this is, but we have pressure damage in some of the buildings of the periphery. The worst-damaged of the buildings in the entire city is the Polyphony Center."

"Damage *and* low energy?" Luercas finally looked directly at Rone. "Then why do we have people in there at all?"

"Because we cannot cancel the festival without serious repercussions to the government. And we cannot move the festival, because there's no place else to put it."

"Then we need to move more units into the Warrens."

"We don't have more units, but we have a new energy source we can draw on to make the best possible use of the ones we have." He spread the sheets of spell schematics out in front of the young man and watched, pleased, as Luercas traced along the lines and figured out what the spell was and how it worked.

"But this is excellent. If the output figures on this are correct, we won't ever have to worry about energy underruns again."

"They're correct. Our problem is buffering."

Luercas had reached that part of the diagram, and he winced. "We've never tried working with anything this dangerous."

"No. We haven't. And we have to put it together today. Now."

"We, Master Rone?"

"We. Me . . . you . . . Maidan. She has minimal clearances—she cannot know the source we're tapping, nor can she know the reason why we're doing it today. The citizens' confidence in the safety of the city has to be absolute."

Luercas looked like he might question that, but then he just nodded. "There are things they don't need to know."

"A lot of them."

"Of course. And what shall I do to assist you?"

Rone liked the young man. He got straight to action.

"We're going to set up a triad spell with buffer channels starting straight into the sea, and then switching slowly to our Warrens once we have the flow stabilized. I'm going to be the apex of the triad—the lead caster. I've already done some work with this kind of energy, and I've gotten a bit of a feel for it. It's . . . well, it's pretty unpleasant. You're going to need to brace yourself for that part of it. You're going to be buffer control; you'll direct the energy of the *rewhah* into the sea until the backflow settles down. I had a nasty fifty percent over the anticipated burst with the small spell I started last night. If we get a simple one-for-one increase in energy-to-*rewhah,* you're going to be dealing with a blast of . . ." He took a pen and scribbled figures. "About five hundred thousand luns."

"Enough to incinerate the entire City Center."

"Yes. And if there's some sort of penalty *rewhah*—"

"Which, considering our energy source, could be a real possibility—"

"Yes, it could. Then you could be dealing with—what?—twice that? Maybe three times that."

"One to one and a half sols. Damn."

"You don't want to slip."

"And what is Maidan going to be doing?"

Rone said, "She's going to man the panic button. If things go wrong—"

"*The* panic button?"

"If things go wrong," Rone overrode him, "the only hope anyone will have is if she floats the city. Because if we blow up the department, they'll be without pressure controls and lights in a matter of seconds, and air in about two hours. I don't choose to kill almost a million people today—how about you?"

"Not today, Master Rone," Luercas said. He looked scared. Really scared.

Good. The young wizard would pay attention to what he was doing, and he wouldn't take stupid chances or get cocky.

Rone set up the buffering rods for the two of them. *Rewhah* always returned with equal force to the casting source, but the Dragons had developed a sort of lightning rod that collected it and allowed it to be channeled and redirected. This one mechanism was the foundation upon which the entire Empire of the Hars Ticlarim was built—for without a way to safely channel *rewhah,* no one would have dared handle life-drawn magic in the amounts and types that the running of an empire required.

Once the rods were set, Rone spelled copies of the schematics for Luercas. Then the two of them waited for Maidan to return.

When she came through the door, Rone told her, "We're ready to bring extra energy on-line. Your job is to monitor our results—keep me apprised of the amount of energy we have going into the Polyphony Center, let me know when we're back in the purple."

Maidan nodded.

Rone added, as casually as he could, "And as a precautionary measure, you're going to be running the blast switch. Give me the parameters for using it."

Maidan frowned a bit. "Total energy loss, disruption of more than fifty percent of the inflow channels, warning lights signaling pressure spell failure or pending perimeter collapse."

"That's right. If any of those things happen, don't hesitate. You understand?"

"Are you considering this a possibility?"

Rone looked at her. "Anytime we bring new energy on-line, it's a possibility. Do I think there's any real chance of it? No. But we're not going to do anything potentially risky without having our backups in place."

She smiled, relieved. "Of course, Master Rone. I understand. Oh— and I heard that you've accepted the Grand Mastership of the Council of Dragons."

Rone nodded. "I think Energy will start getting the respect it deserves now."

Rone stepped under the arch of his buffer rods and signaled Luercas to do the same. Beneath Luercas's arc the two of them had placed a series of channel analogs. They would make the complicated process of gathering the *rewhah* energy and directing it into the sea, and then from the sea to the Warrens, simpler. Maidan rested her hand on the blast switch and turned the flowsheet so that she could read it more clearly.

"I'm ready when you are," she said.

Luercas moved all of the analog channels to open. "Also ready," he said.

Rone nodded, and began casting the spell that would bind the souls of ten thousand Warreners to Oel Maritias and begin burning them for fuel.

"*Rewhah* starting," Luercas reported.

Rone nodded, but continued his chanting. Distantly, he felt the little ping of the temporary spell he'd set up in his workroom dissolving.

"First movement in the inflow bar," Maidan said. "We're up two . . . five . . . nine and a quarter . . ."

Rone managed a tiny smile, but he kept his focus on the incantation; he could feel it building around him, and he could feel the wild, angry energy of the *rewhah* pouring into the bar above his head and running down the cage around him like water down an overflowing dam. The spell, cast fully, had more power to it than he had imagined, and he could feel the energy starting to slip. It had an edge to it—dark and greasy and frightening. He'd dealt with the darkest magics in the Empire, but he'd never felt anything like this, and suddenly he was wishing that he hadn't tried to do the spell alone. His whole team should have been with him. Out of the corner of his eye, he could see Luercas sweating, the confidence gone from his face.

"Twenty-five . . ." Maidan said, eyes on the gauges and bars, "thirty . . . fifty . . . seventy . . . good gods-all, I've never seen anything bring energy on-line like this. This is amazing. One hundred . . . one hundred forty-five . . . one hundred eighty . . . two hundred thirty . . ." Her voice trailed off and she looked over at them. "You're overrunning the main system and going into overflow buffers," she said softly. "You need to back it down."

He heard her. He knew she was right. But he did not dare interrupt this spell. He could not temper it, could not stop it, could not alter it. The magic he was summoning came too hard, too insistently, too fiercely, and in the instant that he broke his focus, the *rewhah* from it would smash down on top of the buffer bar and crush the life out of him—and then the magic, loosed and uncontrolled, would flash out from the City Center like an explosion, warping and twisting and destroying everyone in its path.

So he held on, and he kept reciting the incantation, focusing on the controls built into it, praying that he could get through the summoning and the binding without destroying the city or himself.

"It's slipping on me," Luercas said, at the same instant that Maidan said, "Buffers almost to capacity—should I flush the extra out of the city?"

He barely had the strength to nod to her. Yes. Flush the extra. Wild magic pouring into the ocean without any specific target or any specific spell could have its own awful effects, and the fact that it was pouring into the ocean in union with the *rewhah* that it had spawned would definitely cause fallout that people in Oel Maritias would be dealing with for the next several hundred years. He tried not to think about the hell that this moment would leave for the future; he tried to keep his mind on the needs of the moment alone. He could hear Luercas gasping, and he could see the young man on his knees, barely inside the arch of the buffer bar, sweat-beaded brow focused on keeping the *rewhah* pouring through the channels and into the sea outside of the city.

He fought with everything in him, and somehow Rone made it to the end of the incantation. The worst—for him—was done.

But not for Luercas. Closure of the spell released the full impact of the *rewhah,* and it was a thousand times greater than Rone had calculated. Monstrous. Monstrous. And the young wizard trying to control it simply did not have the skills or the experience to keep the backlash energy within the channels and flowing fast enough to keep the channels clear. The *rewhah* bottlenecked, blasted the channel analogs into a million motes, and whipped straight back at Rone. The caster. The sacrificial lamb.

It hit him like a wall of fire, and he felt his bones melting, felt his skin searing off, felt his flesh running in rivulets to the floor. He wasn't enough to feed it—wasn't nearly enough, and it flashed out again, taking in Luercas and Maidan and rolling outward again. His last vision was of Luercas twisting and re-forming into something hideous, of Maidan stretching and bubbling like tar, and of her hand on the panic button, the blast switch, cutting the city loose from its moorings and sending it in an uncontrolled spin toward the surface of the sea.

Chapter 7

Wraith and Velyn came awake in a tangle of arms and legs and covers, to the accompaniment of noise and impossible movement.

"The room is sideways," Velyn shouted. "We're lying on a wall."

Wraith shouted back at her, "We're heading for the surface!"

Velyn scrunched her eyes tightly closed and held on to him tightly.

He looked for something solid that they could cling to—when the city reached the surface it would go back to level again, either right side up or upside down, and either way, heavy things were going to go crashing past them, and they were going to get thrown around. So far, they were both mostly all right. Velyn had blood on her forehead and her mouth, and Wraith thought he might have cracked a couple of ribs, but they weren't seriously injured. He wanted to keep it that way.

There was, however, nothing to grab.

So when the room burst into sunlight, he lay flat, held Velyn tight against him, and hoped for the best. The room began to right itself—slowly. Slowly—that was good. He and Velyn started sliding toward the floor and things above their heads slid, too, but they were going to be able to get out of the way without too much trouble.

The surface of the water had a bad gold-green glow to it, and Wraith didn't want to be distracted, but when the water began to form itself into hands, and the hands began to beat on the windows, he thought perhaps he and Velyn and Oel Maritias had more problems than just the city launching itself toward the surface.

The Automatic Emergency Pressurization lights were on and flashing—that meant, if Wraith remembered his emergency procedures correctly, that no one dared step out of the city into the world beyond yet, or they would die of the "deeps"—a nasty, painful sickness that came to anyone who rose from the bottom of the sea to the surface too quickly. Leg pain, vomiting, confusion, paralysis, and death could hit just minutes, or sometimes hours, after a deeps-dweller came to the surface. Spells usually kept people at the correct pressure so that they could move about freely from city to surface—but if something went wrong with the spells, that would all change. And if the city had launched itself to the surface, then by definition something had gone wrong with the spells.

So no one would be able to use the emergency launches or leave the city yet.

Quiet came to the room, except for sounds of compartment doors slamming shut and those liquid fists drumming on the windows.

He told Velyn, "We need to get out of here."

She stared at the fists and nodded. "Family meeting room, I suppose."

Wraith wanted to make sure Solander and Jess were unhurt, but he nodded. In times of emergency, the people who ended up in trouble were those who didn't follow the plan.

"Let's hurry," he said. "The sooner we get there, the sooner they'll have an accurate count."

Luercas made his way out of the ruins of the suddenly too-bright City Center, for the first time lit by the sun, and struggled toward Artis House. He dragged Maidan with him—she could barely move forward with his assistance, and would not be able to walk at all without it. They'd both been scarred horribly by the *rewhah* from Rone's spellcasting, but while Luercas's scars were uglier, Maidan's were more crippling.

"How much farther?" she asked again, as he lifted her over an area of corridor completely blocked by the toppled remains of a decorative coral arch.

"Not much," he said, hoping that it was true and that he had not lost track of the turns and straightaways, all so unfamiliar beneath their layers of rubble and debris. The sun heated the corridors almost unbearably. Beneath the sea, the clear, flexible mageglass that made up the majority of each corridor simply provided an entertaining view of undersea life for passersby; but on the surface, the sun poured in and baked everything, turning each corridor into a hothouse. And the bulkhead doors that had closed automatically when the city broke free of its moorings and started to race toward the surface kept the ventilation system from setting up an effective breeze.

No doubt rescue ships were being launched from Oel Artis to pick up the survivors of Oel Maritias, however many there might be—but in the meantime, the city was going to become rapidly more unlivable. And with the air pressure warning lights on, no one dared leave, or vent in fresh air from outside, or even blast holes in some of the windows. The only thing he could really do to help himself at the moment was get away from the center of the city. Luercas wanted to get out of Oel Maritias alive—and in order to do that, he needed to be at the periphery, where survivors were going to congregate. And he needed to be in a house that was going to get first pick of rescue ships, that would have its own people from the upper city on hand to make sure everyone got taken, that no one was forgotten.

Luercas hurt. The *rewhah* had turned his skin hard and brittle, and when he moved wrong he broke off pieces of it. His joints didn't hinge in the same directions anymore, and every time he got too confident while moving over the rubble, he would forget and try to bend a knee forward when it could only bend backward, and he would fall flat on his face, taking Maidan down with him.

She bled, he bled, the two of them had to look like something from the lower reaches of hell, and all he could think of was, Am I covered by the city employees policy for the magework that will repair all of this, or is the cost of repair work for my injuries going to end up coming out of my pocket?

He felt guilty that he could not grieve for Rone Artis. Of Rone nothing survived but a bit of ash and a few scraps of bone that had fallen far enough from the main blast of the *rewhah* that they were not consumed; the brand-new Grand Master of the Council of Dragons had died bringing energy to his city. Died badly. Luercas thought he should have felt more than a dull, angry distaste for the man.

Rone would get the gods' serving of attention when the news came out. The city had all the energy it could use—more energy than it and another five cities like it could use. Rone had not died in vain, and because of that, the magic he had done would be done again, and again, and again. Certainly the use of the spell—the clever soul-spell—would get safer. And Rone would become a hero. That, at least, was to the good. If Luercas and Maidan played the game right, they would be heroes, too.

So Luercas, who wanted only to lie in something cool and soothing while waiting for someone to come and make better all the awful things that were wrong with him, headed to Artis House on the periphery of the city, dragging his fellow hero-to-be, to make sure that he announced the death of the most important man in the city to that man's family first. That was, after all, the right way to do things. He would do his duty. He would accept his kudos as gracefully as any shy and retiring debutante, and then he would reap the rewards.

He figured, once he'd had the magework to repair the damage from the *rewhah*, he could ride this thing at least as far as a high seat in Council. Beyond that, he'd have to succeed on merit—but he had plenty of merit, too.

Wraith and Velyn and Solander and Jess arrived in the meeting room from opposite ends of the house but at almost the same time; Wraith saw Jess look from him to Velyn, and watched the expression on her face turn from worry, to hurt, to something he didn't quite recognize. She turned her attention to Solander, and didn't look back at Wraith again as they took their seats.

A very junior member of the family stood on the dais, waiting. As new groups moved in, he kept asking, "Anyone higher than a Four clearance can take over from me. Four? Anyone?" And then he'd wait, and the next handful of battered, shocked-looking people would make their way in, and—ever hopeful—he would ask again.

His relief when a gray-haired Artis—Master of the House Watch—finally came through the door was so palpable that Wraith almost laughed. "Master Tromiel, Master Tromiel, so *very* glad to see you. Please, you're the ranking member of the family; you need to take the census and determine our course of action."

And Tromiel, whose bruised face, torn clothing, and cautious, pained movements hinted that what he really wanted to do was sit down, nodded with the grace of a statesman, walked instead to the dais, and took the place of the nervous young man. Wraith heard him say, "How are we doing so far?"

"Badly," the young man said softly. "You're the only person here so far who can actually make a decision for the whole family. I'm Level Four, and I was ranking until you came through the door. And this is everyone—I haven't sent anyone out on reconnaissance yet or to look for survivors. I would have had I remained the ranking member, but . . ."

Tromiel glanced around the room, and for a moment his eyes seemed to glaze. Then he nodded slowly. "You did well. We'll wait a few more minutes, get our count, and then set up a communications station in here and send out parties to find survivors. You're my assistant."

The young man nodded. "Yes, Master."

Wraith, as a newly minted and untried adult, held a rank of One, which was at least better than his previous child-rank of Zero. This new rank, however, meant he was going to be taking orders for a while. He and Solander both, most likely. He suspected that Velyn held a slightly higher rank, but she'd never done any of the favor-mongering that tended to win rapid in-family promotions; she would most likely be slogging it, too. Jess, technically still a child and unranked, would probably find herself in one of the nurseries baby-sitting younger children. That would probably infuriate her.

Wraith tried to focus on the good news—that all four of them were alive—but his mind kept wandering to the inevitable bad news and wondering how bad it was going to be. Those watery hands hammering on the glass, the city being shuttled to the surface, the absence of most of the adults in the family. In a room that should have held seven hundred Artis adults, he so far counted just over thirty. What had happened to the city? To the people? To the surface of the sea?

And then two monsters dragged themselves through the door. One, scaled and horned and black as sea sludge, covered with bleeding crusts and twisted in ways that made each of his movements like watching the unfolding of a broken ladder, dragged the second, who still had a bit of the recognizable human about her, but who seemed to be now a bag of jelly poured into a stretchy and shapeless human skin. A few people screamed softly and got smaller in their chairs. Others stared and paled or whispered to those seated beside them. Solander turned to Wraith and murmured, "Ah, no . . . this is going to be a nightmare."

The black, scaled monster dragged his companion to the dais, climbed with agonizing slowness to the top of it, put the jelly-creature down, and turned to the Master. "I have news," he said.

With horror, Wraith realized that he recognized the monster's voice. In spite of all the rest of the damage, the creature's vocal cords and lips still worked right. Wraith tried to comprehend the truth—that bastard Luercas, who had tried to force him to bow on their first meeting and who had hated him and harassed him ever since, existed now inside that magic-twisted casing. Wraith had a hard time not feeling that justice had been served.

"Tell us," Tromiel said.

"I know you can't recognize me, but I am Luercas tal Jernas, the son of Emi Artis and Gregor tal Jernas, and I am also an associate attached to the Department of Energy. I have come to bring you the news that Rone

Artis, the new Grand Master of the Council of Dragons and Master of the City, is dead."

Wraith's gaze slipped sideways to Solander, whose face had gone slack and pale.

Luercas continued, "Last night, we discovered that the periphery of the city had gone underpowered and was on the verge of collapse. Rone Artis could have waited to get extra help, but had he done so we might have lost the whole city and everyone in it. Instead, he dared to bring a new source of power on-line, and by doing so, warded off the collapse of the Polyphony Center and the resultant chain reaction of depressurization of the city that would have killed us all. However, when he brought the new power up, he couldn't handle it alone, and it killed him and nearly killed Maidan and me."

A new source of power. Wraith had no doubt about what that was. The city of Oel Maritias was now burning souls. He wanted to be sick.

He glanced back to Solander and saw his friend shaking, white-knuckled, white-lipped. And Wraith, who wanted to scream that justice had been done—that people who would burn the souls of innocents deserved to suffer or die—remembered that Solander had been close to his father; even the revelation of the day before that his father's activities fell outside of any acceptable standard of behavior had not diminished the Dragon in Solander's eyes.

To Solander, this was not justice served for evil done; this was, instead, the destruction of his hopes. He loved his father, even though he sometimes feared him. He admired Rone Artis, too, had wanted to be like him, and when Solander discovered what sort of magic his father did, his first hope had been to take Rone aside, and ask him about his work and how and why he chose to do what he did. Solander wanted to hold on to the good in his father. He wanted to understand, to find some extenuating circumstances, some mitigating factors for the horrible magic his father chose to do, that would allow him to keep the man who had always been his hero on a pedestal.

With Rone dead, all hope of understanding and making peace with the man his father had been died.

Luercas was still talking. "Rone Artis risked everything to save the people of Oel Maritias," he said. "He lost his life, and we've suffered tremendous damage—but the new power is on-line and running now. We have enough magic to repair the city and drop it again to the sea floor. We have enough power now to make it safe. He did this for you— for all of us. Rone Artis was a great man, and it was an honor being his associate, his friend, and at the end, his protégé. Maidan and I wish we could have saved him. We weren't strong enough, but we tried."

Wraith listened to Luercas's words, but he watched Solander's face. Solander loathed Luercas. Now Luercas stood before these few people, eulogizing Rone, calling Rone a fallen hero—and in the same breath nominating himself for the role of still-living hero. For if Rone, who had sacrificed his life, was a hero, then surely both Luercas and Maidan, who had suffered such physical torture, must be heroes, too.

Solander looked at him, and the pain in his eyes had been erased by anger. "That bastard Luercas—middle-level wizard bent on aggrandizing a dead man in the hopes that some of the glory will reflect off of him secondhand."

Wraith nodded. "I know."

"It will, too. He'll be a dorfing Master within two years for this—just watch."

"Not if we tell the people of the city how this happened to him."

"Won't make a difference," Solander said bitterly. "They'll never believe it without proof. *I* wouldn't have believed you without proof, and you're my best friend. You're talking about trying to sully the reputation of the *Dragons.* The people who make cities fly, give free food and shelter to the poor, and keep the night streets so safe that in most places, a three-year-old could wander them alone at night and the only thing that would happen is someone would notice and take him home. If we say, *Well, yes, that's all true, but they're burning the souls of Warreners to do it,* do you think anyone in the Empire of the Hars Ticlarim would believe us? Do you think, even if they did believe, that they would *care*? The people of the Empire have been trained to hate the Warreners, and even better, they've been trained to fear them. So if the Dragons are doing something to the people in the Warrens, citizens are going to say, *A good end to wickedness,* and that will be the end of that."

Wraith could almost see the future sprawling before him—the Dragons would cry loudly that Rone Artis was a martyr, a man who had given his life in the search for knowledge, and they would demand that knowledge so dearly gained could not be ignored or wasted. They would disguise their greed and callousness and hunger for more and more readily accessible power as carefully as they disguised the source of that power, and they would talk of bringing the most good to the most people with the least cost.

And they would never count the cost, because neither they nor anyone they loved would ever pay it.

Wraith could not permit them to lie to others. To lie to themselves. To disguise their evil behind a pretty face. He'd thought that he would let Solander discuss the issue with his father before he decided on his own course of action, but now all of that had changed. This disaster in Oel Maritias, and the "salvation" of the new source of magic that would prevent the city from going underpowered again would alter the face of the Empire; he had to be ready.

He wished that he could do magic, that he could fight directly against the people who were destroying the Warreners for their own gain, but such wishes were worse than useless, because their self-pity occluded real actions that he could take.

But what could he do? He'd spent his time learning philosophy and history, writing, poetry, doing equations for theoretical magics that he could never test. He had no skills as a tactician or a warrior. What did he have? He had to have something that would let him fight this horror.

He'd missed the end of Luercas's speech. Now Tromiel was standing on the dais, listening to a wild-haired, blood-smeared young woman who seemed to be stuttering and crying at the same time.

At last Tromiel held up a hand and called the gathered survivors together. "We're getting reports in from the Polyphony Center—some people there dead and a lot more injured and trapped in rubble. We're going to need everyone who is healthy and strong to start digging them out." He pointed to Solander. "You're Rone's son, aren't you?"

Solander, thin-lipped and pale, nodded.

Tromiel said, "I know you are going to want some time to yourself, son. That was a hellish loss—your father was a good man, and we won't forget him, and we won't forget what he did for us. But working will help you to ease your pain. The living need you now. The dead will understand—sometimes they have to wait." He returned his attention to the assembly. "I'll remain here with a few of the older children as runners. We've not yet established contact with Oel Artis, but we will. In the meantime, I need a single detail to go from room to room in Artis House and find anyone we've missed. Three people, one with healing magic skills." Somewhere behind Wraith, hands evidently went up, for Tromiel pointed and said, "Yes, you three. And you"—he pointed to his assistant—"you'll be liaison between here and the servants' census. As soon as they check people off, get them down to Polyphony. You and you"— he pointed to Velyn and Jess—"will take over in the main nursery. Reports are that the children are a bit battered, but none died. They're frightened, though, and they need some of their own with them right now. You may keep a servant with you to assist, but we can't spare more than one. Keep the children busy. Find useful things for them to do, and let them know they're helping. Don't let them have too much time to wonder about their parents. We'll have family come for them as we . . . find them." He stared down at the floor for a moment, then cleared his throat and looked up again. "The rest of you go to Polyphony now. In emergencies, we have no rank or class—you'll will work with whoever will help you and get our people to safety. We'll get everyone out of this city and back to solid ground as quickly as we can." He rubbed his eyes. "One final thing. Stay away from the windows. Something is wrong with the water, and until we know what it is and how to deal with it, we don't want to . . . ah, antagonize it."

He dismissed them and sank into a seat.

The distressed woman led the group toward the Polyphony Center. All the aircar passageways, even the deep transport lines, were too cluttered by debris to permit aircars. But servants had cleared some of the express paths, and though Wraith never wanted to use anything tainted with magic again, he kept silent and stepped on the glidewalk with everyone else.

The two days that followed burned themselves into his brain. In the shattered remains of what had once been a grand and wondrous place lay bodies and bits of bodies, crushed, mangled, torn, and shredded. And alongside them, the weeping, begging living, crying out for a drop of water, for something to ease their pain, for someone to save them, for someone to give them the mercy of death. He had spent little time imagining hell before the two days and two nights he spent moving rubble, picking up bodies in an increasingly hot and unbreathable atmosphere, and carting both living and dead away from the wreckage. He had always thought that, coming as he did from the Warrens, he had a solid understanding of what hell was really like.

He'd been wrong.

He and Solander worked side by side, moving slabs of a fallen floatplatform; they could hear people beneath it sobbing and clawing at the slick surface, trying to free themselves.

Solander said, "Magic did this."

Wraith jammed his thighs under one section of a slab and levered it up enough that three other men could get a good grip. Together, they started dragging the slab to one side. "I know," he said. "Without magic, there would never have been a city beneath the sea. No chance of collapse, no floating platforms, no spells gone wrong to destroy everything. Magic should be outlawed."

"No," Solander said. "Magic feeds the masses, keeps them sheltered and safe, carries them from home to work and home again. Without magic, there could be no Empire. But the sort of magic that draws from other people, that gets its power from destruction, and that rebounds destruction at the wielders—*that* sort of magic should be outlawed."

Wraith grunted and, in unison with the other men, released his section of the slab. "That's the only sort of magic there is."

"But it doesn't have to be. It's the only sort of magic that allows an individual to cast a tremendously powerful spell, but I'm on to something—one of the spin-offs from working with you, actually. I think I've found a way to cast a spell drawn from my own energy."

Wraith kept his voice down and made sure that only Solander could hear him. "I've seen the math. Hells-all, I've *done* the math. The power you can derive from a single human life is negligible. It's only by having whole masses of people clustered together that you get enough power to do anything that would interest the Dragons or that would run the city. Besides, they wouldn't choose to pay for their spells with their own lives. And if you have any sense, neither will you."

Solander glanced at the men to either side of them. None were paying them any attention. "The power the Dragons derive from one human life is negligible because it isn't volunteered. It's taken by force and deception. I can't be sure of the power ratios yet, but I believe that I can get significantly more power from a self-powered spell than from one fueled by a sacrifice—and so far, I haven't had any measurable *rewhah* in my tests. It isn't the breakthrough that I wanted—it isn't the answer to what makes you the way you are. But it could be the answer to the Empire's energy needs."

Wraith shook his head. "Have you tried anything big yet?"

"Big? How big? I'm almost certain what I'm doing can work."

"Big. Have you floated a house? Run an aircar? Routed traffic without a mishap?"

Solander sighed. "One person couldn't do that alone. It's too much."

"So the . . ." Wraith grunted as the load they were shifting slipped suddenly onto him. For a moment he thought he would collapse. Then the other men caught their part of it, and Wraith staggered upright and caught his breath. "So the Dragons would not only have to offer themselves as sacrifices for your magic—with the real and painful costs that would entail—but they'd have to do it in collaboration with each other."

"Well, yes. I suppose things like the floating cities and the underwater cities and the aircars would have to go—they're awfully wasteful of energy."

Wraith looked at him sidelong and said nothing.

Solander flushed. "They won't do it, will they? They won't give up the things that they love to save the lives—or the souls—of strangers."

Wraith slowly shook his head. "Not unless we make them."

"We? You mean you and me?"

"You, me, Jess, Velyn . . . and the people we manage to rally to the cause."

"What are you thinking?"

"I'm thinking of getting the truth out there. Of proving to the citizens of the Hars that the Dragons don't get the energy to run the cities from the sun or the earth or the sea. I'm thinking of showing them the insides of the Warrens, letting them look at the people that are being sacrificed so that they can live in the clouds. I don't know how we can do it, but we have to find a way. The Dragons will never walk away from sacrifice-magic on their own—but they can be pushed, I think."

Solander said nothing through the next two pieces of rubble that they moved. Then he asked, "What if the Dragons push back?"

Luercas, his body crusted and in terrible agony, lay on a stretcher on one of the converted docks among the thousands of surviving injured.

"Last count is over fifteen hundred stolti dead," Dafril said. Dafril had been Luercas's only real friend and greatest admirer since the two of them were children. He squatted in the blazing sun beside Luercas, dipping a towel into a bucket of fresh water from time to time and rinsing off the worst of Luercas's crusts. They were waiting for the rescue ships.

"They're still pulling bodies out of the rubble," Luercas said.

"Oh, of course. Will be for days—it's a nightmare in there. But only the chadri and the mufere are cleaning up the mess now—someone finally saw reason and released the stolti to go about their lives."

Luercas glanced at his fellow survivors and made a face. "I can tell right now that the disaster didn't get the right people."

Dafril leaned close and grinned at him. "More than you'd think. We've found the bodies of some of the ones who you know were voting to keep you out of the Council. Next time you come up for a position— especially considering what a hero you are for getting us all out of that mess alive—I'm guessing you'll get a seat."

"And if I can sit in it, it will be a miracle."

"The wizards will get you back to yourself in no time. A good body-mage will be able to fix this."

"I hope you're right."

Luercas heard soft cheers from all around him, and raised his head enough to look out to see. One grand ship, and then another, and then a third, rose on the horizon.

"Excellent," Dafril said. "You'll be out of this heat in no time. The injured are to go in the first ship—the best bodymages are already aboard to make sure all of you are fit by the time you get to Oel Maritias."

All three vessels moved forward with incredible speed. And then the first encountered the circle of glowing sea around the floating remains of Oel Maritias, and the sea formed itself into hands that reached up on powerful arms and gripped the ship's bow. In the path of the ship, a mouth opened. The arms pulled the bow downward, beneath the surface of the water—the stern of the ship lifted into the air and, as it lifted higher and higher, began to collapse backward. The air filled with the sound of rending metals; the ship ripped in two; bodies with flailing arms and legs flew into the air, crashed into the sea, and vanished; and in an instant the poisoned, angry water pulled down both halves of the broken ship.

Not a single head bobbed above the glass-smooth, glowing surface when it vanished. Not one survivor swam toward the city or back toward the two remaining ships.

For an instant, on the deck where so many awaited rescue, silence as deep as the sea itself greeted the shocking finality of the disappearance of the first rescue ship. Then people began to scream, to shout for someone to come get them, to take them back into the corridors of Oel Maritias, to save them from the sea.

"The bodymages," Dafril whispered.

"The *rewhah*," Luercas said. "Gods-all, what kind of magic could turn the sea into a living, vengeful monster?"

The other two ships managed to turn before they hit the green-gold shimmer that marked the living sea as something other than mere water. On the deck of one, someone used a voice amplifier and announced, "We're turning back. We've already sent for help by air. Airibles are being cleared for your use and sent for you now."

"Bad magic," Dafril said. "But we aren't going to worry about that right now." He helped Luercas to his feet, supported him, and started moving him toward the port that led inside. "We're just going back inside until better transport gets here."

Airibles? Luercas wondered. Huge, gas-filled throwbacks to a more primitive age. Using them did make sense, he supposed. An airible could anchor to the floating city without landing, and could transport more than a thousand people at once rather than the several dozen that the largest aircar could hold.

But airibles were slow—and who had any that were ready for use? Poor merchants, perhaps, who couldn't afford the more expensive fast-ships or aircars to ship their products. Bulk shippers, maybe.

Help would arrive, if the sea didn't decide to pull the battered city of Oel Maritias beneath it. And if it came in time, Luercas decided, he would leave with gratitude and never live beneath the water again. He doubted that he would be the only one to give up Oel Maritias—or, more realistically, to give up the new city far from this patch of poisoned water that would become Oel Maritias, as the Dragons carefully rewrote history so that this disaster became something that had never happened.

Chapter 8

Within a year, Oel Maritias the broken wallowed at the bottom of its poisoned sea, never mentioned and mostly forgotten, and Oel Maritias the new and fair lay glittering like a gem tossed by gods, thirty furlongs to the east of its old location and on a fine solid shelf of rock at the edge of a great drop. Life moved on. Wraith turned down the covils in favor of the study of literature and history in a fine old school; Solander took his first steps toward the future he yearned for in Research; Velyn kept company with Wraith when the two of them could find the time; and Jess finished her mandatory classes.

Luercas traveled from bodymage to wizard to healer in search of the reversal of the damage done to his flesh. Dafril buried himself in the study of old magics and dark paths.

And the Empire grew. And grew. Beautiful, graceful, hungry for energy. The Hars provided for its citizens. None were ever hungry, none wanted for shelter. At its need and convenience, however, the Empire rewrote its definition of "citizen." Those who failed to meet its current preferences paid their taxes in more than money; they paid with their lives, and with their souls.

Grath Faregan finished the meeting with his keppin—his immediate superior in the Inquest. His keppin was to be raised to Mastery, and he, Grath Faregan, was to become the new keppin, with a squad of solitars of his own, and access to a vast array of single agents who would do his bidding without question.

He was on his way up.

Thoughtfully, he returned to his play chambers, hidden in the top floors of his private quarters in Faregan House, where he kept his collection. He thought he might . . . But for the first time in ages, his collection left him cold. All of his dolls, magically frozen in artful poses, waiting for him to choose one and wake her for a bit of play, seemed dull and common to him. He studied his whips, his prods, his chains and pincers and brands and knives, and all he could think of was the beautiful young girl from the festival. Jess Covitach-Artis.

His collection would have a gaping hole in it until he added her—until he decorated her with his tools, and posed her, and suspended her in time in the prized center position of his gallery. He closed his eyes and he could see the artwork he could make of her. He could taste her terror. He yearned, he ached, he throbbed for her.

She lived in a fortress to which he had no access, however—he could not hope to get through the doors of Artis House in Oel Artis; it stood alone, with no common through-corridors like the Artis sector of Oel Maritias. His spy told him the girl always had friends with her and never left the house alone.

Faregan did not think he'd be able to get to her by force. Which left finesse.

He worked out a spell that would permit him to watch her whenever she was out from under the shields of Artis House. He determined that he would win her trust.

"I'm free from the Academy for the week," Solander said. "We've a surprise holiday; the Master of Subliminals is to take vows with a harine from Bainjat, and they're having a giant do. We're to be invited, but because she's Bainjati, they've a week of purification rituals, meditation, and testing before the big day. All the Masters are involved, so none of us students have any requirements." He grinned at Wraith. "So that gives me some time to work on my private projects for the first time in months. How are yours coming?"

Wraith sighed and stretched and pushed himself away from his desk. "I'm lost, Sol. My head hurts, and I've discovered that I can write bad poetry all day, but the second I try to write something that matters, I get all awkward and the words refuse to go in the right places. I've done a play. But it's dreadful."

"Let me see."

"I'd rather you didn't. I'd like to still have your respect tomorrow."

Solander looked at his friend and laughed. "Here's my deal. I'll show you what I've done, but only if you show me what you've done."

Wraith said, "You've had a breakthrough?"

Solander just smiled. "You show me first."

Wraith went to a cabinet and opened the bottom drawer. From it he pulled out a sheaf of papers. "At least you can't say I haven't been busy." He handed the pages to Solander and sat back in his chair.

And that was the danger of being the friend of someone who fancied himself a writer, wasn't it? Solander dreaded the idea of working his way through a play, no matter what rhyme scheme it was done in or whether the gods declaimed in Akrenian or Common, and then being forced afterward to say something polite about it. Every time he thought of actors on a stage, spouting the words of some much-lionized playwright, he wanted to flee in the other direction—and if the works of the greatest playwrights in the world could have that effect on him, he could just imagine the horror his friend the amateur was about to inflict on him. But he couldn't think of a graceful excuse. He had, after all, put Wraith through years of grueling experimentation to fuel his own career. So, with the air of a man condemned, he began to read *A Man of Dreams—A Play in Three Acts*.

After a quick description of a very plain set, Wraith started in with a child from the Belows wandering through the street with a basket on his back, from which he was trying to sell something he called *daffiabejong*—casually translated as "fruits of dreams." A young wizard met the boy in the street and asked if he could be assured that the dreams he bought would be good ones, and the boy told him that if his conscience was clear and his heart was pure, his dreams would be good ones—but that under no circumstances should he eat of the fruit if he carried a guilty secret with him.

"Um . . ." Solander looked up, a bit puzzled. "When I saw the first page and everything was written in Common instead of Akrenian, I thought you had your gods declaiming in Common. But you don't actually seem to *have* any gods. . . ."

"No gods," Wraith said. "Keep reading."

"No gods at all. Oh. I thought gods declaiming at the beginning of a play was a requirement."

"I didn't follow the form," Wraith said. "Keep reading."

Interested in spite of himself, Solander returned to the play and to the boy selling dreams. By saying that only the guilty dared not buy his fruits, the boy selling the dreams forced the wizard to buy one—for who would ever admit that he carried a guilty secret when others were walking past, listening to what was said, and looking at him?

The wizard took the fruit of dreams home and attempted to dispose of it by burying it, only to discover that it grew into a tree in his yard in merest moments, and that new fruits sprang forth on the branches, and that the fruits cried out to the man to eat them. Their voices haunted him day and night, leaving him ever more haggard and desperate. When he tried to cut down the tree, two grew in its place, and when he tried to burn the two trees, the flames scattered the seeds so thoroughly that a forest of the trees filled his yard, and what had once been a bright and beautiful place became a dark and haunting miniature forest that moaned and wailed and gave the poor wizard no rest.

The wizard used all sorts of enchantments to avoid the fruits of his tree, of course—but the *daffia-bejong* were nothing if not persistent, and finally, unable to stand another moment of their presence, he fell to his knees, swearing to the little grove that he would eat one of the fruits if they would simply allow him to rest.

The trees agreed.

Thus to the second act, where the man ate, and fell asleep, and his dreaming self suddenly confronted the ghosts of the damned crying out for retribution for the tortures and the suffering that he had caused them. Solander discovered that the wizard had found a spell by which he could turn convicted prisoners into a special form of water that kept anyone who drank it young. But when he ran out of guilty men on whom to use his spell, he had to either find innocent fuel or tell his many customers that they could no longer be young.

He had decided that he would continue supplying his customers, because they made him very rich, and sat him at the center of the table during their great feasts, and applauded him in the streets—but the souls of those who had been so badly used would not rest, and hunted him down in the form of fruit from the magical *daffia-bejong*. And in his sleep, those whose deaths he had caused finally got a chance to protest their treatment in his hands. They haunted him, and swore that he would never wake until he repented his evil and cast a special spell to free them from the limbo to which they had been consigned.

In the third act, the wizard, haggard and changed, cast the spell to free the dead from limbo, and all the ghosts of innocents appeared before him and began to follow him, telling him that he was not done with them. Other wizards had found the secrets of his spell, and they offered the same magical water. For him to gain his freedom from the dead, he would have to sell one of the fruits of dreams to other guilty wizards. The play ended with the wizard, his cart loaded with the *daffia-bejong* he had grown from his tree, wandering the streets, selling his produce to unsuspecting wizards who shared his guilty secret.

Solander sat there staring at the last page for a long time—not reading, just thinking about the souls of the damned in the play and the souls
of the doubly damned in the Warrens of the Empire—souls that would
not even have a chance to cry out for vengeance. Finally he put down
the play and looked up. "The way you have it written, I can imagine
watching it on a stage—but it would be more like being secretly inside
someone else's life. People would love to watch this. Not even just the
stolti, though. I bet if you offered cheaper tickets to the chadri, maybe
even the mufere, you could sell them. It's a good story, and even they
could follow it since it's in Common. And the fact that it isn't told in poetry . . ." Solander shrugged, at a loss for a clear explanation for what
prose gave the play that poetry wouldn't have. "It would have been more
artistic if you had done it in poetry, and you would have been looked at
as a better writer. But I don't know that you truly would have been a better writer, because people would have slept through your play just as
they sleep through the plays of all the so-called greats. I think if you can
actually get the audience interested in what is happening on the stage
rather than in what the other people in the audience are wearing or who
they came with, you might be the better writer. The fact that this doesn't
have any visits by gods doesn't hurt it at all—after all, who really believes
in the gods these days? And as for it being written in Common . . . I
thought that made it all the better." He paused. "The people in it
sounded real—only a lot more interesting in the way that they said
things than most people anyone ever hears speaking."

Wraith managed a smile. "So it wasn't the worst thing you've ever
read. That's reassuring, anyway."

But Solander had only half heard what Wraith said. He'd been capti-
vated by a sudden, certainly ludicrous, but also delightful inspiration. If
he wanted to, he *might* be able to put *A Man of Dreams* on a stage. Since
his father's death, he'd had a monthly allowance that came to him as payment from the Council of Dragons—support based on the fact that his father had died in service to the Empire, and that had he lived, he would
have continued to contribute to his son's education and welfare. This was
money over and above investments that his father had put aside, Solander's share of the family money—which was extensive—and Solander's
own fledgling investments. Because his father had been nothing less than
the Grand Master of the Council of Dragons of Oel Artis and Oel Maritias
at the time of his death, the stipend was almost breathtakingly generous.

Solander could not be seen funding the play personally, of course; in
order to continue with his education in the Academy and to keep from

alienating the Masters whose recommendations he would need when he got ready to find his place within the ranks of the Dragons, he needed to keep his distance from anything that so clearly questioned the always sacrosanct nature of the work of wizards. If he wanted to change the Dragons from the inside, first he had to get inside. And he would never get there by being patron to a play that suggested a wizard (and a stolti) might also be a murderer.

And of course Wraith, in his stolti persona as Gellas, student in the Materan Ground School and respected member of upper society, couldn't be known to have written such a piece of inflammatory prose. But Wraith could deny any connection with the thing. Could attribute it to some other writer, and produce the play as part of his graduate projects for the Materan School.

Solander could fund the staging of the play in a moderate venue if he used third parties that would be difficult or impossible to trace back to him. That would be . . . He smiled. That would be a challenge, and a great deal of fun. As for finding actors to take such interesting parts— well, because the play had been written in Common, it wouldn't have to be acted by the stolti Poets' Presentation Covil dilettantes who were fluent in half a dozen dead languages—but who would, no doubt, insist on proper structure, Skursive rhyme, and coma-inducing content. Instead, Wraith would have his choice of people from all walks of life—anyone who could speak and read Common would be a potential actor.

Solander suddenly realized that Wraith was talking to him.

"What?"

"Where did you go? One moment we were discussing my pathetic play, and the next, you were a world away and deaf as the dead."

"I'm going to underwrite *A Man of Dreams*."

"You're *what*?"

"I'm going to underwrite it. I'm going to put up the money, channeled through a couple of reliable people I know so that no one knows I'm the one who's paying to produce it, and you are going to produce the play on a stage. You're sure no one knows you wrote it?"

"Very sure."

"Good. Attribute it to someone else. That way, if anyone has problems with what it says, you're just the fellow who thought it was clever and who decided to give it an airing. Your imaginary writer can take the heat for its actual production."

"You don't think people will wonder?"

"Give your writer a life of his own. Create him as you'd create a character in a play—know where he lives and who he knows and how he gets around. Set up a way to pay him, and always remember to pay him. Send him notes by messenger, and make sure to read his replies. Make him clever. Make him careful. Make him solitary. And never forget that he is someone other than you—not with anyone. Not even me."

Wraith nodded thoughtfully. "That should keep me from being banned from the Empire or sent to the mines."

"What shall you call him?"

"I don't know. Something. Something from the Warrens, to stick a finger in the Empire's eye." Wraith closed his eyes and thought. Finally he shook his head. "I don't know. I'll think of something sooner or later."

Solander shook his head and crossed his arms over his chest. "This secretive writer of yours needs to come to life today, because I'll give you money to start financing your theater, and some of it has to go to him to pay for his work."

Wraith suddenly laughed. "Here's something. Why not? Call him Vincalis, for all that it will ever matter."

"Vincalis?"

"The name of the gate the beautiful and unsuspecting Shina and I went through, when I first discovered the nature of the Warrens. The gate you and Velyn came through to take Jess and me out. The gate my family is going to walk out of one day."

"Doesn't sound much like a person's name."

"Doesn't matter, does it? This Vincalis is a fellow who's concerned with his privacy. No one's ever going to think that's his real name, anyway."

"Vincalis it is, then." Solander raised his glass. "Here's hoping he doesn't make a fool of all three of us."

Wraith raised the bottle he'd been drinking from and said, "From your mouth to the gods' ears." They drank. "And now, what of the break-through you've been hinting at?"

Solander grinned. "Actually, I've had two."

"Damn braggart."

They both laughed, and Solander said, "Personal or professional first?"

Wraith's eyebrows rose. "Oh, personal, of course."

"You're as much a gossip as any covil-osset, aren't you?" He leaned forward and his voice dropped. "This is good, though."

"Well . . . ?"

"Jess and I are a couple. Or will be tomorrow, when she becomes a legal adult."

Wraith rose, lifted his bottle, and said, "A prayer answered." He drank the remaining contents in one long, hard gulp, and wiped his mouth with the back of his hand. Then he smashed the bottle into his trash basket. "That was to your happiness, and mine."

Solander said, "You're too hard on her."

Wraith just looked at Solander from under his eyebrows and said nothing.

"My other news, then."

"Please. But I'm not sure my heart can take it."

"I think I may have figured out why you are the way you are."

"You're joking."

"Didn't say I'd learned how to use it yet. But with those documents you . . . acquired, I've been doing equations, trying to figure out the effects of all those different spells that are pouring into the Warrens all the time. The spells on the food, the shield spell around the place, the control spells that go in through the daily lessons and daily prayers. And I hit on something."

"Toxic magic overdose."

Solander pointed a finger at Wraith. "Close. I was using the school's equipment after hours, running all the equations and testing them at different power levels. And suddenly I got what I thought was an artifact. All my waveforms went flat. I got a paper copy of what was running at that instant, and saw that it wasn't really an artifact at all. All those spells, and all that power, blasting through the Warrens—and all that energy being drawn back out of the Warrens—and all those levels constantly adjusting themselves. I think, just once . . . or maybe more than once, but you're the only one who got hit by it, I don't know—anyway, in your Warren, at the moment you were conceived, I think everything hit that single flat note that I discovered, and the result was that you were saturated with every conceivable form of magic for one critical instant. You probably shouldn't have lived. Most babies conceived at that instant—if there were any others—probably didn't."

"It was a fluke, then."

Solander looked at Wraith and shook his head. "Was it? I think I found the mechanism that made you the way you are—but the fact that you survived something that I think should have killed you might have been . . . fate. A higher destiny."

"The gods?" Wraith laughed. "It's interesting, anyway. Theoretically, then, I might not be the only one in the world like me."

"Right. But you probably are. I couldn't find another series of power levels that had the same result, and I ran up and down the scale in every

direction as far as I could—for as long as I could get away with using the
school equipment without having anyone ask me what I was doing, anyway." Solander shuddered, recalling more than a month of nights when
he'd used every spellchecker in the student lab, all the while listening for
footsteps and knowing that if anyone came in, there was no way he
could hope to get everything shut down in time—and knowing that the
spells he was checking were government secrets, and that the penalty
he'd incur just for having them in his possession was death. Bad memories. He'd finally decided he'd found as much as he wanted to find.

"Will what you discovered finally give you what you've been looking
for all these years?" Wraith asked after a moment. "Is it the key to magic
with no *rewhah*?"

"I don't know. I think it's a start."

With Solander in the Belows visiting Wraith, Jess found herself with
too much time to think, and too many things to think about. She walked
slowly through the Rone Artis Memorial Starpark, watching the starsetters changing the seasonal displays to either side of the thin ribbon of
translucent pathway that led around the starpond. The following day
would mark her last day of childhood, according to her forged documents, and her last day of tutoring within Artis House. As an adult, she
would be at loose ends. The stolti could not hold paying jobs, as this was
below them; if she had been good at theoretical magic, she could have
found a position in government, which was considered the realm of the
stolti. But she'd hated the necessary maths, and had no real aptitude for
the poetic forms of spellcasting beyond the simplest spellwork. So government would be out. She might develop and manage a business—a lot
of stolti did that to augment their family fortunes. Her Artis stipend, plus
a few investments that Solander had made and then turned over to her
management, would keep her going. She could live in Artis House as
long as she wanted. But what was she to do with herself?

She liked art and music and dance. She could join a covil, perhaps,
and spend time with other stolti who liked the same things. Maybe she
could find some direction there.

"Pretty, aren't they?"

Jess jumped, and turned to find a gray-haired man behind her, smiling at her with an expression of mild amusement on his face.

"Pretty?" she asked. And then realized he meant the displays. "Oh,
the starpond and the staryards. They're lovely. Considerably more dramatic than ours. The comets are especially nice." She turned away from

him, hoping that this brief exchange would satisfy his urge for conversation, and that he would move on. She didn't like him, though she couldn't say why.

But he didn't move on. Instead, he said, "You look terribly familiar."

She studied him and shook her head. "I don't think we've met."

"Then let's meet now. Come with me to Ha-Ferlingetta, and I'll buy you a meal and a drink, and we can get to know each other. You're a lovely young woman."

Jess suppressed a shudder and forced a smile to her face. Everything about this man sent her skin crawling and scared the breath out of her. "Actually, I'm a child," she said, and managed to put a note of apology into the statement. "I'm afraid I can't accept your kind offer."

He frowned. "A child?"

She pulled the locket from beneath her tunic and showed it to him. It glowed—proof that she was, indeed, still under the protection of the Childlaw.

He took a step back, nodded, and said, "My forgiveness, then. You look older than your age."

Which was a lie. She looked considerably younger than her age and knew it. But she merely nodded and said, "No harm done." And then, with a smile and a bow, she excused herself, and hurried back to Artis House, trying to figure out what it was about the man that so filled her with dread, and thanking all the gods of her childhood that she'd had the locket for one more day.

A spring, a summer, an autumn, and a winter. And back again to spring, as Wraith and Solander walked through the theater in the New Brinch District. "Hard to believe it was a warehouse a year ago."

"Not for me," Wraith said with a laugh. "I've been here every day. I have no trouble believing it at all."

"It's beautiful." Solander pointed to the tiers of seats that rose up almost to the ceiling. "But those don't look very comfortable."

"They aren't supposed to be. They're fine if you're sitting up in them, but not at all friendly if you try to take a nap."

"Still determined not to cater to the covil-ossets, eh?"

Wraith shook his head. "I'm not trying to win their awards. I want to reach people." He paused, vaulted onto the raised circular stage, and sat with his legs dangling over the edge. "True what I heard about Jess?"

"Depends on what you heard, I suppose."

"I heard she joined a covil."

Solander wrinkled his nose. "Music Council—spreading pretty sounds and telling the stolti what they're supposed to think about them." He chuckled a little, but Wraith didn't.

"Why is she wasting herself with a thing like that? Endless committees, arguments about which music is appropriate and should be accepted as part of the canon and which is somehow unworthy, nasty little in-groups, petty backstabbing. . . ." Wraith frowned and drummed his heels against the stage. "She could be doing something worthwhile with her life."

Solander hopped onto the stage beside him, and sat staring up at the vast dark cavern of seats. "Scary," he said. And then, after a moment, "You think she should be working alongside you and Velyn—that she should be here every day, directing the workers, planning the production, trying to figure out how to save the Warreners, whatever the cost. But that isn't what she wants. She can't stand to see you and Velyn together, she doesn't ever want to have anything to do with the Warrens again . . . and what is she supposed to do with her life? She's stolti; she can't take employment, she has no particular talents to follow like you do—or like I do, for that matter—and I think her days are starting to stretch out in front of her now, looking all much the same. She doesn't want to take vows—I asked—and the covil is *something*. She talked about an exploratory covil that does digs all over the world, but they'll be working in the ruins over in the territories east of the Strithian Empire for the next several years, so I finally managed to talk her out of that." He shrugged, looking a little ashamed of himself. "I didn't want her to be gone for so long."

Wraith lay back on the stage with an exasperated sigh. "She's with you, but she resents Velyn being with me?"

"She's with me," Solander said. "But she doesn't love me—she never has. I'm just her fallback position from you."

"I'm sorry," Wraith said after a while. "I truly thought she would outgrow that infatuation of hers."

"She loves you," Solander said. He sounded testy, and Wraith looked at him with surprise. "She's always loved you. At least have the courtesy to call it what it is."

"I know. But I can't love her," Wraith said. "She's a memory of every failure, every lost friend, every death I caused in the Warrens. I look at her and all I can see is everyone who *didn't* get free."

"Just as well for me that she doesn't know that, then," Solander said after a long silence. "Because if she did, she would probably be here helping you—in the hopes that if all the Warreners were suddenly free, you might find a way to love her."

Wraith looked puzzled. "And . . . ?"

"Don't be an idiot, Wraith. Just because she doesn't love me doesn't mean that I don't love her. I have only as much of her as she'll give me—but I don't want to lose that."

They were two days from the first open call for actors when Wraith finally came to a decision. Velyn was bent over a piece of the third act backdrop, painting. Her hair fell around her face, and paint speckled her hands, and the graceful curve of her back made his mouth go dry.

He sat beside her and for a while simply watched her, while he tried to consider which words he could use to ask her the question that had been driving him to distraction for so long. At last he said, "Velyn?"

She looked up at him and smiled—the smile he loved so much. "You've been quiet today. Having doubts about our little enterprise?"

"No doubts," he said. "Not about the play, not about the theater. But . . . yes. I've been doing a lot of thinking."

Velyn laughed her soft, low laugh, shook her head with mock seriousness, and said, "You shouldn't do too much of that. It isn't good for you."

"I shouldn't," he agreed, "but I can't seem to stop myself." He took her hand in his and said, "You and I have been working toward the same goals. We want the same things from life—to bring freedom to the people of the Warrens, to make a difference in the world. To leave Oel Artis a better place than we found it."

Her expression seemed to him a bit bemused, and he thought, I'm not saying this right. I'm not saying any of this the right way.

"We fit each other, Velyn," he said. "And I love you. I love everything about you—the way you move, the way you talk, the way you keep surprising me with things that you know I never, ever heard of. I would spend an eternity with you. I would spend two eternities with you, if I could have them."

Velyn laughed. "I love you, too, Wraith. But you already know that."

He nodded. "I want to offer you vows, Velyn. I want to offer you myself. I want to be your love, your partner, your companion and friend, for the rest our lives and beyond into eternity if the bonds of our vows will transcend death."

He had done it in a rush, hoping to see in her face receptivity, excitement, joy. But what he saw in her eyes was . . . evasion.

She smiled, and her smile was sad. "I love you, Wraith. Can't having *now* be enough? Can't it be enough that we have this moment, this work we share, our nights together for as long as we have them? Can't we find what joy we can in that and hold it to ourselves—create memories that we can keep, and accept the days that come?"

He didn't understand. "You love me. Don't you?"

"With all my heart. With my body. With my soul. I have loved you since we first met."

"Then why won't you say you'll join in the nutevaz with me?"

What he saw next in her eyes he liked even less than the evasion. He saw pity, and inwardly he shuddered.

She sighed deeply and looked down at her paint-speckled hands. "I'm stolti," she said, not looking at him. "I couldn't take vows with you if you were chadri—not even if you were rich and powerful and had your own house in Oel Artis Travia."

Wraith stared at her as if he had never seen her before. "Wait just a moment. I don't think I quite understand this. You love me. You agree that you and I are wonderful together. But you wouldn't even consider taking vows with me because I'm not stolti? You aren't legally obligated to choose someone from the stolti class as your vowmate, and even if you were, my papers and my identity disks and everything else identify me as stolti."

"Your papers say you're stolti. But you aren't. Not really. You're a Warrener. That's even worse than if you were a parvoi, for God's sake. Beyond your false papers, Wraith, you don't even *exist* . . . legally."

"But you love me. I love you. We could spend the rest of our lives together."

"Wraith—members of the highest class of families in the Empire can't just join in the nutevaz with *anyone*. Vows introduce a contractual obligation into the relationship, and contractual obligations put family fortunes into play. They give both members of the relationship rights in regard to houses and properties, accumulated wealth, businesses, political seats, hereditary seats."

Wraith didn't like what he was hearing at all. It made him feel sick. But he wanted to hear all the lovely little things she'd been keeping inside for all the years that he had known her. "And do you think I'd take your money, Velyn? Try to walk off with a property willed to you by your grandmother, or some such thing?"

"Wraith, we'd never even get that far. I'd go home, tell my father that you'd asked me to take vows, and he'd say, 'Have his parents send me their opening contracts. And we'll have to find a mutually convenient place to meet, and we'll have to each bring a property appraiser to assess each other's accounts and standings.' And then I would say, 'Well, actually Wraith doesn't have any parents, or any property.' And that would be almost the end of the discussion. The *end* of the discussion would arrive in the form of people coming to take you away to the Southern Hellhold Greenskeld mines because you are not who you say you are, and have for years been masquerading inside a place you have no business being, taking advantage of the hospitality of the house."

Wraith sat there thinking about this for a moment, almost mollified. "So your concern is for my safety. If we presented this issue to your parents, they would . . ." He closed his eyes, his vision suddenly cleared, and he smiled broadly. "Wait. You're well past the age where I would have to ask your father's permission. You and I could simply take an aircar to Falkleris City in Arim, present our papers, and take vows there without any interference with anyone."

But Velyn didn't return his smile. Instead, she looked away from him, but before she did, he saw again the evasion on her face. "We could. But that isn't what I want."

Wraith said, "Then you don't want me."

"I do want you. But I also want the blessing of my parents. A vowmate that won't be at risk from any too-careful scrutiny of his papers or an indepth check of his past. Someone who is who he says he is—who doesn't spend every moment of every day living a lie." She patted his wrist. "Not that you can help that, Wraith. Obviously you couldn't have stayed in the Warrens, and you'll eventually do so much for your people. But . . ." She wrinkled her nose the tiniest bit. "Your people are not my people. And frankly, I wouldn't want them to be. You're unique, but knowing that I had a responsibility not just to you but to those . . . those creatures within the Warrens . . ." Her voice trailed off, and she turned her face away from him and closed her eyes. He cringed at the distaste on her face.

"Velyn, I don't understand you at all. I mean, I'm understanding you better, but . . . you're working alongside me to help free those *creatures* from their involuntary slavery. If they don't matter to you, why are you doing this?"

"It's the right thing to do. The fact that helping them is the right thing to do, though, doesn't mean that I want them to be my family."

"I see." He wanted to crawl into a hole and die, but he did see.

"Wraith—we have wonderful times together. We are closer to each other than any vowmates I know. If it can't last forever, what does that matter? Nothing lasts forever, and at least now is good." She put a hand over his and tipped her head in that fashion he had always found so winning.

This time he found nothing winning about it. Wraith pulled his hand away and said, "You said you hope someday to take vows with the blessing of your parents. But you've clearly demonstrated that you'll never take them with me. Am I correct?"

She had the nerve to look hurt. "Someday, Wraith, yes. I want to have a vowmate with whom I can have children—children my parents will be able to accept. Children with two sets of grandparents that are . . . human. Wraith, *I love you*. This doesn't have to affect us right now, maybe not for years. But if you could stand where I am standing, you would see that there are other things besides love that have to be considered."

He stood. "So I see." He started to walk away, then turned and glared at her. The urge to hurt her, to cut her as deeply as she had cut him, overwhelmed him. "Maybe this wouldn't have to affect us. But consider this: If you don't start looking for the man you want to keep right away, you're going to be too old to have children without the help of some very nasty dark magic. I'm betting you're pretty close to too old already. So why don't you get going? Start looking for your . . . your *acceptable* vowmate." He turned and walked out of the theater. He'd heard her gasp, and he knew that his dagger had hit its mark. She'd always been sensitive about her age—about the fact that she was not just older than him, but at the outside edge of the age range by which time most men and women had chosen their vowmates.

Perhaps she did love him, Wraith thought—to some degree, anyway. Perhaps she hadn't started looking for a vowmate because she wanted to spend every minute—until the time that she could no longer put off her search—with him.

But he didn't want her for some brief, pathetic liaison. He wanted her forever—he wanted to be able to say to anyone who might ask that she was his vowmate, the person who had chosen him as much as he had chosen her. He wanted to have a real, tangible claim to her. He'd always thought they were heading toward that.

Since the first time he saw her, he'd never imagined himself with anyone else. Never.

He walked, along streets heavy with commercial traffic, past vast buildings that housed impersonal businesses that created wealth of one form or another for the people crouched in the houses they'd built on air like petty and vindictive gods. He had hidden himself within their ranks for too long. He needed to move away from the Aboves for good. He needed to keep his feet on solid ground from now on.

She would be gone when he finally got back to his rooms, he thought. He doubted that he would ever see her again—no need to, really. If he never went back to Artis House, they would have no mutual point of contact. He could send for the few things that belonged to him. If he made good with his theater, he'd have enough money to get by on his own. Solander wouldn't have to keep pouring money at him as if he were trying to fill a bottomless well.

He glanced around the neighborhood, trying to get his bearings. He was lost. Well and truly lost. Good. Maybe, if he tried hard, he could lose himself for good.

When Wraith killed Shina with his stupid attempt to take her out of the Warrens, he'd wanted to die. He'd wished that he could simply summon the rage of the gods to devour him in one mighty blast of fire. But the gods had been cruel and he had lived. He'd never let himself invest too much in his hopes and expectations for people after that, though. He'd learned that the person who cared deeply was simply asking to have everything he loved crushed and destroyed—the best thing to do was to never love.

And then, fool that he was, he had broken his cardinal guideline. He had let himself truly love Velyn. He had let himself care about the outcome of their relationship. He had let himself hope, and dream, and want.

And for a second time, life had demonstrated that love was rewarded only by hideous, excruciating pain.

So. He wanted to die, but he wouldn't. This time he wouldn't because he still had something to do that only he could do. He had to free the Warreners—not just the Warreners of Oel Artis, but Warreners from every city in the Empire.

He had to write his plays that would show the dark side of magic, that would present to audiences the price paid for taking the easy road; he had to plant the seeds of doubt about the benevolent Empire of the Hars Ticlarim and its guiding Dragons; he had to make people understand that by moving away from unthinking magic use, they could save lives. He would live without love because he had no choice—but his life would still matter. He would still exist for a reason.

The cold of the air bit through him, and suddenly he realized that full darkness had fallen, and he'd reached a part of the city unlit by anything save fire. He would have thought such a place could not exist in the closely watched, minutely controlled Empire, but it did. So odd, so impossible was the look and feel and even the shape of this place, that he stopped and stared. He heard laughter in the distance, and the sounds of music—drumming and chanting and singing, and deep harsh bells and something stringed and bowed that sounded like cats fighting. He looked around him—the street seemed safe enough. The inhabitants of this place lit their streets by flames—enclosed lanterns hung on posts that cast an oddly comforting blue-gold light. He did not see anyone lurking, and the area was clean and pleasant-smelling—wood fires and food cooking and incense burning, a rich and wondrous sweetness in the air.

He knew he should try to find his way back to the theater. Or to his suite in the Materan Ground School. Or . . .

Laughter, and singing, and wood fires. Something about the place, about the scene, proved more compelling than his wish to nurse his pain and revel in his own misery. What in the hells where people doing burning wood for heat? Burning oil or some other liquid for light? Why were their houses built of what looked like common rocks stacked one atop another, instead of the beautiful, almost weightless, translucent, nearly indestructible whitestone that was the product of Dragon magic and that was the ubiquitous building material of the Empire? Who were these people?

He found his feet again, and with them his curiosity. And he set off toward the sound of music and laughter.

The houses in this odd neighborhood had been built around a central circle of open ground, and in the center of the circle, he found the source of light and noise, laughter and music. A whole tribe of people dressed in clothing as different as their houses stood or sat around a fire as tall as a man. Some of them sang, some played instruments, some danced, many just clapped their hands and laughed as they watched.

Wraith stood in the darkness at the very edge of the circle, hidden in the shadows of the houses, and watched them. A girl in a pale green tunic and matching tights, with heavy cloth boots that tied just beneath her knees, stood up and began to spin and leap and kick her feet high into the air. With each kick, her foot went higher than her head. Wraith found himself holding his breath against the inevitable disaster when she lost track of the positions of the other dancers and her foot went into someone's nose—but she was fast and agile and she never even grazed any of the rest. Nonetheless, many of the dancers moved to the edges of the circle to give the girl room. When she had it, her movements became even more incredible. She ran on her toes, launched herself into the air, right leg pointing an arrow in the direction she sailed, her left leg trailing behind like a flame in a high wind. Her arms arched over her head, and at the highest point in her leap she let out a shout that would have woken the armies of the dead and stirred the warriors of old to blood-lust and magnificent feats of daring. She leaped again, and spun in the air this time, her body a living impossibility. Wraith tried to understand how she could be doing what she was doing. He would have suspected magic, but this place bore no artifacts of magical origin; it seemed a place built in defiance of magic. Wraith could not think that in this place the girl's tremendous feats of agility and strength were anything but her own skill.

He simply had never seen such skill before.

She made two circles of the fire, and at the end of it retired to stand to one side, and a young man, who seemed to be waiting for her to clear the makeshift stage, took her place. His dancing was as wondrous as hers. He was shirtless in the cold night air, and his baggy pants and soft cloth boots only emphasized the perfection of his movements. He seemed to Wraith to be not a man, but a creature of energy and light, as if he cast the light in the circle and the fire was merely his reflection or his shadow. His muscles stood out as he spun and stamped and jumped, sweat-slicked and shining, and Wraith felt a stab of pure envy. He tried to imagine himself in that circle, dancing, and groaned as he thought of his skinny, pale, weak chest and arms, his thin legs, his big clumsy feet.

"You really shouldn't be here, you know," someone said at his back.

He thought for an instant that his heart had stopped beating, so sharp was the pain of his fear in his chest. He turned and looked at the woman who had come up behind him. Plain-faced, of middling years, lean and muscular as any of the young women dancers, she stood watching him with an expression cast between wariness and curiosity.

"I . . . hadn't intended to," he said. "I got lost."

"Lost?" She looked at his clothes, his shoes, his face, and said, "I would have thought, stolti, that such a thing would be impossible for you. A simple question asked to the air should set you right and take you to your destination."

"I don't use magic," he said before he'd had a chance to think that perhaps he should not be confiding in strangers.

But those four words seemed to cast a form of magic of their own. "Who *are* you?" she asked, but she smiled when she asked it, and took him by the arm and dragged him toward the circle, toward the beautiful dancers, toward the fire.

Chapter 9

What do you mean, he told you to get out of his life?" Solander stared at the sobbing Velyn, and then around the darkened theater. Jess sat on one of the benches, pretending she wasn't listening. Pretending she wasn't gloating.

"He told me I ought to start looking for my perfect vowmate immediately, before I was too old to have children normally."

Solander glanced over Velyn's shoulder at Jess. She clearly loved every new detail in this confession.

"Why would he *do* that?" Solander asked. "Or did he find out about your . . . um, other interests?"

Velyn looked startled. "You mean the other men I see? I don't think they had anything to do with it. He's never asked about them, and I've never mentioned them in so many words, but certainly he's known that I've had other men in my life all along."

Solander was shaking his head. "I'm rather sure he believes he was the only man in your life. You were the only woman in his. Ever."

Velyn looked like she'd just fallen from a roof in the Aboves and was on her way to the Belows with a clear view of where she would land. "No. That's nonsense."

Jess laughed softly. "Not nonsense at all. I happen to know that he's never been with anyone but you in his life."

"You can't know that."

"Why couldn't I? He told me about it. I have no reason not to believe him. It isn't like he had anything to lose by telling me the truth, or anything to gain by lying. He just told me, as part of a conversation we were having."

"Oh . . . gods . . ." Velyn whispered. "But then, that makes the way he acted make a little more sense, anyway."

"Why?" Solander asked. "All you've said so far was that he told you to get out of his life and tore out of here like a crazy person."

"He asked me to take vows with him. I told him I couldn't—the thing about me being stolti and him not, and how someday I wanted to have a vowmate with whom I could raise stolti children—but I told him I wasn't considering this anytime soon. I thought he would understand. But if I'm the only woman in his life—the only woman he's *ever had* in his life . . ." She closed her eyes, and Solander saw the tears starting to fall again. "I thought he understood all along that we could never be a permanent pair. I thought he realized that."

"I would say he didn't. In fact, if you had ever asked me, I would have told you that he had more plans for you than just a few years of spending time together." Solander sighed. "So . . . he proposed, you turned him down in the worst possible way, he got his feelings hurt, said some things he's going to regret tomorrow, and left. By any chance did you see which way he went?"

Velyn shook her head. "Out the front door. That's it. I . . . I was still in shock from what he'd said to me."

"We ought to try to find him," Jess said.

Solander considered how Wraith would react to him and Jess and Velyn going out and tracking him down by shouting. He'd be embarrassed and humiliated and angry, and Solander figured Wraith didn't need to get any angrier. And shouting would be about the only way they could hope to locate him, assuming he wanted to be found. They couldn't track Wraith with magical devices—he simply didn't show up on them. He was very possibly the only man in the Empire who could disappear in plain sight without the use of magic.

"We're going to have to wait for him to get over his hurt and come home. One of us can wait here, one of us can wait at the Materan."

Velyn said, "I'll wait here, I suppose. At least I can still work on backdrops and scenery until he gets back."

Solander stared at her. She really didn't understand how much Wraith loved her—or how much he had been sure that the two of them were going to be together forever. She was going to sit here painting scenery while Wraith crawled around the city with a broken heart, and when Wraith came back, he would see that she was so little hurt by what had happened that she'd just kept working. "I think Jess had better wait in Wraith's rooms in the Materan School, Velyn," Solander said. "And I'll wait in here. And I think you probably need to go someplace else for a while. I'll talk to him—tell him that you didn't mean to hurt him, try to smooth over the rough edges. But I don't think that you're going to be the first face he wants to see when he comes through the door."

"He'll get over it, won't he?"

"*You* would get over it. But he's . . . different. He's different about everything. I don't know that he will."

She looked stunned. "You mean—you mean you think he might truly not want to see me again? To be with me again? But . . . that's ridiculous."

Solander looked around the theater that Wraith and Velyn had designed together, that embodied so many of Wraith's dreams and so many of Velyn's interests, and all he could think of was Wraith talking in dreamy tones about how he and Velyn were going to do this and that, how he would write plays and she would create the sets to make them come to life, and how the two of them were going to change the world together. But Velyn, who Solander thought did love Wraith in her own way, had no passion for changing the world. Because it had been challenging and fun, because it had been something that Wraith had made powerful and intriguing by his passion, she had wanted to be a part of it. But it hadn't been her dream. For Wraith, saving the Warreners and changing the magic system of the Empire had become—along with Velyn—the air that he breathed.

Velyn rose, gathered up her brushes and paints, and carefully cleaned everything. She didn't say anything to either him or to Jess; she just cleaned and straightened. And then, when she had finished, she gathered up her belongings. "I'll be at the house," she said. "If he wants to talk to me. For a while, anyway."

Solander said, "If he wants to know, I'll tell him."

She didn't look happy about that "if." She nodded without saying anything else and left.

After Velyn left, Solander turned to Jess, who sat quietly on the edge of the stage. He shook his head. And then he waited for her to say something about Velyn, because in all the years he'd known her, she'd been rock-solid on one thing: She hated Velyn.

But Jess said nothing.

"You aren't happy he got rid of her?"

"She broke his heart. What sort of friend would I be if I could be happy about that?"

Solander walked over to the stage, vaulted onto it, and wrapped Jess in his arms. With his face buried in her hair, he said, "And that is precisely why I love you."

She kissed the side of his neck and said, "And I love you because you would think to ask." And then she said, "I hope he's safe."

Just for a moment, chilled by the worry in her voice, Solander wondered if this was the moment that would take her away from him and carry her back to Wraith. He forced the fear aside. After all, he was concerned about Wraith, too.

As the fire began to die down and the dancers pulled on robes and settled around the fire, the time came for the singers and the talkers to begin their turn. Wraith sat in the circle, watching a small carved stone being passed from hand to hand, and listened as, one after another, the recipients of the stone told stories. Their stories were of the ways of the Kaan, the name these people named themselves, *kaan* meaning "powerless" in the ancient tongue of the Brigomen, whose descendants this small village of men and women claimed to be. This night they told their stories for him, because he was an outsider, but also a guest; so their tales were of the settling of the islands of middle Arim by the Brigomen, and of the capture and enslavement of the people, and of their clever escapes, successful protests, and delightful evasions and trickeries played upon authorities.

Wraith listened, enchanted, and then the stone passed into his hands, and after a moment's thought, he told them who he was, where he came from, and how he came to be among them that night. His was a long story, but no one protested, no one left, and as the flames dropped lower and the Kaan moved their circle closer around it to conserve heat, more and more of them met his eyes with understanding in their own.

If he had never felt that he belonged within the Warrens, if he had always felt that he was an outsider in the grand houses and high cities of the stolti, in this place of hard and heavy stone dwellings, wood fires, and men and women who eschewed all magic he felt he had at last found his place in the world.

When his story was finished, with the brief telling of the creation of his theater, his plans to make the people of the Empire see the price of the magic they used so carelessly, and his sudden and painful loss of the woman he loved, the men clapped him on the back and the women, with tears in their eyes, told him that a spirit such as his had not been born to wander alone.

And then one of the men said, "So—who will act in this theater of yours? Have you filled the roles? Have you found people who can do the effects you hope for without using magic?"

He had to admit that he had not—that he would be holding the first open tryouts for actors, stagehands, makeup artists, and others soon. That is, if he could find his way back in time.

"Why don't you fill your major roles with the Kaan?" the same man asked him. "We could do everything you need, couldn't we? Perhaps there would not be enough of us in this village who were free to do everything you needed, but with some of us there, you would have less trouble with your magic cripples, who will have to learn the simplest of nonmagical skills from the beginning."

Wraith laughed. "You'd consider this?"

"We've finished our harvest of the foods that we plant and grow. Our larders are full enough, but winter money comes hard to us. I suspect that those among us who have no children to tend would be happy to join this endeavor of yours."

One of the younger women said, "We'd be happy to get you back to your theater, too—but only once morning has come. There are areas around us where we don't willingly go after dark. We . . . well, we are not always well liked by the magic-using majority."

They gave him food to eat and a comfortable bed to sleep in. He fell asleep to the sound of a fire crackling in the hearth by his bed, and the sweetness of wood smoke, and with a freedom of spirit that he had not imagined he could ever feel. If he could only free them, his Warreners could find a place among the Kaan. He and Velyn . . .

But he had, in his happiness, managed to put aside for just a while the grief that had brought him to this wonderful haven. He would not be bringing Velyn here; he would not be seeing her again, touching her again, talking to her again. The pain that had eased for just a little while rolled back over him like a smothering blanket.

Luercas, still scarred beyond any recognizable connection with humanity, sat in private council with his old friend Dafril Crow-Hjaben. He finished a lengthy account of his endeavors to regain his old form by saying, "So that's it. The top specialists as far away as Winter City in Ynjarval; most of the funds that the Council gave me in compensation for my injuries—and this is it. This is the best that the best of them can do—that the best of them will ever be able to do."

Dafril held a new-model spell-minder in one hand—a little hand-sized recorder that could hold and play back tens of thousands of spells, or simply project the words of them into the air as text so that the spell-caster could put his own focus and inflection into them. He kept playing with it instead of giving his full attention to Luercas, something that annoyed Luercas almost beyond reason. Dafril pressed the stylus against an item on the list and told Luercas, "See what I've been working on?"

Luercas exploded. "Did you hear a single word I've said? Have you been listening, or have you been so engrossed in that gods'-damned toy of yours that you've managed to miss it all?"

"Heard every word," Dafril said. "Look, Luercas. Look. I think you'll find this interesting."

Luercas glanced at the words of the spell spun of light that hung in the air before him—preparatory, he thought, to taking Dafril's toy from him and smashing it to pieces. But one of the stanzas of the spell caught his attention.

Draw from flesh, soul,
Draw from flesh, soul,
Two bodies, two souls,
And a single exchange.
And new flesh I claim,
New flesh I claim,
And old flesh I relinquish,
Old flesh I relinquish . . .

It went on from there, but Luercas did not keep reading. Instead he started at the beginning, and partway down he began taking notes, checking and cross-checking parameters, figuring energy constants and flux and *rewhah* controls.

By the time he finally made it to the end, he sat in stunned silence.

"Decent, don't you think?" Dafril finally asked him.

"Have you tested it?"

"Animal tests only. But you know how untrustworthy those are—especially when you're doing something as large and complex as this."

"I can't figure out where you send the *rewhah* for the whole thing."

Dafril laughed. "That has to be the best and cleverest bit of spell design I've ever done. You take every bit of it into your own flesh. Every bit."

Luercas said, "That's insane, Dafril." He held out his arms, pointed to his own horribly twisted, inhuman visage. "This is what happens when you take the *rewhah* yourself."

"But that's the beauty of it. You're trading bodies—so the body you're getting rid of takes the hit, and you get the one that comes through unscathed. If you're lucky, your old body will die, releasing the soul, so that you own the new one free and clear."

Luercas began to laugh, softly at first, but then louder and more merrily. "You . . . are . . . a . . . dorfing genius!"

Dafril looked pleased. "I thought you might like this. I've been working on it ever since you gave me the copy of the spell Rone did that caused your problem."

Luercas felt his heart accelerate. "You based this spell on that?"

"No. Well, partly. I got the majority of my preliminary work from texts I unearthed that were used by the Three Sleeping Stones when they transferred their souls into inanimate objects as their bodies neared death. That's *the* baseline spell for soul usage—the only part I had to use Rone's spell for was the transfer of a soul from an unwilling subject; that is difficult, and the part where we're going to generate the most *rewhah*. We won't have the sort of backlash that we would have had if we'd destroyed the soul in our target body; I'd played with the idea of using our target's soul for the energy to run the spell, but the feedback numbers just got to be horrendous."

Luercas leaned forward and looked at the sheets of computations that Dafril shoved toward him.

After long moments of studying the equations, he nodded. "Your payoff by simply swapping out the souls is well worth the risk of having someone in this body who wants revenge. It makes the whole procedure almost . . . safe."

Dafril sat there grinning like a lunatic. "But I haven't told you the best part yet. I've found a way to cover any evidence that we've even done this. We can get you a body that will never be missed, we can dump your body where it will never be found, and the person inside of it won't even be able to tell."

Luercas studied his friend with disbelief. "I'm listening. I don't believe what I'm hearing, but I'm listening."

"We can kidnap a Warrener—a young, healthy one, so that you don't get a body that's too fat. We can inject the antidote to the Way-fare toxins, so the body doesn't die on you—pretty pointless to do this if you have to live on Way-fare and spend your life in twilight. Then we start pumping your true body full of Way-fare. I think I read in the revision paper the developers presented when they changed the formula that it now only takes three doses to become addictive to the system. So we hide you and our transplant until the third dose is in, and when your body is addicted and drugged, I do the spell to make the switch. And we dump your body with the Warrener's soul in it back into the Warrens, and we send you to a visage-wizard who can make you look the way you used to, and we tell people that you finally found someone who could completely counteract the spells. In Manarkas, maybe, or one of the island chains."

Luercas couldn't believe his ears. "How long have you been thinking about this?"

"Since I realized that you weren't going to get back to being yourself until I figured out a way around the fact that no one was powerful enough to counteract the *rewhah* that came from the destruction of souls."

Luercas smiled—and really felt like smiling, inside and outside—for the first time since the accident. "You're a friend, Dafril. A real friend. I'll never forget what you've done for me."

Dafril shrugged. "You would have done the same for me."

And Luercas thought, No. I wouldn't have.

But it didn't hurt for Dafril to think otherwise.

Velyn paced through her suite, by turns furious and shocked. How could Wraith treat her like some street girl, put out of sight the moment he didn't get his way? How could he think that he could dismiss her—that she would be put in her place by a Warrener? He could pretend to be stolti for a thousand years and a day, but that wouldn't change the truth.

"This is all because of my fascination with gutter-men," she told her reflection. "My delight in rolling with the pigs—and one of the pigs finally turned and bit me, didn't it? I could have taken vows with any of a dozen respectable, upward-bound stolti men by now; or maybe a rich man. One or two of the older, established men would have been happy to have had me, though perhaps only in the position of alternative mate. I don't want that."

She turned away from the mirror, threw herself onto the bed she occupied so rarely, and stared up at her ceiling.

"But *Solander* will tell *me* if Wraith wants to see me again. Jess will meet him at one place, stupid Solly at the other, and I'm to come wait in my room like a naughty child who's been punished. And young Solander all superior and smug, looking down his nose at me because I led Wraith on, or because I didn't want to take vows with him, or because . . . gods only know what he thinks he has to be superior about. I don't see him taking vows with *his* little street urchin." She sat up, angrier than when she'd flung herself down, far too restless to lie in one place, and jumped to the floor, where she began pacing again.

"Or maybe she wouldn't have him. Hah! Wouldn't that just be the thing? One Warren-rat with aspirations to vow-lock a stolti, and another Warren-rat who thinks she's too good for her stolti lover. That little bitch always did have her eye on Wraith. Perhaps she's trying to unbreak his broken heart right now. Wouldn't that be funny?"

It wouldn't, though. Velyn had wanted Wraith. She'd lusted after him even while she'd been slaking her appetites on aircar drivers and laborers and sons of merchants, and the occasional merchant's daughter. In Wraith she had seen something that she had never seen before in anyone—a fire, a passion, a hunger for something beyond himself, beyond his own greed and his own self-advancement. He'd been the first human being she'd ever met who earned the description "unique." He had come from nowhere, from nothing, and by his wits and his ability to make the right friends and by his odd disability that turned out more often than not to be to his advantage, he had brought himself and his friend out of hell and into a life of luxury. And then he had not even had the good grace to be spoiled by the same luxuries that had spoiled her. He still had his passion, his fire, his desires and aspirations and dreams.

What's more, he projected the goodness in himself onto her, so that while she was with him, she felt special. She felt that she was as unique as he, as deserving of awe and accolades. She'd come to think of herself as indispensable—as someone without whom his dreams would fall to pieces. But she wasn't. He would go on without her; he would make his success of his theater; he might even succeed in changing the minds of a few people, in making them realize that the magic he so loathed truly was an evil thing.

He'd never change the Empire, of course. The Hars Ticlarim was a mighty river, with a bed three thousand years deep. A boy and his lunatic passions would not succeed in diverting even a rivulet of it. But he would make a great deal of noise trying. And he would be interesting to watch.

She stopped pacing when she reached her window for the twelfth time. She placed her hands on the sleek sill and stared down—down through a faint haze of clouds, down to the dark sprawling smudge that was the city of the Belows. How could she ever have been willing to go down there for her amusement? How could she have allowed herself to be given chores like some mufere streetwasher, like some *nobody*? She'd painted scenery; she'd hammered nails; she gotten filthy, had torn clothing, had developed calluses on her hands and aches in her muscles—because of a Warrener.

She took a deep breath.

"I've forgotten who I am," she said to the window. "I've forgotten my place in life, my station, my entitlements, my rights. In my ridiculous search for some transitory pleasure, for a boy who is nothing but a good lay and an occasionally interesting dinner companion, I've forgotten that I have a life of my own. But it's time to start remembering that."

She moved away from the window, toward her room's house-chime. "Past time. Wraith and his confused notions of who he is can go straight to all the hells."

She reached out. Rang the chime. When the servant answered, she said, "This is Velyn Artis-Tanquin. Please tell my mother and father that I will be dining with them tonight."

Wraith returned to the theater by the first light of dawn. Frost glittered on the streets, on the buildings, on the plants, and the pink pale light turned the city into rose diamonds, fairy crystals grown enormous in some madman's happy dream. Though they kept their voices soft, still Wraith and his new friends, all talking at once, all wondrously excited about their new friendship, their discovery of each other, could hear the sudden sharp echoes of their laughter though the nearly silent streets.

When they burst into the theater, Wraith was so excited to show them all what he had accomplished, he sent poor sleeping Solander into a graceless, panicked tumble from the bench he'd stretched out on.

And Wraith realized what a worry his disappearance must have been to his friends. Poor Solander. Poor Jess. Jess, who worried about the tiniest of things, must have spent the night frantic. Solander at least had managed to get some sleep, though he looked much the worse for a night spent on a bench made only for sitting.

Solander, bleary-eyed and still confused, scrambled to his feet and stared at the strangers, and then looked to Wraith for explanation. "You're all right? You weren't hurt or . . . anything . . . last night?"

"I got lost," Wraith told him. "Ended up in a village way at the northern perimeter of the city."

"Bakangaardsvan," Wraith's new friend Rionvyeers said.

Solander nodded. "I've never heard of it. But . . ." He looked down at the floor, clearly annoyed, and said, "You could have let someone know where you were. Jess and I spent most of the night messaging each other, checking to see if you'd shown up anywhere yet."

"I couldn't," Wraith said.

"It takes a minute."

"It takes a minute if you have a speaker. Bakangaardsvan doesn't have speakers. Doesn't have anything that uses any form of magic anywhere in it."

Solander looked disbelieving—and then he gave Wraith's companions a second and much closer study. He looked at the clothes, at the shoes, at the hairstyles—and when he'd finished staring, he turned to Wraith. "They're Kaan," he said, as if that were an indictment.

"I know."

"Wraith. You can't associate with Kaan. They're one of the proscribed peoples. They're tolerated within the borders of the Hars Ticlarim only so long as they follow special laws given to them. They must keep themselves and their kind apart from the general population—they are not permitted to proselytize, nor are they permitted to gather outside of the confines of their villages in numbers greater than twenty-five." He glanced at the group accompanying Wraith, and Wraith could see him counting. "They must, when they are not within their villages, wear clothing that marks them as being from one of the proscribed peoples." He seemed to be drawing away from the Kaan, even though he stood still. "You can't associate with them, Wraith. You're stolti. You're a student of one of the finest academies in the Hars. You're . . . you're on your way to being someone of importance in the Empire, and if you allow yourself to associate with Kaan, you'll carry a taint that won't wash away with time, with explanations, with . . . anything. Just by being with them, they'll ruin you."

Wraith crossed his arms over his chest, leaned against the wall, and smiled just the tiniest bit. "Sol. You're nearly apoplectic. Take a deep breath, and then I want to ask you a simple question."

"I'm fine," Solander snapped. "I'm just praying that no one who matters will come through those doors before we have a chance to get these . . . these *people* out of sight. My . . . gods . . . I could lose any chance I had of making it onto the Council if I were seen with them."

The Kaan looked at each other, their expressions ranging from uncertainty to distaste to outright horror. "He's a . . . wizard?" the woman Bleytaarn said to Wraith.

Wraith nodded. "He intends to change the Council from the inside.

To find a way to do away with the forms of magic that require sacrifice. He's on our side."

"He doesn't sound like he is. He sounds like he's one of them, through and through."

"He hasn't thought yet," Wraith told her. "Patience." And he turned to Solander. "They're proscribed. Fine. Why are they proscribed, Solander?"

"They have disgusting religious beliefs. They practice bizarre and totally unacceptable sexual practices—"

"Like the festival?" Wraith asked.

"And they maintain a belief system that is treasonous to the aims of the Empire, and that, if it were to spread outside of their little groups, could lead to the downfall of the Hars."

Wraith nodded and smiled. "And what belief system do the Kaan maintain?"

"What?" Solander frowned at him. "Treasonous beliefs."

"*What sort* of treasonous beliefs?"

"I don't know," Solander said. "What difference could that possibly make?"

"They believe that magic as used by the Dragons of the Hars Ticlarim is an evil tool that permits the Dragons to have control over the lives of the people who accept its use, and thus they eschew magic in any form. They do not use magic to power their homes or their vehicles, they do not permit magical communication, magical observation tools, or any forms of magic to make their own lives easier or to aid them in achieving their goals or needs." He watched Solander's expression begin to change, and he said, "No medical magic, no educational magic, no industrial magic, no agricultural magic, no architectural magic, no infrastructural magic."

"What about overthrow of the government, beliefs in anarchy . . . cannibalism . . . ?" Solander had lost some of his air of assumed superiority.

The Kaan shook their heads. "No," Rionvyeers said. "None of those. Just the personal conviction to live lives untouched by magic. That in itself was enough for the Empire to proscribe us."

Solander looked bewildered. "But . . . why?"

Guyeneevin, a lean blond girl with a darkly tanned face, said, "Because the Masters of the Hars truly do use magic—and people's dependence on magic—to control them. That which you cannot live without you must pay the price to live with—and the price of magic in the Empire of the Hars Ticlarim is the enslavement of each magic-dependent human."

"Your father paid for his dependence on magic with his life," Wraith said. "And you are dedicating your life to the same pursuit."

"But I'm not. I'm going to reform the system from the inside."

"They're living outside the system. It doesn't touch them, except in the government's oppression of laws." Wraith hooked his thumbs into the catch-rings on his tunic and said, "And the New Brinch Theater is going to help them escape some of the oppression of those laws."

Solander paled. "You're going to . . . employ them?"

Wraith nodded. "The theater will use no magic. I have a grant for its . . . its aberrations from the norm, if you will, from the Master of Literary Application at Materan. I'm granted the right to demonstrate works experimental in form and method of production, beyond and beside the normal scope and scale of the classical repertory, for the enlargement of the arts community and the expansion of the public good."

Solander took a seat on one of the benches and rested his head in his hands. "Oh, Wraith—do you realize what will happen if you're found to have the Kaan working in your production?"

"They aren't just going to be working in the production, Sol. They're going to be my actors," Wraith said.

"But you could be shipped off to the mines. Gods all, you could be tried and executed for treason. Well . . . not as long as you're thought to be stolti, you're immune from major prosecution so long as everyone believes you're stolti, but if they ever find out who you are, Wraith—"

"If they ever find out who I am, I'm guilty of treason anyway. My existence as a conscious being, my entire *life,* is an act of treason. That I compound the treason of knowing that I breathe and thinking my own thoughts by trying to free my people from hell . . . well, what of that? Imprisoned is imprisoned. Enslaved is enslaved. And dead is dead."

Solander looked at the Kaan. "I can respect their decisions. Their beliefs. In a way, I suspect they're right. They are overlooking beneficial magic, and the sort of magic that I've been working on, which doesn't require the sacrifice of others to function—but in their assessment of the Dragons, of the Hars, I suspect that they are more on the side of the gods than the devils." He took a deep and shaky breath and continued. "And I am sure that you will dress them as citizens. I'm sure you will have the sense to make them appear acceptable. Still . . . I cannot come here in any capacity other than as an interested patron once your work is finished. I can't help you anymore, Wraith. I can't allow myself to destroy by carelessness and thoughtless actions the future I have planned for my-self since I was a child—the career that will be the vindication of my fa-ther's life, and atonement for his death. I cannot lose my chance to change the Dragons, Wraith. If I can first join them, if I can become one of their colleagues, then I can show them that the Hars could be better than it is. I won't put that dream aside."

Wraith nodded. "I had thought you would not be able to keep com-ing here anyway. We've hidden your underwriting of the theater, but if you're seen here as people begin to notice what we're doing, our dummy financiers will be easy enough to spot for what they are—and then, for better or worse, your name will be linked with the theater and its pro-ductions. And our mysterious playwright, Vincalis the Agitator. And me."

"My name is already linked with *yours*."

"At this point, we are friends. Distant relatives—at least by our pa-pers. Two young men whose paths traveled for a while together and then diverged, as such paths often do. If I were you, I would play heavily on that divergence."

Solander looked almost crushed. "And what of our work together?"

"Your experiments on me to see why I'm so different?"

Solander nodded.

"Those can continue in secret. We'll find a safe meeting place and es-tablish times when we can meet. You won't lose your opportunity to find out why I'm . . . broken." Wraith smiled a little.

Chapter 10

Jess thought she had come to terms with loving Wraith as a friend. She came to accept the fact that Wraith would never love her while he was with Velyn. Then he sent Velyn away, but Jess had Solander, and Wraith had been . . . distant. But now he was building a wall between his old life, which had at least included her as a friend, and his new life, in which she was supposed to go on her way and not think about him or see him again.

This final separation had done more than hurt her; it had forced her to look at her life with Solander and without Wraith and ask herself if she had any reason to be with Solander if time spent with Wraith was no longer part of the equation. Jess cared for Solander. She'd convinced herself that she loved him. But she didn't love him enough. If Solander told her that he needed space, that he needed to be apart from her, she would have been understanding. Maybe even supportive. She wouldn't have been devastated the way she was devastated by this same news from Wraith.

So what did that make her? Did it make her someone like Velyn—was she using Solander for her own convenience? Because Solander offered security, a place in the world that no one questioned? Because as long as she was Solander's lover, no one questioned who she was in her own right?

Finally, lost between confusion and self-loathing, she went to the theater, where she knew Wraith would be. She still had her key; when he and Solander told her that visiting would be a bad idea and that she should get rid of any evidence that she had been associated with Wraith or the theater, she had kept it, claiming that she didn't have it with her at the time, and later saying that she had lost it.

She found the doors locked, but she heard faint strains of music emanating from the heart of the building. She entered the anteroom, and stepped into a new and wondrous world. Someone had painted the walls in brilliant colors and patterns, and had hung silk and beads and feathers in arrangements that came to life when she moved. She could hear the music more clearly once the door to the street had closed. Strong, masculine singing, the heavy beat of a drum, and then a voice saying, "You missed your entrance, Talamar. Again, from . . . ah, the third verse. And this time, come out with more . . . with more *emphasis*."

Wraith's voice. Her heart constricted, and for a moment she couldn't catch her breath. Her eyes filled with tears, but she blinked them back and bit her lip—hard—until the pain drove away the urge to cry.

The anteroom split, and the passages to both the left and right banks of seats were dark. This suited her. She wanted to be able to go all the way around, enter from the back, and watch for a while without being seen. She needed to know in her gut instead of just her head why Wraith had pulled himself apart from her and Solander and his old life; she hoped that by seeing what he was doing, she would get a feel for this obsession—this madness—that drove him.

So she made her way through the black passage all the way to the back, and cautiously opened the door farthest from the stage, and took a ground-floor seat at the very back of the theater in almost complete darkness. The stage glowed, however; the lightmaster had illuminated it so perfectly that the scene seemed real to her. A group of men dressed as trees stood to the left, singing, and at center stage but well to the back, two trees danced. Jess knew Wraith was not permitting any magic on the stage, and yet she found that hard to imagine, for when the trees danced, they managed to hang in the air as if some carefully wrought spell suspended them, spinning or leaping so high she felt herself breathless for them.

Then, from the right, a man burst onto the stage as if pursued by horrors from his nightmares and roared, "No peace shall I find this night; no peace shall I find ever," and threw himself prostrate at the roots of the singing trees.

They stopped their singing.

"What will you have of me?" the wizard pleaded. "Would you have my flesh to feed your roots? If you want my heart itself, here, take it—it's yours." He ripped his shirt open and bared his chest to the forest, and the lead tree bent forward and touched him over his heart with one branch.

"Of our fruit you will eat, before you find surcease," the tree said in a voice as hollow as death itself. Jess shivered, delighted by the effect, and wondering how Wraith had managed to create it.

"Give, then, your poison; I taste willingly of my own death."

"If there is poison, it exists already within you," the tree intoned. "We will free you from it." And he dipped another branch into the raised hands of the wizard, who plucked the fruit offered to him.

The wizard took a bite of the fruit, and then another, and then a third. With each bite he took, the stage grew darker, and with the fourth bite it went black.

The whole of the theater sat in utter darkness then, and Jess listened to the trees telling the wizard to dream well—to dream himself to the truth. She also heard shuffling noises, and thumps, and something rolling, and the odd sounds thrilled her—they held out a promise of excitement and mystery to come.

Then a single red light illuminated the wizard, lying on the stage, and when the light touched him he opened his eyes and rubbed them and stood. Facing the stage, he said, as if speaking confidentially to a friend, "I feared that I would dream a hell, dream a nightmare, that my sins would catch me up and devour me, but look—I am awake again, rested and unscathed."

The red light spread, and now Jess could see the shapes of horrors behind him, reaching for him with hands twisted into claws. And as he stood with his back to them, gloating in his escape from nightmare, these tangible nightmares came forward and surrounded him. He turned to walk away, and saw them, and tried to find a direction in which to flee, but they blocked his every opportunity to escape.

Jess sat transfixed as they identified themselves as the ghosts of the innocent dead and accused him of their deaths. She shivered deliciously as they forced him to watch the way that they had died, and as they forced him to watch, also, the use to which he had put their spent lives—as an ugly old woman drank the potion he had created and stepped forward, young and beautiful, able to spin and saunter across the stage for a moment before she grew old again and needed another draught of the potion. A parade followed, of the old who became young, and then old again, and of the dead whose numbers grew until they crowded on the stage so tightly that the wizard in the center could not see a single space that did not hold the souls of the dead he had hurt.

Jess sat through the whole rehearsal, and when it was finished, she quietly picked up her jacket, put it on, and slipped away before anyone could see her.

She understood now why Wraith was doing this thing. He had created something amazing—something unlike anything that she had ever seen or, for that matter, that anyone had ever seen. He had brought a story to life without magic—and it was more magical than the best theater productions that had every possible spell and every imaginable device to create their effects. People would come to see this, and they would go away changed. They would . . . She fought for the right definition as she trudged to her aircar. They would *believe*. They would see in magic a danger that they had never let themselves see, and it would nag at them as they returned to their houses built on air, as they rode through the sky in their magical cars, as they vacationed beneath the sea or went to a wizard to have their bodies resculpted in younger and more beautiful forms. That parade of souls crying out for repayment for the sins done to them would haunt them.

And some of them would begin to ask questions—the right questions—the ones they should have been asking all along.

Jess had intended to beg Wraith to at least come back to the house, to spend time with her and his other friends, to become a part of his old life again. But he had moved beyond that. He had found a direction—a wondrous, amazing, beautiful direction.

And it was time she did the same.

She drove herself home—or rather, she drove herself to the place she had allowed herself to think of as home since she had escaped the Warrens—and on the way, she considered her life. She was pretending, and doing it on a lot of different levels. At base, she was pretending to be someone she was not; she did it for her own survival, but that did not make the lie better. Further, she was pretending that she and Solander might have a future together, and letting him believe this for her own comfort and convenience. She knew that by staying with Solander, she was wasting his time and keeping him from finding the woman who would love him the way he deserved to be loved.

She was wasting her own life, too; holding herself in a relationship she did not truly want because as long as she had Solander she did not have to face the truth that she really had nothing, and because she felt guilty about the pain she would cause him when she left. Well, she'd earned her guilt, hadn't she? She deserved to feel guilty. But she could not stay and still be the woman she needed to be. She'd pretended her way through friendships, through her education, through the tedious covil meetings and their stultifying bureaucracy of the bored and the pretentious; had accepted money to which she'd had no right in order to keep her cover as one of the overseas family; and she found, facing herself in the quiet and being brutally honest with herself for the first time in a long time, that she did not like the woman she had become.

So she had to make changes.

Leave Solander. Get a place of her own, and pay for it on her own. Gently break her ties with the Artis family and the Artis name. Figure out what her life meant—what she was supposed to be about.

She had a place to start, anyway. While, as a stolti, she could not hold a job in someone else's employ, she could create a business and have that business pay her. She had learned from sitting around the long table at dinnertime how such businesses might be created, how the money from them might be invested, and how the money, once invested, might be made to work for her.

And from the covil she knew a stolti woman of about her own age who might be persuaded to join her in an interesting venture—a little business in which the two of them might screen, train if necessary, and employ musicians and send them around to perform at the parties of the stolti. She considered the idea and discovered she liked it. Live art—a thing like that which Wraith was creating in the theater. Perhaps the two of them could rent Wraith's theater in the hours when no play was being performed and offer concerts of their best musicians for the people of the Belows. The people of the Belows had their own entertainment after a fashion—but she thought something live might work well. She had not really considered the idea to have real merit until she saw what Wraith had done. If his work had imperfections, it also . . . well, it breathed.

She determined that, on her way home, she would drop by Caywer-rin House to see if Jyn wanted to sign on as her partner.

Once she had a partner and a start on giving herself an income that she had created, she could find a place to live. And after that, she could tell Solander that the two of them were through. She dreaded that. Above everything else, she dreaded that—partly because when Wraith made his break from them and especially from Velyn, she had seen the panic in the back of Solander's eyes. She had felt his anxiety when he mentioned Wraith; he would be bracing himself for her to leave him for Wraith— but he would never think that she would simply leave him, without any-one to go to, because that seemed completely outside of her nature.

She closed her eyes, dreading the days and weeks that were going to follow this day, and let the aircar take her home.

Velyn looked over the final contracts her parents had forwarded to her, checking off each clause she had requested and looking for loopholes in wording that either they or their advocates might have missed or thought unimportant to a woman in her position. When she finished, she calmly signed her name to a document that, in essence, merged two fortunes and two families. Luercas tal Jernas would be returning from an extended overseas stay, where according to his family he had finally found a medical wizard who had been able to return him to perfect health and perfect form.

She had managed to talk with him once by long-distance viewer two days previously, and she thought the medical wizard had been far kinder than nature. He had never been particularly handsome before his accident; now, however, she thought his beauty a perfect counterpart to her own. They would have attractive children, and they would live well. That they did not love each other—that they did not truly know each other—mattered little to either of them. The contracts offered significant room for outside interests once they had their two legitimate children to carry on the family fortunes and family businesses.

Luercas held a good place in the Council, as the head of Research. He had a reputation for brilliance, and for the sort of ruthlessness that created wealth and that would secure his own position and the positions of those who dared follow him at the expense of the timorous. He advocated increased magical use but also increased magical efficiency; he wanted the expansion of the Empire into areas currently held by other powers: Strithia, the Western Manarkan Dominance, the resource-rich Protectorate of the Ring of Fire. He had real goals, real plans, and real ambition. He wasn't trying to save fat, insensate fodder as his life's work.

Perhaps burning souls for fuel was wrong in the grand scheme of things, but it created and held together an empire, and the more she thought about it, the more Velyn thought the magnificence of the Hars Ticlarim and all it stood for rose above petty concerns about the sources of the Empire's magic, or magic's cost. Without magic, the Empire would not exist—and that would be the greater tragedy.

The last of the snows had passed, and around the New Brinch Theater the wondrous aroma of blooming kettlebushes and sweetbriars promised the advent of spring. Light began reclaiming its territory from dark, and the streets filled with people out for the sweetness of the air and the gentleness of the breezes. They wandered to the New Brinch, drawn by the exotic scents on the breeze and by the sounds of music and laughter, and they discovered outside the theater a free street show— men and women dressed entirely in either red or gold who acted out little pantomimes with delightful accuracy and clever wit. These actors directed the bystanders to the entry of the New Brinch, where tickets for the upcoming shows had gone on sale.

The prices for the cheap seats were quite low, and the bystanders, fascinated by the mysterious entry to the theater with its beautiful paintings and hanging ornaments, and wanting to see more, paid their pittance and took home their tickets for any of three day shows or three evening shows.

At the same time, in the higher circles of the city, an art critic friend of Wraith's published an intriguing little review of the play's dress rehearsal. He was careful to neither praise the play nor to criticize it, but only to mention in several different ways that it was completely different from anything he had ever seen, and that, because of its complete departure from conventional theater, it was apt to disappear as quickly as it appeared. He noted that seats were extremely limited, that some of the best of them already could not be had for any price, and that, with a showing of only six days, only a very few would have the privilege of witnessing this rare and surprising performance.

He might as well have told the rich and powerful of the city that he had the secret elixir of immortality but only the first fifty people who applied to him would get any.

The expensive seats outsold the cheap ones, and the clever who had bought more seats than they needed were able to resell their extra tickets for prices that ranged from the extravagant to the obscene.

Word of the rush for the best seats trickled to the lower classes, who discovered that their tickets were suddenly worth much, much more than they had paid for them. Most—but not all—sold them at a profit that made not just their month but, in some cases, their year.

Wraith, from his place in the theater's inner office, watched the money pouring in with some amazement. Before the first show, he had the money to pay all of his actors for the run he actually planned—one month, not six days—maintain the sets, and start to work on the next production.

Every one of his six announced days was a sellout a week before the first show—but no one had yet seen *A Man of Dreams*. Everything depended on what happened when people actually saw the play. If the stolti gave the thing good word of mouth, then everyone would keep coming—the other stolti because they did not want to miss something, and the lesser classes because they would take any opportunity to be seen with the stolti in social situations, and few such opportunities existed. But if they were horrified by what he had done, they would find a way to shut him down, and that would be the end of the experiment.

"You look like the puppy that cornered the bear," Meachaan, one of his "trees," said as she scrubbed makeup off of her face. They'd finished up the last dress rehearsal; the first real show would come that night.

"If I felt half as confident as the puppy, I'd be doing well."

"You'll be fine. You've done something good here," she said. "They'll come; it won't be what they're expecting, but it will be truly good, and truly thought-provoking. I'm guessing most of them haven't had their thoughts provoked in a long, long time."

"You're better off not thinking about consequences when you're stolti," Wraith said, tempering the sadness in his voice with a little smile. "If you think about consequences, you have nightmares." He shrugged. "Maybe they'll see themselves in this, maybe they'll see someone else that they know . . . or maybe they'll just see a fantasy story with no meaning beyond what it says on the surface. I don't know. Now that we're here, this seems like such a stupid, piddling way to try to change anything. What difference can it possibly make? Who will be affected by it? Who will be changed?"

Meachaan laughed. "You can't know that, and you can't worry about it. You've put the food out. Now others must eat—and how they eat is not for you to say."

"But I want this to lead to the freedom of the Warreners. I want this to lead to the end of the misuse of magic."

"You want what you want, and you want it now . . . but life doesn't work that way. One man can move the world, but to do it, he needs a long lever and a lot of time." Her smile to him was enigmatic. "Just wait. Tonight is the first drop of rain. Tomorrow is the second. Rain carves rivers and wears away mountains. Your changes will come; you've started the storm."

He looked at the box of money, at the list of seats sold, and at the longer list of requests for seats that had come in. He'd started the storm—but who could tell whether it would be a sprinkle that didn't even dampen down the dust, or if it would be a typhoon that washed away the city? Certainly not him.

Dafril Crow-Hjaben took his seat next to Velyn, who had somehow managed to acquire two seats in the very best section. He'd accepted her invitation to be her escort; everyone knew that she was preparing for her nutevaz and needed to be seen only with trusted male escorts for a while—and since he and Luercas were close friends, that put him in the position of trusted escort. This amused Dafril; he hadn't had her in years, but he certainly knew his way around her terrain. But he'd act perfectly respectable; he gained no glory from claiming as a conquest a woman as comfortable with her virtue as Velyn.

He found Jess Covitach-Artis seated to his left and immediately felt luckier. He'd heard rumors that Jess and Solander had parted company, and to the best of anyone's knowledge, Jess had never had another companion, either serious or casual. He'd always found her pretty, clever, amusing . . . and distant. He got the feeling that she didn't like him very much, and that intrigued him.

So he leaned back in his seat, trying to find a comfortable position, and discovered that whatever the seats had been designed for, it hadn't been for comfort. Velyn had glared once at Jess and turned away; Jess had looked at Velyn with an utterly blank expression, then stared stonily ahead at the stage. Interesting. Velyn had stopped seeing Gellas, the producer of this whole charade, some months earlier—and everyone knew that Gellas and Jess had been friends since they'd arrived on the Artis doorstep with their apprentice papers in hand. He found himself wondering if the bad blood between Velyn and Jess came from a conflict over Gellas.

Gellas had been absent from Artis House for almost a year. Dafril didn't pay much attention to most of the Artises, but something about Gellas had always struck him as off. Dafril knew Gellas had come to Artis House from one of the territories to avail himself of the opportunities to which he was entitled by birth and kin ties. But in spite of being best friends with that weasel Solander, Gellas never pursued the single path for which the Artis family could open every door—magic. He'd chosen instead to pursue some sort of philosophical nonsense, when the Artises had no ties to any of the many priesthoods or monasteries where philosophers held sway, and he had ended up here, doing theater as if he were one of the covil-ossets, who spent their lives taking trips to dig in the ruins of Fen Han and Crobadi, or producing books of each other's poetry, or translating the lost literature of the Mehattins. Powerless dilettantes, all of them—and Gellas, who had the right connections and the name, was acting just like them.

And Gellas couldn't even get the gods'-damned seats right.

If Dafril couldn't sleep, though, at least he could chat with Jess. She looked like she would rather be anyplace in the world but where she was; he knew this feeling intimately.

"So, Jess—couldn't find an excuse not to make opening night?" he whispered, leaning close to her.

He was startled by the intensity of dislike in the gaze she turned on him. "I'm delighted to be here," she said. "I was tremendously grateful to get such a good seat. Now, though, I think I'd rather change places with one of the people in the cheap seats."

"Why are you looking at me like that?" he asked. "I didn't do anything to you."

"You've shown a real taste for bad company," she said.

He dropped his voice lower. "Velyn. My mother talked me into taking her. Her prospective vowmate hasn't returned from the islands yet, and her family wants her to be seen in the company of . . . well, friends of her vowmate until he gets back."

The change in Jess's face astonished him. She lit up like sunshine. "She's taking vows? With whom?"

"Luercas tal Jernas. Her distant, distant cousin. He spent a few years at Artis House, but I don't know if you know him. On the Council of Dragons, the Master of Research, has ties through the tal Jernas family to most of the really big businesses in Oel Artis and a lot of foreign connections, too."

"The one who got . . . melted? Back when Solander's father died? That Luercas?"

Dafril nodded.

"They'll make a lovely couple," Jess muttered.

"He finally found a wizard who could undo the damage. He looks good. Better than before, I think."

"Does he know about her?"

Dafril grinned and chuckled softly. "You mean about her . . . hobbies? Is there anyone who doesn't know about those?"

He saw Jess glance toward the stage, then back to him, almost too quick for the eye to see or the brain to note. Almost.

So Gellas hadn't realized his woman had been almost everyone else's woman, too? How hilarious.

Just before the play started, Dafril noted three men who looked out of place among the happy, excited theatergoers. He knew only one of them—a terrifying wizard named Grath Faregan, who in the years since his removal as one of the Masters of the Department of Security, was rumored to have gotten involved with a criminal organization. But here they were, with programs in their hands and tickets that they checked as they worked their way up the aisle. Faregan's eyes met Dafril's as he passed, and Faregan glared, and Dafril shuddered. So Faregan hadn't forgotten or forgiven. The three of them ended up with seats two rows behind him.

Dafril could feel sweat sliding between his shoulder blades. His mouth went dry and his bowels knotted. He kept his arms clamped tight to his sides while his testicles tried to crawl back up into his belly, and he prayed that this was just one of those silly coincidences that happened from time to time. He could hear the three of them talking about a rumor that this stood a chance to be nominated for the Delcate Sphere, and that tickets were going to get harder to come by rather than easier.

But Dafril wasn't soothed. He'd made the mistake of laughing at Faregan when he discovered the wizard had been removed from his post—he'd laughed about old men getting caught with underage girls, and how much of an idiot a man would have to be to make that mistake. And now the man and two vile old cronies were right behind him, and Dafril could feel their eyes on the back of his neck.

When the lights went down and music began to play, Dafril breathed a tiny bit easier. But he didn't bother trying to talk to Jess anymore. He didn't pay any attention to Velyn, either. He simply sat there, waiting for the ordeal to end, hoping that he would be able to get out the exit before Faregan could catch up with him.

Except that, as the play wore on, Dafril found himself caught up in it—and not in a way that pleased him. He began to see an anti-magic sentiment carefully couched in marvelous dancing, clever dialogue, humor, pathos, and wonder at the terrible situation into which the poor wizard had gotten himself. As the main character's life went from bad to worse to truly awful, Dafril could see the audience's sympathy going more and more to the lost souls, and less and less to the suffering wizard.

These were people who had been raised from birth to think that magic would be the answer to all their problems—people who had been carefully trained by every controllable factor in their society to look to the wizards for answers. And yet, in the blink of an eye, their sympathies turned away from magic and all that it represented.

That worried him. He didn't think for a moment that any of these people were going to give up their aircars or their fine houses or their magic-run appliances or anything else that made their lives easier—but he found their fickleness deeply disturbing. It made him think that the ground upon which he had stood so trustingly and for so long had a fault line running through it, one that could open up at any moment and turn on him and devour him.

In producing this work by—Dafril checked his program—an unknown named Vincalis, Gellas had taken a strange stance for a stolti. Very strange.

But perhaps it wasn't so strange at all. Look at what else Gellas had done. He had walked away from the woman everyone had been under the impression that he loved, had ceased coming to Artis House even for holidays, and had even seemingly separated from his dearest friends Solander and Jess.

Something about Gellas sat wrong with Dafril. It had something to do with this magnificent theater, converted from industrial space; it had something to do with the play, written by a complete unknown, and with the astonishing actors, not one of whom bore a familiar name or face. . . .

Dafril sensed an opportunity. Neither he nor Luercas had ever liked that scrawny weirdling, Gellas. Luercas actively hated him. But Dafril and Luercas could point the Dragon Council at Gellas and this anti-magic play; if they could raise any question that this *A Man of Dreams* nonsense was more than just a play, they might win themselves promotions. Power.

By the time the play was over, he'd forgotten Faregan and his old cronies. He left in a hurry to contact Luercas and to let him know that an opportunity had fallen into their hands.

After the show, Jess went back two aisles to greet Ander Penangueli, whom she and Jyn had met when they were putting together a proposal for their live-music scheme. "Master Penangueli!" She held out her arms, and exchanged a polite brush of cheeks with him. "Did you enjoy the show?"

"Dear child, what a delight! The young man who wrote that is a genius. But it was a very dark theme—very dark. I found myself laughing during the show, but now it's over and I find myself thinking instead. Such a sad tale—such sad little lives. And the poor wizard, too." The old man stroked his beard and said, "You know the producer, don't you?"

Jess nodded. "We were great friends as children. We don't actually see each other anymore, sadly, but . . ." She shrugged.

"You must introduce us. And perhaps the writer, too?"

"I don't know the writer," Jess said. "But Gellas is around somewhere—I know he'd love to meet you."

Penangueli nodded. "He found quite a work of art in this play. A tragedy that makes one laugh—or perhaps it was a comedy that makes one cry. Quite unexpected." Master Penangueli said, "And now let me introduce you to my friends. This is Jess Covitach-Artis, the girl who will be bringing live musicians to our homes—and evidently touring them around the empire, as well. Jess, Master Grath Faregan and Master Noano Omwi." He turned to his associates. "Jess and the daughter of a dear friend of mine had the lovely idea of gathering up musicians and placing them on stages for a more intimate entertainment. Can you imagine?"

"But then their audience will be present if they make errors in their playing," Master Omwi said. He looked to her for an explanation.

She nodded. "They will. But their listeners will hear the living music, with natural variations and the passions of the moment—it will not have the perfection of a performance preserved for the videograph, but no one else save those who are there at that moment will ever hear that exact performance. It will be like the theater tonight—the actors may play all their parts slightly differently tomorrow night. It will be a different experience for tomorrow's audience. You see?"

And the three men smiled and nodded. Then Master Faregan, who seemed quite familiar, though she could not place him, said, "Covitach-Artis? Which branch of the family is that?"

And she felt the same fear that had plagued her since she'd come to Artis House. "Most of the Covitach-Artises are in Ynjarval," she said. "We're from the Beyron Artis lineage that settled in the area about three hundred years ago."

She chatted about the lineage—patter she had memorized years ago—and they smiled and nodded, smiled and nodded. And then she noticed that two of them, Penangueli and Omwi, were looking past her as they smiled and nodded—that something down around the stage seemed to have their real attention, and that while they were pretending to give her and her dull family history their attention, they were in fact surreptitiously watching something behind her that interested them much more.

The same could not be said for Faregan. He watched her—watched her with such unblinking intensity that she began to feel sick to her stomach.

She did not turn around, either to avoid Faregan's stare or to see what the other two men were watching, though the impulse to do so was almost overwhelming. Instead, she claimed a prior engagement for which she was rapidly growing late, and gave cheerful good-byes.

When she finally dared to turn away, Wraith was accepting the congratulations of some of the members of his opening-night crowd in front of the stage. Some of the actors stood with him. They were all in the right area to have caught the old men's attention.

She suddenly wondered at the business of the three old men. Jyn had only introduced Master Penangueli by name, not mentioning that he held a position anywhere, so Jess had assumed he was a covil-osset.

Somehow, now she thought he might have some other interest—something unpleasant, though she could not imagine what. That he could choose to be in the company of Master Faregan made her think him not such a nice man after all.

And this outing might not have been as casual and friendly as it appeared: Three old Masters braving the Belows after dark could speak well of the play—or it could suggest that after all these years, someone was starting to have questions about Wraith. Or her. Or both.

The Silent Inquest gathered in the Gold Building, named not for its color or its construction materials, but for its putative designer, Camus Gold, said to have been the greatest architect of the Third Age. The Gold Building gathered its aura of power around itself like an ancient goddess; it stood atop the highest of the Merocalins, the seven hills that had been the heart of Oel Artis before the wizards built the Aboves and sent them sailing into the clouds, and stared haughtily down onto the lower city that had been the whole of the city, once upon a time.

Many of the old buildings had lost their luster and their pride of place as the true heart of Oel Artis moved into the sky, but the walled and mazelike Gold Building was different. For more than seven hundred years it had been the place where little cabals of powerful old men gathered secretly to decide the fates of those beneath them, and its soul echoed with the resonance of those old men, that power, those choices.

Now a Dragon of the Council, a man of great power and respect, came with his face hidden to stand before three old men dressed in green and black robes.

"You saw it?"

"We saw it," Ander Penangueli, Grand Master of the Inquestors, said.

"The play presents a view of magic that I am not sure we in the Dragons wish to permit to exist. The writer was reaching for metaphor, I believe, but he has managed to lay bare an unfortunate literal truth by doing so. He used magic as his metaphor, and used the sacrificing of lives as fuel for a wizard's petty spell as the engine that ran his story."

Heads nodded. "We saw. Get on with it."

The Dragon swallowed hard and said, "*A Man of Dreams* is going to make people think. It's going to point them straight at the things we don't want them to think about, and it's going to make some of them ask some very dangerous questions."

"Then close the play," Penangueli said. "Why should we even be here on this late night for this discussion? Close the damned thing and be done with it, and let's get home to our beds and the sleep we're missing."

The Dragon said, "If we step in and order it closed, we raise curiosity about why the Dragon Council would choose to involve itself in harmless entertainment. We don't want to raise curiosity."

Master Omwi said, "You say you think the writer trespassed accidentally on this issue. Is there any chance he knew what he was doing?"

The Dragon shrugged. "No way to tell. We don't know the writer. The producer is an Artis. He's spent his life surrounded by magic—learned the mathematics of it, as does every child with an Artis tutor, and lived in a house where magic was the sun, the moon, and the stars. But he has never—and I have checked this carefully—absolutely never, done anything with magic of any sort. His interests have always lain within the realms of literature and philosophy, and even his best friend for years, who is a rising young wizard heading toward a place in Research and before long, I'm sure, a seat on the Council, has said that he tried for years to get the boy to choose a more practical course of study. Apparently, clever though he is with words, the lad has no aptitude for even the simplest of spells."

"But you don't think he's aware of the Warrens?"

"Why would he be? That is information never available to anyone who is not a Council member or working directly the spells that actually fuel the city—and the people who do *that* job always become Council members. It's one of the perks, and they know it. There is no way he could get to that information."

"You want the producer killed?" Penangueli asked.

The Dragon swallowed again. "I'd rather not take that step. He's stolti. But I need a way to get rid of this play quietly."

The Inquestor Triad sat silently for a short while. Finally Penangueli said, "Use money. And a diversion. Commission the boy to produce something else in the style of this one. Something less volatile. He can hire a different writer, or have the same one work on a theme of your choosing."

Faregan asked, "And what of the writer of this play? What might he know?"

Here the Dragon faltered. "We do not know any Vincalis, nor have we had good fortune in finding out about him. He takes his pay in cash, has someone pick it up for him, has never attended rehearsals, sends changes and corrections via courier from a variety of courier stations, none of whom know him personally or can describe the person who brought them their package."

Faregan began to laugh softly. "Ah. Those are not the actions of an innocent man. This Vincalis, I wager, knows exactly what he is about. I think in Gellas Tomersin he's found himself a convenient sheep. A front. I'd guess he might be a disgruntled member of the Council itself—perhaps his money funded the renovation of the playhouse."

"We've checked that. A group of dummy investors funded it. They don't know where they received their funds, only that they got a twenty percent commission for handling the deal."

Murmurs around the room. Old voices whispering through the chamber that had heard nothing but old voices, carefully measured tones, thoughtful whispers, for seven hundred years and more. The Silent Inquest, not even known by most of the people of the Empire to exist, dreaded with reason by all who knew it, had predated the building it occupied by nearly two thousand years. The Silent Inquest had survived dynasties, revolutions, wars, famines, disasters, and periods of vast, sloth-inducing abundance by being slow, patient, careful . . . and right.

"Yes," Penangueli said at last. "Vincalis is your problem, I think. Give young Gellas Tomersin a commission, then. Let him give you a great comedy—something light and frivolous and far from souls and wizardry. We will have people watch him. And watch his friends. And we will see who he hires as a writer, and see if, in this second work, we find the same threads of treason. If we do, we will know that the first time was no mistake, and we will act."

"And of the current play?"

"Let it run its scheduled handful of days. But make sure the pressure is on Tomersin to get the next one out immediately—that it is needed for some close holiday for which he must meet a specific date. Give him no option but to close this one when its initial run is finished."

The Dragon bowed. "Yes, Inquestors. We will do this—or, if necessary, I shall do it myself. If we have a traitor on the Council, better he or she not know anyone suspects." With his palms sliding back and forth over each other, the Dragon then asked, "And the price of your assistance, so that I may draw your fee from the private funds?"

Penangueli smiled slowly, no longer looking much like a sweet, charming old man. "You can owe the Silent Inquest a favor at a later date. You may leave us now. We have implementations to discuss."

The Dragon grew pale, but bowed and backed his way to the door, and hurried from the chamber.

When he was gone, Penangueli leaned back. "We'll hold this favor for the day that we need a vote to go our way in Council. Or possibly for something greater. Its worth will depend on what we can discover—so make sure that the Dragons owe us greatly." He smiled again.

Faregan said, "The girl who came up to you tonight might be a key."

Penangueli raised an eyebrow. "Jess? She's harmless, I suspect."

"I'm sure she is. But she is and always has been great friends with Gellas Tomersin. They're from the same part of Ynjarval. And until recently, she was none other than Solander Artis's lover. Solander is the only son of the late Rone Artis."

"You knew her? I never would have guessed."

Faregan gave a dry laugh. "I had reason once to find out about her. If I may, I'd like to put some of my people on her. I suspect she may bring our investigation some luck."

Penangueli, who knew something of Faregan's interest in young women, but not of his collection, said, "She's stolti, Grath."

Faregan nodded acknowledgment, but said nothing.

"Very well," Penangueli said. "Remember that she is not our target." And with that injunction, they moved on to other matters.

Dark, and silence, and in the primarily outlander Perhout District of Oel Artis, peace—but peace soon shattered, as the city guards set up a perimeter around the district and began marching through the streets, knocking on doors, bringing sleeping people out into the street.

"Your papers," they would say at each house, and when the papers were produced, would look at them and either say, "By edict of the Dragons, since we have ceased diplomatic relations with the Camarins, you and your family will be temporarily interned in a house in the Warrens." Or they would say, "You're Kaan. You're not in the Kaan district, and you're not wearing the mandated Kaan garb. You're going to have to come with us—you and your family."

Half the district vanished that night. And the neighbors who remained trembled, and stared out windows, knowing that the others would never be back. Everyone knew, no matter what the guards might say about temporary internships, that no one came back from the Warrens.

In a week, all the emptied houses would have new outlander families in them—families from places that had uncertain relations with the Empire of the Hars Ticlarim. These families would settle down and live their lives, until the next harvest from their district, when some of them, or maybe all of them, would be collected to feed the gaping maw of the Warrens.

Chapter 11

The negotiating agent for the Dragon Council sat across from Wraith in Wraith's office, a broad, false smile on his face. "The city will celebrate the three thousandth anniversary of the birth of Greyvmian the Ponderer, who has been considered the father of mapping, and whose work led to the exploration of much of Matrin. And thus to the greatness of our magnificent Empire. Secure within, secure without." His name was Birch, and though Wraith had managed never to cross paths with him before, he didn't like him at all.

Wraith nodded. "I vaguely remember hearing of Greyvmian the Ponderer, I think. He is not much celebrated these days." He smiled at the man and waited.

"True. True. We have been remiss over the years in our celebration of Greyvmian's memory. But this is a special anniversary—the three thousandth—and the Masters of the City have decided that there will be great public festivals to honor this year. And for that, I have come to you, representing not only the Masters of the Dragon Council, but the Landimyn of the Hars himself."

Wraith, with his hands folded on his knees, raised his eyebrows and waited.

"You have done something new. Something fresh and different. Your play in Common tongue stirs the imagination; it sings to the heart with a passion the old forms have put aside in favor of . . . of prettiness. Though you gave us a tragedy, it was a fine tragedy. Some of the lines of it still ring in my mind." His eyes focused far away for a moment, and Wraith realized that the man was telling him the truth. Something about the play had reached in and touched even him, and had left some part of him moved, shaken . . . uncomfortable.

This startled Wraith. He had not thought that those who held power could be disturbed from their positions of comfort. He had never even considered the possibility. And now, with the truth facing him, he felt real opportunities opening up and sprawling out before him. He said, "So how may I be of service to you, Master Birch?"

"The city would like to commission a play from you. One that will run the whole of the year of Greyvmian's celebration. We would like something stirring, passionate, but also . . ." He stared off into space pensively and at last said, "We do not wish another tragedy, nor do we wish a piece of bombast—the glory of the old dynasties, the greatness that lay behind. We want something contemporary. And . . . ah . . . funny. Humor is very important. Something that people can come to and spend a few hours learning a grand story and laughing at the funny bits, and that they can take home with them and . . . and *cherish*. You can bring this play to us. You have already presented such a play—but it is a tragedy, and a tragedy will not work for a year-long celebration."

"But I'm not a writer," Wraith said. "I merely produced a play that came to me from . . . well, I don't actually know where it came from. I can't guarantee that I could get hold of another so fine . . . unless, of course, you know how I might reach Vincalis?"

"No. I had hoped you would know that."

Wraith shrugged. "I don't. But he obviously knows me. Perhaps if I make the need known, he will choose to fill it." Wraith rested his chin on the palm of his hand and said, "Perhaps it would be well, too, if you commissioned one of the Empire's great playwrights to produce something, in case Vincalis doesn't."

"You would put on a play by one of the known Masters?"

"I might. If it were written in the style of Vincalis."

"Ah. They'd just love that, wouldn't they? To be the acknowledged Masters of their field, and to be commissioned to write something in the style of a complete upstart."

Wraith smiled thinly and held his hands out, palms up. "People don't come to Vincalis's play to sleep, Master Birch. You've been to as many of the Masters' plays as I have, I'll wager. I'm sure you recall the delicate undercurrent of snores that filled the theaters that held them?"

Master Birch sighed. "I'll see what I can do to get a suitable play to you, if one is not forthcoming from Vincalis himself."

"And what of the take from the house?" Wraith asked. "If you are commissioning the project, how much of the sales from the door do you wish to claim?" He knew that the city could claim any amount and he would not dare to refuse, but he did not want to let Master Birch know that. He wanted to appear to be considering it, and to do that, he had to mention the money. No theater owner would fail to question who got to keep what percentage of the gate.

Master Birch smiled. "The Dragon Council and the Landimyn want to give this play to the city of Oel Artis as our gift. This is a . . . a good-will gesture. An *anonymous* goodwill gesture. The Empire has profited greatly thanks to Greyvmian and his mapping discoveries; we trade and own across Matrin's continents. This is . . ." Master Birch laughed gently. "This is a way for old men with much to be thankful for to give something back. So ten percent of gross."

Wraith hid his smile at Master Birch's definition of a gift. Ten percent of gross was, in fact, a dreadfully steep cut. He would have to pay his actors, his overhead on the theater, his costuming and staging expenses out of what was left, and after that, he might find that he would be in a money-losing position.

But he knew business. One did not grow up around the Artis table without hearing about deals and watching deals made—and though he knew he could not refuse and he could not set his terms, still he would play the game as if he believed he could.

"Master Birch," he said. "A cut of gross that vast would leave the theater a money-losing venture—and I am not an old man with vast fortunes to tend. I am a young man still bent on making his fortune. If this theater does not pay everyone else and still pay me well, I'll have to join the dilettante philosophers in the great houses above, and dicker day in and day out about whether or not man's place is in nature or nature's place is in man. A tedious future, I swear, and one I hope to escape." He smiled and said, "But I have my profits and losses for this first week written down if you would like to see them. And I think you would be well pleased with your return on investment at, say, ten percent of net."

Now Master Birch laughed. He leaned forward, eager, for this was a game he had played all his life. He would not spoil the fun by telling Wraith that he was not truly playing—that Wraith would take what Master Birch told him to take. Wraith maintained Master Birch's fiction, and Master Birch maintained Wraith's. "Let me see the numbers."

Wraith brought them out, and for a while they went over rows of figures and dickered consequences, and Birch raised all sorts of hell about the amount of money Wraith had spent on costumes when a single wizard could have spelled the whole thing for much cheaper.

"But, Master, the reason this play touched you as it did is because there was no trickery to it. It was exactly as you saw it. And I think there is an integrity in that gut-level reality which makes the use of magic a liability, not an asset."

"Ten percent of net won't even get us to the door," Birch said. "But . . ." He leaned his head close to his handboard and engaged in furious scribbling with his stylus, doing figures and checking results at a speed that suggested long practice. "But in the name of those who sent me, I can accept twenty-three percent of net. And do remember, we'll be financing your expenses—even the costs of your extravagant costuming—so you'll not be hurt by your overhead."

Wraith drew out paper and a pen and did his own figuring. When he looked up, he was smiling. "Then that will be fine. So, assuming that I can even reach Vincalis, or that you can present a suitable alternative, when should I start? When do you want to have this play ready?"

And Birch named a date that Wraith could not hope to make.

"Two months?" he gasped. "Vincalis has not written it yet. Once it is written, I will have to find actors, and rehearse them, get the costumers to make costumes, design the stage sets and the lighting and perhaps a musical score and . . ."

"The date, I'm afraid, is quite rigid. Greyvmian's birthday falls when it falls. We would have come to you sooner, but since we found you on your first night and have only been discussing this among ourselves for a week, I do not see how we could have discovered you any quicker than we did. The play must open on the eighth of Nottrosy, and be ready for a one-year run from that date."

A strangled, inarticulate cry of disbelief erupted from Wraith.

Birch studied him nervously, then bent over his handboard and, after another round of scribbling, said, "We're prepared to offer you a significant sum to drop everything you're doing right now so that you can begin work the instant your current play is done."

"But *A Man of Dreams* is sold for another week. And I have no doubt I could sell seats for it for at least another year."

"The city wants a play about Greyvmian the Ponderer, and wants it from you, and is willing to compensate you quite handsomely in order to get it."

"I'll have to remove *A Man of Dreams* entirely so that we can use the space to begin work on the next one." And that, of course, was what Birch and his anonymous backers wanted. He saw it in the man's eyes— the sly, subtle satisfaction of a man who played one game to get an unrelated result, and who pulled it off.

At that moment Wraith determined that the play they commissioned would be as thought-provoking as *A Man of Dreams,* but that it would keep its message more deeply hidden within layers of humor, within quick dialogue and clever action. They would have their funny play, and it would be everything they asked for and everything they dreaded all in one fine sweep.

Young men could play games as well as old men.

The starsetters came out early that night, to put finishing touches on the staryard that would grace the ceremony in which Velyn would exchange vows with Luercas. She'd spent some time with him at last, and found beneath his attractive face and handsome body a cold and ambitious man. He spoke with enthusiasm of his determination to hold the Chair of the Council of Dragons in Oel Artis, of his plans to create a union of cities that would bring the governments of each giant city-state under the governance of one central Council, and of his desire to one day become the head of *that* Council—the single man who would rule the whole of civilized Matrin, and much of the wilds that surrounded it. He told her these things because he wanted her to realize that she was getting a man who was already someone of importance, but who would someday be of even greater importance. He told her these things because he wanted to . . . to control her, she thought. Not because he wanted to share his hopes or dreams with her, not because he wanted to talk with her about something that he loved—but because if she knew his importance, she would have a better and clearer understanding of her place.

She thought of Wraith, and for a moment she had to fight back tears. When he told her of his plans for the future, he had been sharing his dreams and his passion with her, and he had wanted to include her in those dreams.

She took a deep breath. Wraith was an idealist. A fool. A child who did not belong in the life he was living, and who would sooner or later misstep, and be found out, and take down not only himself but everyone around him. She was better off without Wraith.

She watched the starsetters lighting the stars all across the yard—the great sweeps of a nebula spinning beneath the house itself, the arms spiraling out, and comets and shooting stars and glorious arches and sprays of light spun out above, so that the guests would dance on air, with stars beneath their feet and stars over their heads. She wished she could appreciate the beautiful effect. She wished . . .

But she did not wish for anything save that she get through this night and its attendant challenges without embarrassing herself. She had kept most of her sexual conquests well away from home and from the Aboves, but a few still hung on in the house, and any of them might come out and join in the crowd of well-wishers and make sure that they said something to Luercas in front of her that would cause her embarrassment.

Her father had often told her, "Live your life so that you can tell the worst thing you've ever done in front of the people you respect the most, and still hold your head up after."

Unfortunately for her, she hadn't liked her father, so she'd spent a great deal of time and effort living her life in a way that would cause him as much humiliation as possible. Now, however, she discovered that he was old and truly didn't care anymore, but she still had to live with everything she had ever done—both the things that people knew about and the things that they didn't but that she had to dread them finding out about. Her father's advice suddenly made a great deal of sense, but she'd come to that realization far too late to do anything but wish she'd liked him more when she was younger.

Her mother came out onto the balcony and stood beside her. "They'll be ready for you in a few moments, you know."

"I know. I was just watching the starsetters. Don't you wish sometimes that you could do that?"

"It's common labor," her mother said, and shrugged. "They make a pittance for their work, and can only enter the Aboves with passes. If they lived a thousand years they could never hope to live here."

"I just thought what they were doing was lovely."

"Of course it's lovely," her mother said. "Elsewise we would not have hired them. Come in and change—I have your outfit ready for you."

"What do you think of Luercas?" Velyn asked her.

Her mother shrugged. "He came highly recommended. Beyond that—he's rising through the Dragons quickly, his family has a great deal of money, and he's presentable. What else do you want?"

"A friend? A companion?"

"Why? We were careful to negotiate your vows so that you will be able to pursue as many 'friends' and 'companions' as you choose, after the two of you produce two healthy children."

"I love feeling like a breeder," Velyn muttered.

Her mother glanced sidelong at her and said, "And if I had not been willing to feel like a breeder, you would not exist, and you would not be heir to a sizable estate. If you don't have children, you cannot pass on the estate within the family. Lineage matters."

Velyn had to wonder why. At that moment, so much of everything her family believed in and stood for seemed pointless. Her parents had given birth to her and her brother because they needed to designate two heirs in order to make certain investments and to own certain pieces of property; those who could not guarantee continuity could not be entrusted with great treasures, since without continuity those treasures could fall into unworthy hands.

She had been born for financial purposes, and her own children would be born for the same financial purposes. She had no real desire to try out motherhood. She'd thought about it, but had discovered too late—that is, once she'd signed all the papers with Luercas—that she'd only thought about it when she was with Wraith. Now, facing a future in which she *would* give birth to two children and the father *would* be Luercas, she found herself facing the miserable truth that she did not want what was coming.

She tugged off her clothing, and put on the soft black robe that her mother handed her. She wrapped the silver, gemstone-beaded girdle over it, and her mother cinched the girdle tight. Her mother unwrapped the crown of stars, a tiny magic-spelled clip that pinned into her hair and created dancing pinpoints of colored light all around her head and shoulders.

Her mother stood back and studied her for a moment, and then she smiled. An actual, genuine smile—and Velyn thought she could count on the fingers of one hand the times she had seen a real, human smile on her mother's face. "You look very pretty," she said. "And your father and I are both quite . . . pleased . . . yes . . . pleased with you. You've grown up a bit."

Velyn managed a smile, but her heart wasn't in it. She knew in her gut that in going through with this, she was making a mistake; she didn't know how that mistake was going to manifest itself, but she didn't doubt for an instant that it would. But her parents were pleased with her. She could not remember the last time she had heard that.

Someone tapped on the door. "Everyone is ready," the muffled voice on the other side said.

Her mother drew herself erect and said, "Well, then. Shall we go out?"

Velyn couldn't back out. The contracts were binding—if she went into breach, she and her parents would be liable for vast sums called restitutionals, punitive fees that the reneging party paid. Luercas and his parents would walk away with property, money, and an increase in their societal rank that would come at the expense of her family, which would suffer a compensatory fall in rank. She would take her vows, then, and she would have the two children required of her.

She lifted her chin and nodded. "Let's do this thing," she said.

The two of them went out the door side by side and down a long and gleaming corridor. They met Luercas and his father at the back of the Treaties Hall, and the four of them walked up the center aisle between the two long banks of feast tables together. When they came at last to the patriarchs of the Artis and tal Jernas families, who sat side by side in the center of the head table, Velyn's mother and Luercas's father stepped aside.

Velyn and Luercas walked the last three steps together, but they did not touch, they did not look at each other, they did not even truly acknowledge each other's presence.

Wraith would have held her hand. Would have smiled at her, whispered something to her to ease the tension in the room, would have, perhaps, commented on the ludicrous clothing that most of those present to witness the final act of the nutevaz wore, and in doing so he would have made her laugh.

She did not think that Luercas would ever try to make her laugh; she doubted that he much valued laughter.

The two patriarchs rose and spread the presentation copies of the vows before the two of them on the table. This step was really just for show—the real copies had already been signed and sealed and filed. Velyn held her ground; she would get through this.

The tal Jernas patriarch spoke first. "Today the contract you two have sworn and attested to becomes binding—you have both vowed that from this day forward, for a period of one hundred years, you will share common property, common space, and the rights and duties of common life as stolti within the Empire of the Hars Ticlarim. You further agree to fulfill your familial obligations to present to the stolti for confirmation two infant heirs in good health, of sound minds and bodies, on the first day of their fifth year. . . ."

He droned on. Then the Artis patriarch took over, going over the details of their contract, making what was private public so that it could be more easily enforced.

Velyn started feeling sick. She looked around at the people seated at the banquet table, at the witnesses who had come to give the vows social binding. And Wraith was at one of the far tables, sitting passively, his face a blank mask, watching her.

No. She had thought that she would not have to see him again out-side of polite trips to his theater. She had never thought that he would exercise his right to come to her vows ceremony. She had been sure, in fact, that he would stay away—that if he had heard of it at all, he would be so hurt, so crushed, so devastated by what he had thrown away that he would not be able to bear his grief. She'd harbored fantasies that he would be so wounded by her quick recovery and by the brilliant con-tract she'd taken that he would come to her, begging to be let back into her life on whatever terms she was willing to offer.

That face staring at her without emotion was not the face of a man who had come to beg.

She turned back to the patriarchs, back to her decision, back to the cold, self-absorbed Luercas, and the tears began to slide down her cheeks. She didn't move to wipe them away; she kept her back to all the people who had come to bear witness to her stupidity. She would not let them see her behaving in this fashion. She stood a little straighter, and breathed as steadily as she could, and pulled her shoulders back. She held her birthright as stolta. She belonged in this house. She belonged in the Aboves. She was not—would never be—some parentless Warrens rat, some young opportunist who'd found shelter and safe haven among generous and unsuspecting people, and had then gone on to take ad-vantage of them for years. She ought to turn around, point to him, and say, "He's really from the Warrens. He doesn't belong here."

Except, of course, if she said that, it would mean that she knew. It would mean that she had kept this information from people who would have wanted it—and that would put her just one step above Wraith. She wouldn't be taking vows anymore—but she wouldn't be living in the Aboves, either. At barest minimum, she could look toward being ban-ished to one of the outlands and living on a remittance. At worst, she could find herself working the mines, stripped of her birthright, no longer a stolta. The stolti covered for each other—but they did not stand for betrayals within their own ranks.

She said nothing. Sooner or later the truth about Wraith would find its way to the right ears; when it did, she would pretend to have been just as taken in by him as everyone else.

Wraith watched her take her vows, and felt the last shreds of hope that he had clung to shrivel and blacken within him. He'd known when she told him that she would never take vows with him that he had to let her go—but some part of him kept hoping that she would come to him, that she would tell him she'd made a mistake, and that she wanted to be with him for the rest of her life, and that if it wasn't safe for the two of them to take vows in a grand public ceremony in Oel Artis, that they could travel to someplace where no one checked papers very carefully, and where they could promise themselves to each other with only paid witnesses.

Luercas. She chose Luercas.

Or had he chosen her? Had he wanted her in order to get back at Wraith for all their years of growing hatred, for all the times they'd exchanged hard words and Wraith, master of words, had come away the winner? How could she want to spend the rest of her life with that bully, that manipulative bastard, that power-hungry cretin—the man who was known as much for his endless sexual forays as for his determination to become the head of the Council of Dragons within the next ten years? The worst rumor Wraith had heard about Luercas was that he could have saved Rone had he wanted to, but that he decided letting Rone die a martyr would be more beneficial for his own career. And look at him now. His scars from that accident completely gone; standing in the full favor of the Council of Dragons; head of Research, the department that Solander so coveted; and now creating a contractual life-merger with the woman Wraith loved.

If Wraith could have murdered Luercas where he stood and hoped to get away with it, he would have.

And then the ceremony was over. Velyn and Luercas signed their public contract, turned, held hands, and lifted the contract over their heads as if it represented some great personal victory, instead of a gods'-damned financial merger. Wraith seethed inside, but outside he applauded along with the rest of the witnesses.

He'd been a fool to come—but he had to see her go through with it. He kept thinking that she wouldn't; that at the last minute she would realize that having a man who loved her was more important than having a man who felt that her family's monetary assets complemented his own. He could not believe, even as he stood there watching her smiling through tears at the crowd of well-wishers, that he had so misjudged her. He'd thought she was the other half of his soul, the person who made him complete. Now he had to face the fact that to do what she had just done, she had to have been almost a stranger to him. There had to be parts of her he hadn't seen, or had seen but hadn't understood.

He wanted to hate her. Instead, as he waited in line with the other witnesses to offer his congratulations, he only hated himself.

*   *   *

Jess sat across the room at the nutevaz and watched Wraith dying inside. She'd debated telling him that Velyn was going to take Luercas to vow, and had convinced herself that he deserved to know. She'd been so sure that if Wraith could see Velyn moving on with her life, he would be able to move on with his. But as she watched him suffer, she had to question her own methods. She could have told him after the deed was done—she could have passed the news on to him in a casual little aside: *Oh, Wraith, I'm sure you've already heard, but Velyn took vows with that ass Luercas last month, and by the way, I just heard that both Jain and Torva are expecting their first registered children.*

He would have been shocked. He would have been hurt. But he wouldn't have been sitting there staring at Velyn like a man who was having his heart ripped out of his chest one still-beating piece at a time. Everyone kept things from Wraith, because everyone thought he was too sensitive to know the hard truth about people, about situations, about anything. So he didn't know that the woman he was so visibly mourning had never been faithful to him, or that she had never even considered faithfulness an issue.

She'd wanted to tell Wraith about Velyn's other men as soon as she found out about them. She hated the fact that everyone laughed at Wraith for thinking Velyn loved him.

"He loves her," Solander had said. "He won't thank you for telling him that the woman he loves is not who he thinks she is. He'll just hate you for destroying his illusions."

But if he could discover the truth about Velyn—if he could just find out that she wasn't worth all this anguish and grief—perhaps he could at last be free of her. Maybe he could find some peace.

Or maybe Solander was right.

If Solander was right, though, then this meant all of them had done the best for Wraith that they could—and that the fact that he was in pain and mourning someone who didn't deserve to be mourned was the best he deserved. Jess did not believe that.

She could show him who Velyn really was, she realized. He wouldn't be happy to find it out—but maybe a brief unhappiness was kinder than this lingering anguish. She glanced around the room. The people there were all stolti, of course—not the chadri or mufere who made up most of Velyn's conquests. But among the hundreds of witnesses, Jess saw two young men with whom Velyn had entertained herself while sharing quarters with Wraith. When the last of the banquet had been cleared away and everyone headed outside to dance among the stars, Jess caught one of them and said, "Kemmart, Velyn was hoping to see you privately before this party is over."

Kemmart jumped a little, and a guilty smile flashed across his face. "I didn't think she'd forget me too easily."

"Of course not. I heard that it was you she had in mind when she was negotiating her contract. Just a rumor, but . . ." Jess shrugged.

"When did she want to meet me? And where?"

"Zero by Dim—out behind the fountain."

He glanced up at the clock on the wall, marked the time, and nodded. "When you see her, tell her I'll be there."

Jess smiled.

She worked her way through the crowd, caught Velyn's attention, and gestured toward a quiet alcove. Velyn nodded almost imperceptibly and when she got a chance, broke free of the throng of well-wishers and joined Jess.

"I can't believe he came," were the first words out of her mouth. "Your fault, wasn't it?"

Jess held up a hand. "Truce, Velyn. I'm on your side. Wraith cut Solander and me out of his life, too—remember? Or didn't you know about that?"

Velyn looked shaken. "I'd heard that you left Solander right after . . . well, after. And I assumed the two of you would get together. I mean, you've had your eye on him all these years."

"Solander and I separated when we realized that we didn't have anything in common anymore. The timing looked bad, but . . ." She managed a tiny, amused smile that she didn't feel at all. "But Wraith and me? No. I never intended to be upstaged by a theater. Any more than you did. I could understand completely your decision not to take vows with him." Jess shrugged. "As for why Wraith came tonight—he thought it would be polite, I suppose. But I didn't call you over to talk to you about Wraith."

Velyn watched her with a wariness that Jess had to respect. Velyn might have had the morals of an alleycat, but she knew how to watch her back. "Why did you want to talk to me?"

"Your friend Kemmart said he wanted to meet with you in private for a few minutes. Zero by Dim behind the fountain. He said it was important."

Velyn looked surprised, and then—as Jess had hoped she would— pleased. "Kemmart," she murmured.

"He didn't seem too terribly pleased that he'd lost you to Luercas," Jess added.

Velyn's little smile became broader. "When, again?"

"Zero by Dim."

Velyn nodded. "Thank you. Oh—and if you see Wraith, you might want to suggest to him that tonight wouldn't be a terribly good night for him to try to make amends. Luercas truly despises him, and would be more than happy to start looking for ways to destroy him, should he think that Wraith doesn't respect the contract."

Jess nodded. "I don't know that I will see him—or even that I want to talk to him if I do. But . . ." She smiled again, falsely bright. "But I suppose if I run into him and can't just walk on by, I could pass that on."

Velyn glanced at Luercas, standing with a group of his colleagues discussing something that seemed to be amusing all of them, and a look of dismay flashed across her face and vanished. "Don't do anything that makes you uncomfortable. If I happen to run into him, I'll be *more* than happy to pass that on myself."

Jess nodded, excused herself, and made her way back to the main party. She located Wraith and kept an eye on him. She wanted to be able to head him out to the fountain at about the right time—and she thought she had just the right story to get him out there. And when he got there, he would see who Velyn really was, and he might be able to stop hurting so much.

And then maybe . . . maybe . . . he might find his way back to her.

Grath Faregan, dressed in blue velvet from throat to toes, nodded to wedding guests, sipped a drink, and finally, with a smile, turned to his companion. "There. Talking to the bride. You see her?"

"Slender, tiny, dark hair, blue silk traditional robes . . ."

"That's the one. You're to get close to her and stay close to her. Get to know everyone she knows, keep track of everything she does . . . and when I give the order, bring her to me."

"To the Inquest, you mean?"

"I said what I meant," Faregan snapped. "To *me*. You understand that?"

"I do, Master."

"Very well. Off with you, then. I'll want reports weekly. Make them . . . personal." Faregan smiled, imagining Jess in his home, in his hands, in his power—imagining finally doing everything he had waited so long to do. "Not much longer," he said softly. "Not much longer at all, Jess."

Wraith would have been long gone—he'd made a horrible mistake coming—but people kept cornering him and congratulating him on *A Man of Dreams,* or asking if he might get them seats since they could not even find places in the high rows or the aisles for any of the performances.

When Jess grabbed him by one arm and dragged him free of a woman who was complaining that he should have planned for a longer run, he could only be grateful.

"You look absolutely gray, Wraith," she whispered, dragging him out of the grand banquet hall, down a well-lit corridor, and out into the star-filled yard, where couples danced on air to the strains of one of Jess's live musical groups.

"I feel like baked death with plantains," he muttered. "And over-cooked, at that."

She said, "You need some quiet for a moment. No one will see us back behind the fountain." She led him through the yard, using her elbows like weapons, yet managing to make every well-placed strike look like an accident. He couldn't help but be impressed. As they worked their way through the crowd, she said, "You were insane to come here; you know that, don't you? It's like you want to hurt yourself. Like you're reveling in the pain."

"I just kept hoping she would realize that she was making a mistake."

Jess patted his arm and sighed. "You would think that, of course. But you're a romantic."

"I love her, Jess. I wanted to be with her forever. I kept hoping that she would finally discover that she loved me enough to . . ." He shrugged. "I'm an idiot. I already knew that I was an idiot. But tonight really proved the point to me."

"You aren't an idiot for loving her," Jess said grimly. "She's an idiot for not loving you."

And they broke free of the last of the dancers, and reached the tall shrubs that surrounded the grand fountain, and moved behind them.

And there was Velyn. And one of the distant Artis cousins. They were jammed up against the fountain, in a state of partial undress, focused only on each other—engaged in an activity that put Velyn in breach of her contract almost before the ink had dried.

Wraith said nothing. Velyn didn't see him—her eyes were tightly closed—but the cousin did. He grimaced—jerked his head at Wraith, telling him to go away without saying any words—but he didn't forget what he was about. Velyn moaned and shivered and told him, "Oh, more. Oh, more. God knows when we'll get this chance again."

Wraith couldn't see. His vision had blurred to virtual blindness, and only when he felt the tears burning down the back of his throat did he realize he was crying.

He felt hands on his elbow, pulling him away, and heard a voice in his ear saying, "I'm putting you in a car and sending you home. Should I go with you, or will you be all right to be alone?"

"I'd rather walk," he muttered, but Jess was steering him through the crowds again, and he couldn't see well enough to choose his own direction, and he didn't have the will to fight her.

The car took him home. The driver delivered him to the door. And the proctor saw him to bed, and gave him some hot wine to burn away the pain.

In that manner he passed the last night he ever spent in his suite in the Materan Ground School.

Chapter 12

Greyvmian the Ponderer—A Play in Three Acts
by Vincalis

CHARACTERS
(in order of appearance)
Truuthman the Ruthless—pirate
Greyvmian the Ponderer—mapmaker
Shetha the Avaricious—landlady
Crobitt the Confused—envoy to the Empire
Nalritha the Beautiful—the pirate's lady but the
mapmaker's true love
Winling the Wise—Greyvmian's friend and advisor
Dal the Seventh—Master of the Empire of the Hars Ticlarim

Act One—Pirates and Heroes Seek Common Ground
Scene 1

Time: The Old Calendar Year of Queh, Raunde 15, in the month of Gehorlen.

Place: A cluttered office of ancient style, built not of fine whitestone but of wood, full of scrolls, quills, calligraphic brushes, and reed-papers, the walls covered with maps drawn by hand with colored inks in the old fashion. The lamps burn real flame, and water pours into a stone sink from a trough that pokes through the back wall. At left stage sits a heavy wooden drawing table, its top angled toward the audience. It is covered with a map in progress—clearly the continent of Strithia, though also clearly out of proportion and with vast gaps in the coastline and interior.

In front of the drawing table sits a tall drafting stool, while at center stage we see several chairs and a small desk on which sit the half-eaten remains of a poor meal and a glass tankard still almost full of weak beer.

A steep and narrow stairway rises at right stage from the working area up to a loft, which holds a narrow wooden bed with a thin and pitiful mattress covered by a tattered blanket.

Doors open to both left and right stage, and through the window backing center stage, we see a bay full of ships, and beyond, the sea.

The curtain rises to reveal TRUUTHMAN, a pirate dressed in full pirate regalia, as in the ancient scroll side-illuminations, who paces at center stage. He glares at the left door, at the audience, at the right door, and then sees the meal and the beer. Glancing around, for he is clearly not in his own home and the meal clearly is not his, he sneaks over to it and raises the beer to his lips. As he takes a huge gulp, GREYVMIAN bursts into the room through the right door, panting hard and startling the pirate, who spews beer across the room.

GREYVMIAN: (still panting, but looking with mournful eyes at his now nearly empty tankard) My *beer.* (And then, noticing that some of the beer has speckled his maps) My *maps.*

TRUUTHMAN: (putting the beer down behind him) You're late.

GREYVMIAN: My landlady was after me for the rent. I found a good dogfight and jumped into the middle of it, and thus lost her— but it was a near thing. The dogs mistook her for one of their own and most fled in fear. (Pause) Were it not for one big fellow—more a lover than a fighter—who took a fancy to her, I would not be here yet.

TRUUTHMAN: (laughing) For just such reasons do I keep to the sea. All landladies are an evil brood, I swear—worshipers of dark and vengeful gods. I'll take my chances with monsters, typhoons, and the bottomless ocean. Which brings me to my purpose: You have my map?

GREYVMIAN: If you have my coastline. The Golden Chain of Manarkas for the southern tip of Strithia—that was our agreement.

TRUUTHMAN: I remember it. And I have made a true copy of my logs for you—my reckonings each day we sailed along the coast, and the positions of the stars at night. I found a lovely bay at the northern edge of my journey this time that is full of islands—I did not chart them, or even try. But south of that, you should get a good line. (Offers a sheaf of loose papers.)

GREYVMIAN: (taking the papers and glancing through them) These look good. Very good. You write a nice hand, and are remarkably concise with your whereabouts for a pirate.

TRUUTHMAN: (looks around nervously, as if afraid the two of them will be overheard. GREYVMIAN, infected by his nervousness, also looks around, though clearly with no idea what he is looking for) Have you a close tongue in your mouth?

GREYVMIAN: Close as a bound trunk with no key. Why?

TRUUTHMAN: Because you aren't the only one to get copies of my logs. I make a copy as well for the Master of the City—from here I go to meet with his man Crobitt. But none may know the Master of the Hars puts gold in the coffers of pirates.

GREYVMIAN: (astonished) Truly! My head rolls if any find that you have stepped one foot into my house, but the Master of the City keeps you on his payroll. It simply proves that one should be born a Master, not a mapmaker.

TRUUTHMAN: (grinning) I hold the gods accountable for such things. I tell them what they shall give me, in women and wealth and weather fair, and because I am Truuthman the Ruthless, they listen.

GREYVMIAN: (kissing his palm and pressing it to his forehead to ward off the evil of such hubris) Don't play on the gods' fields—you won't like their games, and in any case, they cheat.

Wraith sighed and pushed away from his pages. He needed to get both the landlady and the pirate's beautiful mistress on the stage quickly, and while he had a grand idea for the landlady—perhaps in a ripped dress and with a huge dog still panting and grinning behind her—for the life of him, he couldn't think of any circumstance that would bring the fair Nalritha into Greyvmian's humble abode.

Wraith rested his chin in one cupped hand and listened to the dancing down the street from the little room he'd taken in the Kaan village. He wanted to be out there with them. He wanted to be dancing in the night air—or at least learning the steps, which was all he could claim to be doing, really. He wanted to be listening to the stories and the songs, sharing the evening meal, laughing and celebrating life. He wanted to feel the freedom that the Kaan felt.

Greyvmian the Ponderer sat on his shoulders like an evil giant, weighing him to the ground and sucking the joy out of him. He liked his ideas for the play. He even felt a current of excitement about the way he was going to sneak his subversive messages about the dangers of magic and the truths of government abuses of regular citizens and men's right to control their own lives into this seemingly funny bit of fluff.

But he wrote to a hellish deadline, and he wrote to the specifications of the Dragon Council, and he wrote under the shadow of Velyn's betrayal. And he kept seeing Nalritha as Velyn, who loved a poor mapmaker but chose a rich and cruel pirate. It would take everything he had in him to keep *Greyvmian the Ponderer* from becoming a tragedy.

At his door, tapping.

He pushed his pens and sheets away and rose, suddenly conscious as he did of the dull ache between his shoulders and the throbbing at his temples, and the fact that two of his three lanterns had run out of oil and guttered into darkness. He remembered at the same time that he had forgotten to eat, and realized that his bladder had filled to the point of pain.

He shouted at the door, "Just come in—I'll be with you in a moment," and ran to the back, to the mechanical toilet that did not magically purify waste but merely moved it to a leach pit on the downhill side of the village. He considered, as he did every time he used the odd toilet, what effect such toilets would have on the Empire if everyone were forced to use them—plentiful clean water would become scarce, while leach pits sufficient to cleanse waste for the hundreds of millions of people living under the rule of the Hars would take valuable land away from agriculture and at the same time would foul the air. He tried not to think about that too much—about the Hars without magic. He kept telling himself that if everyone lived without magic, they would still find ways to keep the air and water clean; they would still find ways to grow crops in the desert instead of using prime land for farming; they would still find ways to transport the uncounted millions where they needed to be. They would have enough food, enough space, enough of everything.

He didn't believe himself when he thought it, though, and so his second fantasy was that people would find ways to use magic responsibly, without human sacrifice or the destruction of men's eternal souls.

He heard his guest moving around the little room that acted as living room and bedroom for him. He wondered which of the Kaan had come to visit—one or another of his actresses and dancers would appear from time to time to see if he could be enticed into bed for a bit of fun. He couldn't. He knew he should go ahead and take one or two up on their offers, if nothing more than to start the process of changing Velyn from ever-present agony to distant memory, but he didn't care for the idea of using any of the young women who came to him, and in his current state of mind, that was all he would be doing.

So he had a polite no already framed when he came out the door and found, not one of the Kaan women, but Velyn, standing nervously in the center of his little room, carefully not touching anything.

"I had a hard time finding you," she said.

"You shouldn't have looked."

"Solander gave me a general idea of where you might be. Beyond that . . ." She shrugged. She was studying him, as if trying to read his thoughts from his face. He saw dark circles under her eyes, and noticed that her eyelids and nose were red and swollen, as if she had been crying. He saw lines of little round bruises on her upper arms, too, as if she had been roughly grabbed—more than once—by someone with strong hands. "I shouldn't be here," she said. "I shouldn't have come at all, but . . . but I thought you ought to know."

Wraith could not see her standing in his room without also seeing her by the fountain on the night she took vows, with someone who was not him and who wasn't even the man to whom she'd sworn faithfulness, however temporary the term of that faithfulness was supposed to be. He turned so that he wasn't looking at her, but instead at his desk, and said, "What should I know, Velyn? That I never really mattered to you? That you always had other men—that the whole time we were together, you had other lovers? I know all of that now. After your nutevaz, I spent a little time looking. Stupid of me, I know, but I think it's helped me to come to terms with losing you."

He glanced at her and found irritation rather than remorse in her expression. "Be quiet a minute," she said. "I haven't much time, and if I'm found here—well, that would be disastrous. Both Luercas and Dafril are working to discredit you. Luercas hates you—I suppose partly because I was with you before I was with him. But there's more to it than that. He's hired men to check into your background, to see if you've been involved with any illegal activities."

"I haven't."

"You're here, in this proscribed village. You've hired these villagers to work for you. You could be banned from Oel Artis for that—possibly from the whole of the Hars." She sighed. "But that isn't the thing that worries me most."

"No?"

"Your papers are good, but if the men investigating you decide to write to your family in Ynjarval, they're going to discover that the people you and Jess are pretending to be both died in a tragic airible accident at about the same time that you appeared here and moved into Artis

House. And if they discover that, they'll find a way to track you back to the Warrens."

Wraith didn't want to listen to her. He needed to be a playwright to free the Warreners. He needed to be able to go to and from the Warrens to gather images to feed to his allies who had access to the nightlies. He needed to have access to the equipment that produced the anti-magic flyers he wrote. And if he were being watched, investigated—hunted— he wouldn't be able to do any of those things.

Solander would soon be in a position to help him—as soon as he got his position in Research, he would be able to create diversions. Another year, Wraith thought. Another year, and Solander would have finished his exit project and would be declared a Dragon.

Another year. Would Wraith be able to hold out for a year?

He had the patronage of the Dragon Council—but would that be of any value? Not if anyone in power discovered that he only pretended to be stolti. The Silent Inquest would turn on him between two beats of a heart.

He didn't want to listen to Velyn—but he didn't dare ignore her. If people were checking into his background, he needed to have a background that would withstand deep checking.

Which probably meant that, as soon as he had *Greyvmian the Ponderer* on the stage and running smoothly, he needed to take some of the large amount of money he'd accumulated recently and spend it on a trip "home" to Ynjarval to buy himself an alibi. The dead parents would never betray him; he just had to be sure that the rest of the "relatives" would come through for him in his moment of need.

And while he was at it, he thought he ought to make sure he covered Jess's background, too. No sense making his own alibi perfect and leaving a hole in hers that would destroy them both.

He took a deep breath, and turned and actually looked at Velyn. "Thank you for coming to tell me this. I'm sorry for the . . . the rudeness of my reception. I appreciate your concern for my well-being—" A smile flickered at the left corner of Velyn's mouth; Wraith recognized that smile as one of superior amusement. He stopped his placating apology in midsentence. "What's so funny?"

"I didn't risk my neck for your sake, Wraith. You—a Warrener— treated me, a stolta, as if you had both the right and the justification to question my actions. If Luercas and Dafril could find out the truth about you without that truth also implicating me in the keeping of your secret all these years, I wouldn't whisper a single word of protest. As far as I'm concerned, you deserve whatever is coming your way, and I'm quite sure sooner or later something will get you." She laughed softly. "Just know that I'll be smiling when I get the news." She turned toward the door. "My sole interest in this is in keeping myself out of the little circle of people whose lives you destroy when you and your schemes are discovered."

"Ah." Wraith nodded and let himself look at her and really see her— not as he had wanted her to be, but as she was—a high-born woman who had been slumming with him for the secret thrill of it, who may or may not have cared a little about him but who had never cared enough to make a commitment to him, who felt certain that she was a better person than he was simply because of an accident of birth; and, he had to admit, an unpleasant, vindictive bitch. He crossed his arms over his chest and said, "Nice bruises, by the way. Luercas give those to you?"

She flushed and opened the door.

"Don't come back," he said. "I'd hate to have anyone I know see you here. You might give me a bad reputation."

She stared at him and her mouth dropped open—and then, with an inarticulate growl of rage, she slammed the door behind her.

Wraith sagged against the wall and closed his eyes against the welling tears. Gods, he wished he could hate her.

Three years. Three sweet springs, oppressive summers, glorious autumns, bitter winters that rolled across Oel Artis, changing lives, ending lives, and adding new ones, as seasons do. As time does.

In three years, Wraith made *Greyvmian the Ponderer* the cornerstone of a growing repertoire of plays that touched peoples' hearts and made them think long after they finished laughing. Or crying. He eluded any connection between him and Vincalis, other than the obvious one of the plays that showed up at his doorstep at regular intervals, neatly bound in silk. In three years, he created an unassailable alibi—a carefully tended and bought stolti family in Ynjarval who had managed its finances poorly and was more than willing, for regular infusions of cash, to provide proof and testament that they had known the boy Gellas as a child and had sent him off after his parents died so tragically. In three years he wrote more than twenty plays, built two new playhouses to add to his first one, hired managers and actors, accountants and lawyers, and made the names Vincalis—and, to a lesser extent, Gellas Tomersin—as well known as any Dragon's, and better loved. In three years, he owned a fine house in a fine neighborhood in the Belows, and entertained in it often.

In three years, he never replaced Velyn, nor did he try. His heart remained broken and his soul scarred, and he kept chaste as any fanatical follower of Toth.

He and Solander grew further apart with the passing of each day. Solander buried himself in magic studies, got his position in Research, got his own workroom, won grants and accolades for his early work in *rewhah*-less magic, and began to be suggested as a candidate for the Council.

Jess took her musicians around Oel Artis, and then around the Empire. She and Jyn parlayed their initial investment into a massive entertainment concern, and created an interest in the live arts that spread not just through the stolti class, but through all the classes. Both women became very rich. Jyn claimed her share of profits, sold her portion of the business to Jess, and took vows with a charming man she'd met while booking tours in Arim. Jess took lovers, but did not keep them long. She kept looking for something, but not finding it. In all the world, her only constant companion was her assistant. She found this a sad statement on the emptiness of her life, but accepted it nonetheless.

And Velyn. Ah, Velyn. Her mistakes compounded, but Luercas was her first and greatest mistake. She was his revenge against Wraith—and with every new success that Wraith had, Velyn got another opportunity to suffer.

Luercas in his stolen body rose in influence among the Dragons, and his vowmate lived in fear and misery. They had no children, not because she never became pregnant, but because each time she did he claimed the child was not his—even on those occasions when he knew it was. Each time she came to him with her news, he cast a spell to determine the legitimacy of the child, and each time worked the spell so that it would "prove" her unfaithfulness. Each time he demanded, by the articles of the contract, that she terminate the pregnancy. When finally she knew that the baby could be none but his, and his test still lied to her, she realized that he had found a way to keep her forever in breach of her contract, and forever unable to dissolve their vows without ruining her family financially. As long as he could manipulate the paternity tests, she could not hope to leave him on favorable terms.

Velyn was trapped. And when she realized it, Luercas's treatment of her grew just that much worse.

Three short years, and the seasons passed oblivious to the lives of those who lived through them. For every change that happened in view of everyone, another change occurred beneath the surface, hidden in the darkness. These were the dangerous changes, changes that crept toward chaos and evil and pain and grief. They began to surface with a single crack in the veneer of one lovely day.

Book Three

Vincalis the Agitator

All men die, Antram. All men age and wither and creep at last into their dark graves, and from thence into the flames of Hell or cold oblivion, as their theology dictates. But to only a few men do the gods give a task, a burden, a road to greatness that can, if they take it, raise them above the thick clouds of complacency that blind most eyes and plug most ears. To only a few men do the gods give true pain, which removes the bloated cushion of softness and brings sharp awareness of the preciousness of life; which raises up heroes and strips cowards naked before the world. You, Antram, will do great things. You will see, you will feel, you will breathe and touch and revel in each moment you are given. And you will suffer great pain. And someday, whether soon or late, you will die.

But all men die, Antram. Few ever live.

FROM *ON A FAR HILL*
VINCALIS THE AGITATOR

Chapter 13

Dark, and silence, and city guards moved through another out-lander district of Oel Artis. But no one answered the doors upon which they knocked, and when those guards kicked in doors and searched houses, they found no one at home—though signs in the homes showed that people had been there, sometimes so recently that food sat hot on tables—so recently that chairs or beds were still warm to the touch. The guards should have come away with a full complement of fodder for the Warrens from the district they had been sent to harvest—but they left empty-handed.

Lights flashed from rooftops when they passed, and aircars dropped out of the sky and silently deposited people back in their homes—to pack, for they could not hope to survive in their old homes in their old districts once the guards had come hunting them. They had friends now, though, and they would find other places to live—would move through a chain of hands, get new names and new papers, find new homes and new jobs. Many of them, knowing that they and their children owed their lives to the nameless people who dropped out of the sky to pull them away from disaster, joined the underground. These rebels knew only one name for certain among those with whom they fought, but that one name gave them hope.

Vincalis.

On such a morning, with the breeze fresh and sharp and scented by the sea, with the sunlight warm on his uplifted face in wondrous contrast to the frost-brushed wind, with the sounds of the city all around him shaped and transformed by a bell-like resonance of the air, Wraith wanted nothing more than to walk away from Oel Artis to his home in the countryside, to revel in the day. Perhaps he could do that tomorrow. Today—today he would have a full schedule.

He smiled slightly at the facade of the West Beach Experimental Playhouse, the newest of his creations. This building he'd designed from the ground up; no more refurbished factories, no more cutting corners. He had three major plays going on in the city at any time, and fifteen troupes of traveling players on extended tours throughout the rest of the Empire. Managers took care of most of the day-to-day work, so that he was free to write in secret the plays that kept the machine in motion. But some things only he could handle.

His assistant greeted him as he stepped through the private side door, her usual smile oddly missing.

"You've received invitations to several First Hallows parties, and the Benedictan envoy from Kirth has asked to meet with you to discuss the touring of one troupe of players; the Kirthans are most especially interested in the comedies, but understand that the tragedies usually come as part of the repertoire; they have made *quite* a substantial offer. Your bookkeepers have finished the reports for Pombolen, Falzan, and Sheffen, and request some of your time to go over the profits and losses— they seemed quite pleased, so I'm assuming the news is good. You have a meeting with potential investors in the Round Hall at naught-and-half by Work. And last but certainly not least, a woman is sitting behind your desk crying. She says she knows you and is quite sure you'll remember her. I suggest you do not go into the room alone—you'll want at least one reliable witness present, and perhaps several."

Wraith, who had been walking up the stairs to his top-floor office, stopped at that last comment and said, "A witness? Why? Has she accused me of something?"

"No. But you'll want people who are able and willing to testify that she was in that condition when you walked into the room, and not just when she walked out of it."

"Condition?" Wraith had hired Loour because she was dependable, ungodly efficient, and trustworthy. He wouldn't second-guess something she told him in seriousness. He said, "You'll come in with me. Also Dan and Murin. They're both in the finance room. Go get them."

Loour said, "You need to do that. I'll stay here and make sure she doesn't leave—but I don't want you to be alone with her for a minute. There is something . . . something terribly *wrong* about her."

"We could just have her removed."

"She's stolti. *High* stolti. You aren't going to be able to send her any-where."

Wraith nodded, went to the finance room, and returned with his witnesses. He hoped that the woman would be a stranger; he feared that she would not.

The poor, battered creature curled in the corner shocked him, though. This was no one he had ever seen before. Half starved, bruised, cut, with dried and crusted blood caked on her arms and legs, she lifted a swollen face to look at him, and stared at him out of the single eye that would open. She had glossy copper hair, beautifully cut, perfectly groomed, and the finest of clothes; on her, they were a travesty, a horror.

He stared at her for a long moment, trying to see past unimaginable damage to the woman she must once have been, and as he did, she pushed to her feet and stood there, weaving and shaking. And he recognized her necklace.

Gods in hell, he recognized her by her necklace, and if she had not been wearing it, he would never have known her at all. And he had loved her for years, and some part of him loved her still.

"Velyn?" he whispered.

She tried to smile—her cracked lips made the expression dreadful. "It's been a while, hasn't it?"

"Gods above, Velyn—I can't pretend to polite conversation while you stand there looking like death. What happened to you? Who did this to you?"

"My vow-lock was . . . not the best decision I ever made," she whis-pered. She laughed just a little.

Wraith clenched his fists. "Luercas did this?"

"Luercas has been doing this since we got together. It has always been bad. But last night he tried to kill me. I . . . I didn't really have any-place else to go. I need help."

And what was he supposed to say to that? That she hadn't wanted him all those years earlier? That she had chosen the life she ended up with? She hadn't chosen this—to be beaten and starved and . . . How in the names of every deity had Luercas been able to do this to her without anyone knowing? Without anyone stepping in and helping her?

He took a deep breath and looked to his associates. Loour had gone to Velyn's side, had offered her a light blanket to wrap around herself, had brought her a good hot mug of tea. Dan and Murin were consulting over against the west wall, their backs to Wraith and Velyn, their bodies stiff and tight and radiating shock and fury. Wraith understood. Looking at Velyn, he wanted to go out the door right then, find Luercas, and murder him.

"I don't know how to help you," he said softly. "But I'll find a way, Velyn. I'll find someone for you to stay with while I talk to my legal people to see if they can offer any suggestions on how to proceed." He lost the cool, professional demeanor he'd been fighting to maintain and said, "How could he do this to you? How could you stay and *let* him?"

"I have not lived a respectable life, Wraith," she said. "I've made errors. A lot of them. And he is the sort of man who is willing to use every mistake I ever made against me. I would cost my family everything they owned if I left him without providing the two children called for in our contract. And he has made sure that I will never be able to bear those two children, and that I will remain forever his . . . his whipping post." She stared down at her hands; Wraith could see that some of her fingers had been broken before and had healed badly. He tried to understand how Velyn—who had never admitted to flaws or weaknesses, and whose defining characteristic had been her absolute certainty that she was right—came to be so meek. So shattered. He'd realized when she told him she would not take vows with him that he did not know her and had never known her, but now he was looking at a woman so different from *that* Velyn that he was having a hard time seeing them as the same person.

Time changed people—he knew that. But it never changed them as completely as they wanted to believe; core parts of them remained. He found himself staring at her, trying to find anything about her that survived of the woman he had once loved to distraction.

She started sobbing, her face buried in her battered, twisted hands, and he looked helplessly at Loour. Loour frowned, then nodded and crouched beside Velyn. "Come on. Let's get you out of here. I have a good friend who does healing magic; we'll take you to him and get you taken care of. And while we're doing that, Gellas can see about finding you a place to stay until you get everything worked out." She gave Velyn a little tug to help her to her feet and started steering her toward the door. "In fact, I'll get my healer friend to take a look at you and then come with us before the Board of Contract Review. He can testify to the damage that has been done to you. If Luercas tried to kill you, you *cannot* be held to the conditions of your contract. I'm certain of that. And I would guess that, because he treated you like this, the contract could be voided, or even terminated in your favor. . . ."

Then they were through the door, and Wraith couldn't hear any more of what Loour said.

He leaned against the wall and forced himself to breathe slowly.

Dan walked over to him. "I would guess that the man who treated her that way is on his way to being sent to the mines."

Wraith shook his head. "He won't be punished. He probably won't even be fined. Loour wants to think that he'll be made to pay for what he did, but he's a Master on the Council of Dragons, the head of the Department of Magical Research for the entire city of Oel Artis, and if he was secure enough to do this to her, he has some sort of information about her that she can't let get out." Wraith sighed. "Loour can take her before the Board of Contract Review, but at most they'll request Luercas to be present so that he can offer his side of the story—and then whatever he has been using against her will come out."

"That isn't right."

"It isn't. But if you think the most powerful people in the Hars play by the same rules as the rest of us, you're dreaming. And you aren't going to be happy when you wake up." He turned to look out the window—he had a good view of the street, and his timing offered him one quick glimpse of Loour and Velyn getting into an airtaxi that had pulled to the curb.

Wraith got a sick feeling in the pit of his stomach. It wasn't just the pain he felt at seeing Velyn so badly treated—it was almost a premonition; he wished that she had not come to him for help, he didn't want to involve himself in her problems, and yet he could not see any way to be the man he was and still turn her away.

He leaned his forehead against the cool window and briefly closed his eyes.

She would not be able to go home. And when she had been to the healer, and had gone before the Contract Review Board, she would most likely need a place to hide. A new name. A new face.

He knew how to arrange such things; he'd built quite a respectable underground in the last four years. He would be able to move her away from the city, turn her into someone completely new, and—so long as she listened to the rules and followed them—protect her from Luercas.

He wondered how well she would do with being told where she could go, who she could associate with, and how she could behave. Had she been the old Velyn, he would have considered her hopeless. He couldn't begin to guess what he might expect from the new Velyn.

Wraith straightened and turned to Murin. "I need you to cover my morning appointments," he said. "I'm going to need to make sure that Velyn is adequately represented, and I'm going to have to see if I can find a good guest house for her to stay in until this whole thing is worked out. I have a busy schedule today, but . . ." He shrugged. "For reasons I can't even explain to myself, I think I need to take care of Velyn and her problem first."

Murin nodded. He could cover for Wraith without too much difficulty—he had done so on a number of occasions before.

"The big thing on the schedule today is the meeting to arrange a troupe tour of parts of Benedicta. Try to get them to agree to Fourth Troupe—Fourth has been short on engagements since they got back from the Manarkan Coast tour. And see if you can get a commitment for the full repertoire—I especially want them to get another run through *Prime and Nocturne* and *The Fall of the First Sun*. I know they're going to want the comedies, but Fourth needs to be ready to take over for Third Troupe here when they finish the tour. Third needs a break. And I don't want them rusty on the tragedies."

Murin nodded. "I'll take care of it."

"Get us a good price, too."

He left, regretting lying to Murin about what he would be doing—he would find representation for Velyn if she didn't have someone from the Artis family who would take care of her. And he would find her a good guest house. But it would be a guest house from which she would be kidnapped once he and his people were out of the picture, on a night when all of them had good alibis.

He would let Vincalis arrange her kidnapping; have Vincalis's underground arrange a safe house for her; pick the team that would pose as the kidnappers; decide which of his underground contacts to endanger with her presence. Which wizard to send her to for a new face, a repaired body. Which town to hide her in.

And before, posing as Vincalis, he did any of this—before he let his heart and some emotion from his past make his decisions in the present—he would have to find out how much he could trust her, because the second she moved into his underground, she was in a position to betray him and everything he had worked for since he escaped from the Warrens.

If she could not follow instructions, if she would not hide, change who she was, or break all ties with her past, she would destroy his work. His real work.

*　　*　　*

"Master Faregan, our first break in a long time." The voice on the secret channel was soft, as if the speaker called from a place where she might be discovered.

Faregan recognized the voice. "What break, Loour?"

"His old lover, now vowmate to none other than Luercas tal Jernas, came to Gellas for help today. Luercas had beaten her, tried to kill her, by her account. And Gellas is going to help her."

"Good. Watch him. See who he contacts. See if this stirs anything up." Faregan sighed. "If anything interesting happens, let me know in time for me to get everyone over there. We've been waiting a very long time for someone to make a mistake."

Solander ran his final set of numbers on the test and leaned against the console. "Impossible," he whispered.

His partner and fellow wizard, Borlen Haiff, glanced over from his own worktable, caught a glimpse of Solander's expression, and put his work down. "What happened?"

"It worked," Solander said. "I just cast a four-input spell, and did not draw a single bit of magic from the grid. And you want to guess my rebound level?"

"Standard four-input? Flesh, blood, bone, and life force?"

"Right."

"Well . . . give me your energy input readings."

"Three-twenty, three-eighty, forty, and two."

Borlen hunched over his magic pad, scratching away with his stylus. "Duration?"

"Two minutes, no error."

"Standard, then." He scratched some more. "Using Devian's Formula, you should have experienced *rewhah* at one-twenty-five RU, plus or minus ten. But from the look on your face, I'm guessing that your results were better than expected."

"Somewhat."

"How much better?"

"Try zero."

"No."

"Yes."

"Zero *rewhah* with a four-input spell. That can't be. The input-output formulas don't offer any parameters that would let you get results like that. Maybe the guards froze or something and gave you errant results."

Solander was grinning so hard he thought his face would split. "I just isolated the new law. I have it—this is the thing that brings my entire new system of magic together."

"What—you mean that fantasy theory of yours that magic can be done for free, without any *rewhah*? You've been working on that for longer than I've known you and haven't gotten anywhere. If I were you, I wouldn't put too much hope into this single result; I'd be looking for the error in my instruments. Something shut down, something . . ."

Solander was shaking his head. "I'm telling you, this is it. I'm sure of it. There are things that you just know in your gut—you can feel them fall into place, you can tell when you finally get it right." He wanted to jump up and down and shout and throw things around the workroom, and go out and race up and down the corridors of the Research Center screaming, *I did it! I did it! I did it!* He felt like he could fly. Actually, if this newest approach to the formula were correct, he might be able to fly. Damn.

Borlen sighed. "You're obviously not going to listen to reason on this."

"Reasonable men never changed the world. I'm going to."

Borlen grinned at him just a little. "And *that* is why I work with you. Your modesty always leaves me in awe."

"Shut up and let me show you what I have here."

Solander spread out his sheets of equations on the main worktable along with his theory write-up and his ideas for applications, and started walking Borlen through the points.

About halfway through, Borlen suddenly caught on. "My gods, Solander. I think I see what you've done here. You've used yourself as the sacrifice, but you have eliminated any harm or offensive positions from the spells. Completely. You've developed an entirely defensive system of magic. And you can generate additional power . . ." He was running his finger across the lines of figures, squinting a little at Solander's tiny numbers. "Yes. By banding together groups of wizards who each volunteer their own power into a common pool for a common goal." He lifted his head, stared off into the distance with an odd expression on his face, and seemed to Solander to go off into his own world.

After a moment, Solander said, "What is it?"

Borlen raised a finger, a "wait a minute" sign. His eyebrows furrowed and a tiny vertical crease appeared between them. "Mmmm. If the numbers are right . . ."

"What?"

Borlen went scurrying for another sheet of paper, spread it out beside Solander's work, and said, "Application. Idea. Just a moment." He started scrawling numbers and symbols across the page, checking his work, erasing, writing more—faster than Solander had ever seen him do anything. Borlen was steady, but until that moment Solander would have said he was not built for speed. And all the while he muttered. "No . . . that wouldn't work, but maybe . . . Right. And . . . No. Damn! Need three times more power, but . . ." And then he grew very still, and very quiet, and for a moment his eyes closed. Solander watched him, fascinated. Seeing Borlen work hard was such a miracle he almost thought he ought to call a few of his fellow researchers in just to witness it, in case it never happened again. Then the eyes opened, and the hand started moving again, and in complete silence Borlen sprawled an equation across the page that showed such brilliance in concept that Solander felt a stab of envy.

"Shield," Borlen said.

Solander went over the equations. "Yes. Almost. You have the right idea, but you've missed critical inputs here . . . and here. . . ." He shook his head, amazed. "Still, for just roughing it from a raw start, you've done a real piece of work here. There's something missing. . . ." He went over Borlen's formula again. Some part of the application of the magic didn't quite fit with the system Solander had developed—it felt like a reuse of the Dragon-style magic. But Solander would find that and fix it. It was the concept of the thing that was so beautiful.

Borlen hadn't designed a shield that would merely buffer—the sort of shield that wizards always used to try to keep down the *rewhah* damage to themselves. If Solander could figure out the off bit of it, the damned thing would be impermeable to any attack, sending one hundred percent of the *rewhah* plus one hundred percent of the spell itself in a tightly focused beam straight back to the attacker: purely defensive magic with a brutally offensive kick. No doubt an attacker would be able to bleed off some of his rebounded *rewhah* onto available sacrifices, but that *rewhah* would be hunting for him specifically, and the harder he'd tried to hit the shielded parties, the harder he was going to get slammed in return. And if he hadn't calculated getting hit with his own spell . . . "The poor bastard would fry himself," Solander muttered. No normal shield had ever been able to send the attack back alongside the *rewhah*. That was simply beyond the known laws of magic. Until now.

"What poor bastard?"

"The attacker who came at this thing thinking he was attacking a normal spellshield."

"That's sort of the idea. You have a defensive magic here that actually eliminates the need for offensive magic. You're attacked, you simply send the attack back to the attacker. You huddle under your little shield and the harder they hit you, the more they hurt themselves. And you expend almost no energy." He paused. "Assuming you actually got your base theory numbers right and your new form of magic works. I mean . . . we still haven't done tests to make sure that you weren't just getting error readings on the instruments."

Solander was staring at the formula for that shield. A single person could hold off the attacks of an army of wizards and send the weight of their attacks straight back at them—and they would know nothing but that they were attacking a fierce and determined enemy. They wouldn't know that they were getting hit by their own fire.

His skin started to crawl. He tried to imagine what the Dragons would say about his self-powered spells, about his magic that did not permit attacks but only defense, that did not permit the caster to cause any harm in order to work without *rewhah,* and that required the caster to take on the *rewhah* for any harm he caused himself. And he had an unpleasant moment of clarity.

The Hars Ticlarim was an empire built on the suffering of others. It was built that way because the builders wanted it that way. They didn't want to take responsibility for their own spells. They didn't want to limit what they could do to defense, to passive positions, to things that would cause no harm. By such limitation, they would no longer be able to use magic to expand the Empire, or to keep the parts of it already acquired in line. Magic would cease to have an element of fear about it—for what wizard would use magic as a form of public punishment and torture for wrongdoers if he had to take the cost of the spell from his own flesh and blood and bones and life? What wizard would pay that price, and *then* take all of the *rewhah* from the spell he had cast onto his own body? Why would he do that, when he could channel both the power to fuel his spell and the rebound from it into caged creatures that he had convinced himself were not truly human, that he had convinced himself were mindless and of no other value to anyone—even themselves?

Who was going to overturn three-thousand-plus years of "this is the way we do things" for a system that might be morally superior but that was self-limiting and required individual sacrifice? No one, that was who.

And what was going to happen when he took this system before the Council of Dragons and said, *Hey, look, people, I just found a better way to do things, and now we can free all the Warreners and shut down all the Warrens and close down all the power stations. We won't be able to do half the things we can do right now, but . . . ?*

He could envision several outcomes to his revelation of new laws of magic—and none of them were good. The Dragons could simply ridicule him and refuse to review his work. That happened sometimes with promising theories that offered challenges to current and in-favor theories. Or they might remove him from the Dragons. Or they might accuse him of treason and exile him from the Empire.

He couldn't envision a single situation in which they would look at what he had done and say, *Solander, great work! This is what we've been waiting three thousand years for someone to discover.*

Solander turned to Borlen and said, "You know, I think the two of us need to take off for the rest of the day. Go get a drink, develop a testing schedule that we can carry out over the next few days, and just talk."

Borlen wasn't smiling. He'd caught something in Solander's tone, and suddenly he looked nervous. He nodded slowly. "I'm good for a beer. I even know a nice quiet bar with big tables where we can spread out our work and no one will bother us."

Solander started rolling up the sheets with the formulas and equations and theories on them. "Excellent. I'm buying. We can get a good night's sleep and get in here early tomorrow and hit this hard. But I want to make sure we've covered all the safeguards before we do any live testing—and I want to triple-check the equipment. If it's just a calibration error, I don't want to embarrass myself in front of the Dragons, spouting off about finding some whole new law of magic."

Borlen said, "Right, then. Let's get that beer."

They left the workroom, and as he always did, Solander sealed it. He told himself that he had to make it look like he planned to come back in the morning. He had to do everything the same as he did every day when he left. Borlen walked beside him, still looking a bit nervous. They waved to a couple of colleagues who worked with their doors opened. One called, "Knocking off early, you slackard?" and Solander managed to laugh. "Beer calleth, and methinks I must listen." He shrugged and added, "We have a huge workload tomorrow. We want to be rested before we start doing live testing."

The colleague grinned and waved him on. "The beer would be good enough reason for me. See you tomorrow."

At the access gate, the young wizard who did the workroom monitoring said, "Got something big today, eh, Master Solander?"

Solander said, "I'd like to think so. But there's always a chance that I didn't calibrate my instruments correctly—and if that's the case, I have another big nothing. Tonight we're double-checking equations so we don't accidentally fry ourselves. Tomorrow we're doing testing."

"Well, good luck to you, then. I won't see you—I have a two-day off."

Solander smiled. One lucky break, then. He nodded to the intern and he and Borlen exited through the guard portal. He felt the slight buzz as the spell slid over his skin—but he hadn't done anything wrong. Yet. He and Borlen exited safely.

As soon as they were safely in the aircar and away from the Research Center, Solander told Borlen, "We aren't going to get a beer."

"I didn't think we were, Master Solander. Something is the matter, isn't it?"

"I think so. I think we're in trouble. The question is, how much trouble are we in, and is it too late to get out of it?"

"So where are we going?"

Solander, who had the controls, frowned. "I don't know. We can't go anyplace that the Dragons routinely monitor—which means that I can't go home, and you can't go home. We can't go to any of the places we usually go."

The color drained from Borlen's face. "We're . . . we're monitored?"

"Certainly," Solander said. "We are working on the most sensitive information in the Empire. The procedures we develop, in the hands of the wrong people, could overturn the current government, could destroy lives . . . could topple the Hars Ticlarim. Three thousand years of the most magnificent civilization ever to grace the planet threatened by a few men working in secret on a few projects." Solander laughed softly. "There are probably no portions of your life that are not under constant outside scrutiny. The watchers for the Dragons of the Council have distance viewers with capabilities that exceed anything you or I might be able to get our hands on. They use secret spells, and there is one division of Research that is responsible for keeping those spells ahead of anything that anyone else can counter."

"Except maybe us," Borlen whispered.

Solander looked at him, and realization dawned. "Yes. Except maybe us. Gods-all, are we in trouble."

"You don't think they'll be happy with this new law you've discovered?"

"I think if they find out we've actually got something real, they'll have us killed. The more I think about this, and the more I consider what our work would mean to established magic, the more I think they wouldn't be satisfied with sending us to the mines, or even into the Warrens. You and I and what we know represent a threat to them."

"We *are* them."

Solander shook his head. "We *were* them. And then I discovered something that they are not going to want to use, and are definitely not going to want anyone else to use, and you added a refinement to it that I could never even have imagined. You think the Empire uses the best magical paradigms? It doesn't. It suppresses the best ones because they are so good it can't counter them. What we are taught, what we are directed to develop, are techniques that are just good enough to accomplish what needs to be done without threatening the established seats of power. And we have just jumped way outside of our bounds."

Borlen leaned back in his seat and covered his face with his hands. "Why were you working on non-*rewhah* magic?"

"I thought it was important. And I was thinking about it from a power-usage standpoint. I had never even considered military applications. But the first thing you came up with, after looking at my work for practically no time, was a military application. If you could use my theory to develop that, so could someone else." He glanced over at Borlen, who even in the midst of this disaster took the time to look offended. "You're brilliant, Borlen—but you aren't the only brilliant research intern around."

They were down off the Aboves, cruising along the back streets of a district of the city that Solander did not know well. It was a pretty part of the city, he thought. A lot of trees, a lot of fountains, an old air to it that made him think of the First and Second Dynasties. Because the buildings were all of mages' whitestone, they hadn't aged—they might have been three thousand years old, or three. But they had ornaments on the archwork, and decorative, lacy spires far out of the current sleek architectural fashion.

Wraith had mentioned putting a theater in one of the oldest districts of the city. Solander wondered if it could be anywhere close.

He'd fallen out of touch with Wraith. They'd both gone their own ways—Wraith had fallen away from the Aboves and the people who inhabited it, and Solander had found most of his life sequestered not just in the Aboves, but in the few rooms of the Research Center that offered the equipment and space that he needed for his work. Once in a while Solander would go to one of Wraith's plays and speak to him afterward, but Wraith seemed to have let go of his dream of freeing the Warreners from their prison. Truth be told, Solander hadn't given it much thought, either.

But Wraith would have an idea of what to do, Solander thought. Because Wraith had to constantly pretend to be someone he was not, he had never lost that edge of wariness that kept him alive. He produced his plays, he made his money, he did whatever it was that he did in his spare time—but he had never made the mistake of thinking the Empire existed to serve him or help him. Wraith had always considered the Dragons of the Council and the Hars Ticlarim evil. He had never lost that image of them, and so he had never relaxed.

He would be able to tell Solander what to do. Wraith would have some ideas for how Borlen and Solander could disguise the importance of what they'd discovered; or perhaps he might be able to suggest some method by which the two of them could safely disappear.

Solander started actively looking for the theater. Wraith might not be there—probably wouldn't, really. He had three theaters in the city and a number of other business interests now. But someone at the theater would know how to find him quickly, and that was the thing that mattered most to Solander at that moment.

He saw a cluster of well-dressed women standing in front of a large building talking, and pulled the aircar to the curb. "Do any of you know where the playhouse is? The one where Gellas Tomersin presents the plays of Vincalis?"

Several of them giggled, and one walked to the aircar. "I'll take you and your friend there . . . for a price," she said. She gave him a sultry smile, and Solander realized that he had chosen just the wrong group of women to query. "And I can give you two a wonderful experience on the way."

Borlen flushed pink all the way to the tips of his ears. Solander felt the collar of his tunic constricting around his neck. "I'll . . . um, pay for the directions," he said, "but I don't . . . ah . . . we aren't . . ."

She laughed. "You really aren't, are you? I thought you boys had come up with an interesting new line."

Solander shook his head, for the moment speechless.

"You don't need to pay me." She smiled again, and this time it was a real smile, and rather pleasant. "Straight down this road, cross two intersections, turn left, it's on the left. Easy to find." She shrugged. "But the play they're doing right now isn't one of his best. It's the new one. *Girl of the Winter City*. It felt kind of . . . I don't know. Cynical. I think he's sort of lost the heart that made his early work so good."

Solander thanked her and drove off, bemused. Whores as theater critics. He supposed he shouldn't be surprised. Wraith had been writing for everyone, and it seemed everyone had seen something of his at one time or another. His popularity was the reason the city could support three theaters that rotated his plays through them at regular intervals.

Luercas returned home late, and found the servants scurrying around like panicked ants in an anthill just stirred by a stick.

"What's going on?" he asked.

"We can't find the stolta," one of the servants said. "She left this morning—she told the cook she would be gone briefly and gave a list of the meal items for the day. She did not tell Dorsea where she planned to go. And then she did not come back. The Payswi two-seater is missing. But none of her things are gone. We've heard nothing from her all day. And we have been scouring the house for a note, or a message, or anything that might tell us what happened to her. We fear she might have been . . . injured." He averted his eyes from Luercas at that last word, and Luercas understood. The servants feared that *he* had somehow done away with his wife.

Luercas nodded. He did not let his fury show; no matter what they might be thinking of him or what they might believe he was capable of, good servants were hard to come by, and some of these had been with his family for most of their lives. He valued them. He said, "Do not worry about her. She is thoughtless and erratic, but I am sure she has come to no harm. She does things without considering the consequences or who she might inconvenience. She didn't mention any plans to me today, but then, she rarely does what she should." He waved a hand in dismissal. "Call off your search. I'll take care of this personally. And . . . thank you, Otryn. I will not hold any of the staff responsible for my vowmate's thoughtless behavior. Please pass that on to them for me."

Otryn nodded and faded out of the way.

Luercas considered the beating he'd given her the night before. He'd outdone himself, really. He usually tried to keep most of the marks from showing—inflicting deep and lasting pain, but making sure she could not gain sympathy for it by showing her injuries, had a better effect than leaving cuts and bruises that might encourage the staff to pity or support her—but she had utterly incensed him and he had let his anger loose. He'd wanted to crush her.

He stared down at the floor. Actually, most of the time he was beating her, he had wanted to kill her. And last night he'd come close to doing it. He took a slow breath and stared at his hands—at the scrapes on his knuckles that he'd left in place to remind himself of how close he'd come to doing something he wouldn't be able to take back.

He hated Velyn. He hated her tawdriness, her dreadful, embarrassing past, her fascination with the lower classes. How she, who had been born to the highest and the best that life had to offer, could have ever bedded the long list of chadri, mufere, and parvoi ground-grubbers—not to mention her horrifying tendency to take up with family members—was a source of both bewilderment and irritation to him. The only acceptable man he'd ever been able to find among her long list of conquests was Gellas Tomersin; and Luercas hated Gellas more than he hated the nonstolti.

But for all Luercas's hatred of her, he could not lay blame for his violence entirely on her.

In the past years, he had been subject to terrible rages; he had allowed himself to be violent with Velyn, but he had felt an equal fury for the wizards with whom he worked, for the councilors on the Dragon Council who cowered in fear of taking progressive action, for complete strangers who inconvenienced him or did things he did not like.

Luercas did not think that the rages came from him. While he had always had a short temper, he had never been subject to violent and even murderous impulses until he acquired the stolen body. Only a few days after he had finally been released from the horrible travesty of a body in which the accident had trapped him, he had fallen into a fit of blinding rage and broken the neck of one of the inept, stupid servants in the house of the healer whose guest he had been. That had been an unpleasant and expensive fiasco. And since then, those rages had only gotten worse and more frequent.

Luercas believed his true body was trying to get him back into it, and that the lovely body he had stolen wanted to creep back to its rightful soul, and he lived in fear. He felt the tug of his true flesh pulling him toward the Warrens—toward the place where he had hidden the scarred monstrosity he had cast aside, and the soul he had wrongfully trapped in the prison he had escaped.

At night sometimes he woke to find that he had sleepwalked toward the door, toward the Warrens. He dreaded the time when someone should come upon him and catch him at this sleepwalking, and wonder what demons might possess his soul that could drive him to such disturbed behavior. He promised himself that he would never inhabit another body that did not truly belong to him. He could not think of any manner in which he might acquire a body that could truly belong to his soul—he would never take back that scaly, horned nightmare in which he had been encased for so long. But . . .

But he frightened himself. He seemed less and less in control of himself. The body wanted to murder, strangle, torture, destroy. The body. He was its victim, he decided. And it used him, and would continue to use him, until he got rid of it. That was it. He had acquired an evil body. He needed to find a way to get one that had no taint of evil in it.

He closed his eyes, and leaned against the cool whitestone wall, and listened to the soothing hum of the house, the soft chiming that all such houses made when the wind played over them. He was stolti. He had power and wealth and freedom; he had his native intelligence, his fine education; he had the strength of character to control both himself and the people around him. He had to accept the fact that he could not control Velyn, however. He'd spent the last three years trying to convince himself that sooner or later she would learn to obey him and would understand that he was in charge. But she did not. She would not.

So he needed to put her aside—but in a fashion that would not jeopardize his fortunes, that would make her clearly the party at fault. Since he did not wish to murder Velyn—well, since he did not wish to be punished for murdering Velyn, or to have to pay the massive fines and punitive damages he would have to pay were he to take that rash action—he would decide on some more palatable method of getting her out of his life.

First thing in the morning, he would speak to an associate who knew useful people. One of those people would certainly be able to help him.

Chapter 14

Wraith wished he could have pawned Velyn off on one of his associates, but this part of his plan for helping her escape from Luercas he had to carry out himself. He had to be seen as the one who dispassionately brought her before the justice system of the Hars and asked that she be given justice. Since she had involved him in her unhappy situation, his willingness to follow legal precedent would be his only alibi when she disappeared. Why would he take her before the justices of the Grand Court if he intended to help her disappear?

So he walked beside her into the House of the Landimyn's Justice, and led her through the maze of broad, ornate old corridors to the Court of the Family. And there he presented her to an old man whom he had known since he was a boy in the Artis household—a man who now called him from time to time to ask for tickets, better seats, and special favors. Wraith called in the first of his debts.

"You bring this woman before the court in what capacity?" the old man asked him privately.

Wraith sighed. "She and I were childhood friends, and she was once my lover. I asked her to take vows with me, and she refused me, so I put her aside. I had not heard from her since, except on the day she took vows with someone else. But today she appeared in my office, looking like this and begging me to help her. Out of old obligation, I am helping her out."

"You had no hand in her situation, either as the man who beat her or as the man over whom her vowmate beat her?"

"My conscience is clear, Sveth. Hire whomever you will to search out the secrets of my life; I have not seen her in three years. Today's visit has been a disruption and an inconvenience—but I once had feelings for her. I would not see her hurt like this again."

The judge nodded. "Very well. I would not have thought otherwise, but I had to ask."

He sent Wraith back to a seat and called Velyn forward. Wraith could not hear what they said, but he could see Velyn's shoulders shaking as she sobbed. Could see her holding out her battered hands, moving aside bits of her clothing to show a cut or a bruise. He could tell how effective her presentation was because of the increasingly stunned expression on the judge's face.

Finally the judge asked her to step onto the verifier, a small raised cube with a dais set in front of it. He murmured the spell that started the verification process. On the dais in front of her physical self, a second Velyn appeared, this time with Luercas. Luercas's expression belonged to a madman. Wild-eyed, his face red with fury, his lips curled back from his teeth, he forced her into a corner. He drew a knife, and with the fingers of his free hand wrapped around her throat, he began to cut her with the knife—little, shallow cuts on her arms and her neck that bled freely. He cut her shirt away, and began drawing bloody lines across her breasts and belly. The whole time, he was calling her his beloved, his darling vowmate, the joy of his life—but in a voice that made Wraith shudder.

"Enough," the judge said when Luercas jammed the knife into a conveniently close chair back and began to smash his fist into her face, her chest, and her belly, over and over. The image vanished, and the real Velyn slumped to the floor, burying her face in her hands and sobbing.

The judge and Wraith exchanged horrified looks. The judge called Wraith forward again and said, "I will issue an edict of nullification of vows, with a rider of failure to abide by the terms of the contract written against her vowmate. That's what I can do, but it won't be enough. She left without money, and I cannot permit her to return to that house for any reason, under any circumstances. She'll need a place to stay, funds, medical assistance—"

"I've taken care of that already. My personal healer will attend to her injuries. One of my staff members will take her to an excellent boardinghouse. Others of my staff will stand guard over her, to make sure that Luercas does not manage to find a way to finish what he started."

The judge nodded. "And what of you?"

Wraith glanced over at Velyn and shrugged. "I will make sure she is well taken care of, that she is safe and does not want. But I have moved on with my life. She will find someone else eventually, or perhaps not. In either instance, I'm out of her life."

The judge looked from her to him, back to her, and settled on staring off into the distance between the two of them.

"What would you say, then?" Wraith asked, just as Velyn asked, "Why do you stare that way? It's . . . horrible."

The judge seemed not to hear either him or her—and then suddenly he was back with them again, looking from one to the other. "Velyn," he said, "you are not to contact Wraith again. He may seek you out if he has reason to do so, but because of the danger that association with you may pose to him, you are to remain well away from him at all times."

Wraith nodded, satisfied. He gave the judge the name and the reservation information for the fine suite in the boardinghouse he had obtained for her. He informed the judge that he had paid for the first week, and that if she had not come to some accommodation with her circumstances by the time that week ended, he would be sure she would have another week paid. The judge carefully wrote out and gave to one of his junior wizards the injunction against Luercas that placed full blame for the incident on him and dissolved Luercas's and Velyn's vows, with severe prejudice against Luercas. And both of them turned to Velyn.

"My healer will be waiting for you in your rooms when you get there," Wraith said. "You'll have everything you need—food, money, shelter, the best care I can find for you, and good guards who will ensure your safety. Please accept my assistance until you are able to care for yourself."

"You're not going to let me stay with you?" Velyn asked. "You could be sure I was safe, but you're going to shunt me off to some shoddy suite of rooms in the Belows, and leave me there while you just go on with your life?"

Wraith looked at her steadily. This was the reaction he expected, and in a perverse way it pleased him. She was doing exactly what he needed her to do to clear him of any complicity in all that would come later. "Yes," he said. "I have forgiven you for not wanting me, and for not loving me. You chose, and you did not choose me—and I have learned to live with that. But I do not wish to have my heart broken again, nor do I wish to die on your behalf in some ill-fated attempt to spare you from your vowmate's ire. You will be safe in the care of qualified guards. Luercas will not touch you—I swear to that."

"But don't you love me?"

Wraith looked at her and calmly and with all the sincerity he could put into his voice told the biggest and most awful lie of his life. "No."

He sent her on her way, and then returned to his office to construct his alibi for the rest of the evening and perhaps the next day.

*   *   *

Solander had made himself at home in Wraith's office, over the nervous protests of the secretary or assistant or whatever she was that he would be more comfortable in the lounge, and so was sitting on the windowsill admiring the view out the huge old window when Wraith walked through the door.

Poor Wraith looked so shocked that—in spite of his problems—Solander almost laughed.

"Sol?"

"I thought I'd drop by and say hello." Solander didn't want to discuss anything sensitive with Wraith in the office, which he knew the Dragons, with their special distance viewers, would be able to observe. "Actually, I have a colleague with me, and I thought I would invite you out to dinner."

Wraith started to turn him down—Solander could see the words forming—and then the oddest look crossed Wraith's face. A secret little smile, there in an instant and then gone; and Wraith said, "I'd love to go to dinner with you and your colleague. We can talk about old times, or I can tell you about the theaters I'm building in four other major cities right now. I have all evening." That strange smile grew broader. "In fact, I know the perfect place. It's a bit crowded, but the food is a miracle, and the service is flawless. My treat." He leaned out the door and said, "Cancel my appointments for the rest of today—reschedule as necessary. My old friend Solander Artis has invited me to dinner, and I've decided to take him and his colleague to the Abundant Harvest."

"But what about—" the assistant started to ask, but Wraith made a quick, sharp movement that silenced her. "We'll probably be out all night. I have a sudden lust for good food, great wine, and a long night of talking."

Her "Yes, Master Gellas, of course" sounded strained to Solander.

Odd and odder. What did Wraith have going on? Not as much as Solander and Borlen did, certainly.

Solander picked up Borlen from the lounge, and the three of them walked out of the theater and down the street. This theater was, to Solander's surprise, in a well-kept and busy neighborhood. Little shops and restaurants lined the main street, and well-dressed couples wandered along the walkways looking into windows at exotic imports, fine silks, elegant leathers, and other expensive goods. Some of the things he saw as they strolled toward Wraith's choice of eatery looked as fine as anything that could be obtained from the private designers of the stolti. The lower classes in this part of the Belows seemed not much different from the stolti; Solander knew that fact should neither shock nor bother him, but somehow it did. Wraith wasn't truly stolti, nor was Jess—but they were different. They'd been brought up stolti.

When they reached the restaurant, Solander discovered that Wraith's comment about it being crowded had been complete understatement. A line came out the door and halfway around the block. But Wraith ignored the line. Instead, he walked alongside it, and the people waiting to eat waved to him and shouted his name.

The man who stood at the elegant desk just inside saw Wraith as he walked up the stairway, and rose and came out to greet him. "Master Gellas, you honor us with your presence. You don't come nearly as often as we would like to see you. And these are your dining companions tonight?"

Wraith nodded. "Thank you, Wyn. Just the three of us. Have you a table?"

"For you? Always. My mate told me the next time I saw you that I was to thank you for the seats you got for her and her sister—she said it was the first time in years that the two of them managed to spend a pleasant evening together, and she credits you."

"My pleasure. Deera is a lovely lady. I was only too happy to help her out."

"She has a cousin," the greeter said, leading them into a wide and well-appointed dining room, "a stunning young woman who has just completed her education in Arim. Shanit finished in literature and hopes to become a modern playwright in the style of Vincalis—and she's both witty of speech and charming of manner. She's not promised to anyone yet—and Deera says if you do not find a vowmate soon, you shall wither away like a raisin, and that will be a tragedy worthy of your friend Vincalis."

Wraith laughed. "Promise her that I shall not wither. I may be alone, but I am not lonely. She must not worry on my account. But, as hard as I work and as much as I'm away, I fear any vowmate but my theaters would find me sadly wanting."

The greeter said, "Deera told me you would find a way to avoid this introduction, too. Well, you may be a wise man. For all of Deera's many charms, there are times when I miss the life of the bachelor." He smiled and showed them through a door into a dining room where they could be seen by everyone on the main floor, but not heard. "Your table, Masters. One of the staff will be with you shortly to recommend something to your taste from the night's specialties. In the meantime, I'll have the winemaster come right over."

And then he was gone.

"Is it always like this?" Solander asked.

"You mean the admirers, the best tables, the special service?"

"Yes."

"Yes," Wraith said. "Sometimes more so. They don't make much of a fuss over me here, and they always let me have a table away from the main room so that I can eat without people constantly asking me if they can get tickets, if the person with me is the great Vincalis, if I might look at something they've written and see if I'd consider producing it . . . *especially* that last. I think there isn't a soul in Oel Artis who doesn't harbor a secret desire for being a playwright."

Solander was, for just an instant, deeply envious. He thought it would be wonderful to be so beloved by strangers, to be so widely recognized and so fawned over and pampered. And then he tried to imagine taking a woman someplace, hoping to have a romantic meal with her, and having instead to smile and engage in endless conversations about his private life with complete strangers—and suddenly he did not feel envious at all. In fact, "I'm sorry," he said. "That must get quite wearing."

Wraith shrugged. "If the plays were not reaching them, they would not even notice me."

"But are they? Reaching them? The way you . . . hoped they would, I mean?"

Wraith's glance flicked from Solander to Borlen and back to Solander, and he managed a small, strained smile. "Vincalis has given me good material. Some of it gets through, I think. Most of the audience doesn't look any deeper than the surface, of course. We tell a joke, they laugh; we send a lovely girl to her tragic death and they weep. They don't look beneath the story for the meaning of it all. But . . . a few people in every crowd walk away with a thoughtful look on their faces."

Borlen said, "I've seen several of your plays. I've been lucky enough to get tickets for some wonderful performances—even if I didn't get particularly good seats. I always wanted to ask Vincalis—does he mean to imply some danger in the general use of magic, or is that just something that I misunderstood?"

Wraith smiled at Solander and said, "See? Some people pay more attention than others." He shrugged. "What Vincalis means in what he writes, I don't know for certain. I've never so much as met him, much less had the opportunity to talk with him about his intent or philosophy. I know what the plays mean to me, and I'm satisfied with that. I think every viewer has to find his own meaning in them."

"I think he's fairly clear in some of his work, and I think that's . . . rather brave of him—and you, too, for producing such dangerous plays, of course—suggesting some flaw in one of the keystones of the Empire." Borlen rested his elbows on the table and leaned forward. "Or perhaps it's simply foolhardy."

Wraith frowned. "As I said, you would have to ask him what he means by his work. I know he has never said anything that was blatantly anti-Empire; I would not have produced it if he had. Still, as a citizen of the Empire, I don't think anyone who understands the complete cycle of Dragon magic can do anything *but* question the way magic is used here. The . . . the cost of magic is too high, and the use of it too profligate."

Solander winced. "This is one conversation I would really rather not have tonight," he said softly. "I have much that I would discuss with you, but not your politics, Wraith."

"Wraith?" Borlen asked.

"A silly boyhood nickname," Solander said, feeling heat rise to his cheeks. He had not made such a careless mistake in years—but then, he had not felt himself in such dangerous straits in years.

He had to tell Wraith why he had really come to see him. He was going to have to lay out his final success, and his realization that success was much worse for him than failure—and Wraith was going to tell him, *I told you so.*

But Wraith still might be able to help. They'd grown so far apart—and Wraith had achieved such stature on his own since—that Solander couldn't really claim a favor for debts owed. He could only appeal to an old friendship that had fallen by the wayside, and hope that Wraith might be able to see a way clear of his dilemma.

He glanced at Borlen and nodded, and the two of them whispered in unison the final two words that cast a small, sound-blocking version of the shield Borlen had devised earlier that day. Nothing visible happened, but Solander could feel the bubble swirl to life around the three of them. Wraith frowned and said, "*Now form?* What does that mean? Or have to do with anything?"

"We have to talk quickly. If they're watching us, and I'm sure they are, they'll notice the sound drop-out on their distance viewers and have an agent arrive in person to see what the problem might be. I need to drop the shield before anyone can do that."

Wraith stared at him, and Solander could see the moment when comprehension hit. "The Dragons are watching you. Us. But you've done something so that they can't hear what we say."

Solander nodded.

"Talk, then. But be fast, because there's more going on tonight than you can imagine, and I dare not lose my alibi of being in a public place with friends."

Solander did not question this; he knew Wraith would not answer him, and they had little time.

Quickly, he explained how the final pieces of his new form of magic had fallen into place, and how Borlen, looking at the formulas, had devised a shield that would serve as its own weapon, and then he told Wraith why he thought the Dragons would have him quietly killed if they found out about his new magic.

Wraith considered the dilemma only a moment. Then he said, "If it doesn't work, you have no problem, right?"

"Of course. But it does work."

Wraith said, "Not anymore, it doesn't. You change a few essential parameters in your formulas so that they will fail. You go in tomorrow, calibrate all of your equipment as you said you were going to do, bring a slew of your colleagues in to observe your tests—and then fail miserably."

"We'll look like idiots," Borlen muttered. "We'll lose our prime workrooms, we might lose our patronage—"

Solander was grinning, though. "No, no. We'll be fine. We announce preliminary and questionable results, state that the more we think about it, the more we think we were getting artifact, bring in the tester group to help do the calibration and double-check our results, and *then* we fail miserably. If we go in skeptical, state ahead of time that we are expecting no results, and then test with no results as the likely outcome, we'll be doing what ninety percent of the other Dragons . . ." A thought occurred to him. Chilled him, actually.

He glanced at Borlen. Then at Wraith. Wraith, he thought, had jumped to the same idea, because the corner of his mouth was twitching in a suppressed smile. Borlen looked blank—but then, Borlen didn't have a devious mind.

"I'm guessing at least some of the 'dead results' I ended up signing off on were successes that the discoverers didn't dare report."

Wraith said, "I'm guessing that many of your colleagues are developing all sorts of fascinating technology at the Empire's expense, and then hiding the results to sell off the record."

"That's not a good thing to know," Solander said softly.

"It would be a wise thing to forget," Wraith agreed. "And it would be wise, also, to stop silencing our conversation. I have a feeling you might not have much more time."

Solander did not turn his head, but looked out of the corner of one eye at the front entry. He caught the movement of robes—an upper-level Dragon, by the colors, one who would get his choice of tables.

Solander dissolved the shield with a whisper and said, "And then she told me that she wanted to have a dozen children, and that was the end of *that* relationship. I could imagine fathering one. Maybe. But a dozen?"

Wraith laughed. "I've managed to avoid romance, too."

"I don't want to avoid romance," Solander said. "But there aren't very many women out there who are . . . who are Jess. You know?"

Wraith smiled. "Only the one, I should think. She seems to be doing quite well. The last I heard, she'd bought out her partner and had gone on tour in Arim as manager for one of her orchestras."

Solander said, "Oh. Maybe I shouldn't even mention this, but I've heard some strange things about Velyn lately. About her and Luercas, I mean. Things that . . . ah, drift up the stairs from the servants' quarters, if you know what I mean."

Wraith looked down at his hands and sighed heavily. "She came to see me today," he said.

"Velyn? You jest."

"No. Luercas had beaten her. Badly. Tried to kill her. I took her to see a judge friend of mine, and she gave spelled testimony, and on the basis of it, my friend dissolved their contract with prejudice. Luercas is going to owe Velyn and her family major reparations. I suspect it will get . . . ugly."

"With the temper he has, I suspect you're right." Solander tried to figure out Wraith's angle on all of this—Wraith still sat there staring at his hands as if they'd suddenly done something fascinating, like twin themselves. It wasn't like Wraith to say anything without looking his listener in the eye, and Solander thought he kept his head down this time because he was hiding something. But what? The fact that he still had feelings for Velyn? Anyone who truly knew him knew he still loved her.

"Considering your past history with her, I'm surprised you involved yourself."

"I didn't have much choice," Wraith said, looking up and straight into his eyes. He looked hurt, but not evasive. Well . . . maybe his hands really had been doing something interesting. "She was waiting for me in my office when I went in today. Rather like you, actually, except she looked like a rag trampled by a mob. I couldn't just turn her away, in spite of the fact that I suspect Luercas will come looking for me."

"I wouldn't want to have him after me," Borlen said. "I've heard some terribly nasty things about him lately."

Wraith said, "I helped her, I paid for bodyguards and a room for her, and I sent her on her way. I don't have a place for her in my life; I have no wish to have my heart broken again, and that seems to be what she's best at. So I gave her the help I could."

Solander didn't believe what he was hearing. "And that's it? She comes to you, surely hoping that she can correct the mistake she made when she took vows with Luercas, and you give her a room and some protection and kick her out of your life?"

"Yes. It seems to me to be the best thing I can do, for her and me." Softly, he added, "Especially for me."

"And that's why you were hiding your eyes. You feel guilty." Solander leaned back in his padded chair and stared at his old friend. "And you *should* feel guilty. Good gods! If Jess came to me and asked me to take her back, I would in a second. I wouldn't have to think about it. If you love someone—"

Wraith held up a hand. "You didn't want to discuss my politics, I don't want to discuss my love life. Not even a little bit. She's safe, she's out of my life, and that's the way I want it."

Solander shrugged. The three of them sat at the table, looking everywhere but at each other, until the silence grew agonizing. Finally, Solander said, "I suppose we should pay the bill and be on our way. Borlen and I have to check the work on our formulas before we go in tomorrow to present our findings. I'm not at all comfortable with what we have—I'm suspecting errors. But I got some strange readings on our equipment today, so I feel that I really must request observers."

Wraith nodded. "If you must be going, I understand. I'm heading back to the playhouse. We've been working long hours on a new production, and my set director, my score writer, my choreographer, and I have been staying at the theater nights to put all the pieces together. I haven't been home in days."

"You're headed back there?"

"We aren't even close to finishing our work." Wraith raised a finger, and one of the waiters hurried over to see what he needed. "We'll be leaving now."

"Yes, Master Gellas. The owner has instructed me to tell you that you and your friends were our guests tonight. I hope you will have a pleasant evening."

Wraith rose. "Please tell Daymin that I cannot permit him to pick up every check. Next time, I'll expect the bill. And in the meantime, I'll send him some good tickets to my newest work."

The waiter smiled and bowed. "I'll tell him."

Jess had long given up listening to the wild rumors she heard about Wraith. He seemed to attract attention to himself the way high places attracted lightning; she'd learned not to put much faith in any of the wild tales people whispered in her ear about the eccentric Master Gellas. Yet something about this latest rumor set her teeth on edge, and sent little shudders of apprehension scurrying down her spine.

She leaned against the park bench and stared out at the grassy glade; people walked arm in arm along the edge of an artificial lake, their heads dipping and bobbing as they talked, as if they were somehow bound to the swans that swam in the lake's center. Her young assistant, Patr, paid no attention to her change in mood or her sudden cautious silence. In between bites of his steaming benjor, a long hard roll filled with cooked pickled cabbage, three types of spiced meat, and a half dozen melted cheeses, he continued his tale. "So then Buelin says that Gellas is supposed to have garnered this private army of his through his theaters, where he's using magic to control the patrons' minds and seduce them into his clutches. And his actors are supposed to be some sort of subhuman creatures who wear their costumes to hide their monstrous true natures."

"Ridiculous," Jess said.

"Isn't it? But Buelin has heard several variations of the tale, and the main points that each version agree on are that he's raising his own private army to overthrow the Empire, that he's hiring outcasts or freaks of some sort as his actors, and that he's controlling the minds of his audiences and making them do things they would not otherwise do."

Jess laughed, but it came out sounding rather strangled. "Why would people say such things? Gellas is a . . . a treasure of the Empire. I've heard he is to be given the Star of the Hars Ticlarim. He single-handedly revived interest in live theater—people actually go to watch the plays now, which I don't believe they'd done for a hundred years. He's brought forth something wonderful, and now there are a hundred playwrights working to emulate what his discovery of Vincalis has done—to create new, living forms of theater instead of just copying over and over the static form that served for centuries."

Around a huge bite of his meal, Patr laughed. "And there, I think, is your answer. Don't you suppose the Masters of Literature—all those vile old covil-ossets who held the field all to themselves for centuries, and who dictated what was and what was not a play—are furious to find themselves shoved into a corner and relegated to a position of irrelevance? Don't you think they resent being shown up? Being made fools of?" Patr took a seat on the bench where she rested her foot, and balanced the remains of his benjor on his knees while he tried to remove the stopper from the disposable flagon of beer he'd purchased from the vendor. "If I were looking for creators of rumors, the jealous old Masters would be the first to whom I'd look."

Which would have been good advice, Jess thought, and something that would have allowed her to put Patr's recitation of the rumors behind her as mere vengeful gossip—except that, last she had heard, Wraith *did* want to overthrow the government, or at least overthrow the way that it used magic; and he did hire outcasts as actors, even if they were fully human; and he did try to change the way his audiences looked at their world, even if he didn't cheat by using magic. There was more truth to the rumor than she dared to discount; for all the trappings of hysteria and nonsense, someone had gotten the core of the story right.

That suggested a traitor, to Jess.

She watched the Arimese men and women who had come out to enjoy the unseasonably lovely day; she watched the swans. She tried to tell herself that Wraith would be fine, that rumors meant nothing, that his position as a beloved presenter of popular entertainment created by the most reclusive genius in the Empire would save him from anyone who would want to hurt him. A traitor, though, might know more about Wraith than his plans.

Jess considered her schedule, which would keep her out of Oel Artis for another five months, touring Arim, Tartura, and Benedicta. Chances were good that these rumors would lead to nothing; if she returned to Oel Artis to talk with Wraith, she would be inconveniencing herself and her plans, and probably inconveniencing Wraith as well, and with nothing to show for it but a discussion of a story that both of them could easily dismiss as silliness.

She walked away from the bench, down to the water's edge. The delicate spires of the heart of the city of Granorett rose before her, reflecting in the lake like gold-tinged daggers. She had come on this tour to see the world; she'd spent so much of her time working that she had almost forgotten about the wonders that existed beyond Oel Artis. She'd thought nothing could compare to the grand old city with its magical Aboves and stunning, historic Belows. But she'd been wrong.

Every single place she'd gone had offered her something wonderful, a new world, a new way of looking at herself and the people around her, new vistas, new customs, new languages. Music spoke to everyone, and she'd met people she would cherish for the rest of her life. If, at that moment, someone told her that she could never go back to Oel Artis, she would have shrugged and spread her hands in a gesture that encompassed the rest of Matrin. She'd seen almost nothing; she could not imagine what wonders awaited her on each breaking morn.

If she went back to Oel Artis now, she would be walking away from . . . everything.

Yet she owed Wraith her life. She owed Wraith her ability to look at Granorett and wonder at its beauty. Without him, she would have been a caged and insensate prisoner, living fuel without even the sanctity of a soul that she could call her own. How could anyone ever repay a debt that great?

By going home, she thought. By making up some spurious excuse and returning to Oel Artis, and finding a reason to meet with Wraith alone for a few minutes, and passing him the information that he might need to start looking for a traitor within his own ranks. She owed him her soul—her chance at eternity in whatever form it might take. The vast and varied wonders of Matrin would wait for her return.

A week, she thought. A week to return, create some business that would require her to sit down in conference with Wraith and pass him a note that he could then destroy, cover that meeting with a flurry of other, seemingly equally important meetings with other creative and business people, and then she could rejoin the Live Classics Orchestra. The orchestra, in a week, would have traveled to Bastime, in the southern Arimese Islands. She'd miss two cities, Winehall and Saviay. They would still be there when she was ready to revisit them—and when she did get the chance to tour them, she would do so with a clear conscience.

Two weeks. Sixteen days. She owed that to Wraith, for giving her the world.

A girl came into Wraith's office without knocking at seven-and-forty by Dark, and said, "Ah. I thought this was the jakes. I must have taken a wrong turn out in the corridors." She turned and left without another word, and Wraith looked after her for a moment, bemused. He had never seen her before, yet at some level she worked for him. She had given him the code phrase that stated that Velyn had been successfully kidnapped away from her boardinghouse and hidden with members of Wraith's anti-magic underground. She had to be a member of that underground, and the fact that he had never seen her before and might never see her again vaguely disturbed him. It had grown past him— more people belonged now than he could know. They'd spread beyond Oel Artis to other Harsian cities, and no one person knew who they all were or where they all were. Not even him, though at the beginning he could have said with confidence that he knew every single person who had joined him, by name and face and even history.

Perhaps this meant that the movement was a success, even though not a single Warrener had yet been freed. Undergrounders sabotaged magic-channeling installations; inserted messages and dimensionals that showed life in the Warrens and the horrible conditions of the captive sacrifices held prisoner there into public broadcasts; ran businesses that didn't use magic or trade with people who did; and a hundred other things that were slowly, slowly reshaping little pieces of the Empire.

Perhaps freedom for the Warreners would not happen in his lifetime, Wraith thought. Perhaps he had to resign himself to the fact that what he was doing was working, but with glacial slowness—and that maybe that was the best he could hope for.

Souls were dying, though—being erased as completely as if they had never been, and not just from one lifetime, but from the whole span of eternity. That knowledge kept prodding him to find a way to do more, to bring the situation to a head. The Empire had to stop using human beings as fuel. He alone could move anywhere without fear of magical reprisal; that made him not just the best choice but the only choice to bring about change. When he grew too old, or when he died, who could carry on what he left undone?

No one. No one else like him existed.

So he could not let himself find comfort in the fact that people were becoming more aware. He only had one lifetime to accomplish his work, and far too much remained undone.

He rested his head on his desk, using his forearms as a pillow.

Why couldn't he be ten men, or a thousand? Why did the weight of uncounted hundreds of thousands of souls rest on his shoulders alone? Why had the gods singled him out?

His eyes drifted closed, and his last conscious thought was that if the gods wanted everything done immediately, they should have made more of him, or made him impervious to exhaustion.

Chapter 15

Velyn paced from one side of her tiny room to the other. Healed, fed, bathed, and wearing bizarre new clothes and with newly colored and cut hair, she didn't look like the same woman who had gone to Wraith for help. She didn't feel like the same woman, either. She'd thought he would help her—give her shelter in his home, protect her from Luercas, fight for her. Instead, he had passed her off to strangers, and those strangers had passed her off to other strangers who had pretended to kidnap her in order to remove any taint of liability for her vanishing from Wraith's famous and oh-so-pure hands.

He'd dumped her without even asking her how she felt about being dumped. Oh, he'd asked her how she felt about the Warreners, about the Empire's use of magic, about Luercas and all he stood for, about her own patterns of magic use, about whether any of the things she'd professed to care about back when they had been together had truly mattered to her.

She'd told him what he wanted to hear, because she'd thought all those questions meant he wanted to take her back. That he wanted *her*.

She was a fool.

But she was a fool with eyes and ears and a sharp mind, and she could see what she'd fallen into. This was some portion of Wraith's underground; the movement he had dreamed about creating only those few years ago was now a reality, and one unsuspected by the Masters of the Hars. Or, if it was suspected, at least its presence remained unproved.

"Are you ready, Sister?" A young man had entered the door behind her without her noticing him. He stood there now, looking eager and trusting and full of idealism.

She put a smile on her face and said, "I am. Where are we to go, and what are we to do?"

"You'll talk with the head Brother. He'll tell you what you need to know to help you build a new life for yourself. You need never return to the people who hurt you, or to the ones who allowed you to be hurt." He smiled broadly at her. "This is a good place, Sister. You'll find much of comfort here."

She flexed her fingers, reveling in being able to move them completely and without pain for the first time in at least a year. "Comfort. Yes. I could do with comfort."

She stepped out of her cool, tiny room into a broad corridor lined on both sides with doors to dozens of identical rooms. The boy led her past people dressed in clothing of the same cut as hers—loose tunic with draped hood, fitted leggings, soft, ankle-high boots—but where her clothes were of palest green, theirs ranged from deep, vibrant ruby reds to earthy browns to jewel-tone blues to the green of the finest emeralds. All the clothes had the same cut, the same graceful draping—but she noticed that the colors tended to cluster together, with little knots of reds standing and talking in whispers, and deep greens dragging something down the hall together, and blues walking silently in the same direction, hoods up and heads lowered.

The boy, dressed in the same pale green that she wore, moved out of the way of each of the others with a quick, deferential nod of his head. Velyn did not. Whatever these people were, they were not stolti—and stolti neither moved for nor bowed to anyone.

Some of them looked at her in surprise—and each time the boy whispered, "Master Gellas's friend."

And at that, comprehension flickered in their eyes and they gave her polite little smiles and went on their way. Almost as if they were humoring her.

Beneath the fixed smile on her face, she seethed.

At the end of the long corridor, they went left. Straight ahead lay a garden with stone fountains and fixed sources of water, little paths carved through the deep shade of ancient trees, straight-backed wooden benches. Velyn thought it austere. To the right, another corridor. The path they took led them to an office, and a man dressed as Velyn and the boy were, but in gray.

"Welcome," he said, not rising from his seat. "Please, make yourself comfortable." He glanced at the boy. "Joshen, you may go now. Be back by third bell, please—I'll need your assistance." The boy nodded, smiled, and scurried out the door, closing it behind him.

All the chairs in the room were straight-backed, uncushioned, hardly created with comfort in mind. Velyn took the one farthest from the door, turned it slightly so that she could face both the desk and the door, and settled cautiously into it.

The man said, "I am Brother Atric. That is not, of course, my real name. None among the Order of Resonance keep their names; we give them up when we join, and burn our pasts."

"Hardly legal," Velyn said.

"If one does not avail oneself of the services of the Empire, it is entirely legal. We are an independent order of artists, musicians, writers, philosophers, builders, creators—some of the finest minds and greatest talents in all of Matrin reside within our walls. We offer shelter and privacy for those who create to do so free from the Empire's tendency to dictate content, form, and presentation."

"How long have you existed?" Velyn asked.

"I'll assume you mean the Order, and not me personally." He smiled a little at his joke, but did not seem in the least disconcerted when Velyn did not smile back. "The Order of Resonance has held lands in the Hars Ticlarim for over two thousand years. In Manarkas and Ynjarval, we have been around for even longer."

Velyn tried to keep her surprise from showing on her face, but knew she'd failed. She'd been sure Wraith had abducted her into the underground about which he had once spun such enthusiastic plans. Instead, he seemed to have dumped her into a well-known artists' colony.

Gods-all. He didn't even trust her enough to put her someplace where she might learn something she could use.

"How did I come to be here?" she asked. "I was in a boardinghouse, awaiting the resolution of legal actions that I took against my vowmate. Several men dressed in black kicked in my door, blindfolded me, bound my hands, and held something over my nose that smelled atrocious and I have to assume made me sleep, for my next memory is of waking in the room here, with a bath drawn for me, clothes waiting, and my hair already cut and colored pale." She sighed. "Actually, I have a good idea of *how* I came to be here. What I don't understand is why."

"You needed a place to stay, where you could be protected adequately from the considerable power and fury of your ex-vowmate. Gellas sent a messenger to me telling me that you would be arriving, and that we were to give you shelter and treat you as one of our own until he could be certain that you were no longer in danger."

"He was concerned?"

"I got the feeling that he was very concerned." The man looked at her with eyes as gray as his tunic, eyes that got lost in the creases around them when he smiled. "He said that you were the woman he had once loved, and that we were to protect you at all costs."

"Why would you do this?"

"Protect you?"

"Yes. If Luercas can figure out what happened to me, he could do terrible things to your Order. Why would you put yourselves in danger on my account?"

"Master Gellas has been tremendously generous to our Order, both in terms of financial donations and in terms of placing our actors in his plays, and utilizing our musicians and our painters and our builders and even our writers in his ongoing projects. He is our finest patron."

"That's all?"

Brother Atric laughed gently and shook his head. "We have never been a destitute order; we have resources of land, property, and creativity from which we reap a significant profit. But until Master Gellas came along, we held no center spotlight in the affairs of the world. Now we do. Now . . . now our artists and writers and dancers and actors perform before the broad spectrum of society, both in the Empire and beyond. That's more than anyone else has been able to do for us in two thousand years. To me, it seems to be enough."

"But you aren't part of Wraith's underground?"

The blank look on his face might have been feigned, but the timing of it was so perfect, so without pause or break, that she did not believe it was. Even if Brother Atric were a great actor, she did not think he could have hidden the initial flicker of awareness that she felt sure would have been there had he been in on the truth.

"Wraith?" he asked. "Underground?"

"Wraith. Master Gellas's real name. The underground is the group of people he has gathered together to overthrow the magic system in the Empire and free the Warreners."

Brother Atric's expression changed from bewilderment to horror. "You're suggesting that . . . that Master Gellas is a traitor? Do you know this to be true? Can you offer proof of his identity, or his subversive activities? Gods be damned—we cannot permit ourselves to be associated with someone who is . . . who is involved in treason."

"You didn't know anything about Wraith? About where he was from, or . . . anything?"

"If what you say is true, we will cut ourselves off from him entirely. We survive at the tolerance of the Empire. We do *not* seek its overthrow.

And what do you mean, where he's from? He's from the Aboves—from the Artis family."

"He's from the Warrens," Velyn said. "I pulled him out of there my-self, when we were both children, more or less. I was less of a child than he was, but . . ." She shrugged.

Now he was looking at her with horror. "You're a traitor, too? You admit to assisting a Warrener in escaping from the Warrens? Woman, are you mad?" He pressed the palms of his hands to his temples for a moment and closed his eyes tightly, as if his head pained him. "You know what you did as a child—I would not think to question the truth of what you say. But you cannot stay here. You . . ." He sighed and opened his eyes, and the gray of them no longer seemed warm. To Velyn, this man suddenly looked frightening.

"It was a stupid childhood prank." She shrugged, making little of it.

"And yet, if it is true, you have kept the fact of it secret as an adult—for many years, in fact. Had you confessed to your actions as a child, I doubt anyone would have held your actions against you. But by hiding your actions into adulthood, you have changed a childish prank into treason."

"Nonsense," Velyn said. But it wasn't nonsense. She'd been so sure that Brother Atric was a part of Wraith's underground that she had not considered the price she might pay were he not.

"I'll arrange transport for you," he said, standing. He pulled a plain black silk cord above his head, and out in the corridor a bell rang in clusters of four. Clang, clang, clang, clang. Clang, clang, clang, clang.

"Transport where?"

"Out of some misplaced remainder of loyalty to Master Gellas—or . . . Wraith," he said with distaste, "I will not turn you in to the Dragons. I will, instead, send you out with a troupe we have leaving for the Southern Manarkan Chain. You'll travel as a prisoner, and my people will leave you on one of the isolated islands. I suggest that you stay there. Should you ever return here, I will be forced to declare your confession to the Dragons."

"And your complicity?"

"Not at all, dear." His smile this time was cold. "I'll say that you confessed your transgressions while in the islands, and we abandoned you there immediately."

Velyn felt sick. She had no wish to go halfway around the world. No wish to be trapped on a primitive island, far from the comforts of her home. She couldn't believe that she had so misjudged the man. "And what of Wraith?" she asked.

"We will no longer associate with him. He does not need to know why. We will create a dispute over contracts—such things are easy to arrange, and can be impossible to resolve. If he is guilty of treason, his actions will reveal him soon enough."

Four large men in deep green ran into the room. "This woman, who has no name but is no Sister, is to be put into the robes of a Dispossessed and sent out with the troupe leaving today to tour the Southern Manarkan Chain. I will send orders along with her. You are not to speak with her, nor are you to permit her to speak. Use whatever means you must to accomplish this."

He looked at Velyn. "You understand what I just told them?"

Whatever means you must. Yes. Velyn understood that. She nodded, not saying a word.

Brother Atric stood. "I would wish you good luck, traitor, but you have not earned it. Rather, I wish you an end fitting with your actions."

The men marched her out of Brother Atric's office. She did not look back. She was too busy berating herself for her own stupidity for thinking she knew the game, the players, and how to make herself look like one of them.

"We sent her to Bair's Island," Brother Lestovar told Wraith.

Wraith's head ached. He sat down on the long bench in his great hall and said, "I went to a great deal of trouble to send her to *you.*"

"I know that. But in the first minutes of her conversation with Brother Atric, she mentioned the underground, referred to you as Wraith, and said that you were from the Warrens and that she was the one who had pulled you out of there. No matter whether she was trying to get us to admit to something or whether she was merely being stupid, she's more of a risk than we can keep in anyplace as high-traffic and open to the outside as Resonance House. A slip like that to the wrong ears could get her and us and you executed for treason superior."

Wraith rose and walked to his fireplace, where he had a fine little wood fire burning. He took a poker and stirred the logs and watched the sparks fly up the chimney, and he thought. "I cannot tell you how she feels about me, or what her intentions were in telling you so much that should be secret. She was quite angry with me for not giving her shelter in my home. I suspect she feels that I have treated her poorly. Perhaps she mentioned the things she did because she thought she was among friends; I can't swear to that, though, and don't know that I would believe it if someone said it to me."

"Do you want us to leave her on Bair's Island?"

Wraith thought about the woman he had once loved. After she'd been healed, she had looked unchanged from the time when he knew her. A hardness had lain behind her eyes, though—a cynicism that placed a barrier between the two of them. He could care about what happened to her; he suspected that he always would. He could love her; he seemed incapable of putting that love behind him. He would not replace her with another woman; as long as the two of them lived, he would never want someone else. But he could not want her. He could not want what she represented: something cold and shallow and conniving and dishonest. He was a fool to love her, but not such a fool that he would let his love for her destroy him.

"Bair's Island will be fine," he said. "Resonance House has a small chapter there, correct? One that can keep track of her and keep her out of trouble?"

Brother Lestovar nodded. "All that's on Bair's Island is the chapter—which is run as a village where none wear the cowl and cloak—and a collection of old ruins that keep some of our Brothers entertained. And jungle, of course. More jungle than anyone could ever hope to see. We'll make sure that she doesn't come back to haunt you or us."

"Be kind to her," Wraith said. "Make sure she has whatever she needs—food, shelter, someone trustworthy to talk to."

Brother Lestovar sighed. "We could have one of the mute Brothers—"

Wraith laughed. "No. You want someone who can tell you what she's up to. Make sure she doesn't know her friend is a Brother or a Sister." He turned away from the fire and said, "A moment." He left Brother Lestovar standing in the great hall, went into his library, and from his hidden vault pulled out enough money to cover Velyn's stay on Bair's Island for the rest of her life. He handed the cash to Brother Lestovar and said, "For her upkeep. She'll probably be quite . . . difficult. I've added a bonus to, ah, make keeping her on more palatable."

Brother Lestovar laughed. "She fought well. She impressed all of us."

Wraith didn't laugh. "I suspect she's had a lot of practice of late." He shook his head and rested a hand on Lestovar's shoulder. "Thank you for taking care of this."

"You're a friend, Wraith. The Kaan stand beside our friends."

"I'm grateful."

Lestovar—who had given up his Kaan name with his old identity and life—was a dancer, one of the best who graced the stage. Along with many other young Kaan, he'd left the village to help Wraith fight against the magic that all of them despised. When Wraith lost hope, Lestovar carried on with a conviction born of a lifetime of living free of magic. And because Lestovar's belief was never shaken, Wraith always found the strength and the hope to go on.

"I'll be on my way, then." Lestovar smiled. "Breathe easy. She'll be fine in our care—and best of all, she'll never know it's our care that she's in."

Wraith saw Lestovar to the door and closed it behind him thoughtfully. He wondered if he should put some sort of fail-safe into place; after all, Velyn had a way of turning left when everyone was sure she would turn right—and with what she knew and what she thought she knew (an even more dangerous category), she could destroy the underground if they didn't handle her correctly.

"She's simply gone," the investigator told Luercas. "We tracked her as far as a boardinghouse in the Bellhareven District; none other than Master Gellas paid for her room and her court hearing. But apparently she said something wrong, or made enemies other than you, for her rooms were broken into in the middle of the night and someone kidnapped her. A few witnesses have admitted to seeing several men dressed in dark clothing carrying a large bag that looked like it might contain a body from the room, but none of these witnesses stopped the men or questioned their activities."

"Of course not. People aren't fools—or if they are, they manage to avoid being fools when it could get them killed." Luercas sat in the central garden, the one Velyn had preferred above all others. He didn't miss her. He didn't miss the constant irritation of her presence around the place, of her voice, of her face; in truth, he didn't miss anything about her. But he'd received the judge's ruling against him, and with it an assessment of the penalties that he would be required to pay to her family. Were she not found, he was likely to be held accountable, and the penalties would be increased. So for the first time since the two of them had taken their vows, he found himself truly wanting her back.

Just for a while. Just until he could figure out a way to get the penalties that had been assessed against him reversed by a sympathetic judge. To do that, he'd have to have Velyn back in his possession—and he would have to find a way to make her look like the whole of the problem. He had no idea how he would do that, but he was certain that if he thought about it long enough, he would come up with something.

"Pay whatever you have to pay," he told the investigator. "Do whatever you have to do. But locate her, and get her back here. Check Gellas

Tomersin first—I find it strange that she should visit him and immediately thereafter disappear. Check anyone with whom he has regular contact. If you need to take on associates to follow leads, then do so. You have only a week to find her—if she isn't back here by then, I'll have to pay the penalties and any added judgments her family seeks because of her absence."

"Then you need her back here alive?"

Luercas stared at the man as if he had sprouted a second head. "Yes. Alive. Unharmed. Unscratched. Un*insulted,* even. She needs to be back here looking and feeling perfect, and if you find her in less-than-perfect condition, make sure she sees a healer on her way here. I *cannot* risk her being seen in my presence with a mark on her."

"I can do what you want. But I'm going to need a large advance. Hiring colleagues away from their own investigations will not come cheap, and considering the people I'm going to have to bribe to find out about the people you want to have watched, I'll also need cash. Lots of it. Small denominations. Silver, small gold, and perhaps untraceable paper promissories."

"Fine. You'll see Woljis on your way out. He'll have orders to give you an initial supply of money." Luercas stood up and glanced around to make sure that none of the staff was watching from indoors. "Do keep track of expenses. And don't play with the numbers. If you steal from me, you'll have the opportunity to regret it. I don't know if it will be a long opportunity or a very short, intense one. But keep in mind that you want me to . . . to like you."

The investigator nibbled at the corner of his lower lip and nodded politely. "I'll be on my way, then."

Luercas waved a hand, and into the tiny sphere of light that appeared, he said, "Woljis, give this man the money he needs to help me. Be generous." To the investigator, he said, "Follow the light. It will lead you to Woljis, wherever he might be. And remember. Eight days. Beyond that, I'll have to start looking for you."

When he got her back, he would make sure that she told him who had helped her. Then he would have his revenge, just as he would make sure that Velyn would pay for causing him public humiliation and the threat of financial distress. He stood in her little garden for a long moment, fantasizing about different ways of discrediting her, her helpers, perhaps even her family. He didn't have anything solid, but he was sure he would be able to find something. If he couldn't find it, he would create it.

Master Faregan, whose meteoric rise through the ranks of the Silent Inquest had left some envious and others nervous, sat in the anteroom of the Hall of the Triad in the Gold Building, preparing for his next promotion. The poison in his ring had not the faintest taint of magic to it, and was an excellent, slow-acting drug—whichever of the Masters who received it would not begin to show symptoms for a full day at minimum. As much as a week if he were hearty and hale.

Faregan rose as the tea boy came in bearing his tray and three cups. Faregan willed the contents of his ring into the nearest of the cups, then sat contentedly, as if waiting for an audience. The boy went into the inner chamber, and the secretary came out, his expression puzzled. "You were not called for, Master Faregan," he said.

Faregan frowned and looked at the summons—which he had written himself—and then at the secretary. "If you're certain, I'll be on my way. I have the summons, but if none of the Masters wrote it, then none of the Masters wrote it. This is a shabby trick someone played on me, though."

"I'm most sorry," the secretary said. "The Masters apologized—they told me to tell you that they promise to find whomever it was who played this trick on you."

Faregan bowed. "Tell them they mustn't worry about such a small thing when they have matters of great import to attend to. I'm more than willing to find out myself who was responsible." He bowed again and exited.

Behind him, the tea boy came out carrying the empty serving tray.

It was the funniest thing. Or not, perhaps, but definitely odd. Wraith had seen the same man with the shabby blue tunic and the mismatched eyes twice earlier that day—once while he stood in the market buying himself a few fresh vegetables for his dinner, and once as he was walking in the door of the Cinder Hill Theater. And now, going up his walk to his home, he saw the man again—standing down the street a ways, and not looking at him, but still there, and unmistakable.

It's just one of those odd coincidences, he told himself. I must pass the same people dozens of times each day, and the only reason I noticed this man is that he is so shabby and his eyes don't match.

He didn't fool himself for a second. He didn't believe in coincidence, and after his visits with both Velyn and Solander, he had not one but two likely candidates to suspect of hiring spies. He couldn't decide which was more likely, though: Luercas had reason to hate him, but the Dragons, if they had any suspicions of Wraith's activities or his true nature, had reason to fear him. He thought he would rather be hated than feared.

He wondered if he should just walk up to the man and ask who had hired him. Or if he should hire someone of his own to follow the man and find out who was watching him, and perhaps why. Or if he should decide that this was a very good time to take one of his troupes on tour personally, claiming that too much work had left him in need of a rest and a change of scenery.

He lit the fire in his stove, diced his vegetables, put his steaming pot with a little water in the bottom on the flat stovetop, waited until it boiled, then tossed his vegetables in. And all the while, he kept watch through the window. The man moved away from the street corner, came up to Wraith's house, and used one of the popular little hand-voxes to talk to someone. Probably to his employer.

Wraith started running his day's activities over in his head—he'd been in contact with his undergrounders on and off, but since they were primarily his actors and other creative people, he didn't think that would trigger any suspicion. He'd met with Brother Lestovar briefly, but it had been to go over his newest grant to the Order of Resonance—that shouldn't trigger any trouble. Solander had been by the day before, and he knew the Dragons had been monitoring that, but they'd been watching Solander, not him. And aside from that, he'd met with wealthy patrons of the theater, interviewed potential managers for the New Brinch Theater so that he could transfer the current manager, who had done brilliantly, to the still-under-construction Terus Theater in Terus, the fastest-growing city in Arim.

He'd done plenty that the Empire would like to know about, but he'd done it in such a way that it all looked innocent.

He hoped.

Had Velyn told her story to anyone else? Had someone decided that it merited checking?

His "family" in Ynjarval were living well, thanks to him. If anything happened to him, their source of income would dry up like surface water in a drought. He believed he could count on them to protect him.

His employees received better-than-average compensation, interesting work, chances to travel if they so chose, and opportunities to exercise their own creativity.

His friends shared dreams and passions with him, common loves and common hatreds. He could not see any of them betraying him, even if they did find out the truth about him.

He had enemies, and from them he would expect anything—but he'd always been sure he knew who his enemies were. He'd done his best to make sure none of them could hurt him.

And yet, as he leaned against the side counter in his kitchen, eating his steamed long beans and yam cubes, he could see the man who had been paid to follow him setting up for an overnight stay—hiding up against the house in the shrubbery, with a few little bits and pieces of magical apparatus that looked to Wraith like listening and viewing devices.

Charming.

Perhaps he should hire someone to kill the man and be done with it. Except he might not see the next one. And he didn't want to be someone who operated that way.

Early bed tonight, he thought. Early out of bed tomorrow. His first objective would be to find someone who could locate the people following him and find out why they were doing this, what they wanted, and what it would take to get rid of them.

"I have not yet found your vowmate," Luercas's investigator said, "but I've found something that will lead me to her. And I believe it has such value to you that I had to meet with you to tell you what I've found."

They stood at one of the rails of the Rone Artis Memorial Starpark, looking down past the stars to the shore of the sea, which glittered like a blanket of gemstones on that sunny day.

"If you're wasting my time," Luercas said, "I'll throw you over. I feel unwell today—I would rather be anywhere than here."

The investigator didn't look worried in the least—though Luercas thought that more a demonstration of stupidity than confidence. Luercas meant it when he said he would throw the man over. The rages held him firmly in their grip, and he found himself once again yearning for his own body, for flesh unbound to the soul of some stranger.

"You'll like this," the investigator said. "I have a reliable source inside the Order of Resonance who swears to me that none other than Gellas Tomersin hired men to kidnap Velyn from the boardinghouse where he paid for her to stay. And that the people who took her were members of the underground that has been causing such trouble to the Council of Dragons."

"Which would tie Gellas in with the underground."

"It gets better."

"How does it get better?"

"On the very night Velyn disappeared, and during the time that she was being kidnapped, guess who Gellas was having dinner with?"

Luercas turned to face the investigator and in a low voice said, "I don't like guessing games."

"Gellas Tomersin ate dinner that night with Solander Artis, and Artis's assistant from the Department of Research."

Luercas smiled just a little. "They're Tomersin's alibi."

"Yes."

"Tomersin and Artis were inseparable from the time that Tomersin came over from Ynjarval. Skinny little bastard. And if they're both tied in with the underground, it would only make sense that they'd avoid each other most of the time."

"The underground is trying to overthrow the government. They want to free the Warreners—they're lunatics."

Luercas merely smiled. "If both Gellas Tomersin and Solander Artis are involved in their activities, the more trouble they plan, the better for me. I'd love to see both of them executed."

The investigator nodded. "I can understand—if someone made off with my vowmate, I'd feel the same way."

Luercas didn't bother to correct the man's error. He said, "Find Velyn for me, of course. But if by chance you or your contact in the underground could funnel any information to me about just how exactly the underground plans to free the Warreners—or, for that matter, how they're keeping the city guards from collecting insurgents and illegal aliens—pass that on to me, too." He reached into his pocket and pulled out a generous credit tab. "And this is to thank you for your work so far. You were right. That was worth getting out of the house to hear."

Jess stepped out of the chartered aircar behind a dozen other passengers, wishing that she had been able to sleep at least a little during the flight. "I'm going to hire an aircar to take me home," she told Patr. "Listening to you snore the entire trip over exhausted me." She smiled to let him know she was teasing him. "I have several things I need to have you do immediately—essential things. And we're going to be incredibly busy the whole time we're in the city. I expect to be working as close to night and day as the two of us can manage. So if you don't mind, I'll ask you to stay in my guest room this trip. You'll be comfortable. The room's large and airy, and has everything you'll need." She gave him an apologetic smile. "Probably isn't the way you intended to spend your trip home—"

He waved off her apology. "I expected to spend my time acting in my capacity as your assistant. I knew you had a full schedule planned. I'll be fine staying at your place. Anything I can do to make your work easier." His smile managed to be both tender and concerned.

"Thank you." Jess was relieved. "This is everyone I need to see while we're here." She handed him the list she'd put together during the long flight. "You'll be able to use the hand-vox for most of the appointments, but not for the one with Master Gellas. He's . . ." She shrugged and gave Patr an apologetic smile. "Well . . . Gellas is eccentric. He doesn't use any magic in his productions, and apparently not in his personal life, either. He can be a bit difficult to contact. So take care of that appointment first."

"First?"

"I'm going to be sleeping for a long time," she said grimly. "You'll have the time to do everything on the list. Oh, God. I don't have a bite of food in the house. There's a grand restaurant on the corner that will deliver—tell them we're going to want a light meal for tonight, and one for yourself for this midday if you don't want to take your chances while you're out . . . and, I think, something for early tomorrow morning. They'll deliver, and it will be wonderful. Once we have a tentative schedule of appointments, we can make better plans for the rest of the week."

He looked at her and sighed. "You look positively gray. You're running yourself too hard, and you aren't paying a bit of attention to your health."

"I don't have time."

"You had better find time. You're going to run yourself into your grave." He glanced down at the list she'd given him and said, "How can you hope to fit in meetings with all of these people in one week? Even if I can schedule them all on short notice, how are you going to see them all?"

"I want to secure patronage from half the people on that list. I want to see if I can work out a deal with Gellas to use some of our musicians in some of his productions, both touring and at home—I'd have to say that rated my first priority. And if I don't see the other half of the people on the list, I'm going to lose friends."

"If they were really friends, you wouldn't have to worry about losing them. They'd want you to catch up on your rest."

Jess snorted. "You think so? Try it with your friends sometime. Come into town and don't see the people you really like and do see people you don't like, but whose money you need, and see how long you have any friends at all."

He handed her the list and a pen. "Number them, 'one' for most important, down to 'twenty-five' or whatever your least important visit turns out to be. I'll make the first batch of appointments today, and see how you stand up to the strain. If you're still gray tomorrow, I'm going to have to lock you in your room for the day." He gave her his sad little smile and said, "I'm only joking, you know."

"I appreciate the concern. You'll be amazed at how fine I am once I've had some sleep, though."

Those sad eyes never left hers. "No, I won't. I've always known how fine you were."

She turned away, and he didn't say anything else. She pretended most of the time not to know that he cared for her, or that he would have been happy to become her lover in an instant, and he pretended most of the time that he thought no more of her than any assistant felt for his employer. Every once in a while, though, the masks slipped, and Jess was always the first one to back away.

He wasn't Wraith. Nobody but Wraith was Wraith, and she knew she was an idiot and a fool, but her few lovers since Solander had been disasters, simply because she couldn't put Wraith aside. She wasn't going to destroy a perfectly good working relationship for a romance that would end in ruin.

"Well, I guess I'll go ahead and hire that aircar now," she said. "You find Gellas—or one of his secretaries—and make that appointment. A good hour, please—no less. I don't believe we'll be able to get to contracts on a first meeting, or even on this visit, but I think we should be able to work out the majority of the details, provided he's interested."

Patr nodded. "And then I'll order a meal to be delivered to your home for the two of us."

"That sounds wonderful." She reached out a hand and flagged down one of the passing aircars-for-hire. "Then I'll see you tonight. Good luck."

She fell into her bed without being aware of how she got there, and dropped into darkness still fully clothed and wearing her shoes.

Chapter 16

Morning. Wraith had slept poorly, woke tense, went out into cool break-of-dawn air, and discovered that the odd-eyed man who had been watching him the night before had been replaced by an attractive young woman with dark, swept-back hair and delicate features. She did not meet his eyes when he passed her, and when he glanced back, she was talking into a hand-vox.

At the New Brinch Theater, he checked receipts for the previous night, went over the day's problems with his manager, headed out to the Galtin District Theater.

And the attractive young woman was waiting. She sat on a bench beneath a fashan tree, reading a book. She did not look at him.

His heart raced, his skin felt clammy, and he felt light-headed. Knowing that he was being watched made his blood feel like ice in his veins.

At the Galtin, he checked sets, glanced over the short stack of scripts from new writers that his on-site manager thought would be worth giving short runs, and ate the meal his Galtin secretary had waiting for him. When he stepped out into the midday sunshine, he didn't see the watcher, and he breathed a little easier. Perhaps she had lost track of him.

But then he saw the odd-eyed man again, and his heart slammed up into his throat and for a moment he couldn't breathe.

They couldn't touch him. He was stolti. He had people who would swear to it. He had covered his tracks.

But there were people who knew who he was, too—who could sell him for their own gain.

He proceeded to the West Beach Experimental Playhouse, this time hiring one of the aircars he so hated. He stepped out, saw the odd-eyed man step out of a car half a block down the street behind him. Did they think he didn't see them? Or did they not care?

"You don't look like you're feeling well," his assistant, Loour, said. She brought out a list of items that needed his attention. Halfway down the list, he saw an appointment with Jess scheduled for midday on the morrow. One hour. At the West Beach.

"I can't do this," he said.

"Oh, I'm sorry. I knew she was an old friend of yours, so I didn't even question it."

"Contact her, tell her I won't be able to make the meeting."

"I can't. She didn't leave a contact address. But when she comes tomorrow, I'll convey my apologies."

Wraith closed his eyes. He didn't want Jess linked to whatever was going on in his life. He didn't want her seen at any of the theaters, didn't want her followed, questioned, considered as suspicious by whoever it was that was watching him. She couldn't come to the West Beach. And he couldn't go to her.

Or could he?

He was in a theater, for the gods' sakes. Every sort of costume, makeup, and appearance-changing artifice in the world was within his reach. He had talented costumers and makeup artists—and he could damned well pull one of the junior makeup assistants off of a character and let him try out his wings for the evening, while Wraith became someone else.

Wraith smiled. "Don't worry about it. I'll get word to her somehow. We'll set up her meeting for another day."

Loour looked relieved. "I'm so glad. Her assistant said the meeting was quite important. He mentioned a plan for increasing your business and hers, though of course he didn't have many of the details—or if he did, he didn't give them to me."

"I'll find out what she has in mind." He gave her a quick hug. Of his several assistants, she was his favorite. She always seemed to care about what he was doing and how he felt. He sometimes wondered if he ought to ask her to dinner sometime. He thought it might be nice to have someone to talk to in the evenings. She would never be Velyn—but that was a good thing, wasn't it? He didn't love her, but he liked her a lot. If he didn't love her, she couldn't hurt him.

He smiled to himself, just a little. How easy it was to think to the future now that he'd come up with a plan that would let him leave the theater without being followed. How easy to pretend that not being himself for a night would be the same as just disappearing. Someone was waiting to follow him, someone who would be waiting when he reappeared.

"I'll see you tomorrow, then." Her smile seemed special to him. Personal, deeper than the smile of an employee.

When he got his life in order—when he solved the problem of the person or people who were having him followed—he needed to think about Loour. About possibilities. He'd spent long enough mourning his foolishness.

Down in makeup, Wraith told Brenjin, who did makeup for several of the secondary characters, that he needed to be a convincing woman for the evening. Brenjin brayed, and then flushed bright pink when he realized that Wraith was serious.

"Gellas, I think I could make a great girl of you—but is there something you haven't been telling us? I mean, we all just assumed that you were avoiding women because you still hurt from Velyn. None of us really considered that you might . . ." Brenjin leaned in and whispered, "If any of us would interest you, I promise you'd have a line waiting to proposition you come morning. And I'd be at the head of it."

Wraith hadn't even considered anyone wondering why he might want to dress as a woman for the evening—nor had he considered that he might know people who would consider that a good sign. He shook his head. "Everyone was right about me—this is just for a trick I'm playing on an old friend. Make me as convincing as you can, will you?"

Brenjin sighed. "You have no idea how you gave me hope there for a moment. Certainly. Thin and fine-featured as you are, I can make an excellent woman of you. Pity you're so tall—that will ruin the illusion a bit, but you aren't impossibly tall for a woman. We'll just make you wonderfully beautiful, and hide your larynx—gods-all, you have enough of that for two men."

Wraith sat in the chair, and Brenjin started applying makeup. "Have you been in to see Kervin about a costume yet?"

"No."

"You're going to need big breasts to offset your shoulders—it may take him a while to make some for you that hang right. Let me call him in, and he can measure you while I do your face and hair."

Breasts. Wraith thought this was going to turn into a fiasco. He'd hoped for a bit of makeup on his face and a good wig, and something voluminous and vaguely female that wouldn't require a great deal of effort. But he did want to be convincing. He wanted to be . . . perfect. And for that, he was going to need breasts.

He sighed. He hoped he would be able to get Jess to open the door for him.

The makeup and costuming took far longer than he'd anticipated. It tied up two of his best people from their work for the better part of an afternoon. But when they stood him in front of a mirror—barely breathing because of the thing they'd cinched around his waist and ribs—he couldn't believe what he saw. Brenjin and Kervin had given him auburn hair, voluminous breasts, a tiny waist, an outfit that showed off curves the two of them had created out of some amazing materials. He couldn't believe how pretty his face was, nor how completely the illusion obscured the truth. He would be able to walk out the door and down the sidewalk and take an aircar to Jess's home without having to worry about anyone connecting her with him. He might have to worry about men trying to pick him up—he projected a definite air of moral laxity. But perhaps, he thought, it was because he looked very much like Velyn had looked when she'd been younger. Had Brenjin done that on purpose?

"What do you think?"

Wraith looked over at Brenjin and said, "It's perfect."

"No, dear. It isn't. You open your mouth and that voice comes out, and you're going to ruin the whole thing. Let me see you walk."

Wraith walked.

"No. No, no, gods, no! Women walk with one foot directly in front of the other. They pivot from the waist. They don't swing their arms so wide. You want to think small. Try to take up less space. Long strides are fine if you can keep your feet lined up and watch your arms."

Wraith tried the walk.

"Still not it." Brenjin sighed. "Watch me. I'm good at this."

He walked across the room. Wraith would have sworn that a woman's soul had just reached out and possessed Brenjin's body.

"How did you *do* that?"

"Years of practice, Gellas. Years and years of practice. I didn't get this job because I had theater experience. I got it because I can turn myself into a girl even prettier than you—and in about half the time." He grinned.

Wraith was shaking his head, disbelieving.

Kervin said, "It's true. We got these jobs together because we had so much experience with costumes and makeup and creating illusions—we just didn't admit at the time where we got that experience."

Wraith pitched his voice softer and throaty, and didn't try to raise it too much. "I know true magic when I see it."

He walked across the room, turned to the two men who watched him, and asked, "Better?"

"Much." Brenjin tipped his head to one side and studied Wraith for a long, intense moment. "And the voice was acceptable, too. Try not to talk too much, try not to walk too much, and stay out of bright, harsh lights."

"Why? Will my face melt off?"

"No. But any little bit of beard stubble might show through the makeup."

"Ah." Wraith winced. "I'll stay out of bright light. And now I must go. Luck with the rest of the evening—I'm sorry to take you away from your real tasks."

Brenjin and Kervin grinned at each other, and Kervin said, "You jest. You were a wonderful challenge. If you decide you'd like to keep that look, let me know. I know someone who could do some fabulous outfits for your height and build and . . . figure."

Wraith smiled thinly. "Thanks. I'll keep that in mind."

He heard Brenjin and Kervin laughing behind him.

Wraith strolled into the theater, and waited until the intermission—when the curtain fell and the bell sounded and most of the theater's patrons rose from their seats. He rose with them and followed them into the lobby, but unlike most of them, he continued outside.

The boy at the door said, "Shall I mark your ticket, stolta? You won't be able to enter unless it bears tonight's mark."

"Not at all," Wraith said, a bit shaken by being addressed as "stolta." "I have to leave early tonight."

He stepped to the curb and waved a hand, and an aircar dropped down and the rear door opened for him before he had stood there half an instant. He tried to recall ever getting such quick service and couldn't. Perhaps the driver had not had a good night and was desperate for a fare.

"Where to, stolta?"

Wraith gave the address.

"Show not to your fancy?"

Wraith started, realizing the driver was speaking to him, and then had to try to figure out what the man was talking about. Drivers usually wanted to complain to him about their last passengers, or regale him with the racing scores, or the details of their last gambling spree, or their philosophies of life and beer; they never asked him questions.

But this driver kept turning around and smiling at him. And then it snapped into place. The driver was smiling at the *woman* in the backseat. Asking her questions about herself, because she was a woman. Wraith sighed. "The play was good. I got a call that a friend of mine just had terrible news; I need to go see her, and I decided not to wait."

"That's a shame." The man concentrated on his driving for only an instant. "Then I don't suppose you'd want to stop off for a little drink at this charming place I know. I'm buying."

"If I was in too much of a hurry to watch the rest of the play, I'm certainly going to be in too much of a hurry to stop off for a drink."

"Maybe after?" He evidently caught the look on Wraith's face, for he shrugged and turned around.

Wraith couldn't believe this. Did women have to put up with this sort of nonsense all the time? Was just getting a driver to take them from pick-up to destination always an ordeal? Probably not for the plain ones. He thought if he let Brenjin and Kervin turn him into a woman again, he'd make sure they made him as homely as possible.

The aircar left him in front of Jess's house. But Jess didn't come to the door when he knocked. Some man did—a tall, heavy-boned, bovine-faced young man with thick lips and unnervingly shrewd eyes.

"I've come to see Jess Covitach-Artis about a matter of great importance. It's an emergency."

The man leaned against the door and said, "Sweet lady, you could have come to tell her that the world would end on the morrow, and I would not wake her from her sleep. She was gray with exhaustion, and if you're any true friend, you'll tell me whatever message you have to pass on and then be on your way."

"I can't tell you," Wraith said, dropping his voice so that he no longer sounded like a woman. "I've risked my own life to come here, and if I tell you, then you're likely to die, too. If I don't get this message to Jess, she's likely to end up working in the mines."

The man stared at him for a long, shocked-silent time. "You're a man."

"Only way I could get past the people who were watching me without being followed. It is . . . it is life-and-death. If you care about her, and I have to believe you do, wake her."

The man licked his lips, glanced out into the empty street, and then nodded. "Get inside. Sit in the kitchen—pull the blinds. I'll go get her for you."

"Thank you."

Wraith had never been in Jess's house. It didn't seem to have much of her in it—at least not the her he'd known. It had a somber feel to it, all muted colors and carefully placed furniture and expensive pieces of artwork that lacked much in the way of character. The front room, the great room off to the left, the broad arched hallway that led off into an office and an atrium . . . He walked in the direction her friend had pointed him in and suddenly found the kitchen. Unlike the rest of the house, it was truly Jess. Fish everywhere—little statuettes, and hand-painted tiles on the counters, and fish peeking out from behind forests of coral on the hand-painted walls. It looked like her room in Oel Maritias had looked, back when the two of them were children. The rest of the house had left him unmoved, but this nearly tore his heart out. He missed their childhood. He missed the hope for the future that it had held.

He sat at the table, looking at two little painted carved-wood fish that were holding hands and dancing. They had sweet faces—they smiled at each other as they danced, and he could almost imagine them laughing and carrying on a conversation. He held them up to see if the artist had signed them.

"They're clever, aren't they?"

Wraith jumped. He hadn't heard Jess coming up behind him.

She was smiling, but it was her polite, distant business smile. "Patr told me there was some emergency. For him to have gotten me out of bed, it must have been impressive . . . and I didn't catch your name, stolta."

"Wraith," Wraith said.

Jess's mouth dropped open and her eyes went wide. Wraith would have accused any of his actresses who gave such a broad reaction of over-acting. In Jess, the reaction was right, but comical. She put her hands up to her breastbone and shook her head slowly. "Oh . . . gods . . . what happened to you?"

Wraith said, "I've had people following me. If you come to the meeting you scheduled tomorrow, they're likely to follow you. It . . . it might get you killed. I'm not sure who they are, but I have potential trouble from two different sources that I know of, and might have offended someone I don't know about. Any meeting to discuss business needs to wait—it simply isn't worth the risk."

"The meeting wasn't to discuss business," Jess said. "That was a cover to let me get to you without raising suspicion. Everything I'm doing on this trip was a cover for my visit to you."

Wraith felt suddenly cold. "What's going on?"

"There are rumors about you that could get you killed," Jess said.

"Rumors?" He smiled a little. "I have worse problems than rumors."

"I don't think you do. You see, these are the rumors that I've heard: that you've acquired or created a private army, that you are using magic to control the minds of your audiences and to force them to work for you as traitors to the Empire, that your actors aren't truly human but are sub-human creatures that you've costumed to hide their monstrous natures. That you aren't who you appear to be, but someone else instead. Perhaps a Strithian agent. Perhaps something even more insidious."

Wraith sat in the kitchen, listing to Patr moving about down the hall in one of the other rooms. Wraith breathed in and out a few times, hampered by the tight contraption that compressed his ribs and forced his waist into an inhumanly tiny shape. "That's not good," he said at last.

"It sounds to me like you have a traitor. I mean, none of the things I've heard have been exactly correct . . ."

"But none of them have been exactly wrong, either," Wraith finished. "Yes."

Wraith started to rest his chin in his hand, remembered the makeup all over his face at the last minute, and stopped himself. He would hate to be a woman, he thought. At least one who caked this itchy slop all over her face all the time, or wore ludicrously uncomfortable clothing just to alter her appearance. What a miserable pain it was not to be able to sit comfortably, to have to think about face paint, and the hang of clothing, and the way each foot had to go to make hips swing correctly, and . . . pah! Life was too short to be hampered and caged and con-stricted by such nonsense.

He leaned back, making himself as comfortable as he could, and said, "I cannot imagine who might be spreading these rumors. I have good people. Truly good people. I screened all of my employees carefully before I hired them, I've been careful never to mix my private goals with my public persona, or to have people who know me in one capacity also working with me in the other. I have been careful."

"It doesn't matter. Perhaps there's money involved. Blackmail. Sex. I could think of a dozen reason why people would turn on an employer. Two or three that would encourage them to turn on a friend."

He nodded. "So can I. I just don't want to believe that someone I trust could be capable of such treachery."

"Just so long as you *do* believe. . . ."

"I believe. But it adds another question to the identity of the person or people who hired those investigators to follow me."

"You sure they didn't follow you here?"

"They would have had to recognize me. I left in a small crowd, and I didn't look like myself."

"True." Jess had been fidgeting with something over by the window. Now she turned and sighed. "Wraith, you need to have friends around you right now."

Wraith stood up. "That's exactly what I don't need. You haven't done anything wrong, Jess. You've had no part in any of this; you don't know who's involved, you don't know what we've done, you don't know what we plan to do. And that's the way I want it. If I have a traitor somewhere in my organization, the last thing I want is for him or her to make a connection to you. So go back on your tour, and stay away from here for a while. Keep up with the nightlies; if you hear anything about me, figure that at least you're safe."

"I know a few things. I know about the Kaan . . . and the Warrens—"

"Shut up."

"What?"

"Shut up. You don't know anything. Leave it at that." He leaned toward her and in a whisper said, "Whoever is watching me has placed magical listening devices around my house . . . and my office. I've left them in place because as long as I know where they are, I don't have to try to find ones that are better hidden. But . . . you don't know who might be listening to us or watching us right now."

"That's . . . silly. Why would anyone be watching us? Why would anyone have placed listening devices around my house?"

"Because you made an appointment with me. If the traitor has access to my appointment calendar—and I must assume until it is proven otherwise that he does—then you have created a fresh connection from you to me. And since you were a childhood friend of mine, you're going to have raised some suspicions anyway."

"No. I refuse to live my life thinking that the world is such a devious place."

"Don't be stupid." Wraith stood up. "Think about everything you know of the Hars. Of magic. Of the Warrens. Have you gotten so careless or so soft—or so trusting—that you could think that the Masters of the Hars would quibble over crushing someone as insignificant as you?"

Jess winced. Wraith felt like a fiend for being so harsh with her, but she'd spent too long feeling secure, popular, and loved. She'd managed to move herself away from her dark origins and the horror that she knew to be truth. It was easy to do that; the past burned so horribly, the present comforted so completely.

"I'm sorry," Jess said. "You're right, of course. I don't know, and don't need to know, what you've been doing. I only felt that you were in danger and I did not want to let the danger come to you without warning."

Wraith nodded. Jess had turned around and was staring out the window again. Wraith could see the tension in her shoulders, the way her body had gone rigid, the way it used to back when she was a little girl, when she was afraid.

"I still love you," she added.

"I'm sorry," Wraith said. "I'm sorry we never worked out. I was young and stupid, and now that I am older and wiser, I can look at you and see what I missed. Only now I can't have you because I don't dare have you near me."

"Do you think you could love me? Someday?"

Wraith did not want her to keep hoping he'd someday find his way to her. If she could let go of that hope, she could find love elsewhere. "I still love Velyn," he said, putting misery into his voice. Not too difficult, that. "As much as I wish I were free of her, I don't think I'll ever be."

"Ah. She never deserved you." Jess turned back to face him, and Wraith saw the tears streaking her cheeks. He didn't dare touch her—the ruin of his makeup could prove fatal to him, and anything that revealed his true identity too soon could prove fatal to her. He needed to be well away from this place before he stopped being the woman in silk and became Gellas Tomersin—Gellas, Master of the Theater.

"I need to leave now," he said.

"I'll have Patr drive you wherever you want to go." Jess wiped her tears on her forearm, just as she had when she'd been a child. Wraith had another moment of sharp memory, a moment in which it hurt to breathe. Why couldn't he have loved her? Why couldn't he have seen in her the companion who would stand by him, instead of falling stupidly for the faithless Velyn?

Because he was blind. An idiot. A fool.

Because he was human, and that seemed to sum the rest of it up perfectly.

He left as quickly as he could—sat next to Patr in the front seat of the elegant aircar and said, "The Cordorale, please. At least I'll blend in there." The two of them had little to say to each other, but finally Wraith said, "Do you care about her?"

Patr glanced away from the corridor through which they floated, surprise on his face. "I work for her."

"I know you do. But this is important. Do you care for her?"

Patr swallowed hard and looked away. "I love her."

"Good. Get her away from Oel Artis by whatever means you must, and keep her away. Hide her if you have to—from everyone. Ugly things are going to happen here, and I don't want them to happen to her."

Patr's jaw tightened. "You've been her friend for a very long time."

"All her life. What happens to her matters more to me than what happens to me."

Patr said, "You've managed to keep your distance pretty well, for someone who cares so much."

"I've managed to keep the people I care about out of the parts of my life that could hurt them."

"You have a lot of secrets, do you, Gellas?"

"None that need concern you. Except this—I love her, too. I was a fool not to pursue her when I could have. Now I can't. But I still love her. I want to know that she'll be safe."

"I'll protect her with my life."

"That's all I ask."

Patr pulled the aircar into an empty lot, far from where Wraith needed to be.

Wraith glanced over at the bigger man, suddenly uneasy. "This isn't the Cordorale."

"We'll get there," Patr said. "But I have something to ask of you."

"And that is?"

"Never go near her again."

"What?"

Patr's knuckles whitened on the controls, and he glared at Wraith. "You heard me."

"I did. But when this is over—"

Patr waved him to silence. "It will never be over. I've heard the rumors. I have an idea of what you're involved in. Perhaps you'll slip free of the Empire for a while, but sooner or later they'll catch up with you. You will never be free of the poison that you have drawn to yourself, and that poison will touch the lives of everyone you let yourself get close to. You had the sense to stay out of her life before. Trust that same sense. Let this be the last time you see her—for her sake."

Wraith leaned back on the seat of the aircar and closed his eyes. "You offering any alternatives?"

"Certainly. I could kill you now and save everyone a lot of trouble. Should look interesting on tomorrow's nightly—Theater Master Gellas Tomersin found dead, dressed in women's clothing and in a notorious neighborhood."

Wraith opened his eyes and studied his companion sidelong, warily. "Or I could kill *you*. There's never much of a guarantee in situations like this."

"More than you think. I decided to kill you when I heard her crying, and when I heard you telling her that you were involved in something that could get her killed. Don't look all horrified—I listened to the two of you. I would be mad not to—a man I don't know who's dressed as a woman comes to her house in the middle of the night, claiming emergency and demanding to see her. I had no proof you were who you said you were. I had no intention of leaving you alone with her unsupervised. So I heard what you said, and discovered that you've put her life at risk, and for a while I wanted to destroy you with my own two hands, just because your existence is a danger to her existence. I came prepared. But I don't want her to ever be able to think that I might have had a hand in your death—and I'm certain enough that the Masters of the Hars will dispose of you for me. And then she'll be safe."

Wraith smiled a little. "At least you care for her. I'm out of her life. I swear that as long as the Empire is a danger to me, I won't see her again."

"Then I'll take you where you wanted to go." Patr started up the aircar again, and pulled out into the empty corridor.

Chapter 17

"The truth does *indeed* come to those who wait." Master Noano Omwi, raised to the seat of prominence upon the death of Master Penangueli, bowed his head slightly to his two fellows, Masters Faregan and Daari, and leaned back in his soft seat.

"Penangueli was too soft with Solander Artis," Daari agreed. "I thought as much at the time."

"So how do we want to deal with this?" Faregan asked. Though Faregan had been an investigatory member of the Silent Inquest for nearly twenty years, he'd held his post in the Inquestor Triad for all of three days, and he did not yet presume to make statements. Omwi tried to keep this from annoying him—he had been new once, as well.

Omwi said, "We have a number of alternatives, depending on further investigation. Obviously we need to bring in all of his close contacts and all of their immediate contacts. I expect the roundup operation will be quite large; our challenge will be to accomplish it quietly and with a minimum of outside notice. After all, we now have proof from his own mouth and his own actions that he has committed treason in falsifying data and instructing his associate to lie, and we have him linked to another of Penangueli's questionable decisions. The old man was getting soft in his last years."

"Should we bring Solander Artis in immediately, then, before he bolts?" Daani seemed troubled.

"No. He ruined his test results yesterday, so we have complicity and conspiracy to hide secrets of vital interest to the Empire. But he doesn't know that we know what he did—he thinks that he's achieved some level of safety. He'll take a few days to convert assets into cash, to research places where he thinks he can hide, and to make sure that anyone he trusts is safely secured away from our reach. As he does that, we simply tag the people he contacts. If Artis were to disappear prematurely, we would scare some of his fellow conspirators into hiding. But of course we cannot give him too much time, or he could get away." Omwi drummed his fingers on the fine wood table and stared at his own reflection in its glossy surface. "Two days. Anyone he hasn't contacted in two days is of minor importance."

"And those he's already contacted?"

"The only person he has already contacted is Gellas Tomersin—and we already have someone looking into him. We'll need to step up that operation in order to gather up everyone and question them in a timely fashion. I'm uncertain that there are links between Artis and Tomersin, but my gut tells me their childhood connection has remained stronger than it would appear on the surface." He folded his hands together in front of him and willed them to be still; his excitement at this potential catch made his heart race and his muscles twitch. He'd wanted for years to be responsible for a huge haul—something even better than the Circle of Fellows of Freedom, which Penangueli had pulled in the second year he held the top seat of the Triad. This looked like his great catch, if he could coordinate his people and keep them from making mistakes. He could barely keep himself in the chair. He wanted to pace, to shout, to kick things, and instead all he could do was sit there looking calm and reasoned and in control.

A knock sounded on the inner door—it would be someone cleared for the highest level of access, but well trained enough to give the Triad time to remove any evidence of what they were doing.

The three Masters looked at each other. All nodded, and Faregan, junior man in the Triad, rose and went to open the door.

"Agent Jethis! You have news?"

"It pertains," the man at the door said softly.

Faregan waved him in. Omwi didn't recognize Jethis, but Faregan obviously did. Faregan bowed low to Omwi, Jethis bowed lower. "Master Omwi," Faregan said, "this is Agent Patr Jethis, who has been working on a corollary of our investigations of both Solander Artis and Gellas Tomersin. He's my man, who has been keeping track of the young woman who was a friend of both of theirs in childhood—if both of them are guilty, then I suspect we'll find that she's guilty, too."

Agent Jethis was shaking his head.

"Speak for us, Jethis," Omwi said. "You've come here tonight at this very late hour—what have you discovered that will aid us in our quest for truth?"

"My subject knows nothing. She has been out of contact with your subject, Gellas Tomersin, for years, and though she did react by making contact with him when I gave her my planted rumors, she did so only out of concern for him. But I've had a confession to me personally, by Tomersin, of his treason."

Omwi sat back, startled. "A confession?"

Jethis produced a little box and pressed a button on it.

Jethis's voice came out of it. "These are the rumors that I've heard: that you've acquired or created a private army, that you are using magic to control the minds of your audiences and to force them to work for you as traitors to the Empire, that your actors aren't truly human but are sub-human creatures that you've costumed to hide their monstrous natures. That you aren't who you appear to be, but someone else instead. Perhaps a Strithian agent. Perhaps something even more insidious."

And then the unmistakable voice of Gellas Tomersin. "That's not good."

And then Jethis's voice again. "It sounds to me like you have a traitor. I mean, none of the things I've heard have been exactly correct . . ."

"But none of them have been exactly wrong, either."

"Yes."

"I cannot imagine who might be spreading these rumors. I have good people. Truly good people. I screened all of my employees carefully before I hired them, I've been careful never to mix my private goals with my public persona, or to have people who know me in one capacity also working with me in the other. I have been careful."

"It doesn't matter. Perhaps there's money involved. Blackmail. Sex. I could think of a dozen reason why people would turn on an employer. Two or three that would encourage them to turn on a friend."

"So can I. I just don't want to believe that someone I trust could be capable of such treachery."

"Just so long as you *do* believe. . . ."

An odd overlap of the voices bothered Omwi for an instant. But Gellas's next words fascinated him. "I believe. But it adds another question to the identity of the person or people who hired those investigators to follow me."

"You sure they didn't follow you here?"

"They would have had to recognize me. I left in a small crowd, and I didn't look like myself."

"True." A pause, then, "Gellas, you need to have friends around you right now."

And Gellas, sounding sharp. "That's exactly what I don't need. You haven't done anything wrong, Patr." That odd little blurring of voices again. Omwi truly did not like the strangeness of that. But this was first-rate information. He would look into how Jethis had acquired it later. "You've had no part in any of this; you don't know who's involved, you don't know what we've done, you don't know what we plan to do. And that's the way I want it. If I have a traitor somewhere in my organization, the last thing I want is for him or her to make a connection to—" . . . and a blur, completely indecipherable. "So go back on your tour, and stay away from here for a while. Keep up with the nightlies; if you hear anything about me, figure that at least you're safe."

Jethis said, "I know a few things. I know about the Kaan . . . and the Warrens—"

"Shut up."

"What?"

"Shut up. You don't know anything. Leave it at that." A short pause. "Whoever is watching me has placed magical listening devices around my house . . . and my office. I've left them in place because as long as I know where they are, I don't have to try to find ones that are better hidden. But . . . you don't know who might be listening to us or watching us right now."

"That's . . . silly. Why would anyone be watching us? Why would anyone have placed listening devices around *this* house?"

"Because you made an appointment with me. If the traitor has access to my appointment calendar—"

A tiny click, and then Jethis said, "That's all of relevance. We had a discussion about the clothes he chose to wear, and about Jess, but nothing more that gave us relevant information."

"Have we placed listening devices around his house?" Faregan asked.

"No," Daani said.

"Then we aren't the only ones watching him." Omwi felt the excitement of the hunt intensify. This was the one, all right. This was the case that was going to make his name for all time among the Masters of the Silent Inquest. "Someone else is interested in him, too—and that can only mean good things for us."

Patr burst into the room where Jess had been asleep only an instant before and began pulling clothes off of her shelf. The light had come on when he entered, and Jess, bewildered, blinked in the glare and tried to figure out what was happening. "We're leaving now," Patr said.

"No, we aren't. I have a hundred things yet to do here in Oel Artis—I can't even consider leaving the city until—" And then she caught sight of his face, and her throat tightened until she could not breathe.

Sweat dripped from his forehead and from his gray skin, and he wore an expression that spoke of having seen hell.

"Sit," she told him, frightened. "Let me call someone to help you."

But he shook his head. He handed her a cold-weather tunic, heavy leggings, sturdy boots, a hat, gloves, thick stockings. "Trouble coming. We must leave now. I know of a place—but there is no time to talk, no time to argue, no time even to gather anything. You . . . *must* . . . come with me now."

She believed him—not wanting to, but knowing from her gut that he told her the truth. "What about Wraith—I mean Gellas? Is this about him?"

"Probably. Hurry." He swept an arm around her, pulled her free from her covers, put his hands on her shoulders, and looked into her eyes with an intensity that shocked her. "We only have minutes. Maybe less. Maybe it's too late already, but I have to try. I have to save you if I can."

She nodded, mute, and began pulling on the clothes. He had turned away when she stripped off her nightdress; he did not look back until she said, "I'm ready."

He took her hand and dragged her through the house at a run. He did not lead her to her fine aircar; instead, he pulled her to a scruffy little model that had been old before she was born. He leaped into one side, and she followed suit on the other—she barely had the door closed when the little vehicle lifted into the air.

Almost dawn, she thought. She could see the first slivers of gray on the eastern horizon, shading through the tall buildings at the center of the old city, and to the north and south fitting along the curves of the hills. Patr took them up quickly, circling over her house as he gained altitude in the fashion of the old vehicles; and as she looked down at her home, she saw a veritable fleet of cars move in around it, and people tiny as pebbles in her hand clamber out and run toward her house from all sides.

"They didn't believe me after all," he whispered. "I thought they might not."

The aircar reached the altitude he wanted, and he set it running due north, and fast—very fast—at the high speed only permitted in the narrow band that ran on top of the Aboves and just below the point where Matrin's atmosphere became too thin to breathe.

Jess became aware of the fact that he muttered constantly under his breath; an instant later, she finally placed the words he repeated.

"Gods forgive my trespasses,
My moments of weakness,
My choices against good;
Gods lead and protect in this
My hour of darkness,
In this my hour of need."

Over and over. She'd never heard him pray before. She'd never heard from him even the slightest hints of piety. He stunned her with this display, and, watching him drive like a man fleeing the gods themselves, she wondered what he knew that made his fear so deep, so profound, so all-consuming.

She held a silent prayer in her heart—not for herself, but for Wraith. *Protect him,* she demanded of the gods.

She hoped they heard her.

A woman dark as death and a man white as bone came to Luercas in the middle of the afternoon, a full three days after Velyn vanished—both wearing Silent Inquest robes and insincere smiles. They made no sound when they walked, and light seemed to bend away from them as if in fear. "We would like to talk to you about the disappearance of your vow-mate, Velyn Artis-Tanquin."

Luercas felt his skin prickle beneath his thin tunic. If the Silent Inquest was coming after him, they had a lot more to banish him for than brutality to his wife. But once they had someone fixed under their viewing lenses, everything else tended to come out, too. His stolen body—and the way he'd gone about stealing it—would certainly be just cause to win him a life sentence for treason. He frowned to hide the surge of fear that enveloped him and said, "I've filled out the proper reports."

The woman said, "You have. But we're conducting an investigation that seems to have crossed paths with an investigation that *you're* conducting. A very interesting investigation."

Anything he said could be the wrong thing. So Luercas waited.

"Not going to offer to explain why you're having Gellas Tomersin followed and spied upon?" asked the man.

Anger, Luercas thought. That would be the best way to play this. "I have every reason to have that bastard followed. He was the last person seen with Velyn before she disappeared, and I have reason to believe that he's the reason she disappeared."

"But she disappeared from a boardinghouse, and we know that he was having dinner with friends at the time."

"You think he'd be stupid enough to kidnap her himself?"

"No. Nor do we think that *you* would be so stupid, though rumors seem to suggest that you had more reason to want her to disappear than even the judge's verdict might indicate."

"Rumors are worth half what you pay for them. I didn't kidnap Velyn."

The woman smiled gently, and in her dark face her pale teeth seemed predatory. "The thing that made us think you were innocent of her absence was that you're spending a great deal of time and money to look for her—and Gellas isn't. Which is not to say we think you're innocent of anything else."

"So you think he knows where she is?"

"We know he knows where she is. We've found her—right where he had his people hide her. She's on her way here now."

Luercas felt a huge rush of relief—he wouldn't be charged with murder, he wouldn't suffer financial losses worse than those that already faced him, and he might yet find a way to pull the whole mess out of the fire. "Excellent," he said.

"Is it? I suspect she'll have some fascinating things to tell us—and you know we have ways of getting at the truth better than anything anyone else has ever created. She'll be telling us . . . many things." The woman stared at him like a cat who'd cornered a mouse. Had she a tail, it would have been whipping from side to side right then. The man, in contrast, looked over Luercas's shoulder, down at the floor, up at the sky, anywhere but directly at Luercas. His restlessness, his darting eyes, and his gaunt, hungry look sharpened Luercas's fear like a whetstone sharpens steel. The woman said, "So what we would like to know—and we're only asking in a friendly fashion, you understand—" she smiled, and her smile held nightmares in it, "is this: Have you anything to tell us before Velyn arrives? Any little thing that she might be privy to—anything that might bring you grief should we find out about it after she . . . tells us what she knows?"

And how much did Velyn suspect? How much did she know of his activities with Dafril; how much had she seen or intuited or overheard of his struggles with this flesh that did not belong to him? How completely could she destroy him?

He had not been careful around her, because he had never feared her. She lived in terror of him—of what he would do to her—and so he had been free with his speech in front of her, and had not worried when Dafril was equally free. Her cringing, her silence, her head-down submissiveness had always seemed to be its own guarantee. But next to the Silent Inquest, any power he had over her would be nonexistent.

He looked at the woman, at the man, and he said softly, "What is the price of immunity?"

The woman and the man glanced at each other, quick smug smiles flitting across their lips, and then the man said, "You can buy your freedom with either Solander Artis or Gellas Tomersin. Give one or the other to us, and you will live."

"I believe I can give you Tomersin. My investigators have discovered . . . interesting things about him."

"Then come with us to our chambers, and we'll talk."

Wraith viewed the morning with pleasure. No one had been watching him at his home; no one followed him to the Galtin, and the theater hummed with the activity and excitement peculiar to such places. The actors on the stage finished up their rehearsal of *Seven Little Lies* and applauded themselves before they left the stage for their break.

He'd had word first thing that morning that members of the Order of Resonance had successfully infiltrated the high-security Empire Center for Public Education and inserted his latest round of Warrens information into the upcoming nightlies.

Jess had cut short her visit and left Oel Artis. Solander had successfully hidden his discovery and was quickly and quietly putting together plans to get himself and his associate out of the city entirely—and probably permanently.

Wraith smiled a little as he added up the presold seats for the night and tried to determine whether he had already made the necessary take for the day to cover expenses. He could begin to breathe again. Whatever had been going on had apparently not been about him, or if it had been about him, then his precautions and the carefully compartmented way that he lived his life had paid off.

Someone tapped gently on his door. Without looking up—he was halfway through a column of figures—he said, "Come in. I'll be with you in a moment."

His guest opened the door and waited patiently while he added up his figures. When he was finished, Wraith looked up at the stranger and smiled. "I'm sorry about that," he said. "Math and I have never been friends, and once I've started a long column of figures, the last thing I want to have to do is restart it."

The man chuckled. Thin, plainly dressed, with a nondescript face, he was a man that Wraith thought must almost disappear in crowds. "My sympathies. I'm no friend of math myself."

Wraith rose and bowed appropriately to the man, who nonetheless seemed for all his ordinariness slightly familiar to him. "I'm Gellas Tomersin, which you no doubt already knew since you're in my office. And you are . . . ?"

"Davic Etareiff." The man returned the bow, adding a flourish, and said, "I'm the head of a special investigative unit fielded by the . . . ah, the Dragons."

All of the quiet pleasure of the day disappeared for Wraith. "And how may I help you?"

"You may come with me without making any scenes that will disturb your employees. My people are scattered throughout the building, and are both capable of killing and prepared to kill anyone who decides to make a heroic attempt to rescue you from us. The best thing you can do, if you value the lives of the people who work for you, is to pretend that you are coming with us voluntarily."

Wraith stood there for a moment, thoughtful. He could, perhaps, escape the men in his theater; they would try to use magic-powered weapons on him, and those weapons would do nothing to him. However, any of his people who happened to be in the way wouldn't share his immunity.

"I'll go with you," he said at last.

"I'm glad you've reached the right decision," Etareiff said. He smiled a bland, congenial smile, and said, "Just walk beside me. Please don't bring anything with you—no bags or cases or papers. Keep your hands empty and in plain sight at all times. We'll be walking out the back of the theater, where you'll find one of our aircars waiting for you. You'll board it without struggle, and without attempting to give any sign to anyone still in or around the building. Anything you do that is not as I have outlined will result in the deaths of as many innocent people as we can reach within your theater in the time we have available to us. Do you understand?"

"Perfectly," Wraith said.

"Very good. Would you consider yourself much of an actor?"

The question startled Wraith. "I'll do, I suppose. I haven't the talent of the least of the people on one of my stages, but . . ." He shrugged. "Why?"

"Because when the two of us walk out the door, we're going to discuss some of the plays you have produced. You and I will carry on a happy, enthusiastic conversation that will convince anyone listening to us that you and I are great friends, and that everything is going just as it should be. Do you feel capable of doing that right now?"

Considering that if he failed, his friends and employees would be the ones to pay the price, he nodded slowly.

"Then let's go. Tell me about the work you're producing right now."

They stepped out the door and began the walk down the long hall. Wraith nodded to his people but said nothing to any of them. Instead he made it clear by his stance and focus that he was paying attention to his guest, in order to forestall employees who might be tempted to come up to him for just one signature or just one question. He discussed with as much animation as he could muster *Seven Little Lies* and several works that he'd recently put into production in out-of-town venues—works both of Vincalis and of promising young playwrights Wraith had sponsored. He spotted plenty of Etareiff's people in that long walk through the building. Etareiff proved both clever and well read; he was able to quote choice lines from a number of Vincalis plays, and he made entertaining jokes and comments to encourage the flow of conversation.

Wraith thought that, under other circumstances, he would have found Etareiff a likable and enjoyable companion. And that frightened him. He worked with actors, but had never truly considered that the best actors he met daily might not be the ones on the stage.

He hoped Jess was truly clear of Oel Artis, and under no suspicion for her past connection to him. That Solander was safe. That no one had been able to prove any connection between Master Gellas and the invisible, but well documented, Vincalis, or the Kaan, or the Order of Resonance, or the Warrens, or the family in Ynjarval who lied for Wraith about who he was.

He got into the aircar, and both he and Etareiff fell silent. He discovered that he was sweating profusely—the stinking sweat of fear. The aircar lifted off and headed west, toward the Merocalins.

"Any questions about where we're going?" Etareiff asked.

"No."

"I'll tell you anyway." Etareiff smiled a cheerful smile entirely out of keeping with the situation. "You've heard of the Gold Building?"

"Not really."

"Of the Silent Inquest?"

A pause. "No."

"Ah. Then you can't begin to appreciate the honor being done you. Only the very worst traitors in the Empire have ever been brought before an assemblage of the Silent Inquest." Etareiff leaned back, folded his hands in his lap, and stared out the window.

Beads of sweat dripped down Wraith's forehead into his eyes, slipped off of his upper lip, ran down the furrow between the muscles on either side of his spine with an icy and unnerving irregularity.

He looked longingly at the world racing below him; he couldn't help but wonder if this was the last look he would get of Oel Artis.

The aircar settled on the flat roof of one of the ancient wings of a building of tremendously ancient design, landing in deep shadow. Around the roof rose windowless walls three times the height of the tallest man, smooth and featureless and impenetrable. Only one door punctuated the grim expanse of whiteness, and it was toward that door that Etareiff and Wraith began to walk. Wraith knew he could fight Etareiff now—the weapons the agent would have with him would be unlikely to do anything at all to Wraith. But the driver of the aircar would pose a more difficult problem, and there were no other aircars on the roof. He could make things more difficult for himself in the long run by fighting now. If he maintained his assertion that he was an innocent man, a stolti due the respect and protection of the law, and not a criminal who deserved its punishment, he still might be able to walk away from all of this.

"We're going into one of the interrogation observation rooms," Etareiff said as the two of them passed through the single broad door and into a wide, plain hallway. "I'd like for you to hear some things that the Masters of the Inquest—and the Dragons who asked for our assistance—have found very interesting. You won't be listening to these confessions live—you'll simply be observing copies made of the interrogation procedure. I think you'll find some of what we've learned . . . well, frankly, fascinating."

"Learned about whom?" Wraith asked.

"Oh, all sorts of people. You'll see. It has been one of the most interesting days of my career so far, and I must say I can only anticipate it getting more interesting. The Inquestor Triad is simply stunned by what we've been uncovering."

Wraith said nothing else. Anything he said might tell them something they didn't already know. He wouldn't do that.

He followed Etareiff into a small room in which a semicircle of silk brocade and leather chairs faced a raised dais. Men in green and gold robes glanced over at him as he entered, and he was shown to one of the chairs and bade to sit. Etareiff did not take a seat; instead, he retreated to the back of the room and took a position on one side of the door. Another man, clearly armed with several weapons, leaned against the wall on the other side.

"Master Tomersin," the oldest of the men said, standing up, "I am Master Omwi. The Dragons of the Council have . . . yes, *appointed* would be the right word . . . have appointed me investigator into your activities and those of your associates. Welcome to our little circle. We regret the necessity of bringing you here, but as you will see in a moment, serious issues have arisen that require not just your presence, but will eventually demand some form of explanation."

"Master Omwi," Wraith said, and rose and bowed deeply. "I'm sure I'll be able to clear up any questions you might have."

"That would be almost a miracle," Omwi said, "but I do look forward to seeing you try."

Then Master Omwi waved a hand gently through the air, and on the dais in front of the observers Solander Artis appeared, seated in a chair. A column of light surrounded him, so that his questioners of record remained hidden in shadow—he would not have been able to see them, but no one could see them now, either.

"Name," a disembodied voice said.

"Solander Kothern Jans Emanual Artis, stolti, son of Rone Jans—"

"We know your parentage, Artis. It's part of what makes your betrayal so significant. Your father died a hero. You—"

"Enough," another voice whispered. "Stay with relevant matters."

Wraith watched Solander closely. He seemed completely unworried; he sat in a relaxed pose, his hands folded, an expression of calm acceptance on his face. This was a different Solander than the panicked friend who had come to Wraith for help; who had falsified data to save his own life and who had planned to leave Oel Artis as soon as he thought he could escape without drawing any attention to his departure.

Wraith wondered what had changed. Obviously Solander was in trouble. However, he projected an air of such complete confidence that even Wraith, who knew what he had done and who could at least guess at the possible repercussions of Solander's actions, should they be proven, felt himself wondering if perhaps Solander had found a way to prove his innocence.

"You have been brought before the private interrogators because you have refused to agree to cooperate in our investigation. Do you understand this?"

"I do," Solander said.

"You have refused to turn over information on others associated with you; you have refused to explain in any form your own behavior as it has been related to us by our agent; and you have refused to provide us with the complete formulas and background research to explain your new theory of magic, or the law that you claim to have discovered—"

Solander held up a hand to interrupt. "Excuse me, but I haven't claimed to have discovered anything. I've spent years researching *rewhah*-free magic, but my research, while it has provided many useful side products, has failed in its main objective."

"Not according to our agent."

"No. I'm aware that Borlen Haiff has informed you that I was successful in my research. I'm also aware that he has been unable to duplicate the results he claims I obtained, and that while he is vehement in his claims that I have been successful, he has no proof of this."

Wraith heard the long, hostile silence and had to smile. So Solander had figured out who the Inquest's spy was. Of course, the fact that he'd brought Borlen with him when he met with Wraith—and that Wraith had offered what could only be seen as treasonous advice regarding the way in which Solander could prevent the Empire from finding out what he'd been working on—did not bode well for Wraith's future freedom, and certainly went far to suggest a reason why he sat with members of the Inquest watching the interrogation.

Wraith waited, studying the image of his friend. After a moment of silence, the invisible interrogators began again. "Had you not discovered something that you believed the Hars Ticlarim would find valuable, why would you have acted as you did?"

"How did I act?" Solander asked.

"You fled to a meeting with a suspected traitor to the Empire, Gellas Tomersin, and discussed ways of hiding your discovery from the Council of Dragons, and further, ways of leaving the empire with this discovery."

"Nonsense." Solander actually laughed. "Is that what dear Borlen told you? At least now I know why I'm here. He must have had a much more interesting night than I did. I took him to meet Gellas, who is both my distant cousin and a friend of mine from childhood. Borlen had claimed to be a great admirer of Gellas's work, and seemed to enjoy meeting him. The three of us walked to dinner at a fine restaurant, ate our meal, engaged in ordinary table talk, and after Gellas bought us our meal, we left, and Borlen and I went to our separate homes because we needed a good night's rest; we had to check our equipment calibrations and present a public test of my theory on the morrow."

"Borlen Haiff presents an entirely different picture of that evening."

Solander smiled slowly. "And now you're admitting that Borlen is your agent. Thank you. So we're making some progress." He sighed. "Borlen is ambitious. He's also careless, and has, for most of the time he's been assigned to me, proven astonishingly lazy." Solander shrugged. "I made do with his assignment to me because I was told we were short on qualified assistants; I believe my regular written complaints dating back over two years will be on record, making clear the fact that I did not consider him competent help and requested an adequate replacement as soon as one might be found."

"They are. But your complaints about Borlen have nothing to do with your own treasonous activities."

"I have no treasonous activities. What sort of fantasy world do you live in?" Solander asked. "You think that a two-year complaint file regarding the general worthlessness of an ambitious assistant—who just happens to also be a spy for the Dragons, or whatever offshoot of the Dragons you might be—won't have any repercussions? Borlen Haiff finally decided that the bad references in his file and the fact that we weren't making the sort of progress that would make him famous added up to a need for him to take action on his own. So he concocted this story of his and presented it to you; what's more, according to you, he made himself the hero who created some sort of mystical shield that did not lose energy as regular shields do, and that rebounded both *rewhah* and spell force on the sender, making it the perfect defensive weapon." Solander shook his head gently. "It makes a lovely story—who wouldn't want to have created such a thing? But if it had any truth to it, why couldn't Borlen show you his brilliant shield himself? Your questions to me have made it clear that he claimed all along to have created this shield—not even he blamed that on me. Why did you come to *me* and demand that I was hiding something from you, and that I should show you this thing that only Borlen in all the world claims exists?"

"You forget that you had dinner with Gellas Tomersin that night. We'll question him, too."

"Of course you will. And you'll discover that his story matches with mine."

"I'm sure we will. And I'm sure that, when you've been subjected to spelled interrogation, your story will match our agent's. You cannot lie under spelled interrogation."

Solander spread his hands wide. "Then interrogate me."

"We're giving you a chance to tell us what we want to know without interrogation. You are stolti, and of the highest family. If you simply agree to tell us what we wish to know, and if you cooperate with our further investigations, we'll offer you limited immunity, and you won't be subject to full prosecution for anything you've done. At worst you'll have to step down from your position in Research and accept a period of house confinement."

"I'm innocent," Solander said. "And the friends that you want me to give you in exchange for this bargain of yours are innocent as well."

Wraith felt his stomach knot. They knew Solander was a connection to him—and they suspected Wraith of something much worse than concealing information. They suspected him of harboring his own private army and planning the overthrow of the Empire.

They were, for the moment, being quite polite about how they dealt with him, considering what they believed to be true about him. They were about to be less gentle with Solander, however.

"For the record, then, you refuse this last offer of leniency on our part for cooperation on yours?"

"I do," Solander said. "I have done nothing wrong, my friends have done nothing wrong, and I will not sell anyone to you to protect myself from your lies. The truth will be my protection."

Which all sounded very noble, and Wraith had to admire the presentation—but the fact was, Solander *was* lying. He *was* guilty. And spelled interrogation was going to prove that to everyone. Solander was giving up a chance to protect himself, but he wouldn't be able to protect Wraith, or Jess, or Velyn, or the Kaan, or the rebels in the Order of Resonance. It would all come out, and he would be stripped of his citizenship and banished anyway.

And then the image of Solander vanished.

Wraith, who had been prepared to see the spell cast and to see Solander confessing everything that had happened from the day that Wraith had run through his gate to elude pursuers, instead found himself facing a blank dais.

And the members of the Silent Inquest turned and looked at him.

"You can just imagine what he told us," Master Omwi said.

Wraith tipped his head and his brow furrowed. "Pardon me, gentlemen, but I thought the purpose of making a live record of the interrogation was so that viewers wouldn't have to imagine." He put his hand to his chin and stared off at nothing. "All I can imagine," he said at last, "is that you discovered exactly what he said you would discover—that is, nothing. And that, hoping I would think you discovered something more, you brought me here, showed me the part of the interrogation that took place prior to spellcasting and that could therefore only be subjective, and counted on my concern for my friend to put some sort of pressure on me to tell you whatever it is you want to hear."

"We have proof of what you've been doing from a number of unrelated sources. What you have now is an opportunity. If you are honest with us, you will save the life of your friend, who otherwise will be stripped of his stolti class, created a parvoi, and executed for treason along with anyone else we can connect with him."

Wraith couldn't believe what he'd just heard. "The man is innocent. You couldn't even get proof of treason with spelled interrogation, which from everything I've heard, and everything everyone else has heard, is completely and perfectly accurate. If you had proof of his treason, you would have used that part of the interrogation. So why are you telling me that unless I tell you what you want to hear, you're going to execute him?"

The Masters looked at each other, and finally Master Omwi said, "Because we have reason to believe that he has found a way to lie under spelled interrogation. That, in fact, he can do everything our agent told us he could do, and more—and that he used some of this new magic to subvert the course of our investigation. Though it was never considered a genuine possibility, the Silent Inquest nonetheless maintained a law in our annals that anyone who lied under spelled interrogation would be executed."

Wraith stood up. "What you're telling me now doesn't make sense. You're claiming that if I tell you he lied—a thing that you cannot prove—you'll spare his life. If, however, I tell you the truth—which is that he told you the truth—you'll execute him for treason."

"We know he lied," Omwi said. "In spite of the fact that we never use spelled interrogation on our own agents, we made an exception in this case. Following Solander's interrogation, when he demonstrated that everything he'd told us had been true, we brought Borlen Haiff in and questioned him under spellbond. And he proved that everything *he* told us had been true."

Wraith considered that for a moment. "Ah. And now you need to know which one is lying to you, and you think I'll tell you that my friend Solander is the liar. Well, you're at least interesting in your insanity."

Omwi managed a thin smile. "We have a little sense of humor over the strangeness of our own predicament, Master Gellas—but not much. Our humor won't extend very far in any direction if we do not get some cooperation. And quickly. Let me tell you what we are currently doing. We have located your longtime lover Velyn Artis-Tanquin where you apparently had her hidden. She is now on her way here, along with the men you charged with hiding her. We have a fine collection of your associates already in holding cells—men and women from the Order of Resonance, various actors you have employed over the years, a handful of assistants, prop managers, lighting specialists, set designers, and costumers that you have employed on a regular basis since bringing your first heretical play to the stage. We have already interrogated some of them. We plan to interrogate others. We are still awaiting the arrival of Jess Covitach-Artis, whom we are having some difficulty locating—this in spite of the fact that her assistant is one of our people."

Wraith started at that, and Omwi smiled. "Ah. So you've met Agent Jethis."

Wraith thought about his discussion regarding Jess with the hostile Patr and nodded thoughtfully. "I didn't like him. So he betrayed her, too."

"Betrayed her? Not at all. She is apparently innocent of any wrongdoing—but we can always use her as leverage if we need to. No—Agent Jethis merely told us interesting things about you. In fact, he gave us a recording of a conversation he had with you that has been most helpful in pointing us in the direction of people we needed to bring in."

Wraith knew he hadn't said anything of a sensitive nature to Patr Jethis. But he also knew that he had said many incriminating things to Jess. What if Patr truly did love Jess? What if he'd obtained a copy of that conversation, but had protected Jess by finding some way to make the incriminating discussion sound like it had taken place with Patr instead?

The Silent Inquest knew about the Kaan. They would find out about everything else; either Velyn would arrive and tell everything she knew to get herself out of trouble and get even with him, or the Kaan and the

Order of Resonance would, under spellbond, reveal an absolutely horrifying list of treasonous acts against the Empire.

"You have nothing, then, that you wish to volunteer?" Master Omwi asked.

"No."

The Master nodded, and out of the shadows that surrounded the room, burly guards stepped forward. Before Wraith could move, they clamped his wrists into heavy white-metal manacles, and marched him forward onto the dais where moments before Solander's image had stood.

"Certain you don't wish to talk to us voluntarily?" the Master asked.

"Quite," Wraith said.

"Your choice," Master Omwi said.

The guards stepped away from him, and from overhead, the light of a spellshield shimmered to life. Wraith considered walking through it, but decided that if these people didn't know magic didn't touch him, he would be best off to let them think it did.

"Your name," Omwi asked.

"Gellas Tomersin," Wraith said.

"Your class."

"Stolti. Artis family."

"Your occupation."

"Theater manager and producer of plays."

"The identity of Vincalis."

"I don't know."

Silence. Wraith could see nothing beyond the wall of brilliant light that poured down around him. But he could hear well enough. "Check the settings," Omwi whispered, "and increase them by twenty percent."

"Yes, Master."

The light got brighter. "The identity of Vincalis."

"I don't know." Wraith had a hard time not smiling as he answered the questions. He knew this sort of interrogation to be hell on the people who had to undergo it. Those who had offered testimony on only minor matters reported headaches for days afterward, and confusion, and feelings of dread. But he might as well have been standing on a sunny beach enjoying the breeze. As far as interrogation went, he could take this forever.

"He has to know," a voice Wraith didn't recognize murmured, and Omwi responded with a grunt and the muttered, "I would have thought so."

"Where is Velyn Artis-Tanquin?"

"I don't know," Wraith said.

"Damnall, you *know* he knows that!" someone else yelled. "It isn't working on him, either!"

"No magic use coming from him," a voice from high up and off to the left said. "I have us at five hundred luns right now, and all my dials are clear—he's taking everything we're running through him."

"But *he knows where Velyn Artis-Tanquin is, because we know where she is and he's the one who sent her there.*"

Wraith felt a sudden dread. Jess's assistant was one of these people. Solander's assistant had been one of these people. Which of his assistants was the spy?

"All the way to the top," Omwi yelled. "Four thousand luns, and if that cooks his brain out of his skull, we'll apologize to his next of kin."

"Yes, Master Omwi."

The light grew so brilliant that Wraith could no longer see his hands at the end of his arms—could no longer see his arms, for that matter. He closed his eyes, but the light came through his eyelids. As a form of interrogation, this became a bit more real, he thought.

"Is Velyn Artis-Tanquin on Bair's Island?" Omwi asked.

How to answer? That was where she was, and they obviously knew it—he would be giving them nothing that they didn't already have if he admitted this. Then he might be able to win their faith in the rest of his lies. They might think the increased power was working where the lesser dose hadn't. "Yes," he said.

"Good. Who is your main underground contact?"

"What's the underground?" Wraith asked.

He heard a snarl of inarticulate fury from somewhere out in the darkness.

Omwi said, "Who is Vincalis?"

"Master of Transports Camus Pindolin," Wraith said promptly.

"Turn it off," Omwi said, and his voice was filled with disgust. The light vanished abruptly, but Wraith still couldn't see.

"Good attempt," Omwi added. "Unfortunately for you, Pindolin is one of ours. And we know you're involved in the underground, because one of your regular contacts is one of ours, too."

"Shall we kill him?" someone right behind Wraith asked, and Wraith jumped. He still couldn't see anything but the multicolored spots of light that swarmed in front of his eyes.

"No. I'll bring in a few torturers from the Strithian borderlands. We can have them here in two or three days, and we'll get what we need from him then. We should probably use the torturers on all of our prisoners—no telling which of the rest of them can withstand four thousand luns in the interrogator. We'll run them all through the interrogator, and when we're finished we'll torture to get a cross-reference."

Silence. Then, right next to his ear, Omwi's voice. "Your gift to all of your fellow rebels, Tomersin. Because of you, now all of them will get to bleed, too."

"It's just me," Wraith said.

"No, it isn't. The interrogator didn't work on Artis, either. But we could at least tell he was doing something to fight it. The magic never quite touched him. You . . ."

Silence. And the darkness. And then a hand gripping the back of his neck so hard he wanted to cry out, and someone else's voice saying, "Keep up with me or I'll kick you till you piss blood for a month."

Chapter 18

Solander lay on the narrow cot in his cell, staring up at the glossy white ceiling. He could smell the sweetness of ripe fruit in the bowl beside him, and the sweat and piss of the man in the cell down the hall, the one who ranted and howled constantly and incoherently.

His shield had held, and during the spelled interrogation, he'd managed to project excellent, convincing images that ought to have demonstrated the absolute truth of his assertions.

Yet he had failed to convince *someone* of importance, as evidenced by the fact that he remained in captivity.

He wanted to hear some news. He wanted some word that his friends were safe, that Wraith and Jess and even Velyn remained out of the hands of the Dragons' interrogators. Instead, he listened to Big Fly the Madman going through his endless shouted loop.

"Big FLY fall spot SPANK leaf bread BONES meat stick HOT bang GOD dog train flee big FLY fall spot SPANK—"

Every once in a while, he'd stop in the middle of the loop to drink something. Solander could hear him slopping and swallowing. No matter where he dropped out of the loop, he always restarted with "Big FLY . . ."

Big Fly made for an interesting form of torture, and Solander had determined early on that it was a form to which he was particularly susceptible. He hated noise, he hated nonsense, and the erratic nature of Big Fly's lunatic ragings, stopping and starting as they did, were driving him in a quick and efficient manner to the edge of a piece of madness of his own.

So he lay on his cot, staring at the ceiling, trying not to worry about all the many things he could not change, and trying equally hard to figure out some way to get his theory of magic safely into the hands of people who would not only hide it, but if something happened to him would use it to wage war against the parasitic magic of the Dragons of the Hars Ticlarim.

Solander should have known Borlen Haiff was an agent. Borlen had been far too lazy to have come up through the ranks of junior and senior wizards. And while he had shown admirable knowledge of some narrow aspects of the field of magical power utilization, overall he didn't seem to have even such grasp of his subject as would get him through the preliminary magical training, much less the advanced work that created assistants and associates.

A door banged open and then closed in the distance, and footsteps echoed along the hallway, moving closer. Solander narrowed his eyes to slits and made his breathing deep and even. He doubted that this charade would convince anyone who might be spying on him, and he doubted that it would offer any information or comfort to him. But he thought that if he didn't have to talk to whichever guard was coming, he would be ahead of the game.

"Your cell, Master," the guard said, and Solander heard the door across the hall open and close, and heard the bars that locked it shut click into place. He lay where he was, his body limp and his breathing steady, and watched. Initially all he could see was the guard's back. "You'll have a meal coming later," the guard said. "I suggest you eat it, and fast. We come along to pick them up after you've had sufficient time. What you haven't eaten when we return, you don't get. For now, you'll receive one meal a day. I've been instructed to tell you, too, that if you offer to cooperate, you'll receive both larger portions and more frequent meals."

"I doubt that will be an issue." The voice belonged to Wraith. Solander almost lost the pattern of his breathing. He didn't want to alert Wraith to his presence until the guard was well out of the way. Wraith, careful as he was, wouldn't blurt out anything compromising about the two of them, but Solander preferred their first communication in these foul circumstances to be between just the two of them. And whomever might be operating the viewers, of course.

"Well—I told you," the guard said. "How you choose to use the information is your choice."

". . . spot spank leaf bread bones meat stick HOT bang GOD dog train flee BIG fly FALL spot SPANK LEAF BREAD BONES MEAT STICK HOT BANG GOD DOG TRAIN FLEE big fly fall—"

"Shut up, Stotts!" the guard bellowed, thus giving a name to Solander's headache.

". . . spot spank leaf bread bones meat stick hot bang . . ."

"He'll keep you plenty of company in the meantime," the guard said with malicious pleasure. "So you think about cooperating. Stotts drives people crazy. After a while they start to believe that they know what he's talking about. If he gets to making sense, you better ask for a deal. Your brain will be soup if you don't."

And the guard left. Steady footsteps down the hall, the heavy door opening and closing, and a momentary reprieve when he left, as Stotts took a break to drink again and gargle.

Solander stood up and walked over to the barred door of his cell. "This isn't the place where I'd hoped to see you next."

Down the hall, Stotts whispered, with the fervor of an ascetic, ". . . leaf . . . bread . . . bones . . . meat . . . stick . . . hot . . . bang . . . god . . . dog . . . train . . ."

"We *have* to get out of here," Wraith said.

Solander, who had been listening to Stotts for far longer, nodded, then said, "But I won't believe we can until I see the sky again. I've been charged with treason. They've told me if they can find proof—any proof—that I actually accomplished what Borlen Haiff said I did, they'll strip me of stolti class, make me a parvoi, and execute me. For magic, Wraith. For gods'-damned *magic*. For a *theory*, by the Obscure!"

"They aren't going to execute you." Wraith shook his head. "They're after Vincalis. They think he's the head of a conspiracy, that he's trying to overthrow the Empire, and they're going to go through you, and me, and anyone else they can to try to find him. They've already told me if I cooperate with them, they'll drop all charges against you and Velyn and gods alone know who else they've already dragged in, and set me and the lot of you free. If they think you know anything, they'll tell you the same thing." Wraith glanced up and down the corridors—Solander knew that someone would be monitoring everything the two of them said. Wraith obviously didn't want to say anything incriminating, but Solander could tell that he wanted to say more than he had.

"I don't know what they need to know," Wraith said. "They'll find that out. They'll find it out about you, too, and about anyone else they question. Vincalis has never shown himself to anyone. Never."

Solander nodded. "I don't know about anyone else, but I know he's never shown himself to me." He sighed. "Maybe you're right. Maybe that is what they're really after."

"Come on. You come up with some theory of magic that doesn't even work, and they're going to execute you for that?"

Solander laughed weakly. "I suppose not." He signaled to Wraith that the two of them should end their conversation. They'd planted their lies as best they could. The stress of lying for the audience he knew he had, though, was costing him.

Solander had hoped to get a copy of his theory to Wraith so that Wraith could get it to the underground where someone could make use of it, but with Wraith imprisoned, he had no idea where to hide it, or even with whom to entrust it.

If only Wraith didn't have his atypical reaction to magic, Solander could talk to him mind-to-mind. But with Wraith, nothing could be that easy. He thought for a while, and suddenly remembered the hand signals the two of them had used around his father when they'd been boys. The two of them had thought they were so clever—in retrospect, Solander had to think that his father had simply assumed that boys wouldn't have secrets worth searching out.

The code might still work, though, and if he and Wraith didn't overuse it and kept it as disguised as possible, they might be able to work a few things out.

Solander dragged his bed along the back wall, which gave him a clear view into Wraith's cell. Wraith watched him. He stayed put.

"Didn't like the view?"

Solander said, "I was hoping that being right against the back wall might cut down on some of the . . . er . . . noise."

"Ah." Wraith's eyes never left his. "It help?"

"A bit. Not as much as I could have hoped."

"I'll take a little help," Wraith said, and dragged his own cot over so that it lay against his back wall.

Truly, it made no difference regarding the sound. Stotts kept right on babbling—now his voice ran from the prayerful to the demanding, but the text remained the same. Solander didn't care, though. He sat on the cot, his back pressed to the wall, and with his legs sprawled wide, dropped his hands front and center, so his thighs shielded most of their movement. And he signaled, *Do you remember the code?*

Wraith watched the hands, frowned for a moment, worked the movements out using his own fingers, and then slowly signaled, *Yes. But it's not a very complicated code. They'll figure it out quickly.*

Then we need to get to the point.

Fine. What point?

I need a place where I can magically create a print copy of my theory. Someplace both you and I know, where you or one of your people can retrieve it if I don't make it out of here. I have the key. This new magic can free the Warreners. It can change the world—and the Dragons can't even detect it. They can't fight it. They have no defenses against it. You have to make sure that your people get hold of it and use it.

Wraith looked at him as if he'd gone insane. *You have magic they can't even detect, and you're sitting here? Why? Why haven't you just created a spell and let yourself out?*

Because they told me they had Jess, and that if I gave them trouble, they'd kill her.

Funny. They told me they couldn't find Jess, but that they had Velyn and an entire collection of my associates, and that if I didn't cooperate, they would kill them.

Both men stared at each other.

Have you seen anyone you give a rat's damn for in here—besides me? Wraith signed.

No. You?

No.

Think they're lying to us?

Maybe. Do we risk their wrath?

Do we stay in here and let them torture us into betraying the people and the causes we care about?

Solander considered that for a moment. The magical interrogation had failed on him because he'd used his new magic to shield against it, and had magically supplied images that supported his lies. Wraith would be as immune to magical interrogation as he was to any other magical application. He must have driven them nearly mad as they tried spell after spell to force him to confess, and got no results from anything.

Certainly they had put him together with Wraith in the hopes that the two of them would betray themselves in discussion with each other. But Wraith was right. Physical torture would be the Inquest's next step, because it would be their only option. And Solander had no illusions about his ability to stand up to physical torture. He'd led a soft life. He'd crack like an egg.

We need to get out of here now, he signed.

Wraith smiled a bit. *How?*

I can get the locks. I can shield us. We'll need to wait until it's dark in here, though, and Stotts is asleep—I don't want him alerting anyone.

Does he sleep?

Sometimes. Not often enough.

Can you get us past the guards?

I can get us past magical alarm systems. I believe I can put a shield around the two of us that will fool them. I'm sure I can make myself unobtrusive to guards, too—but you're the problem there. Surrounding you with a shield is simple, because all you have to do is stay close to me and you'll be inside of it. Changing your appearance with an illusion, though . . .

Wraith nodded. *Then we'll need to avoid guards.*

Yes. Unless I can make myself seem to be a guard.

Risky.

We're going to die in here if we don't flee. How much riskier does the situation need to be? My gut says we're in terrible danger right now.

Then we'll flee. Our signal will be Stotts asleep.

Done.

Meantime, Wraith signaled, *I know the place for your theory. Create a copy in the Oel Artis Warrens. First house up against the wall by the Vincalis Gate. First apartment on the right. Each unit has built-in seating with storage on the right wall beside the door. Can you find that? Can you do it?*

Solander considered this for a while. He could trance, use the new form of magic he'd developed to draw energy from his own flesh and blood, find the place Wraith described by distance-viewing without the viewer—an uncomfortable prospect, but not an impossible one—and create a perfect copy where Wraith indicated.

But you'll be the only person who will be able to retrieve it, Solander protested. *If anything happens to you, it will be lost forever.*

I know. But I can't think of anyplace else where we wouldn't be compromising someone whom the Dragons and these people of theirs might already have under observation.

True. Solander considered. *I can do it while we're waiting for Stotts to fall asleep. It might take some time, though, and it will definitely cost me some energy. Why don't you try to sleep? You may have to carry me out of here.*

Really?

Yes.

Wraith's forehead creased, but he nodded. *I can do that. I'll sleep. You work. We'll get through this.*

A long pause, with the two of them sitting there looking at each other, friends separated by time, by the abyss formed from their different lives, by the directions they had chosen and the worlds in which they moved. They were friends who had wandered, brothers estranged by nothing more pressing than life; and in that moment Solander realized

how much he had missed Wraith, and how much he hoped they would
find their way back to the close friendship they had once had.

This new magic could give them that. It could give them everything.

Fortune favor us, he signaled to Wraith.

And whatever gods there might be, Wraith replied.

Their fingers fell still. They each stretched out on their cots and
waited for any hint of darkness, and for the babble that was Stotts to
cease.

Velyn paced along the broad, cool breezeway of her island home.
Out in the courtyard the palms rattled, every breeze clattering their
fronds together. Monkeys shrieked and parrots screeched. She hated the
tropics. Palm trees seemed unfinished to her, and monkeys, with their
weird little faces and nasty little hands, made her queasy—and she was
afraid of parrots. Big evil beaks and beady bright eyes.

Her guest followed half a pace behind her, his flowing khebarr,
loosely belted and with the skirts tucked up into the belt, already sticking to his skin.

"Idrik," she said, "I am bored beyond words. Surely there must be
something for me to do on this godsforsaken island."

"Beyond this village there is a jungle. Or a rocky beach that ends in
the sea. Your friends made sure you had things to entertain yourself. You
have paints. Sculpting materials. Books. Musical instruments. Writing
supplies. Cloth and thread and yarns and beads and needles of every
sort. What else might you wish for?"

She glanced at him, trying to assess what he would look like without the body-concealing khebarr. "What can you give me? A wider bed
and a robust young man to put in it. I'll take you if you'd like to volunteer."

He stared at her, stricken, and his face flushed the deep, tortured red
of a tropical sunset. Poor boy—he hadn't been prepared for her to be
honest with him.

Speechless, he looked down at his feet and twisted his hands together, as if by doing so he might wring the sweat out of them.

"Well? You're supposed to be my assistant, aren't you? They hired
you, right? So assist me. Take off the robes and let me get a look at you,
then. I suspect you'll do—I'm willing to be reasonable, after all. I don't
demand a prize stallion—just someone with a little imagination, some
stamina, and a bit of enthusiasm."

Behind her, someone with a very deep voice cleared his throat.

Velyn turned and found a lean, dark-eyed man in a black khebarr watching her.

"Stolta Velyn, don't waste your time teasing the children."

"He's a child? He looks old enough. Barely."

"You're his first full posting. He most certainly isn't prepared to satisfy your lusts."

"Then I'm to be left dry as a barren old woman?"

The stranger smiled slightly and gave a signal to young Idrik. The boy fled at a pace just fractionally slower than an out-and-out run.

"I didn't say that," the stranger said when the boy was out of earshot. "I didn't even imply it. I merely told you that you aren't to be bothering the children."

Velyn sized him up. He was her age. Maybe a bit older, but if he was, he wore the age with remarkable grace.

"So why are you here?" she asked.

He smiled slowly. "I seem to have heard that you were bored."

"You have good ears. Or good timing. Who are you? Really?"

"You can call me Farsee."

"Which doesn't answer the question of who you are."

He chuckled. "It's as valid as your saying your name is Velyn. Velyn isn't who you are, but it's the name you've attached to yourself. Who I am is something that I can know, but you can only discover through experience—not by my telling you." He took a step toward her. "Are you still bored?"

She had to smile at that. She wasn't. Not in the least. She found herself excited, interested, even intrigued.

He nodded at her expression and said, "Good. If you'd like to make the day interesting someplace other than your hot, stuffy bedroom and your hard mattress, come walk with me. I know an excellent place—cool and beautiful and almost . . . enchanting. And we'll have the most excitement you've had since you got here."

"You think well of yourself, don't you?" Velyn was already walking to him, though, not in the least concerned by his answer.

"I know who I am. I'm satisfied with that."

Velyn found his answer delightful. She looked forward to discovering if he could stand up to his own opinion of himself. If he did, wonderful. They'd have a memorable afternoon. If he didn't, well, she'd get some amusement out of the whole thing one way or the other. If her amusement came at his expense, she could live with that, too.

He led them out of the breezeway, through the central garden, and then toward the back of the little compound. Beneath vines, he opened a gate that she had never discovered before.

"I didn't know this was here," she murmured.

"You weren't supposed to."

Behind the compound, the jungle grew hard up against the walls. Beneath the dense canopy of giant ironwoods and blackwoods and snaketrees and vining blooddrinkers, she could see the start of an overgrown path.

"Not many people come back this way. The place where we're going once had regular visitors, but the jungle reclaimed much of the territory after the last civil war in the islands. The chapel remains—is, in fact, better than it was before, since I have made it into my own little home away from the Order."

"So, who knows you're with me?"

"Young Idrik, at least as much as he is capable of knowing," Farsee said. "And when someone thinks to question him, the questioner will know what Idrik knows."

"Then we're likely to have someone charging in on us at an inopportune time."

"Hardly. You have no keeper in the village. If you choose to wander about the island, none will question you. And none are likely to come to your rescue, either—so I suggest you stay out of the jungle unless accompanied. It can be a dangerous place."

Velyn nodded. "I see."

The jungle's darkness seemed oppressive to Velyn. She liked the coolness of the lush, light-obscuring greenery, but she found her eyes straying to movements at the periphery of her vision, and discovered that she kept more quiet than was her wont while her ears strained to pick up the soft padding of heavy, careful feet, or to notice first the hiss that would precede the dropping of a giant snake onto her slender shoulders from the branches that arched overhead.

"You seem nervous," Farsee said after a while.

"I'm a city girl by nature and preference."

"You'll like the city I'm taking you to—or at least what remains of it. It's truly amazing."

"Well . . . a city sounds good. Hard to imagine that there could ever have been one on this little island."

"It once housed a part of a great civilization. That civilization has crumbled to dust, leaving little more behind it than stones and statues and a few carved messages that no one has figured out how to decipher.

The people of this place were artists, though. But you'll see. We haven't much farther."

He was as good as his word. They walked only a few more moments before they reached a cliff along which ran a narrow, paved stone road and a low stone wall no doubt meant to keep passersby from falling to their death as they traversed the high thoroughfare. Farsee stopped her and pointed to her left. "That way, you would find the ruins of many small houses, a once-grand market, baths, and a few other public buildings. Some of the villagers still go there regularly to study the inscriptions on the stone and see if they can make sense of them. I don't busy myself with such things; the words of the dead and dust hold little appeal to me. But to the right, there is a secluded chapel." He shrugged. "At least I must guess that it is a chapel, since it follows the architectural pattern for chapels built by these people. It *doesn't* get many visits from the villagers, since it has no inscriptions carved anywhere around it, and since it is so inconveniently located to the rest of this little city."

"We're going right, then?"

Farsee smiled. "You'll start hearing the waterfall in just a moment. Wait until you see it; to me it looks like a thing alive."

The two of them stepped carefully over vines and roots that had grown into and over the ancient road, worked their way around a steep bend, and then Velyn did hear the waterfall. As they came to a ravine, water echoed through the steep valley. The sound faded again once they were past the bridge, but returned when, on the other side, they went into an unlit tunnel. They had not touched each other until this time, but Farsee took her hand as the utter darkness of the tunnel blanked out the rest of the world. The sound of the waterfall roared through the darkness, providing a hint of the direction they must follow. Farsee, his voice raised over the distant roar, said, "This isn't terribly far, but the stone paving becomes increasingly slippery the closer we get to our destination. Just take your time and hold tight to my hand."

Velyn thought this was going to extremes for an afternoon of amusement. Had he told her how far they would have to travel, that they would be so tired and sweaty by the end of their journey—or that some portion of it would be through a tunnel that she wouldn't enter alone for double shares of her father's fortune—she would have said she could be hot and sweaty in her little room and entirely bypass the entertainment value of fear.

Instead, she let him lead her through the darkness, and she wondered how he navigated. Could he see in darkness, as cats could? Did he have some marks cut into the path that he could follow with his feet alone? She didn't know. She knew only that the sense she got of the place they traveled through was that the tunnel walls were very far away—and that if she pulled free of Farsee, she could become lost in the darkness and never find her way to light.

And then, after interminable creeping along, Farsee asked, "See up ahead?"

She squinted in the darkness, not seeing anything. Then she realized that the little spot up ahead that she thought she'd imagined was in fact real—green and light and growing closer with each step.

"Wonderful," she said, and now she pulled him forward, eager to be free of the tunnel's unending reign of night.

He reined her in with an arm around her waist. "Careful," he told her. "It wouldn't pay to hurry. You step off the path here and I'd have the demons' own time finding you again, assuming I ever could. The tunnel, I suspect, tested the faithful. But it weeded out a lot of the faithless at the same time."

She shivered—the cool and damp of the tunnel would give her an excuse if he should ask her what bothered her, but she felt her fear and a sense of ghostly presences much more.

"I can't imagine anything being worth this sort of a trek," she said.

A moment later, he led them free of the tunnel, and she took back the words. On *this* side of the tunnel, fruit trees and flowering trees grew in rampant, unchecked, glorious profusion. Here, light filtered through a low, sparse canopy and dappled the richly green, grassy ground. Off to her left, she could see a domed building, its windows long gone but the gracefully curving lines of its ancient architecture still as stunning as they had been the day it was built. And behind and to the right of it, perfectly framed by the mouth of the tunnel in a manner that could only have been planned, the waterfall tumbled from high black cliffs—a thin, twisting ribbon of rainbow-tinted living art.

"Oh," Velyn whispered.

"Beautiful, isn't it?"

"I've never seen anything more flawlessly created, or more soothing to the eye."

Farsee laughed. "You will. We're going to the chapel now."

To the chapel? Yes, she'd been in the mood to be entertained, amused, and, if she was lucky, driven out of her body for a short while by a talented lover—but that had been back at the house into which the bastards of the Order had installed her before going on their way, abandoning her in this steaming hellhole. The mood had passed. Now she felt the urge to eat, then maybe sleep—and then she thought she might give some thought to sex.

But Farsee, pulling her forward like an excited child dragging a reluctant parent, managed to impart some of his enthusiasm to her. And when he ushered her beneath the moss-edged arch and into the chapel itself, she stopped and gasped.

A combination of art and nature had turned what had once been a lovely chapel into what could only be considered a bower for romance. Enough of the roof had caved in to permit light for growing things—and the flowering vines that covered the beautiful stone walls filled the still air with a sweet, heady scent as compelling as the musk of sex itself. At the back of the chapel, what might have once been a sacrificial fount or a baptismal font or even a sacred spring bubbled from the wall into a clear, moss-edged round pond. Water poured from the pond into a stream carved into the floor; the stream split into two waterfalls at the steps leading down to the main portion of the chapel, and then ran out in two pretty, softly burbling little rivulets in which tiny, jewel-colored fish darted and flashed. Iridescent birds spun in and out of the vines above, their wings so quick Velyn could only see the blur of them; they darted from flower to flower and hung in the air as if suspended by their own magic before shooting out of the open roof at last, like tiny, fiery festival rockets.

And at the juncture just beneath the twinned waterfalls sat an enormous ivory basin—and in the basin rested cushions and comforters of silk and linen. Right in the falls beside the basin, a bottle of golden wine was chilling. Bread and seppe fruit and taratale pastries, legendary for their aphrodisiac properties, sat on an altar. A lutelle stood on its own little stand, and a gold-bound book lay amid the cushions, an invitation to read. Velyn thought she recognized it simply by its exquisite binding—Carmathi Toruri's *Poetry of Lovers.*

"But for the food, I would think you had this little lovenest ready-prepared for any woman you could lure here."

"And you would be mistaken. When I saw you walking across the compound your first day there, I thought that never had I seen a woman I so wanted—and never had I seen one I was so unlikely to get." Farsee leaned close to her and brushed his lips along the side of her neck, and she shivered, wonderfully. "And yet, here you are, and all my preparations these last few days are suddenly made worthwhile."

She turned into his embrace and whispered, "And yet you could have shared sport with me in my little room."

He nodded solemnly. "And chanced the interruptions of villagers curious about you, and suffered the heat of that tiny enclosed space, where here we have air cooled by waterfalls and the wings of lovely birds, and we have food, and music, and poetry."

She slid a hand down his chest, down his belly, and down—and stroked him through his coarse clothing, and felt him respond. He was all over her then, food and music and poetry forgotten as they shed clothes and inhibitions with equal speed. Their mating, like the rough coupling of lions, had as much of fight to it as of lust. He held her down, bit the back of her neck, and she cried out in the shock of pain become pleasure; she turned and pivoted a hip into him, caught him off balance and threw him into the basin of cushions, and dove on top of him, forcing his hands above his head, riding him hard. They tangled, untangled, crashed together again and again, in configurations new to one or both of them, and at endless last when they lay sodden and spent across the cool linen and warmer silk, he laughed, reached across her, and pulled the wine from the tiny, murmuring waterfall.

"Drink?" he asked.

"I could drink it dry by myself."

"But I won't let you do that, greedy girl." He poured her a glass, handed it to her, and poured one for himself. Then, the effort more than he had energy for, he flopped back into the cushions and said, "My gods-all, what a gloriously beddable bitch you are, woman. You have thighs like pythons; I thought my ribs would break from the strain."

Velyn didn't inhale her wine, but it was a near thing. She coughed a little and said, "Nor have I ever experienced a talent quite like yours. Could we just stay here? At least a day or a week or maybe a month or two? I don't relish the walk back—and you did things I didn't even know were possible."

He sighed. "Well, we don't have to walk back. I hid an aircar here—that was how I got all the cushions and the food here ahead of time and still managed to have them fresh. We can stay awhile longer, but not overnight." He brushed her breast with his lips. "Sadly. Wondrous as this place is during the daylight hours, I would not wish to be here once darkness falls. The jungle has no respect for humans then."

Velyn sighed her disappointment, then brightened. "No matter. You have the aircar. We can fly to civilization and continue our entertainment there."

He smiled and said, "Perhaps we can, at that." She sipped the last of her wine and held out her glass, and he reached over and refilled it for her. He fed her one of the pastries. She had a bit more of the wine. And then she slept.

She woke to find herself still naked, but now bound. The last rays of the sun illuminated the broken edge of the roof; inside the chapel, night had already come. Farsee had gone, and had taken the food, her clothing, the book of poetry, the musical instrument, and even all the cushions upon which she had been lying; instead, she found herself stretched out in the smooth ivory basin like a sacrifice chained and awaiting the knife-wielding priest. She wondered if she had become just that.

Her heart thudded as something big moved outside the chapel. She tried the bindings at her wrists, working to free her hands. But they fit to her as if they were a part of her. She struggled to her feet, and found that, though Farsee—or someone else, if not Farsee—had bound both her hands and feet, she had not been tethered to the basin or anything else that might keep her within the chapel. She could flee. Hobbled, naked, nearly blind in the darkness, and with a headache and a foul taste in her mouth that suggested Farsee had poured more than wine into her glass, she did not, however, think she would get far. If Farsee feared for his own life in the jungle at night, she doubted she would have any chance at all.

She had to find shelter—something she could barricade. She would have to go through that hellish dark passageway to get away from the chapel; would have to find one of the complete, regularly visited buildings on the other side. If she could hold out this one night, maybe one of the villagers would find her in the ruins in the morning.

The last curve of light slid away from the broken roof. She shuddered. Should she cast a light spell? Or would that summon the jungle hunters? Would she perhaps be better off working her way to a corner and hiding, still and silent, until dawn? Or should she seek better shelter?

And then a cheery voice from the arch at the back of the chapel: "Well, you're awake just in time. I have the aircar packed with all my things, and I thought for sure I was going to have to carry you out." He snapped his fingers, and a handful of little lights spun to life around his head. He grinned at her and said, "I swear, I'd have another go at you if we had the time."

"You could take the damned bindings off first," she said, and then she noticed that he had changed. He no longer wore the khebarr of an island villager. Now he wore green and black—and something about the formality of the robes, and the way he wore them, chilled her blood more than any thought of being abandoned alone in the jungle ever could have.

Velyn had thought herself terrified at the thought of a night alone in the jungle. Now the jungle seemed friendly by comparison. "You bastard."

He laughed. "We could have just gone straight back to the city. But I thought that would be such a waste; I'd heard rumors of what a talent you were, and when the Inquest is finished with you . . . ah, never mind. You'll get the bad news soon enough, and why ruin a lovely day by thinking about it now? And all I can say is, the rumors don't begin to do justice to the truth. I'd keep you if I could—really. If the Inquest didn't already know I'd found you, I'd have you tucked away in a private little love nest somewhere." He shrugged. "But they know I have you, so . . ." He sauntered over to her and she took a swing at him. This time he had a mission, and she didn't catch him off guard as she had during their sex play. With an efficiency that shocked her, he caught the binding that held her arms and whipped a second binding around her waist and attached it. As quickly as that, she couldn't move her arms at all.

He smiled at her—a cold, calculating smile—and said, "If you want to walk out to the aircar under your own power, behave right now. If you force me to carry you out, I'm sure I'll find your soft, naked body too much to resist, and I'll simply have to act out my worst and most aggressive lusts on you."

She swallowed, her mouth suddenly dry as sun-broiled sand. She nodded acquiescence. When he pointed toward the door, she walked. When he gestured at the backseat of the aircar, she got in without fight or question. She might find an opportunity to escape from him. If she was lucky, she'd make an opportunity to kill him. When she sat, he threw a blanket over her. She used the cover to begin working at her restraints; she felt certain she could find some way to win her freedom.

As a last resort, perhaps she could buy it.

Chapter 19

Wraith woke to a soft click at his cell door. He sat up, expecting to see Solander, but it was too early. Stotts now sang his maddening babble—three notes, all off-key, all grating. Two guards waited for him, with the cell door open. One of them smiled at him, amused. "You could sleep through that, Gellas? Very, very impressive."

"I spend days and nights listening to actors practicing their lines, all at the same time, over and over and over," Wraith said. "What's one more babbling idiot to me?"

The other guard studied him, eyes curious. "You didn't find him wearing?"

Wraith shrugged. "I find them all wearing. I've learned over the years not to hear them."

"Well, you would have had a—ha, a bit of a reprieve anyway," the first guard said. "You're to be moved."

"Moved?" That wasn't in the plan. Wraith glanced at Solander, who sat in opposite cell, as still as if he'd been frozen, his eyes closed, his hands folded on his lap. "So soon?"

"The Masters have had a breakthrough in finding Vincalis. Some confessions, apparently. We're to have public executions, from what we hear, and the guilty are being separated from the innocent."

Wraith studied him. "Oh? You're separating the innocent, but not freeing them? That's an interesting way to treat innocent people."

"Orders." Both guards shrugged.

They had their attention on Wraith. Behind them, Solander stood silently, and opened his eyes, and clasped his hands together tightly. Light began to curl away from his skin, almost like the fog that curled across the surfaces of warm lakes on cool mornings.

Wraith stood with his head just a little down while the guards stepped into his cell and reached for his hands and bound them in heavy metal manacles. Which, he supposed, answered any question he might care to ask about whether he was presumed to be innocent or guilty. With his head angled down, though, he could see what Solander was doing—and as long as he kept his body angled as it was, both guards kept their backs to Solander.

". . . leaf bread . . . bones meat . . . stick . . . hot-bang-god . . . dog train . . . flee . . . big *fly* fall *spot* spank. Leaf bread. Bones meat. Stick hot. Bang. God dog train flee. Fly. Fall—"

"*Shut up,* will you!" the younger guard bellowed. "At least for a few minutes!"

"Spot," Stotts whispered. "Spank leaf bread. Bones. Meat-stick. Hot bang."

The whispering, Wraith thought, was actually worse. Except, of course, that it created one final distraction that Solander could use.

The light grew very bright for just an instant—bright enough that both guards turned. Solander glowed like a small sun in the center of his cell, illuminated both from the outside and from within—he was, in that single instant, beautiful beyond anything that Wraith had ever seen. Then he vanished, and the light with him, and for a moment Wraith could see nothing but the blazing light that had burned its shape into his eyes. When his vision cleared, the guards were both racing for Solander's cell. Wraith waited where he was—as long as he stayed still, he could hope that he would not draw either of them back to himself.

He hoped that Solander had a plan that included both of them. He hoped. He trusted. And he waited, because if he ran, one of them would be sure to run after him, and . . .

They unlocked Solander's cell. Threw open the cell door and raced in. The door closed behind them with a clang, and a blue fire exploded along the edges, fusing it into an inescapable mass of molten whitestone.

As quickly as that, Solander reappeared. "Let's go. This isn't ideal, but we're out of options."

Velyn fought Farsee and the handful of other Masters who dragged her into the Gold Building; on the way back, Farsee had regaled her with tales of the multitudes who had vanished inside against their will and never came back out.

But, determined though she was, she couldn't hope to win a fight in which she was both bound and hopelessly outnumbered. She satisfied herself that she managed to hurt a few of them, and that if nothing else they would have bruises to show for their meeting with her.

They dragged her into a room where banks of chairs rose up to a high ceiling, and a brilliant—even painful—light blazed down on a clear half circle of floor to the front; and they hauled her into the light and strapped her—still bound, naked, and chilled—into a chair. On the way in, she'd been able to see that the room was mostly empty, but now, caught in that merciless light, her eyes could make out nothing but blackness beyond.

In the darkness before her, silence. They would say something soon, she thought. Ask her questions. Demand whatever truths she might know. She wouldn't answer; she'd already decided that. When they spelled her—and they would—she would tell them what they wanted to know. But she wouldn't volunteer anything. She wouldn't betray herself by choice.

But they didn't ask her anything. She knew they were there. She could feel them staring at her. She could sense them all around her, even though she couldn't see them. She might as well have been alone in that huge room, though. Alone beneath that merciless light. Her heart raced madly, and her mouth went dry. The silence stretched.

Maybe, once they brought her into the room and tied her to the chair, they'd left. Maybe she was simply imagining them sitting above her, staring down at her. Maybe they intended to leave her here. She fought against her bonds, but they'd been applied by someone who knew what he was doing, and who didn't intend to have any mistakes. She couldn't even loosen the straps a little.

Alone? Or silently observed?

They were going to torture her, weren't they? This wasn't just them waiting for her to talk. They could have the answers they wanted from her at any time; so why make her wait here, humiliated and powerless, unless they had a reason to want her scared? This was ugly.

Silence, and the infinite blackness beyond the bleeding white light. She shivered, having a hard time catching her breath. She wanted to go home. She wanted to be with her parents. She wanted to be back with Wraith. She wanted to be anywhere but where she was.

Silence.

And then a single soft voice that signaled the end of silence.

"You've been found guilty of treason, and you're to be executed in three days, along with the rest of the conspirators against the Empire."

And that was all he said.

The silence descended again, and into it she said, "Wait. I haven't done anything against the Empire. I'm no traitor. Look—I don't deserve to die. I'm a stolti, damnall. The most you can do to me is sentence me to Refinement! You can't execute me!"

The silence continued, like a blanket over her.

Her voice, thin and quavering, rose as she tried to push it out through the lights, into the impenetrable darkness beyond, to the ears and hearts of those who had already judged her.

"I'm innocent. But I can tell you who isn't."

Silence, like shuttered windows. And then a laugh. And the silence again.

"Please," she said. And, "Please," she whispered.

Strangers came, unbound her from the chair, untied her, threw a blanket around her, and led her—nearly blind, mad with fear—away from the bright light, into the hellish darkness.

"But I can help you," she shouted. "I can *help* you."

Faregan paced in the corridor. "All of them but her," he said. "I put my most loyal man on her with orders to bring her in to me when this all came together, and the bastard vanishes, and her with him." He punched his fist into the open palm of his other hand. "I was going to offer her the choice between survival with me and death with the traitors. She would have been mine. Mine. So where is she? Where is Jethis?"

He walked faster, up and down the empty hall—a dozen steps, turn, a dozen more, turn. Rage ate into his gut like poison—twisting, hurting. Cheated. He'd been cheated of his prize, his due reward. He'd waited, he'd been patient, he'd taken her refusals and her rudenesses, and each time he'd simply put them aside, for that was what men did. They were patient, they made plans, and when the time was right, they made offers that could not be refused.

"Jethis was a double agent," Faregan said suddenly, stopping in midstride. He stared up at the ceiling. "A double agent. One of them. He's taken her to whatever place these traitors had set aside as a bolt-hole."

Everything was all right, then. Faregan would still find Jess Covitach-Artis; when all the traitors' stories under mage-interrogation and torture started coming in, the locations of the few holdouts would come to light. Then loyal Inquestors could go and retrieve Jess. And Jethis.

After Jess was safely in his possession—the toy he'd waited so long to acquire, the finest of his collection—he thought he would participate personally in the torture of Jethis. The double-dealing bastard would have a long, long time to wish he was dead.

Wraith and Solander moved through empty corridors, and at each intersection Solander had to force open locks by magic. Each time, Wraith expected someone to come after them, yet each time, Solander eventually succeeded with the lock, and they moved forward.

"They've thrown everything they have at these locks," he muttered once. "That's the reason they don't have anyone guarding the corridors—not even the Master of the Dragons could hope to get through all of these locks without a massive pipeline into the Warrens, and they've somehow blocked magic access to everyone but themselves. If I wasn't drawing on my own forces, we'd never have a chance."

"They've got to know we're out," Wraith said. "How could they not? I haven't shown up wherever they were going to take me. The guards are welded into your cell—the Masters are going to miss them soon enough."

"We're not leaving any tracks. The shield I have around us will keep us from setting off any alarms, and as long as you stay close to me, neither of us will even be visible."

"You hope."

"Could you see me when I shielded?"

"No."

"Then it's more than a hope."

"We're really going to just walk out of here?"

They moved around a corner and three routes confronted them. Solander swore. "Assuming we don't get lost, yes."

Wraith spent so much of his time anymore away from magic, he sometimes forgot just how much it could accomplish. "This place is a maze—designed to confuse. I've read the histories of it. Do you have any way of using magic to find a safe way out?"

"Doing it now," Solander said. His face was pale, his forehead gleaming with sweat. "Don't . . . talk. I need my focus. I can't guarantee anything, but . . ." He shrugged.

Wraith nodded and, silent, stayed as close to his friend as he could. They made little sound, walking through long corridors past closed doors, the near-darkness broken only by the infrequent green glow of wizard globes along the walls. This part of the Gold Building had the feel of the abandoned, the forgotten. It gave Wraith the shudders; he could imagine himself or someone else languishing behind one of those locked and barred doors, starving into oblivion, misplaced by everyone. Did the Inquest—this startling group of madmen and fiends that lived and thrived under the noses of the Dragons, almost as a second government—rid itself of its most troublesome targets in such a callous, simple manner?

Solander only spoke once more during their traverse of the corridors. "Every one of these locks is different," he whispered. "Every one takes some special combination of tricks to break through. I'm not sure how many more of these I have the energy to open."

"How can I help?"

Solander laughed softly and shook his head. "You can carry me if we make it outside."

"That's it?"

Solander nodded.

Long corridors, and twists left and right, and the intermittent splashes of green. Then a change. Darker walls, an unexpected older part of the building not built of the mages' whitestone, but of actual stone— of cut and fitted blocks. Wraith had never seen anything outside of the Kaan enclaves even remotely like it. Solander and Wraith stopped, looked at each other.

"Close?" Wraith whispered.

Solander nodded, pointed them onward.

No more gates now. They walked faster, Solander leaning on Wraith and breathing hard. And finally the last door lay ahead. Solid metal, barred. Solander leaned against it, concentrated as he had with the other gates, and finally sagged to the floor. "I can't touch this one."

Wraith looked at him. "The spell too strong?"

"I don't know. I can't get close enough to the lock to see the spell. Something is keeping me back."

Wraith studied the door and the mechanism of the lock with a desperation approaching panic. On the other side lay freedom. He could feel it. But he had no tools with which to manipulate the lock's tumblers, nothing with which to cut through the metal, no way to break down this one last door.

He didn't understand this setback. He could have understood if the door had no magic to it—though in the Gold Building, he would imagine no such door existed. But that Solander could not manipulate it by magic—that he did not understand. Had the Dragons found the secret that would explain what made Wraith the way he was? Had they discovered how to make things oblivious to magic?

A voice behind him said, "Final spell, you see. A magic repeller."

Wraith and Solander turned. They faced what looked like the whole of the Silent Inquest: the three men he recognized as the Masters, with Master Noano Omwi at their head; behind him a dozen or more keppins—middle-aged men who took orders directly from the Masters; the keppins' assembled solitars—young men coming up in the organization; and the solitars' many investigators, watchers, and drones. The mass of black and green robes, of hooded and shadowed faces, of fanatical eyes, caused Wraith's stomach to clench so violently that he had to fight back simultaneous desperate urges to puke and shit himself.

Omwi said, "Not expecting us? Ah, but we've been expecting the two of you. We created a test for you, and you did beautifully. We couldn't see you, we couldn't hear you, we couldn't track you except that each time you passed through a door, our watching spells could see the door open. Had it not been for that, we'd have lost you almost immediately. Lucky for us that doors are such physical things."

And Faregan, to Omwi's right, smiled and asked, "So were you impressed with this last gate? It's something new that we've just tried out—and well that we did, too, though the cost of using the spell with any sort of regularity would bankrupt the Empire's magic reserves in no time."

"But it won't be necessary. We needed it for these two, but the secret of this new magic dies with them, for the good of the Empire." Omwi chuckled. "Quite a little discovery you seem to have made, Solander. You and Gellas both—to all appearances impervious to magical questioning, and shielded from magical manipulation thanks to this new magical system of yours. To have gotten through every other barrier we placed before you—and to do it without setting off a single alarm, or tapping into the Warrens' energy pools—you've had to pull from yourself as much power as we've drawn from at least a dozen souls. And while we've had to expend effort and power in diverting the *rewhah*, you seem to have no *rewhah* issues at all. It's been a breathtaking demonstration." He crossed his arms over his chest. "But now, unless I miss my guess, the two of you are at last reserves. Just as well. We didn't want to have to hurt you before we took you to the interrogation rooms. We want you to be healthy and . . . and, well, cooperative for questioning. After all, we're going to have to have your secret. What would be a disaster in the hands of the citizenry will to us be . . . valuable."

The keppins and the solitars brought up weapons and aimed them at Wraith and Solander. "No," Solander said. "We'll go with you without a fight."

"You will," Omwi said. "But on our terms." And keppins and solitars fired simultaneously.

Gold and green and red and yellow fires erupted from the weapons and exploded around Solander and Wraith, and Solander collapsed instantly. Wraith simply stood there while the cold fires splashed against him and swirled around him, crackling and roaring. He thought perhaps he ought to collapse as Solander had, but he didn't think it quickly enough. Omwi gave a signal an instant before he thought to drop, and keppins and solitars switched off their weapons and lowered them.

"No," Omwi said. "That wasn't a shield. You weren't using the sort of magic he was; you weren't using anything. The spells went right through you, but they didn't touch you." He looked from Wraith to Solander, and back to Wraith. "Him I understand. I don't know how his system works yet, but I know he has a system, and I know I can get the details. But you . . ." He shook his head. "All the time I've been watching you, Gellas, I never noticed anything wrong with you. But you're quite, quite wrong, aren't you? Fascinating."

Omwi turned his back on Wraith, and to his keppins he said, "Take Solander to interrogation. And when you have what you need from him, lock him away with the rest of the traitors." He turned back to Wraith. "You . . . well, you'll have a different fate, I think. We have to find out first what makes you work, don't we? We can't waste someone for whom the laws of magic don't seem to work. No telling what fascinating things we'll find out about magic if we study you."

Wraith closed his eyes. He should have fallen to the ground along with Solander. He should have. Too late to do it now. Now he could only allow himself to be taken back the way he had come, allow himself to be escorted into a single, lonely cell. Could only listen to the heavy, physical, real bar on the other side of the door falling into place, and to the physical—not magical—lock clicking.

One of the lonely cells in one of the labyrinthine corridors, somewhere in the heart of oblivion.

The end of the road, he thought. He'd reached the end of the road, and neither he nor Solander had managed, for all their idealism, to save anyone.

"Why are we here?" Jess asked Patr.

Patr paid the little man from whom he had ordered an extraordinary amount of supplies, clothing, and foods. He turned to Jess and pointed to the little house to which he'd brought them.

282 ☙ HOLLY LISLE

"Inside first."

Jess looked over his shoulder and said, "Wait. That man is taking our aircar."

"That's part of how we paid for the things we're getting. Believe me, we don't want it anywhere around us. My superiors may have ways of locating us through it."

"Patr . . ."

"Inside. I promise, love—this is something that can't be said in open air."

Jess stared at him, then turned and walked into the tiny, run-down house. The three rooms were all empty, the adobe walls cracked, the windows unfettered by any such niceties as mageglass, or simple glass, or even shutters or screens—the wind blew in as freely as it blew across the plains of this bleak, sun-scorched place, bringing with it bits of dirt and sand, insects, and the occasional tiny float-lizard.

"Inside doesn't seem to offer much of an improvement over outside, actually," she said.

"I know. And I apologize. This is the best I can offer on short notice; once I . . . well, once things changed, I'd planned something much better, but I ran out of time."

Jess found the one wall that looked more or less solid and almost clean, and leaned gingerly against it. It held. She said, "You've talked about things changing, and about running out of time, and about your plans—but you haven't given me any details. One last time, then, Patr. Who were in the aircars that surrounded my house? Why did we run, and how did you know to get us out of there before they arrived? And what are we doing here?"

He took a deep breath. "Easy things first. We're here because we're hiding. From the Silent Inquest—a group of evil men, and a group in which I was once a minor but trusted member. I had this place put aside in case I should ever run afoul of them. They . . . ah, they sometimes find the best way to keep a secret is to eliminate everyone who knows it. I've had friends who disappeared right after they worked on something big or sensitive. The Masters of the Inquest and their keppins are vicious; they claim a code of honor, but rarely find it convenient to follow it. So, when I realized what they were and how they worked, I acquired this place. Very carefully, through dummy buyers and layers upon layers of protective cover. I've never come here before." He glanced around at it and wrinkled his nose. "I didn't get much for my money, but if I got our lives, that will be enough."

She nodded. "Fine. Then the people who invaded my home just after we left it were . . . Silent Inquest?"

"Yes."

"And this is about Wraith?"

"Wraith? You mean Gellas?"

"Yes. Gellas is Wraith."

"I don't know if it's about him. It's about treason against the Empire, and I have to think your friend Wraith has some part in that, but I don't believe he's the only one the Inquest is after. I know they want Solander. I know they want Vincalis. And I know they're after the Kaan; they've just been waiting for the Kaan to demonstrate their animosity to the Empire in a way that can be both proven and punished."

Jess cringed.

"And they were after me."

"Yes. Because of your associations with both Gellas—or Wraith, I suppose—and Solander. You had the misfortune to make some, well . . . some ill-starred friendships, to say the least."

Jess smiled a little. Without those two friendships, she would be either mindless magic fodder in the Warrens or already dead. Facts that Patr, secret soldier of the Inquest, would not get from her.

"I understand why you are here, then," she said after some thought. "But why am I here? Why not give me to the Inquest and be a hero, or simply leave me where I was and flee for your life? You would have had a safer and easier trip without me."

"I love you," he said. "I've been falling in love with you since the day Master Faregan assigned me to you."

"Master Faregan is a member of the Inquest?"

"Yes. He's one of the Triad, the three most powerful Inquestors in all Matrin. He sits second, after only Master Omwi."

"He was briefly a member of a music covil with me," Jess said softly. "He asked me to go home with him to listen to some music from his collection—he said he could guarantee I'd never heard anything like it before. But I didn't like the way he looked at me. At other times, he asked me to go places with him."

Patr said, "He collects young women. No one knows what he does with them—though I spent a great deal of time and effort once trying to find out—but most of the Inquestors know he finds strays and takes them home. I think you were to have been part of his collection. I realized early on that I wasn't going to be able to turn you in to him if that ever became an issue, but I also realized early on that you weren't involved in any conspiracies against the Empire. I could have—I *should* have—cleared you with them after the first six months. If your innocence would have mattered to anyone, that is."

"But you didn't."

"No."

"Why not?"

"Because then perhaps Faregan would have taken me away from you, and set me to watching someone else. And I didn't want to watch anyone else. I wanted to be with you—to have an excuse to be with you every day, and to have the approval of my superiors to be with you. It made me happy."

"And it left me under suspicion."

"I told them that you didn't know anything, but that you had friends who might be using you as an unsuspecting contact point, and that if I stayed with you, I might find out something useful. From time to time, I fed them pieces of information that weren't completely true, but that weren't completely lies, either—just enough to keep them on the hook."

Jess stared at him, shocked. "You sound like you're proud of this— like you expect me to be flattered that you left me under suspicion so that you could be with me. You actually think what you did was . . . good?"

He looked at her and shrugged, and she saw in his face and movements a hardness she had never seen there before. "You want me to say I did all this for you? That would be a lie. I did all of this for me. I wanted to be with you, I made it happen." He leaned forward and looked into her eyes. "I never said—I never *implied*—that I was a good man. I'm not. I've killed people, I've had people killed. The people I usually deal with are like me—people who will smile at a friend and kill him on orders from above, and then go out and have a big meal with a couple of other friends and their favorite whores." He looked away from her then, and his voice softened. "In you, though, I see another life. Another world. You're pure. Good. You've never hurt anyone, never allowed yourself to take an easy road. Your people—the Artises . . . bad people. I've worked with them; I know them. Through the Inquest, they've had me do a few things for them. They're as deep into the mire as anyone, grabbing for the same few fistfuls of power just as hard as they can and sinking anyone they can sink just to improve their own footing. You came out of that family, out of that world, and it's like none of it ever touched you. You just walked away from it all—you and Wraith both. It's almost as if the two of you grew up in a completely different world from the rest of your family."

He laughed a little, and looked at her again, and she hoped he couldn't see any of the dismay in her eyes at how close he had come to her real secret. He said, "And, I have to admit, you're beautiful, and you're smart and kind, and you're soft, and you smell good . . . and I hoped if I hung around long enough, I'd get you into bed."

"I'm grateful to be alive," she said, "but from what you tell me, I wouldn't even have been in danger had it not been for you. How are you hoping that I'll react to what you're telling me? That I'll . . . what? Fall in love with you because you saved my life?"

"First," he said, "Faregan had me watching you because he wanted you. He wasn't looking for your innocence. He didn't care if you were innocent; he simply wanted you. And sooner or later he would have either found or manufactured what he needed to have you brought in and put into his power. I stood between you and him. If I'd failed outright or tried to claim your innocence, he would have put someone else with you, and chances are that other Inquestor would have found a way to give you to him. So you would have been in danger. You simply wouldn't have been with someone who cared what happened to you."

"That's horrible," Jess said. "You're horrible."

He watched her without expression, and for a long time said nothing. Finally, he shook his head. "Would you rather I'd lied to you? It would have been easy enough to hide my associations with the Silent Inquest, to simply let you think a friend tipped me off that you were in trouble, and that we were lucky to get away when we did. I could have made myself your hero easily enough; probably could have gotten you into bed the same way without too much trouble. I'm not looking to be some false hero in your eyes—not looking to lie to you about who I am or what I am. I helped you because I could. I love you because I do. I stayed with you because I wanted to. What you do about it—what you *think* about it—is up to you."

He looked out the window at the bleak, hot expanse beyond, and said, "We'll have furniture here soon: beds, food, clothing appropriate for the area, a good supply of water. When it gets here, you direct the people to put things where you want them. Make this your home."

Jess almost laughed then. "You're not with the Inquest anymore, are you? I mean, they'd drag you in as fast as they would me right now, wouldn't they?"

"They'd kill me on sight. There's no 'dragging in' about it. Why?

Thinking about selling me to them for your own safety? Don't. They'll double-cross you as fast as you apparently would me."

"It hadn't even crossed my mind. I was just thinking . . . if you don't have the Inquest behind you anymore, what makes you think the man who took our aircar away from here will ever come back with anything? If he doesn't, what are you going to do about it?"

Now Patr smiled. "I'd like to see him try that." He leaned against a wall at a right angle to her and said, "Jess, I didn't turn into a bad, hard man because I joined the Inquest. The Inquest recruited me because I was already a bad, hard man. If my . . . friend . . . doesn't come back here with the things I paid him for, I'll make sure it's the last mistake he ever makes."

The words, and the pleasant smile he wore while he said them, sent a chill through Jess's veins. No matter what else she did, she decided she would not cross Patr.

Chapter 20

The Masters of the Inquest made Wraith an involuntary witness to the interrogations, and then to the trials. Bound to a chair at the back of the amphitheater that served as courtroom for the whole hellish charade, silenced by a gag, he sat through hour upon hour of watching while friends and colleagues underwent beatings and horrible tortures; he listened helplessly as they confessed to things they had done, and to things they had never done. He wept, and each night when the ordeal was over, he begged to be taken before the Inquest to offer his own testimony. Endlessly he confessed to being Vincalis, whom the interrogators claimed to be seeking.

No one listened. No one cared what he said.

He watched the Kaan broken one by one. Beneath the hands of the interrogators, "Vincalis the Agitator" came to life in shadowy, strange detail; the Silent Inquest's victims first said nothing, and then said anything when the humiliation, the brutality, and the anguish became too much for them to bear. Vincalis took shape beneath these forced confessions as a powerful member of the stolti class and a wizard of some repute, a man so powerful he managed to remain hidden, so well connected that he controlled vast secret armies with a single word. He was varyingly tall and short, gaunt and fat, pale and dark—and even occasionally female, though usually the interrogation victims said he was male.

The initiates of the Order of Resonance came next into the dark room to bleed, and from them the interrogators extracted the details of plans to free the Warreners, and copious information about their search for an antidote to the addictive poisons in Way-fare, and the ways that they subverted art to bring others around to their cause. And they, too, described Vincalis the Agitator—half man and half god, a shadowy overlord so hidden none of them had ever seen his face, though many had spoken to his associates and all knew of him.

And finally they brought in Velyn. And Wraith nearly lost his mind, watching her sit calmly before them and tell them everything about him and Jess and Solander, about how she'd had a part in rescuing Jess from the Warrens, about how Wraith had come from there, too, about how Wraith and Solander had planned all along to use Solander's magic and Wraith's knowledge of the Warrens to destroy the magic of the Empire and free the human animals the Empire used as fuel. She told them that Wraith, who was Gellas, was also Vincalis. She told them that Solander planned to overthrow the magic of the Empire with his new form of magic. She gave them everything, and embellished what she gave them with things designed to make her look better and them look worse. She just handed it to the Inquestors, without a sign of remorse, without a single threat or struggle. And when she was finished, they tortured her as completely and as brutally as they tortured everyone else—and she told them more or less the same thing.

Wraith wanted to die. He loved her and knew he was a fool for it. And she seemed determined to prove him a fool—and to throw his every attempt at helping her back in his face.

The man who sat next to him, who had commented with amused and loving detail on each of the tortures inflicted on Velyn, looked at Wraith with some interest and said, "She hates you, man. If we gave you to her and handed her a knife, I'm betting she wouldn't have the kindness to kill you quickly." He shook his head and laughed. "I'd love to hear what you did to her."

Wraith would have told him. He would have told him about Velyn, about his own role in everything; he would have taken on the weight of every sin committed by every one of the people who had trusted him, as well as the things he had done himself, if only someone would have listened to him. But he remained bound and gagged, given sips of water at intervals, beaten when he attempted to speak.

He had to face a dark, horrible fact. The Inquest didn't want the truth. The Masters of the Silent Inquest could have had the truth in a heartbeat, from anyone brought before them except for Solander or him, for nothing more than the expenditure of a small amount of magic. The truth would have lain bare before them, unembellished, unadorned, untwisted, for them to do with what they chose.

After they got the truth by magic, the Inquestors tortured their prisoners until they forced lies from them—and it was the lies they seemed to most want. But why? What purpose did these lies serve that the truth did not? Wraith worried it around in his thoughts, but could not think of anything that would explain the actions of the Inquestors.

Then one of the guards brought a viewscreen into his cell the evening of the day that the Inquest interrogated Velyn and said, "You're to watch this. It has to do with you."

On the viewscreen, he saw the nightlies. Not the usual discussion of art and literature, or of public meetings for the benefit of one community or another. This was a spectacle, with dramatic music and well-dressed commentators discussing the discovery of a plot against the Empire of the Hars Ticlarim, and scenes straight from the interrogation room, of person after person confessing to crimes against the Empire, and reference after reference to the mysterious Vincalis, mastermind of the entire attempted destruction of civilization. No mention of the Warrens in connection to Vincalis, of course, or of the source of the Empire's magic. No mention of the burning of souls to keep houses afloat in the air, or aircars soaring on their merry way. No. That would never reach the screens.

But the indictment of art made its way into the commentators' discussions clearly enough. They branded art and artists as subversives. They declared that the Empire had only managed to bring in a small fraction of the evildoers connected with this potentially world-shattering plot. They suggested that good citizens of the Empire would search out and bring forward all subversives who had so far eluded their net. And they added the final bit of fear-mongering to their report: Vincalis the Agitator had so far escaped capture, and was thought to be very much active in attempting to carry out his plot against the Empire. No less than the Landimyn of the Hars had offered a massive reward for Vincalis's capture, including money, a grand home in the Aboves of Oel Artis, and a raise of status to stolti for the informant—and all of his family—whose information led to the capture and conviction of the dangerous fugitive.

"I'm Vincalis!" Wraith screamed out the door to the guards. "Didn't you hear Velyn? She *told* you I'm Vincalis. I wrote every one of the plays, I'm the one who plotted to free the Warreners, *I'm the man you're looking for!*"

He beat his fists on the door of his cell, but no one came. No one wanted to hear the truth. Lies suited the needs of the Empire so much better.

Patr had been right: Everything he'd ordered arrived, including a small, decrepit aircar that Jess doubted would carry them much farther than to the village and back—if that. She said as little as possible to the villagers who brought things into the house; she busied herself in finding places for the food, the furniture, the few small amenities that Patr had managed to acquire for the two of them.

The little viewsphere surprised her. She'd never given much thought to the nightlies, but considering her status as a fugitive, she thought she might do well to see if she and Patr got any mention.

As they sat eating a dinner badly cooked over fire, with food much stronger in flavor than any she was accustomed to, Patr turned on the viewsphere, and the nightlies sprang to life in the tiny room. And she saw the roundup of Wraith, Solander, the Kaan, the initiates of the Order of Resonance, office personnel in Wraith's several theaters, lower-level wizards who had worked with Solander. . . .

She stopped eating, put bowl and fork on the table, and stared. People she knew flashed onto the screen, telling unimaginable lies about a huge conspiracy to destroy the Empire, overthrow the government, and place the playwright Vincalis—whom the nightlies had dubbed "Vincalis the Agitator"—at the head of a new world order that forbade magic, made men and women live like animals, and would bring misery, starvation, and war to this peaceful place. She clenched her hands into fists and ground her teeth; she stared from the images to Patr, and helplessly back at the travesty before her, and when the lies were done, and the Empire's plan to eradicate art and artists in the name of safety and to turn everyone against each other as they sought to win some ludicrous reward for their treachery became clear, she closed her eyes and wept silently.

"Madness," she whispered.

"Not at all," Patr said. "What they're doing will serve any number of larger purposes. All sorts of dissidents will be shoved out into the light of day, and from the Empire's standpoint, if a few innocents—or many innocents—get caught in the same net, what of that? There will always be more innocents; the Empire makes them every day. Further, the Masters of the Empire can instill a great deal of fear and respect with very little effort, simply by publicizing the executions and making sure that everyone knows the search for traitors is ongoing, and that everyone is more or less a suspect. Third, by leaving Vincalis the Agitator at large in the public mind, people no longer trust their neighbors and friends—and no new conspiracies will have good ground in which to grow for a long, long time.

"When the Dragon Council made its deal with the Silent Inquest to hunt you people down and turn you over to them, I'm sure they had just this sort of sweeping power grab in mind."

"What did the Dragons pay you for this? What is the price of all these lives?"

"A favor," Patr said with a tiny smile. "A favor to be named later."

"Please tell me they don't intend to execute everyone they've taken. Not really."

"They're planning mass executions. I doubt that anyone they've taken in will live—and the more they know, the more I'm sure they'll be killed."

"But they have Solander . . . and Wraith . . . and so many friends, so many of my friends, so many actors and dancers and singers and writers. . . ."

"They don't have you," Patr said.

A week passed, and in that week the nightlies showed a steady stream of conspirators confessing. And each night, the commentators discussed not only the confessions, but their import: how the success of the conspiracy would have led to famine, plague, genocide, wholesale destruction of the Empire, its citizens, and their children. Vincalis—Vincalis the Agitator, the conspirator, plotter, devil spawned to destroy the hopes and plans of millions of innocents—stayed at the center of the nightlies' coverage.

Special investigators sat with the commentators, discussing methods of ferreting out traitors, of recognizing people who might have passed as solid citizens but who lived secret and dangerous lives beneath the surface. Masters of wizardry described the real danger that unsanctioned methods of magic posed to the Empire's power delivery structure, and ultimately to the very existence of the Empire. Wizard trackers displayed some of their methods as they attempted to use their magic to locate the elusive Vincalis.

Among the population, interest became obsession and obsession became dread as the coverage wore on, and in the streets, both spontaneous and orchestrated marches calling for the deaths of all the traitors began erupting throughout the Empire.

In the second week after the arrests, power outages in a poor section of Oel Artis caused the deaths of hundreds of mufere and parvoi citizens when the river that the magic held back flowed into the homes at night, drowning everyone in that district. Vincalis and his traitors took the blame, and the Silent Inquest rounded up another hundred people from around the city and herded them into the Gold Building. These "conspirators" were never even questioned—they were, instead, moved under cover of darkness to the Warrens.

No one mentioned that the part of the city drowned had been fighting eviction notices and demolition orders for more than ten years, or that the Masters of the City wanted the land for special waterfront resorts of their own. No one seemed to notice that the people who just vanished, taken in by the Silent Inquest—which was working as the secret right hand of the Dragon Council—had nothing to do with the arts, that they were all small property owners who held land in coveted locations.

No one questioned the Dragon Council. No one questioned the hysteria—at least not publicly. No one stood up to the Masters of the City. Citizens from one end of the Empire to the other kept still and quiet and hoped that no fingers would be pointed at them. Which, of course, was exactly what the Masters of the Dragon Council wanted.

Master Grath Faregan stepped into Wraith's cell and sat on the bench that ran the length of the wall opposite him. "I hear you've had much to say," he said. "That you have requested an audience. I find myself with a bit of free time, and a little curiosity about what you might have to say. Would you care to enlighten me?"

Wraith nodded. "I'm Vincalis," he said. "There isn't anyone else. There's no mysterious master conspirator, no one who is waiting out there to strike and destroy the Empire. There's just me."

Faregan said, "Quite a few of your colleagues have also confessed to being Vincalis. Rather generous of you all, considering that when Vincalis is brought before the people, it's likely that he'll be burned alive, or perhaps ripped limb from limb. Public sentiment isn't running much in his favor these days. Funny how people forget how much they loved all those little plays when they think a man's been plotting underneath it all to murder their children."

"But I never plotted any such thing. I wanted to free the Warreners, nothing more. The Dragons are burning their souls as fuel for the Empire; they can't be permitted to do that. But Solander came up with a form of magic that would permit civilization to continue, and neither of us would ever have permitted harm to come to the Empire's citizens."

Faregan glanced at him, started to say something, stopped himself, and then shook his head and laughed. "Gellas, you probably are Vincalis, for what it's worth. I thought it likely when we brought you in. No one has traced any of the work directly to you, and you were careful enough that we could never prove anything . . . but that knife cuts both ways. You can never prove anything, either. And for our purposes, that's infinitely better."

Wraith frowned at him, not understanding. "Why?"

"If you're Vincalis, then the threat to the Empire is over as soon as we execute you. People go back to life as it was—they resume their day-to-day activities and expect all the details of their lives to return to normal. But your . . . well, your *experiment* in conspiracy has highlighted a few weaknesses in our system, and in order to patch them, we're going to have to do away with some privileges that people currently consider rights. In order to do that, they have to perceive a threat to their lives and the lives of their children, and they have to think that the government is the only entity that can protect them from that threat. And as long as 'Vincalis the Agitator' is free and causing problems, we have our necessary threat. The Dragons can eliminate rights with impunity, increase surveillance on the populace as a whole—including the stolti class, which has until now been terribly resistant to such invasion—and increase revenues while we do it. Less for more."

"That's evil."

"That's government, my boy. Government is all about its own survival; it's as much a living, breathing entity as any snake . . . and much more cold-bloodedly deadly." His smile turned sly. "Meanwhile, as we play along, acting the part of the Dragons' allies, the Silent Inquest has its own agenda. We increase our pressure on the Dragons—the Masters of the Silent Inquest watch even them. Once the hysteria is at its highest peak, we intend to put a few Masters into the uncomfortable position of being discovered as part of your conspiracy. We'll supply all the evidence to the public and the rest of the Masters simultaneously to prove that these few chosen ones were deeply involved. Once the Dragons find them guilty—as they must after all their public outcry—and once they hold the necessary executions, we'll prove to the survivors how vulnerable they have become to their own hysteria." He laughed softly. "And the remaining Dragons will be more than willing to fall in line with our objectives."

Wraith's head hurt. "You want people to die."

"The right people—yes. That shouldn't surprise you."

"It doesn't. Nothing surprises me anymore."

The old man laughed. "Such cynicism. Well, you'll live, boy. You'll be our permanent guest . . . and at some point you'll probably wish we'd killed you with your friends. But you'll live. I have a team of the Inquest's private researchers flying in to convene here. Once the executions are over, they'll begin studying you. If we can acquire your immunity to magic, the Dragons will have no hold over us at all—and control of the Hars will once again reside with us."

Wraith turned away. "No truth will stop you. No pleading will stop you. The innocence of your victims won't stop you. What *will* stop you?"

Grath Faregan raised an eyebrow. "Something bigger and meaner than us, boy. That's the only thing."

He rose and said, "If you truly are Vincalis, let me say that I did enjoy your work. You were a talented writer. Pity for your sake you didn't find an acceptable outlet for all that talent—but your . . . ambition, for want of a better word, worked out well enough for us. I won't see you again. You'll attend the executions as a guest of the Inquest, and then you'll go to your new home, which will be your last home. You have any last thing you want to say to me?"

Wraith turned and stared at him. "Only that this won't be the last time we meet. If you hurt my friends, I'll walk through seven hells to come for you."

Faregan nodded politely. "I hear that a lot, actually." He bowed slightly. "I offer you my best wishes, then, and take my leave." Suddenly he stopped. "One thing. Every time I've met you, I've had the nagging feeling that we'd met before. Why is that?"

For just an instant, Wraith managed a thin smile. "You really don't know."

"No. But don't think you'll win any concessions by withholding the information. I've lived this long without it. I won't lose a minute's sleep if you don't tell me."

"I don't imagine you lose sleep over anything, you lizard. But I'll tell you. You met me for the first time in the Oel Artis Travia fresh market, where I was attempting to steal food for my friends." Wraith's smile stretched fractionally. "You tried to stop me with magic. And you failed. So you tried to have me killed. You failed again. And you know something? I think you're going to fail this time, too."

It was sheerest bravado, Wraith knew—but seeing the recognition on Faregan's face, followed by a look of shock, and for one beautiful instant fear, made whatever Faregan might do to him as a result worth it.

Then Faregan regained his composure. "Ah. Yes. Well, let me tell you something, young thief. I'll make you wish you'd died that day—and a hundred times over—before I'm done with you." And Faregan, escorted by the guards at his sides, bowed lightly and left.

"There has to be some way to stop them from executing everyone!" Jess, her fingers claw-hooked into the material of Patr's tunic, glared up into his face. "We can't let them all die without doing something."

"I keep telling you, Jess. I didn't let them *all* die. I saved *you*. Beyond that, there's nothing we can do that won't get both of us killed, too."

They stood in the tiny house's doorway, watching dust blowing in front of the house. Jess wanted to go back to Oel Artis immediately—to disguise herself as some out-country bumpkin if necessary, and find some way to Wraith no matter what it took. Solander, too—but if she could only save one, she would save Wraith.

"If Solander and Wraith die, I don't want to live."

Patr's face creased with pain. Her rejection, Jess thought, of him and his hopes. He wanted her to love him, and she didn't. And every time she opened her mouth about Wraith, she stuck the knife in a little deeper. "Avenge them if you want. I'll help you. But you can't save them."

"You know where they're being kept."

"Yes."

"You must know some way to get in—some secret passage, perhaps, or friends who will let you pass and look the other way. . . ."

He laughed softly. "Friends. In the Inquest. My friends are just like me. They've been told now to kill me, and they took the oath when they were sworn to the Friends of Truth—the Secret and Honorable Society of the Silent Inquest; they would smile at me, and welcome me with open arms, and as soon as I was within reach, they'd cut my heart out. They are men I've loved like brothers, but they are as far beyond my reach now as the moon or the sun."

Jess frowned at him. "Surely you have someone you can trust. . . ."

But he shook his head. "Trust runs downhill among the Friends. The Masters hold all of the trust in their hands and dispense it at will; the lowest of the solitars hold none of the trust, and act out of obedience and hope that someday they, too will be worthy of trust. Obedience earns a higher place, and more chance that a man will live to see the next dawn. But we swear loyalty to the truth above all, and that means that friends, family, everything comes after the truth and the orders of the Masters, and our superiors."

"Have you ever killed anyone?"

He looked away from her and said evenly, "A long time ago I learned not to ask a question if I didn't want to know the answer."

Jess rested a finger under his chin and turned his head so that he was looking into her eyes. "I'm asking. Have you ever killed anyone?"

"To become a member of the Friends of Truth, you have to kill some-one."

"Then the answer is yes."

"The answer would have been yes anyway. I told you, I'm not a good man."

"But you saved me."

"Even bad men are capable of love."

She turned away from him. She didn't want to think that he loved her. She didn't want to hurt him—and she didn't want him to hurt her when he discovered that she wasn't going to love him. She wondered how he defined love; if he had any idea of what love really was.

She said, "Love isn't passion—isn't the heat in your blood and the way your heart races when you see your beloved. Love is . . . sacrifice. Duty and honor. Being willing to give up your own life for the life of the one you love."

She turned and found him smiling at her. Without a word he spread his arms to encompass the hovel in which they stood and the bleak world beyond the door.

She looked at him and felt her face grow hot. Maybe he did know what love was. But so did she.

"I love Wraith," she said. "He gave me my life—you cannot understand this, you may not even believe it, but without him, I would never have known who I was, I would never have walked freely beneath an open sky, I would never have looked at the clouds and the sun, buildings and rivers and the sea, and known what any of them were. I owe him not just my life, but my soul. To him and Solander, really. I have a life-debt to the two of them that I can never, never repay. I have to try to save them."

Patr frowned. "How can you owe someone your soul? That sounds like exaggeration, like words just for their dramatic effect."

Jess swallowed hard, considered her options, and then told him. She told Patr about the Warrens, about magic and where it came from and how she fit into the picture, about Wraith and how he and Solander had found a way to take her away from the hell of her life and how they had given her a new life—one built on lies—and how she had fought to bring some truth and some beauty to the world in repayment for her freedom—but how, when it came right down to the bone of the thing, she did not have the coin to repay all she owed. Or hadn't until Wraith and Solander fell into the hands of the Inquest. *Now* she could repay. Life for life, and soul for soul.

When she finished, Patr stood staring out the door for so long she thought perhaps he'd stopped listening to her—that somewhere along the way he'd grown bored with her story. Or that he was disgusted that he'd allowed himself to think he loved a Warrener.

Finally, though, he said, "I'll take you back to Oel Artis. I'll do what I can to help you get to Wraith and to Solander. We'll probably die in the process, and you may very well end up losing your soul anyway—we have no guarantee that if they catch us, they won't just throw us into the Warrens to use as fuel. But I understand honor, and I understand debts." He sighed and leaned his head against the doorframe and stared up at the ceiling. "Gods-all, what a nightmare. I guess I'll have to find us a re-worked, untraceable aircar. It will take a day or two. I'll do the best I can, but you have to understand, we may not be able to get there in time, no matter what I do."

"I understand. Move the heavens if you must—just give me the chance. Please."

He nodded. "The chance. You'll have that. If we die for it, you can't say I didn't tell you that was what would happen. But I'll do what I can."

Solander paced from one end of his tiny holding cell to the other, frantic. He'd lost track of how long he'd been a prisoner. Days? A week? He had no true day, no true night. He existed in perpetual, maddening twilight, punctuated rarely by meals tossed at him—and by nothing else. The Inquest was taking no chances with him. He occupied a wizards' holding cell—it was designed to be away from and shielded from any connections to the city's magic streams. But the Masters of the Inquest had added an additional shield around him, so that any spell he drew from his own power that attacked the shield would rebound on him. Had he been willing to incur the *rewhah* of an offensive spell, he still would not have been able to attack.

He tried anyway, thinking that if he could break free he might find some way to free the rest of the Inquest's captives, and in the ensuing pandemonium, make his way back to Wraith. But the Inquest had done its work too well. He hurt himself, drained away most of his energy, and when the fireworks died down, he was still a prisoner.

The only route left him was the one that led inward.

Exhausted, frantic, scared to death, he took it. He settled himself cross-legged on the narrow cot, pressed his hands together hard enough that he could feel the rhythm of his blood running through his finger-tips, and closed his eyes. With his eyes closed tightly, he stared upward at the inside of his forehead, and breathed in and out as slowly as he could. The fear began to subside.

Solander had never been one for prayer. Had never seen much pur-pose in the gods, when men could become near-gods by the use of

magic. But now he sat, captive, in a place where magic could offer him
nothing, and he yearned for the comfort of a power beyond his own.

In darkness and silence, he tapped the last of his energy, and offered
himself, not anonymously, as he would have offered payment for a spell
cast—but personally. "I'm here," he told the heavens. "I'm here, and I'm
in trouble. I am alone."

For a long, desperate moment, he shared his fear with the vastness
of an uncaring universe.

Then power not his own flowed into him, and he felt the world fall
away beneath him. *I'm here,* something—*someone*—whispered to his
soul. *You are not alone, nor have you ever been. You are part of a plan.*

"I don't want to die."

*No. Of course not. But you have done almost everything you came to do—
you have achieved the objectives you set for yourself this lifetime. And, as you
had planned, even your death will serve.*

"I want to be part of a different plan. Please. I have so much left to
do—I have people I love, and goals I've set for myself, and—"

*You swore yourself to my service lifetimes ago, seeking to learn the path-
way to godhood. Have trust in me—you are on your path. Do not let fear
throw you astray.*

"Fear isn't the real problem. Dying at the hands of the Silent Inquest
and the Dragon Council, and taking with me my friends and the other
people who fought so long and so hard to free the Warreners and end
the Dragon misuse of magic—that's the problem."

*I've already told you that you've achieved almost all that you have come
to do, and that in dying you will finish your chosen task. That you cannot hear
what I have to say and find comfort in it comes from fear.*

"I don't know you."

I am Vodor Imrish.

"That means nothing to me. Are you a god?"

*I am as much a god as any soul can be—all souls have the potential of
godhood, which is the power of creation. And it means nothing to you because
at the moment you are bound in the forgetful flesh. You will soon be free, and
then you will remember.*

"This isn't quite the comforting experience I'd imagined it might be,"
Solander said.

Do you want comfort, or do you want truth?

"At the moment I want out of here. You're a god. You say you're my
friend. Can you get me out of here?"

You can call on me in your moment of need.

Solander felt the wall at his back and the thin cot beneath him, smelled the stuffy, still air of his magic-bounded cell, and fought off the urge to scream. "This is a moment of need. This is a *big* moment of need. I'm calling on you now."

To do what, Solander, my friend?

"To get me out of here? To open the doors, blow down the walls, free me, free the Inquest's other captives, free Wraith. . . ."

Wraith is as much my servant, my associate, and my apprentice as you are. He, too, moves along the path he chose before he came to this life. His path now diverges from yours, Solander, but this is as you both decreed. Would you have me go against the path you chose for yourself? Would you have me undo in an instant the work of a lifetime?

"Yes," Solander said. "Yes. I wanted to stop the Dragons from burning souls for fuel, but I don't want to be a martyr to them. My death now will solve nothing. Nothing! I haven't trained anyone in the new system of magic. I haven't had the chance to—"

You have done what you came to do. And when you need me—when you truly need me—I will be with you. You will find godhood in your own time and on your own path—but be careful that you remember: Each mortal begins and ends the work of a lifetime in that lifetime. When the time comes to let go, you must resist the temptation to impose your will on the future. The future is for your soul—not for Solander, who is your shape and passion of the moment, but for the part of you that has no name, nor needs one.

"I'm not done here."

You are near a revelation. Very soon, you will have the chance to find it, and with it, your godhood. A door will open for you, and you will either pass through it or not. Fail to go through that door, and you will delay your ascension for a lifetime, or a hundred lifetimes . . . or forever.

"There's only one door I want to go through right now," Solander muttered.

And so you shall.

And the god who called himself Vodor Imrish was gone.

In the next instant, rough hands grabbed Solander and bound his wrists before him with a spell so heavy it must have cost the souls of a hundred men to cast it. He opened his eyes to find the executioners before him.

"Time," one of them said.

Chapter 21

As best he could guess, Wraith spent three days alone in the cell following Faregan's visit. On what he thought was the morning of the fourth day, though he could not be sure, four large men came for him. They put white-metal manacles around his wrists—the same cold bonds that had held him in place while the Masters of the Inquest tried to pry his secrets from him in that first meeting. They stood two to either side of him. And they marched him forward. Silent. Cold. As uncaring as the cold night sky, all of them, and seemingly as far away.

He didn't try to escape. He was almost beyond caring. He would be witness to hell, to the destruction of his life's work and the people who shared it, and if he was fortunate and the gods were kind, he would fall dead with the people he loved.

And if not, he would spend the rest of his life in torment from within and without.

They marched him through a maze of corridors. Out into bright daylight—the first he had seen since the Inquest brought him into the Gold Building. He squinted, blinded by the brilliance of the sun, and for a long moment could see nothing. In that moment, his guards shoved him into a seat, and one of them said, "You'll open your eyes and watch, or you'll suffer worse than any of them, starting now."

Wraith said, "I'll open my eyes and watch, but only because I will not do my friends the dishonor of hiding from the hell they face because of me. I will see, and I will remember. And if I ever can avenge them, I will."

The guards laughed. "Sure. You just hang on to that thought," one of them said.

His vision cleared. He sat in an outdoor amphitheater at the very heart of the Gold Building. The stage below him was covered in sand,

and in the sand stood row upon row of thick metal posts. All of those posts were empty, but he could make out the rings into which the wrists of his friends would soon be clamped.

Wraith remembered the gods of his childhood—the gods in which he had once believed, and that he had once reviled. In a child's act of unknowing hubris, he'd named himself after one of his favorites from among that pantheon, and named the first and pure love of his life after the other. Wraith and Shina, the Unseen One and the Mother Goddess.

At her death, he'd turned away from all gods. But now he prayed that they would intervene. He would find forgiveness in his heart for Shina's loss, if he could just save the many who were about to die—the many who had trusted him, worked with him, and believed in the importance of what he and they did together. He did not want to live if they died.

He clenched his hands together tightly and stared at the killing field, and prayed with everything that was in him, offering himself in exchange for the lives of the many.

And a sudden peace descended over him, and inside him a voice spoke softly.

What is to be is as it should be. What is to come is as each soul has chosen. Grieve for your friends, but not for their choices; their road is not yours, but they walk that road by their own design. And be at peace. You, too, have a place in the changing of the world. Your time has not yet passed—Wraith and Vincalis still have much to do. Be strong. I am with you, as I have always been.

Please just save them, Wraith prayed silently, not believing that he heard anything but the desperation of his own heart, but willing the words in his head to be the words of the god he wanted to believe in.

Watch. And remember. Your voice will speak yet to this generation, and to generations yet to come. Watch.

Wraith shivered. Down on the killing field, commentators from the nightlies stood speaking into glowing blue communication spheres of wizard-fire that would transmit their words and images into each home in the Empire. Because of the nature of the magic, their voices also filled the amphitheater. Wraith tried to shut out the sound of their smug condemnation, but he could not.

". . . and in just moments, the first group of traitors will be led onto Gold Field to hear their sentences read; we expect that among this first group will be a number of well-known stolti—"

"That's ex-stolti, Farvan. Remember, part of their sentencing included being stripped of their stolti class."

"You're right, of course, Cherrill. We expect that among this first group will be a number of well-known *ex*-stolti, including Solander Artis, once a member of one of the highest-ranking families in the Empire as well as being a member of the Dragon Low Council of Magic, and socialite Velyn Artis-Tanquin, vowmate of ex-Dragon Councilor Luercas tal Jernas, who is watching from the stands today, and who may find public support for a bid for reinstatement on the Dragon Council after this is all over."

"That's right, Farvan. We've been told that members of the Dragon Judiciary Association, who sentenced these criminals and who are in no small part responsible for the events today, have received threats against their lives because they were unwilling to overturn the convictions of the stolti-class criminals based simply on their rank."

Both commentators—themselves highly placed members of the stolti class—nodded to each other and exchanged smiles. "Cherrill, this is simply proof that justice in the Empire of the Hars Ticlarim is for everyone. Our government is just—but it will uncover the evil in its midst and root that evil out, no matter how . . . er, no matter how high into the air those roots may . . . ah . . . rise . . ."

Farvan, tangled in bad metaphor, fell silent, and Cherrill doggedly moved to fill the lull in the play-by-play. "We're expecting to see nearly a thousand executions today. This pernicious plot spread from the lowest quarters in the Empire to the highest—a vast, insidious group of malcontents working toward the annihilation of all that we hold dear."

Farvan got his second wind. "It's going to be a long afternoon, I think. We don't know exactly what to expect, but for this level of treason . . . well, all I can say is, I expect we're all in for an education."

All was exactly right, too, Wraith thought. According to the commentators, the entire Empire had shut down for the day in order that everyone could be at home to watch the executions. Watching was mandatory for anyone of the age of citizenship, and suggested for all children older than ten. Wraith wondered what effect watching more than a thousand men and women die in what would undoubtedly be the most creative manner the Masters of the Dragon Council could devise would have on the Empire's inhabitants. No one could know. No one could even speculate; nothing like this had happened before within the long annals of the Empire's recorded history.

Wraith would give his life for it not to happen right then, either—but the commentators had turned toward the huge arch that led out onto Gold Field, and the woman said, "And there it is, Farvan—the music that signals the approach of the traitors. We have to move into the spectator stands now. We've been told that no one who remains on Gold Field once this starts will be safe."

The spheres of blue light floated toward the entrance; behind them, the commentators scrambled for the opposite end of the field and a rope ladder that colleagues hastily let down for them. No one would see their awkward ascent into the stands. Everyone, instead, would see the first of Wraith's friends, colleagues, employees, and associates marched out onto the field, and would see them bound to the posts, and then would see them . . . what? Burned by fire from the heavens? Exploded limb from limb? Flayed alive by magical hands?

Soldiers of the Silent Inquest, no longer arrayed in the green and black, but in the standard uniforms of the Empire—for this hellish mass execution would never be called an action of the Silent Inquest, but instead would be credited to the legitimate government of the Hars Ticlarim—clamped people one at a time to the posts. Wraith could make out the faces of his friends: Rionvyeers the dancer; Meachaan the actress; Korr the Arts Master of the Order of Resonance. Too, he saw faces he had never seen before, and wondered if those were friends of Solander's, or if they were innocents brought in to pad out the numbers and make the conspiracy look bigger than it truly was. But he did not see Solander. He did not see Jess. He did not see Velyn.

And then the last of the first group came out onto the field, and she was Velyn. His Velyn, who had turned against him, and whom he had in turn pushed away. His eyes filled with tears, and he leaped to his feet, thinking to throw himself into the killing field and die with her and the rest. But the men guarding him shoved him roughly back into his seat.

"Move again and find out how much living can hurt," one of them snarled.

Wraith felt a stab of pain at the back of his neck that blinded him and sent his body into spasms. He screamed, unable to stop himself, and sagged forward.

"That was just a taste," the guard said.

They pulled his head upright and faced him toward the crowd.

"You are found guilty of treason against the Empire of the Hars Ticlarim," a deep voice boomed from everywhere and nowhere. "You have plotted against the government of this great realm, but more, you have plotted for the destruction of the lives of the citizens of the realm, and their children. With callous disregard for life, for property, for humanity, you have planned to disrupt the magical underpinnings of this

304 ❖ HOLLY LISLE

realm, and though your plans have come to nothing, your intent is enough to condemn you to death.

"You will, therefore, die as all plotters against the Hars shall die; you will die by the magic that you would have undone."

"*Rewhah*," Wraith heard someone behind him mutter. "They're going to channel the *rewhah* from the Empire's magic use through those posts and into their bodies. I can feel it building."

"Quiet," someone else behind him muttered. "Don't spoil the surprise for anyone else."

Those two voices sounded weirdly familiar, Wraith thought. Out of place, as if they belonged not in this amphitheater, but in . . .

Jess! Jess was the one who felt the *rewhah*. And Patr was the one who told her to be quiet!

They were behind him—a few seats behind, but still, if they were there, then they would not be dying on the killing fields. But had that really been Jess's voice, or was he hearing what he wanted to hear? If next he heard Solander, he would know his heart and his mind were playing tricks on him.

He heard nothing else, though, but the cries of those on the field, begging for mercy.

"You will die by the sword you would have wielded against others," the voice of the judge said with finality. "Prepare your souls; you shall this day meet perdition."

Above the screaming, above the pleas for mercy, Wraith heard Velyn shout, "There's the one you want, sitting in the stands. There's the real traitor, Gellas Tomersin! Gellas! Wraith the Warrener! In truth he's Vincalis the Agitator. Burn him, not us!"

He felt his heart break.

From her position several seats behind him, he heard Jess say, "Brace yourself. Here it comes."

The guards, having finished binding all the first group of sacrifices—martyrs—to the posts, fled the killing field. The instant they were outside the ring, a sheet of green-gold light descended and formed a wall between the spectators and the victims. And in the eyeblink after that, the hideous fires of *rewhah* erupted from the ground, swirled up each of the posts, and enveloped each of the Empire's sacrifices.

Wraith wanted to close his eyes, to hide his face in his hands, to block his ears . . . but he forced himself to watch. To bear witness to this thing that he had done, to this guilt that was his burden. Tears ran from the corners of his eyes and blurred his vision, but not enough to keep him from seeing the bound men and women shifted into ever more hideous parodies of the human form before the *rewhah* finally reduced them to ash. He thought that he would never escape the sounds of their screams, the sight of their destruction. And the vision of Velyn dying a death no human should experience, while on the safe side of the magical shield, Luercas tal Jernas sat applauding and cheering.

After the screaming died, after the dust that had moments before been human beings settled, the green-gold shield that kept the *rewhah* in the killing field disappeared. And the music began again, and into the breathless hush that ensued, the next group of victims marched. Wraith closed his eyes then, and prayed to the voice that had offered him comfort, "Save them. Take me, and save them." If he could have changed the outcome by will alone, the men and women being fastened to the posts would have vanished, and he alone would have stood on the killing field.

But he opened his eyes and saw Solander being clamped front and center, with one of the blue communication spheres floating in front of him. The commentators were discussing him from the sidelines, speaking into a second communication sphere.

". . . Solander Artis—who was expected to be in the first group, and who ends a promising career in magical research. Artis, whose father held the highest position in the Oel Artis Dragon Council before giving his life to save the city of Oel Maritias during a disaster some years ago, was expected to win a seat on the Dragon Council, and highly placed sources suggest that he might have been a favorite for early promotion to the chair occupied by his father. A conviction of treason doesn't just shame him; it also casts shame on his entire family. They'll lose a lot of stature among the stolti because of this."

"They certainly will, Farvan. I can't imagine what the Artis clan is thinking right now. You'll notice that none of them are here watching."

Wraith was having a hard time actually thinking critically—the horror he had just seen and the horror he was about to see had nearly shut down rational thought. But watching the commentators and the hovering communication spheres, he suddenly realized that none of the spheres had moved in on Velyn when she shouted that he was Vincalis the Agitator and pointed him out to the crowd. In fact, the commentators had taken no notice of her either. As if, he thought, they'd been told not to.

Yet the communication spheres were right up against Solander.

So the commentators knew at least enough about what was going on that they'd kept their commentary away from Velyn. And the wizards controlling the viewers knew enough to only catch her image from a distance. Had they known she would point him out and spoil their illusion that Vincalis the Agitator ran free in the Empire?

Probably.

And she died hating him. That was going to haunt him forever, he thought. He'd tried to save her—tried to help her. And he'd helped her to death.

Wraith shuddered as guards clamped the last of the second group of victims in place, and fled the killing field.

This time, the communication sphere stayed in front of Solander. Wraith saw Solander close his eyes. As the green-gold shield of light dropped into place, he saw another fire, a pale, soft white one, shimmer from Solander's skin.

Behind him, Jess gasped.

In front of him, Solander lifted his eyes to the heavens.

He shouted, "Vodor Imrish! More time—I am not done here!"

Jess gripped Patr's arm as they brought Solander out and whispered, "No."

Patr took her hand in his, leaned over, and so softly that she almost couldn't hear him, said, "We can't leave. If we try, we'll draw attention to ourselves and be down there in the arena with them before you can blink. Now sit up, keep your hood over your head, and don't you dare cry, or we're both dead."

Jess nodded.

"I'm sorry, Jess," he added. "I didn't want you to be here for this."

Now she wished that she hadn't come. She couldn't get over the hell of watching Velyn charred to ash in front of her eyes—and she hated Velyn. The nightmare of watching the others in the first hundred die equally horribly would never leave her. But now she was watching Solander, who in all the world was, next to Wraith, her best friend. He was going to die, and she was going to have to sit there and watch, helpless.

Four rows in front of her sat Wraith, with a guard on his left, a guard on his right, and two guards behind him. Jess didn't know why he wasn't down on the arena floor, but she could find only a little comfort in the fact. The Inquest held him, and according to Patr, if they let him live, what happened to him would probably be worse than what would happen if they killed him.

Her world felt like it was coming to an end. She wanted to stand up in her seat and scream, *I'm one of them. Kill me, too.*

But something in Solander's face kept her in her seat, and gave her hope. He didn't look afraid. He looked . . . almost triumphant. He stared up at the sphere of fire that sent his image around the world, and she thought she saw the faintest of smiles cross his lips. She could not imagine being in his place, being merest instants from torture and death, and radiating the sort of calm he did.

Perhaps, she thought, he's found a way to escape.

The shield dropped around the arena, and the people seated in the auditorium leaned forward in anticipation, but the *rewhah* didn't have a chance to touch the Empire's sacrifices. Instead, Solander shouted, "Vodor Imrish! More time—I am not done here!"

Solander had spent his time since meeting Vodor Imrish gathering his energy. Now, bound to the post, staring up at the faces of observers come to watch him and the rest of the rebels die, he considered for one final time the choices he had.

He could shield himself—he could, he felt sure, hold off the worst that all the gathered wizards of the Empire could throw at him. At least, he could for a while. But the Empire could bring in hundreds of wizards, all of whom could call on the nearly unlimited resources of the Empire's many Warrens for their power. And he had what he held inside himself. In the end, he would falter, and he would die.

He might be able to attack the wizards controlling the *rewhah* by drawing on his life energy. But he would have to take the *rewhah* himself, and the force he would be able to throw at them would likely be nothing compared to shields they would already have in place. He would die having accomplished nothing.

For a long time he'd thought that he had no third option; that he would either die alone and shielded or die alone in a futile attack. It was only when he considered the rest of the Empire's intended victims that he realized he did have a third option.

Vodor Imrish said that Solander had accomplished almost all of what he had come to do—and that his death would complete his mission. But perhaps he could do more. If he could not live to fight, perhaps he could fight from the place beyond death. Perhaps he could even find a way back. The god had suggested letting go. But Solander could not . . . or perhaps, he thought, he simply would not.

He felt shields building around the arena, and knew he had only instants before his death to do what he had to do.

He stared into the softly glowing blue sphere of the mages' viewer, and smiled slightly at the thought of what the Empire's reaction would be if his plan worked; and with every bit of power he could gather and offer, he shouted, "Vodor Imrish! More time—I am not done here!" And as he shouted, he gave Vodor Imrish his life, breath, bone, blood—and soul.

Around him, the light of the wizards' shields flared to life, and he felt the *rewhah* coming up through the ground beneath his feet; he could feel the fury of it, the rage born of the deaths of souls.

But before it touched him—before it touched any of the prisoners on the killing field—Vodor Imrish acted. He took Solander's sacrifice—breath, bone, blood, body, and soul—and to that sacrifice added his own unimaginable power, his own righteous wrath. Solander felt the fire of a god burning through him, cleanly and painlessly devouring him, and a terrifying joy spread through him. Cut loose from the weight of his flesh, with his soul for the moment linked to that of the god Vodor Imrish, he suddenly felt love and compassion for the Empire's captives trapped on the killing field and waiting within the wings for their chance to die.

Solander reached out to all of them, and before the *rewhah* could destroy them, he removed them from harm's way, and secreted them safely out of the reach of the Masters of the Hars.

And when they were safe, Solander used the last of the god's touch to re-create his own face in fire, and to speak to the audience in the amphitheater and to the millions who watched the nightlies from their homes. "I am with you still," he said.

Vodor Imrish released Solander from his embrace. Solander found himself bodiless, suspended in a darkness beyond time and light, beyond flesh and need. He could feel the pull of life behind him, and the pull of something else ahead. A door opened in the darkness—a path that would take him forward to the place beyond death.

"Go," Vodor Imrish said. "You have done well."

But Solander could not go. Behind him lay his world, his time, his people, his goals and ambitions, his dreams and hopes. Behind him lay promises he had made to himself and to others. Behind him lay the magic that only he truly understood—and if he did not find a way back, who would lead the people he had rescued against the Dragons of the Hars Ticlarim?

Vodor Imrish had said he was done. But Vodor Imrish was wrong.

Do not make this mistake, the god whispered through his soul. *Your future is ahead of you, not behind you.*

But Solander's hunger and his heart lay behind, in Matrin. The pull of the door into the eternal, of the golden and welcoming light, called to him strongly. *Not yet,* he thought, and turned his back on it. He moved into darkness and felt his way through void back to the world he had so recently left.

He could see it rolling like a river before him—the past, the present, the future. He could dip his thoughts in and pull out pieces that formed a story—and in that story, the Dragons flowed like poison.

He could not reenter the world, he discovered. Not yet. But he would find a way. He would find his way back to life, to a body, to a voice. He would create a way to make the stand against the Dragons that would destroy them.

Solander shouted his demand to the heavens, and in the next instant, Jess saw him light up brighter than a sun—gold as the heart of the world, pure as life itself. The light he radiated shot out and touched every one of those on the arena floor with him. A beam of it blasted through the shield and into the tunnel from which the Empire's sacrifices had been marched. The prisoners vanished in the blink of an eye: One instant there, the next simply gone. Solander did not vanish, at least not instantly. Instead, his body broke free of the bonds that held him and rose into the air, and Jess, squinting at him, watched all the recognizable details about him dissolve into that ever-brightening light. As she raised her hand to shield her eyes from the blinding radiance, she suddenly saw his face fill the arena and heard his voice say, "I am with you still."

The light blinded her. Then, with a roar, the *rewhah* summoned by the Dragons to destroy their sacrifices burst up out of the ground, but without human fuel, it had nothing to contain or control it, nothing to feed it. The *rewhah* hellfires erupted against shields that had not been designed to withstand such all-out fury, and the shields began to buckle. All around Jess, hysteria reigned. People shouted, screamed, fled in all directions. Blinded, she reached out for Patr, and found his seat empty. And the next instant a strong hand grabbed her upper arm and pulled her to her feet, and Patr's voice in her ear said, "We have Wraith, but we have to get out of here now. Keep your hood over your face and don't say anything."

She stumbled, still blinded, at his side as they ran up the steps, surrounded by a stampeding mob. Into the tunnel that led into the bowels of the Gold Building, and into the cool and dark of the main hallway, in the crush of masses of panicked men and women desperate to escape.

Shoved, buffeted, elbowed, and kicked, Jess managed to keep on her feet only through the force of fear.

"Left," Patr shouted, and began forging a path through the herd toward the left side of the hallway. It branched, and when it did, they were in a smaller, poorly lit, less crowded passageway.

Now they moved faster. They tucked their heads down and kept up with the robed men, all fleeing at as near a run as they could manage.

Patr started guiding them rightward, and shoved them into a very narrow, unlit corridor that ran at a right angle to the passageway they'd just been in.

"We're leaving the lights off because I don't want to call attention to us," Patr said. In the narrow space, his voice seemed suddenly close and loud. "Watch your step. We're going to reach the stairs in just a second."

Even warned, Jess stepped off into air and only the hand around her arm kept her from taking a bad fall. "Careful," Patr said.

On the other side of him, she heard Wraith swearing.

"Quiet," Patr said.

"Nearly killed myself on the stairs," Wraith whispered. "No balance at all with my hands bound like this."

"I'll fix that when we get where we're going."

In the dark, the stairs seemed to descend interminably—Jess could almost imagine herself hurrying to the heart of the world. The air began to stink of rot and mold and the sickening sweetness of death; her skin prickled from increasing cold and damp and a crawling, clawing air of malice. She started hearing the faint drip of water, and she got a sense of space opening up in front of her.

"Almost to the last step," Patr said. "The ground is slick once you get past the stairs—but we're almost where we're going."

Jess felt bad magic erupt at a distance. "If you think it will provide some protection, we need to get there fast," she said.

"You felt the *rewhah* break free?" Wraith asked.

"Yes."

"Hell's-all!" Patr swore. He muttered, "*Vey-takchaes!*" and dim lights flickered on all around them. They'd arrived in a natural cavern, huge and arching, with stalactites hanging from the vault like the fangs of demons, and stalagmites stabbing up from the slick floor to meet them, so that Jess felt herself trapped in the massive jaws of death itself. The eerie blue-green lights cast long and twisting shadows that did not successfully hide bloated bodies in all stages of decay, stacked one atop the next and crumbling in on each other. Dead eyes stared at her, dead jaws gaped open in frozen shock. Some faces were human, some might once have been human, some were barely recognizable as faces. Jess thought some of them still twitched.

Jess felt her heart contract, and Patr said, "Don't look. Just run."

They fled, Patr dragging the two of them to a doorway carved into a massive pillar of stone, opened the door, hauled both of them through the narrow opening so fast Jess crashed shoulder, chest, hip, and face into the doorway while getting through, and then shoved the door shut behind them.

He dropped a bar into place, pushed a bright red button just above the door . . .

. . . and all sensation of evil, of malice, of the horror that had been unleashed in the amphitheater of the Gold Building vanished.

"Safe room," Patr said. He leaned against the wall, panting, bathed in pale light for which Jess could find no source. "There are a lot of them scattered around this cavern. Things go . . . wrong . . . quite a bit down here. This room burns power like a floating mansion, but we should live through whatever is going on above."

"Out there," Wraith said. "Those bodies . . . what were they there for?"

"Very specialized . . . research." Patr looked grim when he said it.

Jess rubbed her hip. It hurt bad enough she expected an impressive bruise—but if she didn't melt into ash, she'd take a hundred bruises. "What sort of research?"

Patr had taken Wraith's wrists and was trying various small wands above the opening mechanisms. He didn't look up to answer. "The Silent Inquest considers the Dragon Empire its mortal enemy. Masters of the Inquest will take Dragon money and do Dragon dirty work if that work also suits their needs, but the Inquest antedates the first of the Dragon dynasties by nearly four hundred years, and in eras when the Dragons lost their grip on power, the Inquest has been here to resume its control of the lands and peoples of the Hars."

Jess frowned. "Most people don't even know the Silent Inquest exists. And we've never had an Inquest government."

"Ah, but we have," Patr said. "The Dragons prefer to rule by deception—by making people believe that the Dragons have the best interests of the people at heart. They make a show of all their good works, but they want power just like any other government, and they'll use any methods to get and keep it. They spend a lot of time and money painting their work in pretty colors, though.

"The Inquest has always ruled from the background, and by fear.

Most people don't know it exists because that's how the Inquest wants it. Outside of the Gold Building, Inquestors wear no special clothing, no insignias, no distinguishing marks. We know each other by reputation, but never identify ourselves as Inquestors to others to whom we have not been introduced by those we know are Inquestors. And we never introduce another of our own as an Inquestor to one to whom we have not been formally introduced."

The first lock clicked open at Wraith's wrist.

"But I'd heard rumors of the Inquest before they took an interest in me," Wraith said. "I didn't know the rumors were true, but I heard things."

Patr nodded. "We are a secret society and a silent government, but some of our members—those in higher positions—took a liking to the fruits of fame and became . . . visible. When they became too obvious, the highest of the Masters had them killed, and when even our Grand Master once made a spectacle of himself, lower Masters convened and agreed to his death."

He sighed. "And that is what *this* place is all about. When the Masters command a death, we are required to provide that death—and sometimes the death they want is of a powerful wizard, or someone with access to the protection of powerful wizards. Here is where we learn how to reach powerful people and kill them."

Wraith rubbed his wrists. "And this is what you did? You killed people."

"I mostly provided information. I'm good at blending into places, making myself seem to belong. But . . . sometimes, yes."

Wraith studied Patr without expression. "But you risked your life to save mine."

"Only because Jess asked me to. *I* would have let you die."

The faintest of smiles crossed Wraith's lips. "Thanks for being honest, anyway."

Patr smiled grimly and said, "Anything for a friend."

"So what happens now?" Jess asked.

"We let the *rewhah* run its course. We arm ourselves." He nodded upward, and Jess saw what looked like standard stun-sticks, but with more settings on the handle. "Those will kill almost any nightmare that even a heavy *rewhah* backlash can create," he said. "Take one. I hope we won't need them, but I'm betting otherwise."

"I couldn't kill anyone," Jess said.

Patr looked to Wraith. Wraith reached up without a word and took down a weapon from one of the hooks. His face told Jess more than she wanted to know: not only that he could kill something if he had to, but that he thought he was going to have to. She stood there for a moment, considering. She and Wraith could fight the Empire if they could get out of this place. If they didn't live to escape, though, this desperate rescue became nothing but a waste of Patr's sacrifice of himself to save her.

She looked from Wraith to Patr, and back to Wraith. Then she stood up on her toes and reached for the weapon. She was too short by far. "Give me one," she said. "I'll do what I have to do."

The light inside the room flickered and then went out. The sense of being protected vanished. Jess gripped her weapon with shaking hands. What came in the wake of a magical blast so fierce that it could blow the spells of a wizard's safe room?

"I wish Solander were here," Wraith whispered.

Outside the safe room, something big growled and clawed at the door.

Chapter 22

Luercas lay in the corridor, alive and untouched, but surrounded by masses of the freshly dead. He raised his head carefully, fractionally, ready to drop it and pretend to be a corpse again should anything in the corridor move. But this time nothing did.

So he got to his feet slowly, watching in both directions in case one of the scarred monstrosities that had survived the *rewhah* came back. Those things were known to go mad and turn on people; when the *rewhah* had scarred him, he hadn't—but he'd known what had happened to him, and had felt certain that sooner or later magic would be able to set it right. Most of those in the corridor knew nothing of *rewhah*: thought that the magic the Empire used was a clean source of energy; believed that they would be protected and that their lives mattered to someone other than themselves; thought the world they inhabited was a safe place.

With their beliefs shattered, they could turn dangerous quickly—and some of them came out of the hell of *rewhah* with the equipment to make them doubly dangerous. Three fast beasts with talons and fangs had risen out of the ruined bodies near him—he'd caught a glimpse of them through slitted eyes, and it was enough to make him fear for his life. They all matched—something unexpected when dealing with backwash damage. Not only were their body parts consistent within themselves, but they were consistent from monster to monster. The damage had the look of intent about it, as if . . .

Luercas had lain on the whitestone floor and held his breath and tried to be logical. To the best of his considerable knowledge, no one had ever managed to control the effects of *rewhah* to create anything useful. No one. Many had tried, but *rewhah* resisted the best efforts of talented

Masters—and those who dared push their luck a bit too far found themselves fighting for their survival. Yet here in front of him were three matching monsters—almost birdlike in their movements, featherless, with dark copper hides and teeth as long as his hand set solidly in gaping jaws. They each moved on two huge, powerful hind legs, and had tails as long as their bodies, and long, supple necks, and eyes that glowed like the setting sun. Most times, guards would bring down anything that looked too dangerous—but those three had the air of survivors about them. And the air of the intervention of gods—and of that sort of thing Luercas had seen entirely too much already for one day. He'd been more comfortable in a world where gods were dusty myths, trotted out at holidays to provide a reason for merriment. He did not care to be confronted with proof of active, interested gods; he did not care to have his rules changed.

But at least all the living, viable monsters seemed to be gone.

Nothing like them in the corridor anymore. Nothing but bodies dead, and wreckage that had once been human but was dying. He had drawn from many of them to save his own life—pulled from their living energy to create a shield around himself, and fed the *rewhah* back on them. More might have lived had he not done so, but he'd already borne the scars of *rewhah* once in his life, and had no intention of doing it again.

He hurried through the corridors of the Gold Building, aware that somehow the rules had changed, that in these corridors neither he nor any other Dragon would be an accepted visitor. The Dragons, who had been providing the shielding and the *rewhah* for the day's executions, had lost face badly. Those Masters in the Council who could get to the City Center would have put a curfew into effect, and would have found someone to blame the disaster on, but while they could claim the intervention of some anti-Harsian faction, people had seen what had happened, and without careful handling, they were going to sympathize with the people who had been . . . what? Saved by a god? Or simply removed from the world in a less painful manner?

Luercas had never even believed in the gods; his theology put him near the top of a pyramid of wizards and conceded the existence of nothing higher.

The presence of gods changed things. He wasn't sure how yet, but if the enemy could call on gods for assistance, and actually get the assistance requested, then the Dragons should find a way to do the same thing. Or perhaps they could harness the power of the gods, in the same way that they had harnessed the power of souls. Wouldn't that be interesting—using gods as fuel? What wonders could the Dragons do with fuel like that?

He got out of the Gold Building and took his aircar home high above the streets and out of the usual flight patterns to avoid any trouble. He had a lot to think about. A lot of research to do.

In spite of the day's disaster, he was almost excited. He sensed massive potential, and an opportunity for himself, one he doubted anyone else sensed.

Besides, for him, at least, the day hadn't been a total disaster. He was unscathed, many of the Masters of the Dragon Council were surely lying right there in the Gold Building, twisted beyond all humanity—which made him happy—and Velyn was dead, and he hadn't needed to do a thing to make that happen.

With those cheering thoughts, he went into his workroom, buoyed by visions of future greatness.

Grath Faregan, barred into one of the midlevel safe rooms in the Gold Building, listened with his ear to the door for any more screeching or snarling.

Just outside the door lay poor Omwi, who prior to the *rewhah* blast had been a bit older, a bit slower, and a lot fatter than Faregan. Omwi, who made the mistake of bolting for the same safe room as Faregan, and expecting that Faregan would share. Omwi, who forgot that he was the only obstacle standing between Grath Faregan and the Grand Mastership of the Secret Inquest.

Omwi, who made an unimpressive little pile of cinder, Faregan reflected, peeking out the weapon slit. Poor fellow. Just not quite fast enough to get to the door first, and not quite smart enough to figure out that what he really needed was a different door.

Faregan leaned against the back wall and smiled. He was in charge. He had a favor coming from the Dragons—a big favor. And he already knew what he wanted more than anything else in the world.

"What's out there?" Jess whispered.

Patr peeked through the weapons slot, paled, and pulled his face back far enough that all three of them had a clear view of one huge, yellow eye staring in—before Patr shut the slot. "You don't want to know," he said.

"We're trapped in here," Jess whispered. "Just like in the Warrens."

Wraith looked at her sidelong. If she got to thinking this was like being in the Warrens, she was entirely capable of going to pieces. Rational as she was about other things, she wasn't rational about that. He said, "This isn't like the Warrens at all. We can walk through the door anytime we please. We just aren't going to like what's waiting on the other side."

Patr shuddered.

Wraith wished he hadn't seen that shudder. If it scared Patr, he certainly didn't want to deal with it.

"They evidently still had some live ones in the piles," Patr muttered.

"What do we have to do to get past them?" Wraith asked.

"Kill them before they have the chance to kill us." Patr eyed the weapons still hanging overhead. "No chance we could outrun them. They look fast as hellwinds."

"That's reassuring," Jess said.

"You suppose if we wait long enough, they'll go away?" Wraith asked.

"They might. But they might just settle in to wait us out. They know we're in here. They know we don't have any way to get anywhere unless we go through them."

Wraith heard the clawing on the stone door again, and his skin crawled. "You've dealt with this sort of thing before, have you?"

Patr nodded.

"What do you recommend?"

"Ideally, not to find yourself in this situation." He smiled a little. "That not being an option, I recommend . . . hiding in here until they go away."

Then he shook his head from side to side, silently telling Wraith and Jess this wasn't what he recommended at all. He pointed to the weapons above their heads and indicated that each of them should carry two, then pantomimed going out the door with both weapons drawn, firing at anything that moved.

They can hear us? Jess mouthed.

Patr nodded vigorously.

And understand?

Another nod.

"I get the comfortable spot on the floor, then," Jess said, and pointed to her choice for second weapon. Wraith reached up and handed it down to her. He grabbed one for himself, and Patr got his own.

They eyed each other nervously, checked their weapons to make sure the charge bar showed full.

When they were ready, Patr very, very slowly pivoted the security bar over from the closed to the open position. The red light at the top of the room went out. Jess jerked her head upward, indicating the light. Wraith could guess what she wanted to know: Did the things outside have any way of telling that the three of them were getting ready to come out the door?

They won't know, Patr mouthed. *Security feature.*

That made sense, actually. They had the weapons and the safety rooms because this sort of thing *did* happen; it would only make sense that the wizards wouldn't handicap themselves by designing rooms that would tip off the things that wanted to eat them as the wizards were getting ready to go out the door.

Patr held up a hand, fingers spread. Five. He had his second weapon tucked tight to his side with his elbow. Wraith, closest to the door, put a hand on the handle so that he could swing it open. Patr would go out first, Jess second, and Wraith would bring up the rear.

Patr tucked a finger in. Four.

Jess wiped the sudden bloom of sweat from her forehead and readjusted her weapons.

Three.

Wraith's blood pounded in his ears like a herd of mad drummers.

Two. His hand tightened on the door, his muscles bunched, and he felt sweat slicking his palm. Jess bunched herself tight. Patr's left cheek began to twitch, and his lips thinned into a hard line. In the instant before the final count, Wraith noted, surreally, the tiny burst of blood on the right side of Patr's lip where he'd bitten into his own flesh without knowing it.

One.

For an instant, everything felt as slow, as silent, as surreal as that blood. Wraith opened the door and Patr lunged out of it, both weapons cutting arcs in front of him. Jess charged out in his wake and began shooting left—Patr moved to cover the front and the right. And Wraith raced behind them, not bothering to close the door, swinging around to cover their backs as they ran.

That clarity, that logic and order, only lasted for one suspended instant, though—and then the world erupted into blood and screaming. The Scarred nightmares came at them, all claws and teeth and massive, muscled haunches; the beasts exploded when the spellfire hit them, and Wraith realized that they screamed words. "Mamma!" and "No!" and "Don't kill me!"

His stomach lurched.

They moved along the slick cavern floor, a tight cluster that slowed to a walk as their feet hit moss-slimed stone. "Up the narrow stairs," Patr said.

"The narrow stairs?"

"They only permit one human walking single file. They're easy to defend—a bit nasty when you're downhill having to move up, but these wide beasts won't be able to navigate them, I think."

He no more than said it than Patr's feet went out from under him, and one of his weapons spun across the cavern floor. He grunted, and one of the nightmares leaped at him, a giant bound through the air that would put it on top of him and its claws deep into his entrails. Jess gave a yell that ought to have stopped time itself and blasted the monster out of the air as if she'd been born to such things.

"Good shot," both men said, as Patr pulled himself to his feet.

They left the lost weapon, and Patr led them to the stairs.

"Where from here, though?" Patr asked.

"We probably should have thought of that before," Jess muttered. As they moved onto the comforting narrows of the steps, she handed one of her weapons to Patr, who still had point. In the middle position, she couldn't fire in either direction.

Wraith said, "We need to get to the best aircar we can steal."

"You can steal aircars?" Patr's voice held a note of interest that was almost funny.

"Magic doesn't work on me," Wraith said. "You could blast me all day with one of these things, and I wouldn't notice, aside from the light."

"Damn. So you didn't need to run from the *rewhah*?"

"No. But I didn't want to sit in the arena, either."

"I know where the best aircars are," Patr said. He blasted at something ahead of them, and Wraith heard a chilling scream.

The run through the nearly vacant Gold Building was a nightmare. All that seemed to be left, aside from twisted corpses, were monsters.

"The survivors will be in tomorrow to clean up," Patr said. "They have a protocol for this. The place will be locked up tonight, and will probably receive a few blasts of, . . ." He swore under his breath. "We need to get out of here fast. Blasts of sterilizing magic will be set to go off in here every hour on the hour. I don't want to spend the rest of the day and all night in a safe room, and be here when the cleanup crew shows up tomorrow."

They ran.

It seemed to Wraith that they ran halfway around the world. He'd always been a runner, but of late he'd lost the urge—and now his ribs ached and his side burned and he couldn't catch his breath.

They came out of the maze onto a roof, and on the roof sat a row of gorgeous, gleaming black aircars. Wraith chose the nearest, ran to it, and opened the door. He started the controls. Behind him, Patr swore. "I could have used you when I was a kid."

"I wasn't stealing aircars when I was a kid," Wraith said.

Patr laughed just a little. "I wasn't, either, but I sure as hells-all tried."

They were in the aircar, in the air, away from the Gold Building.

"Where are we going?" Jess asked.

Ever since Solander's sacrifice, Wraith had been hearing two words in the back of his head. "Three Spears," he said. "It's a hunch, but I'm going to trust it. First, though, we have one place we have to stop." He raced them through the city, finally dropping them to the ground on a quiet back street in front of a narrow, massively magic-shielded gate.

Jess went pale as death as she recognized the gate. "Get me out of here," she said.

Patr nodded, but Wraith held up a hand. "Wait. I have something I have to check for. Drive back and forth along this road. Whatever you do, don't stop and wait in front of the gate. If Solander succeeded in what he tried to do the night the Masters of the Inquest put us together, we'll have a weapon in there that the Dragons won't be able to stand against."

Patr and Jess looked at each other, and Jess took over the aircar controls. Wraith waited until they were well away from the gate, and then moved through it. First house up against the wall, he thought. First apartment on the right. Storage under the seating. Where he would find the details of Solander's work, if Solander had succeeded. But Solander's success while barred inside the cage of the Masters of the Silent Inquest was no given. And if Solander had failed, the survivors who might hope to save the Warreners were lost before they began.

Wraith would have considered praying that it would be there, but right at that moment the gods—or at least one of them—seemed closer and more involved in his life than he felt comfortable with. What had been a sort of reflex in bad times for him now seemed like talking out loud in front of someone who might or might not be listening, and he wasn't sure he always wanted to be heard. So he merely hoped that Solander had succeeded, and ran through the shadows to the appropriate door. It opened, of course. Why have locks on doors in a place where none of the occupants had free will, or initiative, or awareness of their surroundings beyond that which was permitted them? He went down the stairs, and found the family at home. The smells hit him first: sour sweat and the awful sweetness of Way-fare, and the closed, stuffy stink of tiny, crowded rooms that were never opened to fresh air. Suddenly he was a little boy again, trapped in a home where no one could see him, where no one would talk to him, where no one would hold him when he was afraid or hurt.

The family didn't look at him—they didn't even twitch when he came through the door. They sat, eyes fixed to the flickering light in the center of the room, looking at the faces of and listening to the voices of their gods. Wraith got a chill when he saw the face of the god speaking at that moment.

It was Luercas—a younger Luercas, but Luercas nonetheless.

Of course the Dragons would do their own controlling programs. But he thought of his childhood, of sitting and watching the gods who spoke to him, of finding in them more comfort than he found in his own family, and he was filled with a hatred so vast and seething that he had to sit down for just a moment. He had worshiped his family's torturers, enslavers, killers. His gods had been his owners. The men responsible for Shina's death, for the deaths of other friends, for Velyn and Solander.

His eyes blurred and filled with tears, his throat clogged, and he wanted to scream and pound the walls. So much had happened so fast that he hadn't really been able to realize that Solander was dead. That Velyn was dead. The first real family he'd made for himself, almost all gone. The realization hit him with the force of a falling house, and he hurt so badly he couldn't breathe. Blinded with tears, swallowing his sobs, gasping for air around the lump in his throat, he stumbled to the place where Solander and he had agreed Solander's formulas and spells would be. He reached around, feeling for them, and came up empty.

Failure. Solander's magic was gone. The Dragons had won—for without Solander's magic, Wraith and his fellow rebels had nothing with which to fight off the Empire. He wiped his eyes on his sleeve, and doubled over with his forehead pressed against the cool wall. His foot twisted, and he heard paper rustle. He froze. In a Warren house, there would be no need for paper. No one who could read, no one who could write. He wiped his eyes again, and caught his breath, and, when his vision was clear, looked down. Sheets of tan paper—large sheets, and glossy—lay scattered across the floor like autumn leaves after the fall. Across them, written in neat rows of Solander's careful, back-slanted hand, were formulas and notations, discussions of variables and their effects, substitution charts, and spell after spell after spell.

Wraith dropped to his knees and gathered up the pages as quickly as he could. He didn't have to worry about interference from the Warreners; his presence would never register with them. But he did have to worry that Jess and Patr would be picked up by a curfew patrol; he could not imagine, after what had happened, the Dragons not declaring a state of emergency and closing down the Belows with a curfew. Until they came up with a good lie to explain away the visitation of a god and the rescue of the traitors by that god, the Dragons stood a good chance of having to fight off riots from one end of the Empire to the other.

He tucked the papers beneath his shirt and took a steadying breath. He could be distraught and devastated on his own time, as soon as he had some. Right now, Jess and Patr were going to need him.

Out the door, up the stairs, along the dead-empty street to the Vincalis Gate, and then through. He held his breath, afraid that Patr and Jess would have already been picked up and taken away, but no. They waited where he'd left them.

He hurried to them. "Now we need to get to Three Spears."

Patr said, "That's on Haffes, off of the Benedictan Peninsula."

"Why Three Spears?" Jess asked. "That's . . . Damn. That's Gyrunalles country. A hundred roving, warring clans, each with its own little king or queen, people who'd steal your eyes if you didn't watch them, and some of the nastiest wizardry anywhere in the world." She frowned at Wraith. "There's a reason the Empire leaves Haffes alone. As long as the Gyrus have their own bit of land, they don't come marauding elsewhere. They keep their wars and their flocks and their thieving at home."

"We'll find help there."

"Are you sure?" Patr asked.

"No."

"It will be the sort of help we'll regret," Jess muttered.

"We're going to have to fly shifts, and unless we go the long way, we'll be spending the whole time over the ocean."

Patr and Jess both shrugged. "Why is that a problem?"

Wraith said, "If the Dragons decide to stop travel between cities—and if I were in their position, I'd at least consider that an option right now—all they have to do is shut down power on the mage-routes. If they shut down power, then wherever we are at the time, we'll go down."

Patr said, "We need to go the long way."

"The long way takes us along the most heavily traveled route in the Empire, at least until we get to Carse Cay in Benedicta. And even by the most conservative route, we still have . . . what? . . . seven water crossings. And . . . the longer we take, the more likely the Empire is to suspend travel. If we go at top speed, and straight there, we'll cut about four hours off our flight. That might be enough to make the difference."

"And if it doesn't?" Jess studied him with curiously calm eyes.

"If it doesn't, we're in trouble. But if we go down on the main over-land route, we're going to be crashing in the middle of some of the most densely populated part of the Empire. And we are not going to have any friends there."

Jess nodded but said nothing.

Patr was clearly considering all sides of the issue. At last he said, "I'm in for whatever route you want to take. Just steal us a faster aircar."

Luercas and Dafril met in the open-air market in Oel Artis Travia, the only part of the city not affected by curfews and identity checks.

"My informant tells me the Council's Grand Master has lost control," Luercas said. "We may never have another opportunity as good as this one."

Dafril smiled gently and said, "We have a good team to finish this—top-level Masters with ambition and brilliant skills who have been bypassed by the current administration or who are in your position—simply out of favor. If the Masters of the Council commit to an insupportable position—if they overextend themselves—we have the perfect way to cut their legs from under them and come back in as rescuing heroes saving civilization for the world."

"If it works."

"It uses the same spell base we used when we . . . ah . . . *transferred* you. It will work."

"Maybe."

"If we disappear for five years while things go to the hells in the devils' own wagons, and then come back—with new names, new faces, and completely innocent pasts—we'll appear to rise out of the common people. We'll step in to set the coming chaos in order, and we'll reestablish the government, but with ourselves at the top. It's the only way we're going to end up in charge. You know this."

Luercas pursed his lips. "I don't have to like it. I'm not comfortable with the technology."

"You're proof that it works."

Luercas shrugged. "You don't know what it feels like from the inside. To feel another soul still tied to the body that ought to be yours. You don't know the ghost rage, the nightmares, the compulsions . . . but if we do this, you will. And so will every one of the people we take with us." He looked away from Dafril, picked up a cluster of grapes, and stared at them as if they held the answer. "When I'm alone, even now, I can feel the screaming."

Dafril looked shaken. "Screaming? But the soul your body originally had is in the Warrens. It was a Warrener soul. It shouldn't be feeling anything."

Luercas said, "Perhaps it resents being burned a bit at a time. The Way-fare may numb the body and the mind, but I promise you it does not reach beyond physical space."

Dafril stared at him, clearly horrified. "I wish you'd said something about this sooner." He buried his head in his hands. "By the Obscure, Luercas, I had no idea you could still feel that damned soul." He looked up, then stared off into space, thinking. "We'll have to revise the design on the soul-keeper—the Mirror of Souls—a bit. We'll add in a buffer spell. Something that will prevent any communication between the displaced soul and the body—or maybe just a suppressor. Keep the original souls in the bodies, but put them in tight cages." He smiled, looking happier. "Don't worry. It's just a design problem. We'll have it worked out by the time we need it."

In darkness a sleek stolen aircar lifted above the unnatural stillness that pervaded Oel Artis. Because of the state of emergency declared by the Empire, alarms should have gone off from one end of the city to the other. City guards and Empire warriors should have scrambled to intercept the aircar, Masters should have received notification of the breach, Inquisitors should have readied their chambers to receive people who were undoubtedly traitors to all that the Empire held dear.

But none of these things happened. Instead, the aircar, carrying the three fugitives most wanted by the Dragon Council and the Silent Inquest moved silently and swiftly to the south and west, out over the ocean. Unseen. Unnoted.

The touch of a god is a powerful gift.

In the Red Water Kingdom, the initial madness had died down a bit. Early that day, twice as many people as lived in the Camp of the Red Water King had erupted out of a cloud-filled sky with a crack of thunder and fire that shattered the Bell of First Voice and scattered goats, women, and warriors alike.

Of all of the recent arrivals, Sunsta Go-Lightly-Overland was first to get her bearings. Sunsta was Gyru-nalle-born; she'd left the Red Water Kingdom—a kingdom on wheels, but a kingdom nonetheless—to seek wealth and a future in the grand cities of the Empire of the Hars, and while disconcerted at finding herself so abruptly back home again, she felt that her mode of arrival would give her standing with the siblings and cousins and aunts and uncles that her Hars job as a census taker would never have conferred. She promptly announced that she and her companions had been transported in the hand of the god Vodor Imrish, who had claimed the lot of them as his messengers—and then gave her relatives and onetime neighbors the message that the god Vodor Imrish wanted his messengers treated well.

Were not the whole lot of them glowing like small suns from the moment they arrived, and had the Bell of First Voice not shattered—a clear sign of divine intervention—people might have been more skeptical. The True People had their own wizards, though they held kings in much higher regard. Gods, though, still mattered in places like Three Spears, and though no one had heard of Vodor Imrish, the majority were willing to give him a fair hearing—and were, at least for the moment, willing to consider as a sign of favor the fact that the god chose their kingdom for this visitation instead of a rival kingdom.

The warriors, the women, the wizards, and even the king pitched in, putting out extra hammocks, sacrificing garden crops and goats to extra dinners, and taking the newcomers into their wagons and the circle of their trust as if they were all as much family as Sunsta.

She felt good about that. These were her people, and for all their terrible reputation among those who did not know them, they had made a good showing for themselves. They had been hospitable, charming, and— at least so far—they hadn't declared undying hatred or war on anyone.

Sunsta at last fell exhausted into the hammock in which she and several sisters had spent many a childhood night. She was home. And alive. Good things, these. The lapping of the waves on the beach in the bay just below the place where the clan had stopped its wagons for the month, and the steady roll of the surf out along the point, soothed her. The singing of the nightchukkar, low and melodious, made her for a few moments a seven-year-old again, and left her yearning for the bony knees and elbows and hushed confidences of her sisters, now married and with wagons of their own, and children. The breeze kissed her, sweet with blooming redweed and childbud. Home, which she'd been sure earlier that day she would never see in this lifetime again; and family, glad to see her and willing not to ask too many questions; and the impossible, wonderful voice of the god that still hung in her head.

Wait. Your time to leave this world has not yet come. I have much for you to do.

She still had a future. She had the promise of a god on that.

*　　*　　*

Wraith brought the aircar down in the bay near the one village where lights still burned.

"Why here?" Jess asked.

Wraith said, "It's where we're supposed to be. I don't know how I know. I just know."

Patr muttered, "I hate that mystical stuff."

"Nothing but clear-cut, sensible magic for you, right?" Jess asked. Wraith heard a hint of sharpness in her voice. "Which has been so good for all of us up until now."

Wraith kept out of it. He floated the aircar up to the beach and grounded it, popped the nose door open, and got out. There was this to be said for packing light, he thought: Unpacking didn't interfere with the hunt for dinner. Or, in this case, breakfast. Along the eastern edge of the bay, the first gray arrow of dawn cleaved sea from sky. Wraith thought it odd that the village still had lights burning at such an hour. In his experience from traveling with the theater troupes, the Gyru-nalles started their days along with the sun or somewhat after it made some headway on its daily trek. He'd never heard of Gyrus who beat the sun out of bed.

Behind him, he heard Patr and Jess getting out of the aircar; Jess still sounded unhappy, while Patr merely sounded exhausted.

"What are we supposed to do here, Wraith?" Patr asked. "As a hiding place, it doesn't seem too bad. I don't know of any of the Inquest's agents who have ever been posted to Three Spears, even for short-term duty. And it's out of the Empire's full-service area, which will inconvenience anyone pursuing us as much as it will inconvenience us."

"Maybe we *are* just supposed to hide here," Wraith said. "Vodor Imrish isn't . . . speaking to me, precisely. I just have this . . ." He faltered to a stop. "I don't have any words for it, really. It's sort of a tug at my gut. When I'm headed the right way, doing the right thing, I can feel it. When I start to drift, I can feel that, too."

"Couldn't just ask him for a map and a schedule, eh?" Patr asked.

Wraith laughed.

"That's not funny," Jess said. "That's disrespectful. You shouldn't question the workings of a god that way, especially not the god that saved your life."

Wraith looked at her. "Why not? As far I can tell, that's the entire purpose of having a brain and free will—to ask questions, make decisions, then act on them. Why should gods be immune to our questions . . . or our opinions, for that matter? I have to agree with Patr. I wish we had a map and a schedule; I wouldn't be standing here wondering if I've dragged the three of us across half an ocean out of idiocy and imagining that the queasiness in my gut was anything more than a mild case of food poisoning. And as for Vodor Imrish saving our lives . . . fine. Yes. He saved *our* lives. But he didn't save Solander, and he could have. He didn't save Velyn, or any of the people who were with her. Maybe he didn't even save the people who were with Sol, though it looked like he did. I think we have a right to question his actions."

The steep, rocky beach provided enough obstacles that none of them could speak until they'd reached the top.

At the top of the rise, none of them could think of anything to say. Masses of the Kaan, and clusters of Wraith's employees, and whole mobs of initiates of the Order of Resonance stood at the edge of the village, waiting in silence, staring back at them. Soft light radiated from the crowd, as if they were mage-lights set in a night garden to illuminate a path without distracting from the stars.

They were the lights Wraith had seen from the air, the lights that had guided him in. He'd known to look for lights. Those had been the only lights.

Wraith's skin felt like ice. The touch of a god was a frightening thing—it had too much of caprice to its nature. He rejoiced to see his people, but the circumstances frightened him.

"It's Gellas," someone said. "He's come!"

Then, like a small sea of light, they ran to him and embraced him, and cheered his survival and his escape from the hands of the Dragons and the Inquest. And his escape from death.

In the Dragon Council, the battle of words raged on. "We have to stop the rebels, agreed. But if we discontinue magic service along the trade routes, we cut our own throats! We won't have food coming into the city, we won't have trade goods, and we won't have our import fuel from the Strithian borders."

"We're still getting slaves in from Strithia?"

"Eight percent of our new fuel supplies come from there," the lucky survivor and new Master of Energy, Addis Woodsing, said. "Would you care to cut eight percent off our power production and see what happens?"

Grath Faregan, new Grand Master of the Inquest, who'd gone straight from his safe room to the meeting, sat upright, his back jammed uncomfortably against an edge of his seat. He'd called in the favor that the Dragon Council owed to the Inquest: He'd demanded a voting seat on the Council in exchange for the conspirators that the Inquest had delivered—and that the Council had lost. The Dragons resented bitterly keeping their end of the bargain, but previous demonstrations of the Inquest's power—family members taken, then returned home in pieces, stolti fortunes overturned, stolti lives ruined—kept the councilors to their bargain.

When the Master of Energy fell silent, Zider Rost, the new Master of Research—who acquired her post by being the highest-ranking member of the Research Department not required to attend the executions, thus now the highest-ranking member of the department, period—stood and cleared her throat. She was a thin-faced woman, clearly uncomfortable with her abrupt lurch into power. "If we destroy the one thing the rebels all seem to want to save," she said, "they'll have nothing left with which to rally others to their cause. Their rebellion will die, and then we can round them up at our leisure."

The Council's Grand Master frowned. "What do you mean, destroy the one thing they want to save?"

"The Warrens—and everyone in them. If there are no more Warrens, the bastards have no grand cause."

"If there are no more Warrens, we have no magic," Woodsing of Energy pointed out.

"You haven't been following recent research, have you?" Rost of Research leaned forward and placed her hands flat on the table. She looked now at every master in the room in turn. "We are mere months away from liquid power. We've finished preliminary testing; we're in the *rewhah*-handling phase of spell development now. It's as neat a spell-set as anything I've seen in my entire career. We got the idea . . ." She chuckled softly. "We got the idea from that play by Vincalis—the one with the mage who turned people into an elixir of youth. We thought an elixir of pure energy would be more useful, and we have the spell now that will do it. Will liquefy a human, and bind the complete energy from blood and bone, flesh and will, and best of all, the entire soul, in a liquid matrix that never evaporates, is insoluble with water or other liquids, and that maintains one hundred percent of its potency until it's tapped."

"Right now our energy from the Warrens is renewable," Woodsing said. "The Warreners breed."

"The Warreners breed problems," the Master of Transport said.

The Master of Cities rose to his feet. "Agreed. We could certainly replace the Warrens and our breeding stock at a later date. Nothing could be simpler. But by eliminating both Warrens and Warreners now—by leaving in their place a pool of liquid fuel that bears no resemblance to people—we could show citizens what was behind the Warren walls, state that all we've ever had in there was fuel derived from the sun and the earth and the power of the sea. . . ." He smiled, a happy, happy man. "Oh, this is lovely. We demonstrate once and for all that the traitors' propaganda against the Empire was nothing but lies, we discredit the entire group of them—and then we hunt them down and kill them."

"And if the rebels are using this new magic of theirs to hide in the Warrens, as seems likely—since you people cannot find a trace of them anywhere else?" Faregan asked.

"Then that's a problem solved, isn't it?" someone said under his breath.

"If we could create the right delivery device," the Master of Defense said, leaning back in his chair, "we could time the . . . ah . . . the conversion of our fuel sources into liquid fuel to hit all at the same time. Air attacks, I'm thinking. And then we could say that the attacks came from the traitors, and that they attempted to destroy our fuel storage areas, but that we stopped them. Maybe we could destroy a couple of the islands off the east coast and say they were hiding there, but that we destroyed their bases and most of them at the same time. Thus, the Empire remains intact, the traitors have been stopped yet again, and justice will prevail. We start a search for the remaining traitors. We make it thorough. People will be turning in their own grandmothers to save themselves."

The rest of the Masters smiled. Except for Faregan. He simply shook his head. "You've been pointing to the Warrens all these years as the source of rioting, violence, criminal activity so bad that you had to keep the perpetrators locked behind walls. Everyone in the Empire knows you have people in the Warrens. You can't just suddenly pretend that every Warren in the Hars is a fuel storage area."

The Master of Diplomacy sighed heavily. "We don't need to pretend no one lives in the Warrens. We can offer a story much closer to the truth. We can claim that the members of the underground set the spells that destroyed the Warrens because not even they were crazy enough to actually want to have to deal with Warreners, and that the underground then tried to make it look like the Empire attacked." He shrugged. "We can create all the evidence we need to prove our statements—and that will cost the underground any sympathy it might have. Or we can claim that the traitors went into hiding within the Warrens and that the Warreners were in league with them and ready to use criminal magic to break out. If we say that the Warreners were about to erupt into cities throughout the Empire, raping, murdering, robbing and pillaging, any measures we choose to keep the Warreners contained are going to receive the full support of the citizenry. They live in terror of the dangerous madmen we keep behind those walls. The citizens of the Empire wouldn't dare protest."

"That works for me," Luercas said.

The other Masters nodded.

"How long," the Master of Cities asked, "until we have the completed liquefaction spell?"

"We thought we could finish it within six months with full testing. If you need it before that," the Master of Research said, "you'll get it, but with the understanding that *rewhah*-handling might not be . . . perfect."

The Masters looked at each other, and it was clear from the expressions on their faces that each of them was thinking of the disaster in the Gold Building arena. Everyone knew what imperfect *rewhah*-handling could do.

"You have three months," the Grand Master said. "Sooner, if you feel confident that the spell won't go wrong."

"But no later," one of the other Masters—Faregan didn't see which one—said.

Faregan weighed their reactions. They were now hot for the chase—hungry for the destruction of the Warrens, ready to hunt down the traitors and wage an all-out war against them. He would have to make sure that they could find the traitors when the time came. Faregan now owned by blood oath the finest network of spies in the Hars; he had no doubt that he would be able to locate the rebels and get the information to the Council. In fact, it would give him a way to get back in the Council's good graces when he needed to. Come bearing an excellent gift, and hope that the bastards didn't look too closely at what it would cost them. Faregan had already decided on the price. The Council was going to destroy Gellas, destroy Jethis . . . and it was going to destroy Jess, because if he couldn't have her, he would know that he had ended her.

And they were going to do this no matter what else it cost.

He would see to it.

Chapter 23

ods inspire. In times of hardship, gods offer comfort. Gods occasionally, in the direst of circumstances, intervene and save their followers—or those they would claim as followers.

But even the most attentive of gods is too distant and too intangible
to carry out the everyday tasks of leadership. These tasks, therefore, fell
to Wraith. And Wraith, in mourning for the best friend he had not been
able to save, felt like he was drowning in anxious demands. The survivors needed permanent places to stay. They needed food. They needed
encouragement and comfort. But most of all, they needed a vision, direction, words to stir them to action, to bind them into a single force,
and to lead them forward.

Wraith tried to give them stirring words, yet to them he was only
Master Gellas, a stolti one step up from a covil-osset, a decent theater
manager, perhaps, and the man who had once been the intermediary between the secretive Vincalis and the masses who followed him—but not
a visionary leader.

To Jess, after another discussion with dissatisfied, worried men and
women, he muttered, "What we need is Vincalis."

Jess looked at him and said, "Then get him."

Wraith said, "I *am* him, Jess."

"I know."

"Then you know why I can't get him. All of these people know me.
I can't stand up now and say, 'Well, yes, I'm Master Gellas, but I'm Vincalis, too, and now I'm going to . . . what? Lead you to the Good
Ground?'" He shook his head. "They have the spells. The ones who will
have anything to do with magic are learning them. The rest are building
shelters. But we have to go back, Jess. We have to go to the cities and free

the Warreners. We have to use Solander's magic to release them from the poisons of the Way-fare and their years of mindlessness. We have to save them from the Dragons' spells. If Solander were here, he could convince everyone to look to that. If Vincalis were real, *he* could convince everyone to move forward. But all we have left is me."

"Then you're going to have to do it." Jess rested a hand on his shoulder, turned him to face her, and said, "Wraith, you know I never wanted you to get involved in this, and I avoided it as much as I could—but I was wrong. I was wrong to try to abandon who I am and where I came from, and I was wrong to try to get you to do that. Do what you have to do. I'm right with you, and I'll do everything in my power to help you. But I have the feeling that we don't have much time. Something bad is going to happen. The Dragons aren't going to just let us get away without coming after us. We have to be ready. Use Vincalis if you have to. Write his words, claim that he is in touch with the soul of Solander . . . pretend you're writing another of his plays. Work at night. Patr and I will figure out ways to cover for you during the day. When you have what you need, just . . ." She shrugged. "Just say that Vincalis sent the messages to you in the dead of night. You could convince them of that. You convinced them that Vincalis was a real person for all those years."

Wraith stared at her. "Lie to them?"

"Well . . . yes."

"About the will of a god, about the words of someone who doesn't even exist and never did? Lie about something that should be . . . sacred?"

Jess hooked her thumbs into the belt of her tunic and shook her head slowly. "When you created Vincalis, why did you do it?"

"So that I wouldn't be the one guilty of writing treasonous material."

"That's all?"

Wraith considered for a moment. "Well, no. I suppose I created him, too, because if no one knew him, he would start with a fresh slate. With the chance for complete credibility—the sort of credibility with the stolti I could never have with people who had known me from the time I was a child, and who would always see me as the young idiot I started out being. And the sort of credibility that I as a stolti could never have with the people of the Belows. The stolti were always sure he was one of them, but in the Belows, people thought that he was really one of them, and that was why he hid his identity."

"You gave him credibility. Tremendous credibility, which he still has among everyone who ever loved his work or listened to his words and took them to heart. When people say the name Vincalis, they say it with a little awe, don't they?"

"Yes."

"Then don't be an idiot, Wraith. *Use* that. You've created him. You created him to reach people you would never be able to reach otherwise—and you reached them. Now it's time to make everything you ever dreamed of a reality, but to do that, you're going to have to use a fiction. A lie. Do you think the god Vodor Imrish didn't know about Vincalis? That you managed to keep your secret safe from even him?"

Wraith felt a bit stupid. "No. Of course not."

"Vodor Imrish needs you to free the souls of the Warreners. This is the task for which you were born. Do you think Vodor Imrish doesn't want you to use your very best tool to accomplish this task?"

Wraith looked out at the palm trees rattling just beyond his window. Vincalis didn't seem like *him*. Vincalis seemed like the interloper who walked off with all his good lines, got all the admirers he deserved, won praise and glory and never shared any of it with Wraith. And Wraith was jealous of Vincalis; even though he had created him, even though Vincalis truly was him, still Wraith held a small, tight kernel of hatred in his heart for this creation who had eclipsed him in a brilliant light that did not even belong to Vincalis, but that shone from him nonetheless.

Once upon a time, Wraith had longed for the day when he could stand up at the end of a play, bow before the assembled audience, and say, *And now, the revelation you've been waiting for all these many years—I, Gellas Tomersin, Wraith the Warrener, am in fact Vincalis the Agitator.*

In his mind's eye, the people leaped to their feet, cheering and shouting, and heaped bouquets of roses and fantams upon him, and lifted him up on their shoulders and carried him through the street, shouting, *Behold Vincalis revealed—behold Wraith.*

When he fled Oel Artis and his old life, he was glad to leave Vincalis behind. But now Vincalis stood beside him, grown yet again in stature, and this time with the promise of a permanence that Wraith knew he wasn't going to be able to shake. If he resurrected Vincalis this time, it would be until both of them died—because he would never, never be able to say, *Oh, incidentally—all those things I told you Vincalis said . . . well, I was really the one who said them.*

Solander had sacrificed his life to save the people who now needed Wraith. Wraith was going to have to sacrifice, too. He was going to sacrifice the part of himself that he most respected, the part he most valued. He was going to have to give that part of himself to his creation, and pretend for the rest of his life that he was nothing more than a messenger carrying his creation's words. If ever what he had done became a part of history, it would wear this false creature's name in his stead. He would die unknown, and the rival he had created would live on in his rightful place.

But his friend Solander had given his life to save these people. Wraith could sacrifice the dubious possibility of his own literary immortality, couldn't he?

Couldn't he?

Or was he so selfish that he would rather have everything he had ever fought for come to naught than let his work bear another's name? He *was* envious. He *was* selfish. But was he that selfish?

"It's just writing," Jess said. "You can do it, Wraith. You do it all the time. I know you can do it."

She misunderstood his reluctance. But, he thought, would he rather have her think he doubted his own talent in this situation, or that he had complete faith in his talent but merely resented his creation?

He sighed and turned to her. "There's still a problem. I came here, and all of these people came here . . . but where is Vincalis? Why wouldn't he still be back in Oel Artis?"

"Maybe he is. Why wouldn't he have some special way of communicating with you? After all, you've been receiving work from him—and communications—for years."

"Yes. Of course. I never had to worry about how we supposedly communicated when I was there."

"Don't worry about it now. You hear from Vincalis. You always have. People will believe. In the meantime . . ." She frowned thoughtfully. "In the meantime, I'll see if Patr can find something impressive for you to write in. Something that will look like it's meant to convey the plans of a god and the words of a great man."

"Thank you," he said, hoping he sounded sincere. "I'll do my best not to let the great man down."

Wraith sat before a small lamp that night, and in a fine lined-and-bound notebook, wrote the first words of the lie that would, he suspected, define his life.

"I, Vincalis, torn from the world and the life that I love, now in hiding for my life, in a dream that was not a dream talked to the spirit of our lost friend Solander. And he has given me the future of the brotherhood of rebels who will from this day forward be known as . . ."

Wraith pondered this for a while. Vodor Imrish's band of would-be heroes needed a noble name. The name should invoke flight—should summon images of creatures who were strong and swift, but nimble and pure. Predators and fighters, but not monsters of immense, terrifying power. They would symbolize the magic that Solander had worked out—magic based on self-reliance, on individual responsibility, on self-sacrifice, on honor. Doves? Willow-brush hawks? Eaglets?

Wraith remembered the bird that symbolized freedom to him when he still huddled in the Warrens with his friends—the bird that came to him in nightmares and woke him to the horrors hidden behind the Warren walls.

". . . Falcons," he wrote in.

Then he wrote of his hopes for the Falcons, and the history of the Empire and the Dragons that they would have to fight. He wrote of the Warreners, too, and of the politics of rich men, and the price of magic.

If sometimes it seemed another force moved his hand, he ignored that. He was a writer and had been for many years; he was used to the power that words had as they gathered their own momentum. He wrote a fiction, as he had written so many fictions before it, and while he put as much of the truth in as would conveniently fit, he did not let himself be hampered by a strict interpretation of fact. He wanted something that would inspire. Lead. Offer hope in these dark days, and in the dark days that were sure to come.

He wrote through the night, one page after another, not counting them, not stopping to consider words, not stopping, in fact, for anything. When the dawn came, with his hand cramped and his body aching, he fell into his cot and slept. He had filled the first of the stack of notebooks Jess had acquired for him, but did not know it. He had never written so much in a single sitting in his entire life, but he did not know that, either.

In the nights that followed, Wraith filled the rest of the notebooks, one each night, a hundred pages at a sitting. He did not read what he had written—he simply poured the words on the page, stopping to consider what he wrote only rarely, occasionally feeling some pride in the deft turn of a phrase or the apt use of a metaphor. But in the month that he wrote, when he filled thirty-four such books, he never once questioned where the words came from, or that they never faltered.

By day, bleary and disheartened, he and the others who were willing to touch magic went over the papers that Solander had left behind, looking for the keys that would free the Warreners from the prisons of the

Warrens that confined them, and from the Way-fare that condemned them to death beyond their cages. Wraith could not cast spells, nor could he offer his energy—he was as immune from the magic Solander had devised as from any other, and as blind to it. But he understood the formulas, knew the principles of the spells Solander had devised, and from years of regular contact had a better feel for the philosophy of the system than any of the magic-talented who had never been exposed to Solander's work before.

So his presence during the day was essential.

In the first month after Solander's death, his usually thin frame became almost skeletal, and his eyes burned with an almost hypnotic intensity that came, perhaps, from lack of sleep and too much pain, but that had about it the fervor associated with the god-touched; the people who cared about him fretted that he mourned those he had lost, and that he would die before he could find some peace and accommodation with all that had happened, and urged him to eat more, to sleep more, to join one or the other of them in their beds for a bit of comfort.

Wraith lived the life of a monk, working by day, working by night, and sleeping only in the few hours on either side of dawn.

And then he wrote the last word in the last notebook that Jess had acquired for him, and suddenly he felt that a weight had lifted from his shoulders. He had no more words, and he knew somehow that he needed no more notebooks. With only the vaguest curiosity, he opened one of the books at random, and was surprised to see the tiny, crabbed hand, so different from his usual writing. He noted the way the words crowded one on top of the next on the page. He read a few of the words, and though they were very beautiful, and though they sounded like his words—like the words he had created for Vincalis before—he found that he couldn't remember having written them, and he couldn't imagine where they had come from. He'd had that reaction before, after especially intense writing sessions—he would find whole paragraphs that seemed to have been written by a stranger.

But here he found whole books that had been—thirty-four of them, with titles and chapter headings and page after page describing places he had never been, visions he had never imagined, stories that were not his.

In that moment, nervously, he wondered if Vincalis was not just a figment of his imagination, but a real man, one who could take over his body at will. One who might choose to replace him.

Then he laughed. He was tired. He was, in fact, bone-tired. For the first time in a month, he realized that he needed sleep. That he ached.

That his skin was feverish, his tongue swollen, his eyeballs compressed by almost unbearable pain.

He got into his cot and covered himself with a thin blanket, and he called for Jess.

"I'm sick," he whispered, his throat suddenly so sore that he almost couldn't push the words past it. "And the books are done. All of them."

Jess stared from him to the notebooks, and back to him, and said, "Oh, gods, no wonder you're a wreck. I didn't know how hard you'd been working." She brought cool compresses and put them on his forehead, and gave him water and cold fruit soups, and took away the notebooks.

He slept eventually, and in his sleep, Velyn chased after him and called to him, begging his forgiveness, telling him she'd been wrong about him, and Solander came and sat by his bed and told him that he had to live—that he had to lead the people to freedom, and that no one in the world could do it but him. He knew he was dreaming, with that vague hazy realization that if he was talking to the dead, he had to be dreaming. But in his sleep he could not decide whether the dreams were true dreams, or whether they were the product of fever, or exhaustion, or simply his own wishes transmuted to dream form.

He awoke a week later, and stepped out into a camp transformed.

"We cannot wait for beautiful numbers to test our results," Luercas said. "Before the Council is ready to attack the traitors—even before it's ready to destroy the Warrens, since that might be the trigger that sets off the god and those lunatics—we need to have tried the Mirror of Souls on one of our people, to make sure that we'll be able to make the transfer, and that the Mirror will then be able to deliver the replacement bodies for us, and that we'll be able to get into them."

Dafril sat in a comfortable chair on a balcony overlooking the long hall in the Belows that Luercas had purchased when he decided that his future with the Dragons wouldn't be as bright as he had always hoped. From Dafril's vantage point, he could see all the wizards and assistants below him, and by virtue of viewscreens placed at each worktable, he could speak to anyone in the hall at any time, and they could each speak with him. In that manner, he kept everyone pushing forward toward the completion of the working Mirror of Souls.

Luercas found Dafril's setup efficient enough, but the languorous pace on the floor below him made him uneasy. He needed results. He'd heard from his spy that the Dragons had a bigger team working on their spell-sets, and were close to completion. When they launched their attacks against the traitors and their god, and when the god struck back, merry misery would erupt from one end of the Empire to the other—and it would be clearly attributable to the Dragons. Luercas suspected the citizens would go wild, and that any wizards in their way would be targets for everything from mobbing to torture to murder. He wanted himself as far away from the disaster he saw coming as he could get—and if he had to tolerate Dafril and a cluster of hangers-on for a while, he would.

"Ah, Gellas—so good to see you up and around again. We feared you would not recover until this last day or so." The Kaan, one Wraith didn't know except by face, patted him on the back and moved on.

Wraith, unsteady on his feet, blinked and squinted against the hard white glare of the sun and tried to make sense of what he saw. Clusters of Kaan men and women sat on the ground, reading passages to each other from a thick book and taking notes. Beyond them, the wizards— who before Wraith's illness were struggling to understand the spells of Solander—now worked together at a table, writing out a spell of their own.

The surviving members of the Order of Resonance and the Gyrunalles worked side by side with others of the Kaan, building an entire row of little boxes with seats in them—boxes that to Wraith looked a lot like aircars, but without any of the mechanisms that located sources of magic or translated that magic into flight.

This busyness frightened him; he felt that the world and all reason had moved forward while he slept, leaving him alone in a place where nothing made sense, or ever would. His vision fogged around the edges, he lost track of where his head was supposed to be in relation to his feet, and with no more warning than that, the ground rolled up to meet him. The next thing he knew, strong hands had pulled him to his feet and Jess was racing across the clearing toward him, worry written broadly across her face.

"Gellas! Why are you out of bed?"

"I . . . felt better," he said, but at that moment he didn't feel better. He felt bewildered, and unnecessary, and lost.

"Help me get him back to bed," Jess said. "He shouldn't be up for another week. We're lucky to have him still alive."

Wraith would have protested that he was fine, but he discovered that he didn't even have the energy to lie. He let the men who'd run to help him haul him back to his cot, then lay where they put him and watched

Jess as she shooed them out and told them that he was not to be bothered under any circumstances.

When they were gone, Jess turned to him, frowning. "Are you crazy?
How could you even think about getting out of bed? You almost died last
week!"

"I did?" He lay there feeling that he might die at any moment. He
didn't disbelieve her; he simply didn't remember.

"You did. You've been seeing ghosts and talking to yourself and
you've had a terrible fever that neither wizards nor herbalists could
break. Patr was ready several times to take you the nearest city, but I
wouldn't let him. He wanted to say you were someone else and have a
specialist look at you—but we didn't dare let you go. From everything
we've heard, all of us are to be killed on sight. The Dragons have declared all-out war, with executions of anyone even suspected of harboring us or other rebels. The cities are nailed down tight, the Dragons have
cut off all travel magic, cities have brought their airibles out of storage
and are using them for essential shipping of food and other supplies.
We've heard of food riots, of people fleeing cities in search of safer
places . . . terrible things. If we'd taken you into a city and someone had
recognized you, that would have been the end of you."

Wraith said, "They're insane, making a war of it. What can we hope
to do to them?"

Jess gave him a funny look. "The books you wrote detailed everything that we could do to them—and everything that we would."

"I don't remember writing them," Wraith said. "Well, I remember sitting over there with the notebooks you brought me—but I can't remember a single word I wrote."

Jess came over and perched on the edge of the cot. "How can that
be? You told the wizards how to make the best use of Solander's magic
to overcome the poisons the Warreners have been given, and how to
pool their magic to make shields to protect them while we find places for
them. You told the initiates of the Order of Resonance how to use their
art to prepare for the invasion of the cities, and the Kaan how to build
the aircars that would get us there."

Wraith closed his eyes, trying to bring any of that back. "I didn't," he
said at last.

"I watched you writing, Wraith. You did."

He looked at her, a little frightened. "It might have been my hand
holding the pen, but it wasn't me writing the words."

"Who, then?"

Vincalis, he thought. Vincalis had made himself so real that he could control Wraith's writing. Perhaps Vincalis really had written the plays that bore his name. Perhaps Wraith had only been the medium through which they had been created.

Except he remembered writing the plays. Sweating over them. The words in the plays were his words. And the words in the notebook? Were any of those words his? Did he remember *any* of that ordeal?

"Falcons," he said suddenly.

Jess looked at him curiously. "Falcons? You want to talk to them?"

Wraith's eyes opened. "Them? Them who?"

"The Falcons. Do you want to talk with them?"

Wraith sighed. "I don't know. Do I? Who are the Falcons?"

"The new order of wizards who take the Oath of Falcons, and who live by the words of Solander."

"Oh, gods. I don't want to know about this, do I? What in the hells did I do?"

"In the books, you had Vincalis claiming to be talking directly to the spirit of Solander, who told him what would happen in the future, and . . ." Jess, watching his eyes as she spoke, stopped speaking and stared at him, realization dawning on her face. "When you say you don't remember this, you aren't just exaggerating for effect, are you? You truly don't remember what you wrote. You really could have been channeling the spirit of Solander, which would explain how you could write one whole book a night, every night for a month."

"I did what?"

"You filled all the notebooks. Thirty-four of them—one a night— every page, every line, both sides, in tiny little handwriting." She considered that for a moment. "The handwriting wasn't anything like your regular writing," she said, "but it wasn't anything like Solander's, either. I thought you were just being careful."

Wraith cautiously told her his theory that Vincalis might be a real person, or perhaps might be becoming one, which he found even more frightening a concept.

Jess waved it off. "This isn't about Vincalis. This is about you, and Solander, and . . . maybe Vodor Imrish. Perhaps the god himself moved your hand."

"And told me to write about invading a city? That's madness."

"Told you how to invade all of them, Wraith. Our people are going in to protect and free all of the Warreners simultaneously, so the Drag-ons won't be able to discover what we've done at one Warren and block us from the rest. We're going to save all of them, and with the help of Vodor Imrish, we're going to bring down the Dragons."

Wraith buried his head in the thin pillow, closed his eyes tightly, and groaned. "All I can say is, I hope what I wrote was dictated by Vodor Imrish. Because if it was the fever talking, we're all going to die."

"You weren't sick when you wrote those books."

"Wasn't I? Did you check?"

Jess grew very quiet.

"Well? Did you? Because I've lost a month of my life—I don't remember anything that happened from the time I sat down to write that first paragraph until I woke up today. So . . . did you check to see if I was sick while I was writing? Because the results could certainly affect the outcome we hope to achieve."

"No. I didn't check." Jess stood and looked down at him. "Don't go anywhere; don't talk to anyone; if anyone comes in here, pretend you're asleep. I'm going to go get Patr, and I'll be right back." She looked ill. "It never occurred to me that you might not have been . . . well, in your right mind when you wrote the *Secret Texts*. I thought you were making things up in them to give everyone hope, but I didn't think you were . . ." She frowned. "I didn't think you were delusional."

Before Wraith could protest that the last person he wanted to see, except perhaps an *active* Inquisitor, was Patr, she'd fled.

Which left him alone with his own thoughts, and with the pathetic certainty that no matter what he did now, he'd already caused more trouble than he could imagine.

Addis Woodsing, Master of Energy, looked at the miniature device brought to him by the junior-level associate from Research. "This is a limited working model," the associate said. "We can test it inside a shield here if you have a prisoner. It's fully automated. A wizard will speak the launching words and then set a timer that will replay the launching words into the device at the right time. We have it set so that it will liquefy everything—flesh, bone, stone, earth, masonry, plant and animal matter—within the confines of a shield. It won't touch air, of course; that might have unfortunate consequences, lowering pressure within the shield to the point where some portions of the shield would implode. We were quite careful not to permit that. This spell-set will run until everything within that shield is liquid fuel; it only takes a bit of initial energy to run, too. We've set it to use a very small amount of the soul matter within its reach once it gets going, so that it will feed itself until it's finished."

Addis took the device in his hand, both compelled and appalled. "It flies?"

"Oh, yes. Beautifully."

"Do the full-sized ones look like birds as well?"

"Yes. We've given them feathers and beaks and eyes—they're absolutely lovely. And the movements of the full-scale models are indistinguishable from real birds. We'll have to reactivate the transport-magic spells to send these to each of the Warrens in the Empire, but the spell systems will be self-delivering. And they're quite fast. Much faster than real birds."

"How accurately can you place them?"

"On the blade of grass of your choice, Master."

Addis, who still wore the mantle of absolute Master of the department with a great deal of discomfort, nodded. "That seems accurate enough, in theory." He turned the device in his hand. "So . . . *why* do they look like birds? Aside from artistic considerations, of course."

"Yes. We thought that by making them look like birds, their arrival would cause no alarm for resident populations."

"The resident populations of the Warrens wouldn't notice them if they were the size of sailing ships and if they dropped directly onto their heads, young man."

"No, Master. But the people who live in the cities surrounding each Warren might. We were under the impression that nothing should be noticed about these devices until they went off."

Addis nodded thoughtfully. "Quite so. Now . . . tell me what will happen if we have a breach in one of our shields."

The associate shook his head firmly. "Master, we cannot permit breaches. We must be quite certain that the shields are impregnable. Should the spell get out, it would turn the whole of the planet and everything on it to liquid, and bind all our souls into the mix for eternity."

Addis put the little bird on a table and said, "Son, one thing I have learned in forty years of practicing magic is that you never—and I mean *never*—develop a system based on the assumption that any other system will be functioning at the time. We cannot guarantee that all of our shields will hold. What if the god who destroyed our shield during the execution, and who is responsible for the deaths of most of the Inquestors and a goodly portion of your colleagues, decides to breach one of the shields we cast around some remote Warren?"

"That would be . . ." The young associate began, then paused and considered. "But what god would aid in the destruction of the souls of potential worshipers? That simply wouldn't make sense."

"You plan not for what the enemy might do, but for what he can. Take your test device back to Research. Before I will clear it to go to the Council, and before I will sanction a demonstration, it will have a self-limiting spell attached. It will abide by the following limits: It will cast itself only upon humans; no animals, no plants. It will have an energy-use cap; that is, no matter how much energy is available to it, it will use only a specific amount to run itself—let's say . . . ah, a thousand luns—that will be controllable by the area Dragons if it gets out of bounds. And each device will have a defined damage radius no greater than the radius of the largest Warren in the Empire. That way, if we have a shield go down on us somewhere, we won't lose an entire city, or even much past the outer edge of our target." He templed his fingers in front of him, thinking. "No, better yet . . . let each device have a damage area no greater than the diameter of its own target Warren. It may take a bit longer to design individual spells—but if you have a good artificer working on the final spell-birds, he could add a spell rheostat to each that would permit us to set the radius before we launch."

Lost in his own thoughts, Addis did not see the expression that flitted across the face of the young associate as he listed his requirements for the final spell-birds. He should have.

"That will be all, then," he said after a final moment of contemplation. "You have my requirements firmly in memory?"

"I wear the badge of Mnemonimancy," the associate said coldly.

"You do," Addis agreed. "I should have spent some time at that degree myself—I wouldn't trust my own memory to get me out my door in the morning without a good minder on my wrist, chirping the directions to get me there."

The associate turned away. Addis would have been disturbed by the young man's expression of fury, more so by the nature of his thoughts.

Chapter 24

Kirbin Rost, promising full associate in the Department of Energy, held not only a badge of Mnemonimancy, but also the ear of the new Master of Research, Zider Rost. Zider happened to be his favorite aunt. Kirbin sat across the desk from his freshly promoted relative—the rupture of the shield the day of the executions had been unlucky for some, but certainly not for all—and placed the spell-bird on the smooth jade surface.

"The Master of Energy was pleased?" Rost the elder asked.

"The Master of Energy is a senile dolt; did you know that?"

"We've met." Zider smiled slowly. "So . . . he had problems. Didn't like the color of the birds, eh? Thought we should model them after wrens, perhaps? Or ravens?"

"Nothing so simple." Kirbin carefully repeated, word for word, his conversation with Master Addis Woodsing—but as he repeated the conversation, he took some liberties with tone. He knew he should not do such a thing, but the Master of Energy had been condescending. Rude. Ignorant and stodgy and unimpressed with the marvelous work the men and women in the Department of Research had done. So Kirbin slightly increased the edge of the conversation—made the condescending responses a bit more snide, made the doltish ones just slightly more nasal and dull. One of his Masters would have caught him, but Zider, like most wizards, had never bothered to obtain the difficult but low-stature badge of Mnemonimancy. If she had listened to both conversations side by side, she would have declared them identical.

And they were, except that Kirbin's version had been designed to increase the chance that Zider would feel the way Kirbin felt about the stupid old man in Energy.

When he finished his recitation, he summoned the Mnemon.

"My words I present,
At forfeit of my life.
Each and all accounted,
None added, none taken away,
By oath of the Mnemon,
That which remembers."

Around him the air shimmered, and the Mnemon spoke from a space above Kirbin's head: "A true accounting. The teller may live."

So he hadn't cut his emotional shadings too fine. One day, he thought, he might do just that—but not today.

His aunt said, "A thousands luns. The moron wants each spell-set to run on just a thousand luns. And a rheostat to adjust the damage circle, when we'll have perfectly good shields all about to keep the damage where it's supposed to be. He'd add another half year to the design work with that damned rheostat spell, by the time we made sure it didn't interfere with the workings of any of the rest of the spells in the spell-set. People see a nice bit of work at a trade show, where someone demonstrates using a rheostat or something similar to control spell workings, and suddenly every apprentice and his half-wit brother wants a rheostat on everything from the toilet pull to the doorbell. As if the damned device will be the answer to all their needs."

"We aren't going to do the rheostats, then?"

His aunt smiled at him. "Of course we'll do rheostats. And we'll do a nice display that permits the user to specify the damage radius. And that's all it will be—a nice display. I'm not limiting the spell-sets to any thousand luns of energy usage, either. That's ludicrous. It would take a week—maybe even more—to liquefy a small Warren." She frowned and began scratching figures on a notepad. "Almost a month for the total liquefaction of the Oel Artis Warren. We're supposed to turn those energy units into liquid fuel over the period of almost a month? That's . . . inhumane. I don't care what they know or what they feel—I wouldn't sleep nights if I did a thing like that. Better it's quick."

Kirbin leaned back in his seat and nodded. His aunt was no old dolt. She understood energy, understood the way spells ought to work. "Then how will we present our handling of the energy cap?"

"We won't. You've given me the information, I have taken that information and made my determinations, based on my expertise—which in this instance does take precedence, and can override a one-to-one vote from Energy, if necessary. I will add a limit to prevent a spell from running indefinitely. A shield somewhere could go down, and I don't want to be eternally liquid, and I doubt that you do, either."

Kirbin nodded. "So you think there might be some danger of a shield collapsing."

Zider smiled. "This is one area where the old fool was correct—and is something our own people need to remember more often. Plan not for what the enemy might do, but for what he can. The god Vodor Imrish probably won't interfere with any of the shields. But he could. So plan for that. The planning costs us nothing, the preparation costs us little, but our failure to take simple precautions could—unlikely though that might be—cost us our lives and our world."

Kirbin considered that; even though he worked in the Department of Research, he wasn't the design and implementation specialist his aunt was. He'd developed a broad range of skills that had made him invaluable to the department—but he couldn't claim the years of intense practical experience in energy handling that his aunt could. If Zider thought a range limit on the spell was reasonable, he would have to defer.

"He didn't have a problem with the cutoff switch?"

Kirbin said, "I failed to point it out to him. And he failed to notice it."

"Ah." Zider smiled. "It's silly of me, I'm sure, but I don't like to build anything that has a start switch but no stop switch. In case we . . . ah, have to change our minds at the last minute."

"Have you ever had to do something like that?"

Zider's face went bleak as death. "Yes."

Kirbin considered asking his aunt for details, thought he probably shouldn't, if the look in her eye was any indication—and then decided to ask anyway. "When?"

"Just a few years after I first joined the department." She shrugged. "The Bird City power outage. It was the worst thing I've ever seen." Her eyes developed a faraway stare, and she shuddered. "You can look it up in the records."

Which meant that she didn't intend to talk about it, but Kirbin tried once more. "Worse than the Oel Maritias disaster?" He'd been in that one. Had been a little boy, and terrified. His mother had been so badly injured in the collapse of one of the floating platforms in the main festival chamber that she'd never been the same afterward. Even with magical reconstruction and a great deal of mind-healing, she still refused to go to underwater cities again for any reason, and eventually left him and his father and moved away to a ground dwelling. Kirbin hadn't seen her in years.

But Zider smiled grimly. "That wasn't a disaster. That was a save. The only long-term repercussions we've had from that are the bad spot in the sea where the city used to be, and having to drag the city itself thirty miles to the south before we could resink it."

"A lot of people died."

"People are the least of your problems when magic goes bad."

They didn't talk about Kirbin's mother, Zider's sister. She was a save, too, technically. Her strange choices after the accident had little to do with reality, and much to do with the paranoia that gripped her and refused to let go.

Kirbin realized their discussion was at an end. "Would you have me do anything else, then, Aunt Zider?" he asked.

Zider frowned. "Have someone get me radiuses and total mass data for all of the Warrens. I want to figure energy expenditures. We've configured for the *rewhah* from all of these spells to go through the Oel Artis Processing Center, but I think, as I consider safety, that we might be better off adding a hand-clasp pass and moving *rewhah*-handling to the area centers. We could have a real mess if we fail to adequately buffer all of the centers."

Kirbin said, "I'll have the information to you as soon as someone can figure it. Do you have a tolerance range you'd like to specify for mass averages?"

"I'd like exact measurements, but if we can't get those in time, then I want the tightest tolerances possible, and in every instance we need to round our estimates up, not down."

"I'll pass it on."

Patr kept watching the sky. He tried not to get caught at it, and so far he had managed to deflect the few comments with generalities about the weather and fear of coming thunderstorms, but with every minute that passed, he knew disaster was racing closer. He could sense the Inquest searching for him. His betrayal would not go unpunished, and his presence would betray the rest of these people. When the Inquestors came, they would come in low, he thought—and no one would have time to react. And the Inquestors would destroy the Gyru-nalles and their pretty, painted wagons. All the warriors would die, and the women and the wild, unfettered children, and the wizards. And with them would die the Kaan, and the outcast citizens of the Empire, and the brethren of Resonance, and the newly minted Falcons, and that lunatic Wraith, and Patr himself. And Jess.

So when Jess came pounding through the brush with her hair wild and her face pale as death, Patr's heart jammed into his throat and he couldn't breathe and couldn't think. They'd come, and it was all over, and he hadn't been able to save her.

But she was babbling something about Wraith.

Wraith.

The din of panic in his ears died down a little, and he said, "Wait. Catch your breath. What about Wraith? Did he die?" That would only be partly bad news for Patr. He'd come to like Wraith, but the fact remained that Jess carried her unrequited love for him around her like a wall, and it wouldn't be until the man was dead that she might see how much Patr loved her.

"He . . . he . . . woke up." She was crying, too, Patr realized. Tears dripped from the corners of her eyes and down the tip of her nose. Her face crumpled when she cried.

Just his luck, then. "Well, if he's alive and awake . . . that's *good* news, Jess. So why are you crying? I'd think you would be happy."

She closed her eyes, took a long, shaky breath, and blotted her face on her sleeve. "I'm scared," she said. "Wraith can't remember writing anything from all of those notebooks. He can't remember a single thing from the time he started writing them until he woke up today. He asked me if maybe he wasn't sick—even delusional—when he wrote them. He'd just lost his best friend, Patr. And the woman he loved since the day he first went to the Aboves. Maybe he was out of his mind with grief."

Patr snorted. "Nonsense." He held her shoulders, turned her until she was facing him, and waited until she looked into his eyes. "Think about this for a moment. He worked all day that whole month. And he wrote all night. He slept a little around dawn—but he never took a rest, he never quit. Remember?"

"Of course I remember."

"He wore himself out. And the ordeal has blotted itself from his memory. The same thing happened to Inquestors who worked with me. They'd take a tough assignment, and they would get no sleep and little food for days on end, and when they finally had a chance to catch up, their bodies would nearly shut down. Just like Wraith's did. And when they woke up, they never knew what had happened."

"Really?"

"Really. It happened to so many people we had a name for it. We said they'd gone losters."

"Did it ever happen to you?"

"No. But I had a friend in an upper level of the organization, and he kept me away from the worst assignments."

"So you don't think Wraith was out of his mind when he wrote the words upon which everyone is basing their lives?"

Patr sighed. "I wish I could say I thought he was. It would mean you and I could walk away from all of this; that we had no reason to stay and involve ourselves with the Falcons or Vodor Imrish or all of these plans against the Empire. We could go to Strithia or Ynjarval or Manarkas and find a place to hide from the Inquest, and maybe we could live long lives. Together. I'd love to have the chance to be happy with just you someplace far from here." He brushed a stray tear from her cheek with his thumb and smiled sadly. "I've read what he wrote. I don't understand any of the things in the books of prophecy, but I understood his battle plan well enough. It's solid. It's the only way I could imagine that the smallest of small forces could have a chance against the massed might of the most powerful organization of wizards in the world. In fact, I could never have imagined it. The wizards who came with us and the Gyru-nalle wizards have both said the spells he wrote out not only work, but work precisely within the guidelines of Solander's magic—the Falcon magic. According to everyone who knows about those things, the work is simply brilliant."

Jess nodded. "I've looked over the spells. I don't have the training the wizards here have, but I've had enough theory to understand the basics of what Solander designed, and to understand that the way Wraith worked with Solander's limitations was . . . amazing."

"Then why are you doubting?"

Her trembling smile made him want to cry. Why couldn't he have that smile turned on him, meant for him? "Because he was afraid . . . and his fear frightened me."

"What's he doing now?"

"Waiting for the two of us to get back. Probably dreading having consigned everyone to death with the things he wrote."

"Then let's go back and tell him he's fine. And that he didn't do anything terrible."

"You'll tell him about the . . . losters?"

"I'll tell him."

He wondered how long he could simultaneously admire Wraith and hope for his death—or even for his public removal from the world by the hand of the god Vodor Imrish—without the duality driving him mad.

"There's a problem," a Research underling said to the associate in charge of his section. "When we implement the liquefaction spell, the damage radius limitation spell, the stop switch, the timing spell, and the guidance spell in one spell-set, *rewhah*-handling goes haywire. We can do any four and keep the *rewhah* under control, but in every instance the fifth spell sinks us like a reefed ship."

The associate read over the spell specifications the underling handed him and began marking out the equations, seeing what might cancel and balance, what might amplify, and what might simply set the whole thing wrong.

He worked for a steady two hours, with an increasing itch between his shoulder blades and sweat trickling down his back. The spell-set was tricky. He found factors in the liquefaction spell that amplified factors in the guidance spell, that canceled portions of the damage radius spell, that wrecked the timing spell, and that caused the stop-switch spell to reverse. In each instance, talented members of his crew had gone in and done very resourceful fixes. But the fixes clashed with each other, too. The problem was the liquefaction spell. It was the nastiest, dirtiest piece of work he'd ever touched, and *rewhah*-handling for it alone was going to be a nightmare. Yet it was the one portion of the whole mess that couldn't be altered or removed entirely for cause. It had to stay.

He found that if he removed the guidance spell, the other four spells and their fixes stayed stable. The equations meshed beautifully. In many cases, the birds could be hand-delivered if necessary, he thought. He would have to present that option to the Master of Research. In the rest of the cases, the alternatives that would still leave a working spell were removal of the damage radius control—and he wouldn't even consider suggesting that one—or the stop switch.

It made sense, he thought, that if the spell-birds were going to deliver themselves to Warrens in the remoter parts of the Empire, they wouldn't have much need for stop switches. By the time they arrived at their destination and the liquefaction spell triggered, everyone would be quite certain that they fully intended to go through with the procedure.

So he could easily leave the stop switches off of them.

And of course the spell-birds that Dragons could hand-deliver would not need the guidance spells. So he could, with some relief, implement stop switches on those and leave the guidance spells off.

He wondered how the Masters of the Dragon Council would feel about canceling the whole project, though. He'd never had a worse feeling about anything he'd worked on than he had looking at that horrid liquefaction spell. It was such an ugly piece of work, he felt guilty even belonging to the department where it had been created.

He considered writing an anonymous message to the Council, telling them what he thought about the project. And then he came to his senses. People had disappeared for much less. He would keep his mouth shut, do his work, and pray that his requested transfer to the Research Department in his tiny hometown of Balgine came through soon.

He took both the problem and his solution to *his* supervisor, two steps below the Master of the Department, who told him grimly that he could do whatever he had to do to make the damned things work, but that the Dragons were ready for their spell-birds immediately, and that he and his people were on notice until they were done—and that everyone could sleep in shifts on cots.

The associate went back to tell his team, knowing the response he was going to get, and swore that when this crisis was past, he was going back to Balgine for good, whether he went there with a job or not.

The Falcons presented their spell-set to Wraith on the same day that the Kaan and the Gyru-nalles finished the last of the aircar shells. At first, Wraith didn't believe them when they told him they'd found a way to eliminate the addictive and deadly toxins from the Warreners' bodies and package that spell with a buffer that would permit the Warreners to eat the Way-fare without it drugging them mindless. It wouldn't be healthy food; it would still keep them immensely fat, because that was a physical, not magical, component of Way-fare. But until the Falcons found a way to get them safely through the gates and into the real world—and found a place to put them and a way to feed and clothe them once they were there—it would serve.

The third and final spell in the spell-set was the one that was going to cause problems.

Wraith looked it over and said, "I can see what you've done here, and why. The shield spell will block the Dragons from using any more energy of any sort from the Warrens, which will protect the Warreners' lives and souls. But the second we put this into place anywhere in the

Empire, the Dragons are going to descend on us like the last demons of Green Hell. If we save one Warren, we lose the rest, and probably all of ourselves in the process."

"The aircar shells are ready," one of the Falcons said. "We're planning to go to the Warrens individually and place the spell-sets, then travel straight to Oel Artis to disable the Dragons' largest energy facility. Once that is done, we'll be able to start getting the Warreners out of the Warrens." He shrugged, as if the plan he described represented neither any great danger nor unreasonable risk. "With fortune and the hand of Vodor Imrish behind us, we'll be able to dismantle the worst of the Empire's evils in a day. And the rest will surely follow."

Wraith stared at them.

"When you cut the power that fuels the Empire, have you considered what will happen?"

The Falcons all looked at each other. "Of course. Energy in the Empire will stop flowing. Or else the Dragons' spells will automatically divert to accessible power sources—which will default to the citizens of the Hars. But they'll have to cut that fast enough—they wouldn't dare run their cities on the blood and souls of their own people."

Wraith, still weak and sick, leaned against a wall and shook his head vehemently. He wished the room would stop spinning, and he wished that he had the compelling presence in person that he had in his writing. "That isn't all that's going to happen," he said softly. "The floating cities are going to fall to the ground, killing everyone in them and everyone beneath them. The aircars will crash to the ground; the cities beneath the sea will either flood or the weight of the ocean will crush them the instant the magic dies."

"But no." The young wizard Mesinna spoke up. She had been a colleague and sometime research partner of Solander's, and had thrown in her lot with the Falcons after the Dragons chose her at random in their final collection of "traitors against the Empire." She'd lost her taste for Dragon magic and Dragon ethics—such as they were—on the killing field, with her hands clamped to a post. "We won't let harm come to the innocents. Didn't you see the power-down parameter we included in each of the spells?"

Wraith had not. "Show me."

"Right here. Wait . . ." She thumbed through the sheaf of papers that represented the equations and spell-chants for the complete spell-set, and finally pointed to a cluster of lines on one of the many pages Wraith had skimmed. "You see—this part of the power-down increases the strength of our shield slowly from zero up to absolute. The Dragons will experience a gradual energy loss over a period of about a month. It will eventually become absolute, but in that length of time we will have been able to warn everyone of what is happening, and people will have time to evacuate from danger areas."

"Some of them won't go," Wraith said.

She nodded. "Some people refuse to leave homes on the sides of volcanoes when lava starts erupting, too. And some won't leave homes at the edge of the sea with a hurricane coming straight at them. We cannot save the stupid. We can tell them what is happening; with the information we give them, they'll have to take responsibility for their own lives."

Wraith felt a little sick. The death toll from this was going to be bad, no matter how well the Falcons and their comrades got the message across. People wouldn't believe until the last minute that the Dragons were not going to be able to save their homes. In the final stampedes, innocent idiots would die in droves. And truly stubborn fools who refused to believe would die in their homes—badly.

The Empire's soul-fed magic had to end, though. Even a god was willing to offer his assistance in ending this unimaginable evil. Wraith knew he and his people stood on the side of right. He just wondered what price the world would have to pay for the end of evil.

It all might come to nothing, of course. If the words he'd written in Vincalis's hand, channeling the words of Solander, were true, at the appointed hour—or should he think of it as the Appointed Hour?—Vodor Imrish would gather up each of the Falcons' aircar-shaped boxes and transport them and everyone in them to the many Warrens around the world. In each aircar, the wizard and his team would deploy the spell-set, Vodor Imrish would take them to the next Warren on their route, and they would deploy their spell-set there. According to Wraith's estimation, each Falcon and his associates would have to deploy five spell-sets before Vodor Imrish took them to Oel Artis for the final part of their plan. Some of the spell-sets would have to go to Warrens in underwater cities. Some would have to go to cities across oceans, mountain ranges, and deserts. The whole process, including the concerted attack on the Oel Artis Energy Department Power Processing Center, was supposed to take a mere one hour.

If Vodor Imrish never showed, it wouldn't happen at all, because the aircar shells weren't real aircars. They simply looked like them—and then only from a distance and when viewed by a noncritical eye.

Wraith closed his eyes, feeling the room reeling around him. He

354 ❖ HOLLY LISLE

could not stop what would happen. He could not change it. He had spent his life fighting for it, and now that the reality raced toward him with terrifying speed, he wondered if he'd been wrong. They were going to bring a great empire to its knees, and they had little to offer in recompense. He dreaded the hardship that would follow. He dreaded the world that he and his colleagues intended to create.

And how it was out of his hands, and in the hands of a god.

Perhaps Vodor Imrish would lose interest, he thought. Perhaps he would go someplace else, miss his appointment with destruction, get busy doing whatever it was that gods did for all of eternity. And Wraith could honestly say that he had tried. His conscience would be clear. And the beautiful, glittering white Empire of the Hars Ticlarim would go on as it had gone on for three thousand years.

Maybe that would be the best outcome after all.

And later by days and a week, beneath the painfully bright lights on the floor of the spell manufactory, the associate dragon from Research in charge of manufacturing the spell-birds stood before Addis Woodsing, Master of Energy, and said, "We have the final bird forms completed, and one working prototype for each of the self-delivering and hand-delivery models. We await only your approval of the specifications we've used to manufacture these; with your signature, we'll begin installing the final spell-sets for the order."

The Master nodded, and looked over the specifications the asssociate provided. Or rather, he appeared to look over the specifications. His finger trailed along the lines of equations and the outmargined errata notes and working fixes, and for all the world he looked like a man intent on his work.

But he'd discovered only that morning that his young mistress, in whom he had taken a great deal of pleasure, had been keeping a young man of her own on the side, and using the allotment money he gave her for her entertainment to keep him available. He had discovered this, unfortunately, in the most humiliating and expensive of ways: His vowmate and her overpriced investigative team had presented him with the evidence of his infidelities in graphic detail, and to rub salt deep into wounds they would be prodding and freshening for quite some time, they had spread before him vivid evidence of his mistress's free-time activities. Then they had laughed, and his vowmate—vile old harridan— placed before him the thirty-year-old contract, in which he and she had most clearly decreed any side-mates would be chosen with the approval of the vowmate, and all financing of consorts and mistresses be done from joint funds, with spending subject to the approval of the vowmate, who held veto.

That damned contract clause had seemed a good idea at the time, when his vowmate had been young and beautiful and willing as a ferret in heat. As time wore on—and as she wore out and became one of the busy society matrons focused on her own stature and lost in her own busy-work activities—he began chafing under her more frequently used veto. She'd agree to mistresses her own age. Plain-faced, dull, charmless . . . those satisfied her.

And now his contract was going to cost him his family's ancestral home in the Aboves, and a massive portion of his investment income, and he was going to be shamed as a contract breaker.

His finger trailed over the specifications, but his mind ran to associates of his who claimed to know people of a certain sort. People who might be approached with money and offers of special treatment, special privileges, and who for considerations might make his vowmate and her investigators and their information simply . . .

. . . disappear.

He signed off on the specifications for both spell-sets, having failed to actually read a single word of either of them.

Such are the events that shape fate and change the world.

Chapter 25

Luercas sat at one of the little tables outside the restaurant Ha-Ferlingetta, sipping cool, herbal jabemeya from a broad, shallow bowl. He'd been waiting already for nearly an hour, growing increasingly annoyed. The oblivious crowds moved past him in two directions, jabbering, stupid, a herd in search of a shepherd. They could not see the disaster that waited to befall them; they did not know that they would, one day soon, bow in gratitude when he rose up from among commoners and saved them from the complacent monsters who owned them.

He noted a flash of bright red off to his right. And there came Dafril, late as usual, running, looking flushed and flustered and wearing something both new and gaudy—he spent far too much money on fashion. But Luercas noted that along with everything else, Dafril looked pleased. Even triumphant.

Dafril grabbed a chair, plopped into it with all the grace of a sack of rocks thrown to the ground, waved for a servant, and, as if he were speaking to everyone beneath the awning and even all the passersby, said, "Give me a casklet of the best ferrouce in the house, and a plate of whitling, rare and spiced, and whatever my friend will have. We have much—*much*—to celebrate!"

The servant nodded, face tight, then smiled politely and said, "My congratulations, Master, and the congratulations of Ha-Ferlingetta." And scurried off like the insignificant bug that he was. Luercas turned to Dafril as soon as the man was out of earshot and said, "Keep your voice down, man. I'm suspended, you're currently far out of main favor, and the last thing we want anyone to think is that we've had some personal triumph."

"My vowmate's test confirmed her pregnancy!" Dafril blurted, and all around him, those who had been watching out of the corners of their eyes, curious and wary at once, smiled knowing smiles and went back to their meals and drinks.

Luercas frowned and his voice dropped to a whisper. "Your *vowmate*? When in all the little hells did you acquire one of those?"

"Pregnant," Dafril crowed. And sotto voce he said, "And we're going to name the baby Mirror of Souls."

All the tension and anxiety and frustration drained out of Luercas in an instant, and he smiled so broadly that he thought he might swallow his own ears. "The test . . . worked, then?"

Dafril grinned. "Like magic. We have one in the, ah, *you* know, right now. Went off perfectly—most beautiful bit of work I've ever seen. Even if I do say so myself."

"You've earned the right to gloat." Luercas thought for a moment. "You've . . . ah . . . talked with the . . ." He fell silent, unable to think of any clever way to say *disembodied soul held in the Mirror.*

But no matter. Dafril knew what he meant. "Had a good conversation with her. She's delighted. Asked only that when she . . . er . . . comes back, we make sure she's prettier than she was." He chuckled. "We could put her into the body of a hell-blevy fisherman just freed from the gill net and she'd be happy, frankly."

Luercas considered that for a moment, then smiled. "Ah. Our volunteer was Mellayne, eh?"

"Guessed it in one. I thought she'd go for it—opportunity to be beautiful, to get rid of that dreadful lump of flesh she's been lugging around her whole life while she waited for someone who could do a spell that could repair everything wrong with her."

"She jumped at the chance."

"She did indeed. And we'll let her be someone pretty; I'm sure we can locate a 'traitor' for her and manage to lose the girl on the way to the Warrens."

"When are we scheduling the reversal, then?"

Dafril smiled but didn't answer. Instead, he greeted the servants who brought his food, dug into his drink and meal with every appearance of delight, and was as gracious as a man could be when the last servant to the table presented him with a tiny baby-cake, so delicate and perfect it seemed a shame to eat it.

Had he and his nonexistent vowmate actually been expecting a child, tradition would have required him to break the thing in two and then devour the entire cake-and-spun-sugar mass to ensure his vowmate's good health and fortune. The tradition had been born in the days when men hoped to fool gods by destroying false infants, praying meanwhile that doing so would draw those gods' attention away from the real infants they desperately wanted to live. The gods were long forgotten—or at least those with any sense of decency were, Luercas thought with some bitterness—but the tradition remained.

Dafril played along, though. He broke the cake, stuffed the pieces in his mouth with no regard for his dignity, and washed it down with his dreadfully expensive ferrouce. Then he raised his hand and said, "To the child."

And all around him, people raised their hands and repeated, "To the child." And they, for just a moment, pounded on the table as if they were their primitive, superstitious ancestors. Luercas went through the charade with them, amused that he was in fact wishing luck to his and Dafril's baby—the Mirror of Souls—and to his own ascent to the post of god of the Empire of the Hars.

When people went back to their meals and conversations, Dafril said, "We're looking for a good body for her. We want to wait a few days, too—the thing used an amount of energy not to be believed. We had the spell-sets run through the main energy grid; it's going to look like the Long Wall District and part of Five Corners experienced a brief power drain. But I want us to link in through a different district when we pull her out, just to make sure that they don't trace the theft to us."

"Reasonable." Luercas took a bite of his salad and chewed thoughtfully. "Make sure it stays connected to power at all times, though, just in case."

Dafril, pin-sticks halfway to his mouth loaded with whitling, froze and frowned. "Whatever for? My sources tell me the Dragons are a minimum of two weeks away from their first strike. They're working hard, but these things tend to get waylaid by bureaucratic red tape, safety worries . . . a million things. Best guess is their attack on the Warrens, and their follow-up against the rebels, won't be for a full month yet."

Luercas said, "I know all of that. I have sources, too. But I'm . . . nervous. They haven't found any sign of the rebels yet. Nothing. Not which way they went, no sightings from people loyal to the Empire. If the rebels strike first, we're going to have to move fast."

"You want to know what I think?" Dafril asked, mouth full of food.

Luercas didn't, actually. But, polite for the moment with this necessary associate, he said, "Of course."

"I think the rebels have vanished because their god Vodor Imrish took them home to the next world. They aren't anywhere to be found because they aren't anywhere."

Luercas shrugged. "You might be correct. But we have to assume that they are around somewhere, that they could hurt us, and that they'll at least try."

Dafril shrugged. "No problem for me. I'll make sure everything stays in a ready state. But I doubt the necessity. With everything moved and in place, I figure we could have everyone on site and transported in two hours, maximum, from the moment of notification, even if we weren't connected to a source."

Two hours sounded like entirely too long to Luercas. "I didn't realize you'd located a permanent home for it already," he said. He didn't appreciate this independent streak of Dafril's. "Where is it?"

"We've moved it to the mainland. There's no wilderness left on Glavia. I have it housed in a protected temple inland from Freyirs City. The acolytes of the temple have sworn their souls to guarding it, and I've bound them by magic. I figure we need to have it someplace where no one will bother it for the few weeks that we're waiting for things to fall to pieces."

Luercas smiled. "How clever of you. I would never have thought of giving the Mirror its own order of priests. How did you convince them to take it in, though?"

"Simple. Mellayne in her current form can make herself look like anyone or anything when she's summoned to speak. So she made herself look like their god. They're dead certain they're housing the person of their deity—that they've been honored beyond words. Good-looking bunch of kids, too, most of them. I figure we can use them as replacement bodies when we come back."

Luercas leaned on an elbow and shook his head, momentarily silenced by genuine admiration. "Gods-all, Dafril," he said at last. "You stun me. What a brilliant stroke."

Dafril looked delighted by the praise. "As long as we talk to them from the Mirror from time to time while we're waiting, we should be able to keep their converts coming—no worrying about the priesthood turning into a few wizened old decrepits in case we end up stuck in there a bit longer."

"None whatsoever." Luercas chuckled. "So everything is in place. I believe I'll fly out and take a look at the . . . ah . . . god today. Make sure I know the route well enough to get there in a hurry." He savored the last bite of his salad. "Meanwhile . . . lovely work, Dafril. Just lovely. You should have been a Master long ago. You have the deviousness and the innocent face for it—and a streak of brilliance far deeper than anyone would believe."

*   *   *

A chill that passed over his body woke Wraith from deep sleep into darkness, and in that moment he knew. The time had come. Time to get everyone who was going into the aircar shells, time to say good-bye to the rest, maybe forever, time to find the words that he would say when the wizards took over the nightlies in time for him to tell everyone what they had done, and why, and how they must leave their homes and their worlds in order to preserve their lives.

Time to find the words that would make them understand that he was doing the right thing, the good thing—when he could not find even the words to convince himself. He would be destroying something three thousand years old, something beautiful beyond imagining, something that offered comfort to the lives of so many, and security for most, and peace, and safety—and in its place he would be offering . . . what? Lives and the preservation of their own souls to some, yes. But to the rest?

He could lie here in the bed and pretend that he did not know the time had come. And if he did, the time would pass, and he would be able to apologize to everyone—tell them the *Secret Texts* had been written by a sick, delusional man, and that he was now better. And sorry. The opportunity to free the Warreners would never be offered to him again. He would be free of it. Someday, perhaps someone else would pick up the burden and carry on. He need never tell anyone that he now remembered what he had written in the *Secret Texts*—every word of it, as if it had been engraved on his brain—that he knew for certain that Solander had used all the energy he could muster to reach Wraith from beyond death, to tell him everything he had been able to guess and understand about the future from his position in the place beyond the worlds. If he so chose, Wraith could simply permit the moment to drain away like rain falling on sand. Someday, someone else would save the Warreners.

Maybe.

But they wouldn't save *these* Warreners. They might save their children, or their grandchildren—but these people, trapped in a hell not of their own making, would die, not just for the time, but for eternity. They would die so that something beautiful might live, but the price they paid was disproportionate. No one should be forced to give up immortality so that others might have beauty and convenience.

Wraith rose from the cot, shivering as if he'd been dunked in a lake and left on an ice field. He bore the weight of an empire on his shoulders, and the lives of uncounted hundreds of millions, and he knew in that moment that he carried too much for one man. He wished that Solander had lived and that he, Wraith, had died, for surely Solander would have been able to divine through his magic the right course, or else he wished that this twin-headed horror that he must choose between would pass from his care to the hands of someone stronger, someone purer, someone who could see more clearly. He wished Vodor Imrish would come to him and tell him what he must choose, so that he would at least be absolved of responsibility . . . and guilt.

But Vodor Imrish remained silent, and the future—the future of the Empire of the Hars Ticlarim on one side, and the future of an unending stream of nameless, dreamless, hopeless Warreners on the other side— lay for that one moment within the grasp of his two hands. He had lived in both worlds, and he had known the hell of one and the heaven of the other, and as much as he had hated the one, he had loved the other. But he could not change one without irrevocably changing both.

Tears rolled down his cheeks. He clenched his hands into fists and wept silently—wept for people he could never know, and for people he did know and would not be able to help. And then he stepped out of the tiny one-room cottage where he had written the *Secret Texts*, and with full understanding of the consequences others would have to pay for his choice, he roused the Falcons and their support team, and told them that they had to get to the aircars quickly—that the time had come to fight.

He was grateful for the darkness that hid his tear-stained face. He did not wish to share his doubts with anyone else. Ever. If they had their own, he sympathized—but he would not try to escape the weight of his own burden. He'd earned his guilt, and for the rest of his life, he knew he would live with the consequences of this choice, whatever those consequences might be.

Jess sat beside him, and Patr across from him. None of them said anything. The three of them would not assist the Falcons in the placing of spells; their job would come when they reached Oel Artis and the Falcons breached the security that guarded transmission of the nightlies. Until then, they would follow, or simply wait, at the whim of the god.

In the dark, Wraith felt a small, strong, callused hand slide into his. Jess scooted closer. Wraith held her hand with gratitude and waited. Finally, when the last of the aircars held all its passengers, a faint gold-tinged spiral of wind swept around all of them, glowing only enough that they could tell it had arrived. Soundlessly, smoothly, the aircars lifted into the air, and then moved through something that felt to Wraith like chilled silk, like a spider's web hung with cold, cold, bone-chillingly cold dew. True silence descended; not the silence of the world, but the silence of a place beyond the world. All light fell away. All sensation ceased.

Wraith knew that he had been sitting, but he could not tell if he sat any longer; his body was gone. He had no arms, no legs, no eyes, no ears. He tried to speak, but no mouth moved, no words formed, no sounds came out. He tried to feel Jess's hand, or even to sense her presence, but for all that his senses told him, he could have been the lone sentient thought in the center of an infinite expanse of nothing.

He should be afraid, but he was not. Blind, deaf, mute, bodiless, lost, he found in the emptiness the presence of Vodor Imrish. He received no words of comfort, no reassurances, no promises that everything would be all right. But he knew Vodor Imrish traveled with him through this place, and with that knowledge, he found contentment.

The state of bodilessness lasted only an instant, and then he and Jess and Patr and the aircar fell through the brush of colder-than-death cobwebs again, and he looked out to see Oel Artis below. And all the other aircars full of Falcons and their assistants flew with him.

"Something has gone wrong," he whispered. "We shouldn't be here yet. Or, even if we were supposed to be here, everyone else should still be at the Warrens."

Jess gripped his hand tighter, her fingers interlocked with his so fiercely that he doubted he could free himself if he chose to. She said nothing, and he realized that she was scared. He hadn't sensed any fear in her the whole time they'd been preparing for this moment, and as she'd been helping organize the teams that went into each aircar, she'd sounded as calm as if she had been giving people instructions on finding the playhouse where one of her groups was playing. He looked at her, wishing that he could see better in darkness. From her profile, sharply outlined against the sea of stars that was Oel Artis below, he could tell that her lips were pressed tightly together, and that she'd squeezed her eyes closed.

"We'll be fine," he whispered in her ear. He didn't know if it was true, but he hoped it was.

"I'm not worried about us," she whispered back. "I'm worried about what will happen to the Empire when we do this. *If* we do this. All these people . . . where will they go? How will they eat? How will they survive?" She turned her face toward him. Now he could see nothing but the silhouette of her hair. "Can we do this, Wraith? Even being who we are, even coming from where we come from . . . can we do this? Is it the right thing to do?"

Wraith squeezed her hand. In that moment, fully and completely, he realized at last that he loved her. She understood a thing he'd thought no one could understand: how he of all people could be ambivalent about what was to come. She understood—but more, she shared his ambivalence. His fear. He'd been silent about his anguish most of all on her account, for he could not help but remember that she—of all the people working toward the freeing of the Warreners—had the most right to hate the Empire that burned Warreners like cordwood, body and soul, for its convenience. To her he could never have expressed his doubts, for it seemed that by doing so, he would be questioning her worth. Her right to live. She had been one of the Warreners in a way he never had—she had been just a unit of energy to be counted and converted. She had earned the right to hate. But she did not hate—or, at least, she could still see parts of the Empire that had value, and she could still understand that innocents stood on both sides of the dilemma, waiting to suffer.

"I don't know," he admitted. "I have to believe we're doing the right thing—that the destruction of souls must stop, no matter what the cost may be in bodies. I know there's no good solution. I don't know if this is truly the best solution. But it's the best solution we could devise."

"Of course it is," Patr cut in. "The Empire is evil—built on evil, full of evil. It has to end. How could you question that, either of you?"

Jess and Wraith looked at each other, and Jess said, "How could we not?"

Wraith caught a flash of light behind Jess and said, "We're landing already."

Jess's fingers felt like iron as they clung to his. "We could still turn back," she said. "No one has had any time to do anything—we could still turn back."

The aircar thumped lightly on the ground—a mildly imperfect landing for a god, Wraith thought. And Patr charged out of their aircar first, running toward the one that had landed beside them.

"I know where we are," Wraith whispered to Jess. "This is the transmitting center for the nightlies. At this hour, everyone but the technicians who keep the transmission going should be at home."

"We're where we are supposed to be, then," Jess whispered back.

"Yes—but not when." He rose. He needed to go see if any of the Falcons had been able to figure out why Vodor Imrish brought them all here instead of taking them to the Warrens first. "Do you want to stay here?"

"No." Jess sounded emphatic about that. Well, he couldn't blame her. He wouldn't want to be the one sitting in the dark waiting for an explanation, either. They both got out. The aircars had all come down on one of the side landing roofs. Wraith saw that one of the Falcons had already tried the door and found it open. "Bad security," someone said behind him.

"Or the work of Vodor Imrish," another said.

They were all moving toward the opened door—the Falcons, their handpicked assistants, Patr. Wraith grabbed one of the Falcons by an arm and said, "Why is everyone going in already? You have to set the protective spells around all the Warrens first."

The Falcon turned to him. "We've done it. We've been working for hours, Master Gellas. It took my team far longer than we'd anticipated because something about the spell the Dragons had around the Warren in West Shadowfall interfered with our spell initially. It finally gave, and we were able to place ours, but—"

"Hours?" Wraith couldn't believe what he was hearing. Hours? That meant they had irrevocably cast the die. The Warrens were shielded, the magic was going to start failing all over the Empire, and all that remained was for Wraith to tell people to get out of the way, and then to follow his own advice.

No turning back. No turning back. The impact hit him hard—all at once and all over his body. He looked desperately for a rest room as his bowels knotted and he clenched and fought a simultaneous urge to vomit.

He pushed through the doorway into the transmission building, dove into one of the marked alcoves off the main hall, and found a privacy chamber. He barely made it.

He retched and heaved and clutched his belly as everything let go. And then he vomited some more. Too much for one man—too much guilt, too much responsibility, too much hanging in the balance. *Make it all not true,* he prayed. *Make the Warrens not true, make the fall of the Empire not true—simply change things to make them good. To make them fair, and just, and right.*

His body calmed, but the spasms left him trembling, sweating, pale. When he was done, he felt almost too weak to move. Feet milled about outside the door of the chamber he'd raced into—people worried that he'd lost his nerve, or his mind; he knew that with every minute he stayed, he raised the chance that all of them would be captured and taken away before they could accomplish the final—and now essential—part of their plan.

He dragged himself to his feet, rinsed his mouth, and headed out. "I'm fine," he said before anyone could question him. "Not over my illness, but I'm strong enough to go on."

The Falcons had cast a shield around the rebels before they went through the door. Now they began the process of undoing the magics that prevented anyone but authorized personnel from going into the sensitive transmission rooms. Wraith would have been able to pass through without this—but alone, Wraith knew he would not last long against more than one or two defenders. And no one knew exactly how many people would be in the transmission center at this hour.

While the Falcons took down the Dragons' barriers, their helpers readied weapons. They fully intended that no one would be injured—but in order to prevent the transmitter operators from making a heroic defense, the attackers needed to look like they were willing to do whatever was necessary.

With stun-sticks and illegal mind silencers ready, they braced themselves to kick in the doors. The Falcons crouched to either side, chanting in whispers, offering their flesh and blood and bone and will as sacrifices for the success of the mission. Nothing happened. Wraith felt his heart racing. Jess stood by his side, tense and pale. And still nothing. Then, without a warning sound, without any apparent change, the two doors through which the attackers had to move glowed golden, and the Falcon nearest the door nodded. The attackers kicked in the door and poured into the room, weapons pointing forward and ready to fire, having no idea what they would encounter on the other side.

Three young men and an older man yelped and leaped to their feet from comfortable, cushioned chairs, and bits of meals scattered in all directions along with plates and drinks.

"Don't hurt us," one of the young men shouted.

But the older was reaching slowly behind him toward a black switch.

"Don't touch it," Patr said. "Don't touch anything. I'm from the Silent Inquest—your chance to walk out of here instead of being carried out on a stretcher is directly related to your cooperation. If you do what we tell you, you'll live. If you don't—"

"You're the rebels," the older man said. "You're trying to destroy the Empire."

"Actually," Wraith said softly, "at this point, we're trying to save lives. Please move away from the transmission equipment."

The four men did as told, and the one helper who'd come along because he'd spent some time working in the transmission center said, "You stand on the dais across the room, Gellas. I have to override the transmission of the nightlies—when I give you the signal, start talking. People will be able to hear you."

"Are we safe from intrusion?" Wraith asked.

Jess said, "The Falcons have us covered, but we need to keep this short. You have the right words, Wraith. Just don't waste any time getting to them."

Wraith nodded, crossed the room, and climbed onto the dais. A transmission sphere hung in the air in front of him, glowing dully. He watched it, having no idea what he would say when he got the signal to go ahead. He had never been more completely without words in his whole life.

Luercas wasn't even paying attention to the nightlies on the viewscreen in one corner of the room. He'd decided to attend a party thrown by a number of the Dragons who'd assisted in the development and deployment of the Mirror of Souls. The party had turned into an orgy, and Luercas, who considered himself above that sort of behavior, amused himself by watching the people who would one day make up the reborn government of the Empire, and trying to figure out how he might gain some advantage from the couplings going on before him. So intent was he on matching names to partners and trying to recall if any contracts were being violated that he failed to note the abrupt cessation of a debate by two commentators on the state of diplomacy with Strithia. He did not note the silence; he did not note the abrupt appearance of a single gaunt, pale face.

But others did. One woman gasped, "Oh, no, it's started!" and pointed to the overhead display, and the orgy died an immediate and ugly death. Luercas saw Gellas's face staring down at him, and he knew she was right. It had started.

He wanted to stay—to hear what the bastard had to say, find out where the spells were going to fall, and why. But he knew he and these idiots might already be too late.

"We need to leave now," he said. "Bring nothing. You'll need nothing."

"We haven't had time to do a successful reversal yet. We don't know how well the automatic search features work, or if the emergency low-power stasis feature acts the way it should!" someone called, but though he heard what the man said, he was already running for the pad where his aircar sat.

To his surprise, Dafril caught up with him. "You were right," he panted. "You were right to keep the thing ready."

"We aren't all going to get there in time," Luercas said.

"You and I will get there in time. Everyone else will either make it . . . or not."

The two of them dove into Luercas's aircar and Luercas slammed it to maximum acceleration—something that would make the manufacturer and the spell designers cringe, but some things could not be helped. His exquisite aircar would be his sacrifice to the exigencies of getting himself out of harm's way at the best possible speed.

"How long is the Mirror set to hold us?" Luercas asked.

"Right now?" Dafril considered. "Ten years, so long as power remains steady. If there's a drop below critical levels, it will go into stasis mode automatically and only return to active mode when the power comes back again."

"Stasis mode. I don't like it. I would have liked an active power-source search feature better."

"But people would see it as hostile if it started melting down anyone who wandered too close to it. This way, it looks like a gift of the gods at best, and a nice piece of furniture at worst. And as long as we have the priests to protect it, we should be fine."

"I just don't like the idea of the stasis mode."

"It's nothing major, Luercas." Dafril spread his hands wide and shrugged. "We won't be able to communicate with anyone on the outside, but no one will melt the thing down for metal because they mistake it for a weapon. It seems the perfect way to deal with brief power outages."

Luercas looked at him sidelong. "I suppose. But with an active power-search feature, we would always be in complete control."

Dafril sighed. "It's not an issue. The stasis feature is only there at all because I'm a worrier. I got to thinking about what might happen if the Dragons overused energy in fighting the rebels, and this seemed like a reasonable precaution. It will keep the lot of us alive, no matter what."

Behind them, the air filled with aircars all aimed toward the mainland, all streaming at fastest possible speeds.

"Someone is going to notice this," Dafril said suddenly. "Someone monitoring traffic is going to see the lot of us and send interceptors to investigate."

"Probably. But maybe Gellas will keep them entertained long enough for us to get all the way out of their monitoring range."

"Let's hope he's got a bit of theater tucked in there, then," Dafril said, and smiled thinly.

Chapter 26

A moment in time—crystalline, perfect, beautiful because it is true . . . honest . . . real. One moment, sliced thin as mountain air, held up to the light, examined with sadness, because it is the last—the last moment of its sort that the world of Matrin will ever know. Here—look.

In the floating city nicknamed the Aboves in Oel Artis, the finest diamond in the crown jewel of the Empire, a girl accepts her first dance from a suitor in a hall with walls of midnight hung with stars, and all around the dance floor, men and women long past their first dance smile and glance at each other, remembering.

In the underwater city of New Oel Maritias, the full-time residents of Kaldeen District debate, with passion and animation, the addition of a new wing of the city, outlying their own current edge district. They worry about the decrease of property values when they lose their unobstructed views of the sea, and want a setback for the closest new construction that is farther than visibility on the water's clearest day, and they want a one-year study to determine the precise distance, and a moratorium on building until the distance is determined. The consortium of builders and potential buyers, on the other hand, wants to start building right away, and they don't want the setback, which will increase building costs and make the addition less stable. No one is happy.

On to the mainland now, where in the city of Tarz, the Festival of Remembrance is under way—men and women dressed as incarnations of Death, dancing in the streets, drinking, singing mournful songs, copulating in alleyways, visiting the Memorial Hall, where pictures of their beloved dead adorn walls. A vast citywide celebration, ironically, of the fact that they are all alive.

Down to Haffes, off the western peninsula of Benedicta, where the clans of the Gyru-nalles have met for the semiannual month-long Bride Trade, an archaic tradition in which those men whose wives fail to please them may trade them off to men from other clans, but only to married men who are also exchanging a wife. Trades must be one for one, but trades in series, in which a man from one tribe will trade his wife to a man whose wife he doesn't fancy at all, simply because he can then exchange this second wife for the wife of a third participant in the deal, who has already made arrangements with him in advance—are common. Men put a great deal of effort into making their wives look good and themselves look unreasonable, in the hopes of getting takers. For the most part, the traded wives are as happy to go as their husbands are to see them go. Still, as with horse trading, people often end up a month or two later resenting the deal they had made. It is often speculated that the bad blood between so many of the clans might stem directly from the Bride Trade.

Or it might be the horse stealing.

One clan, and only one clan, is notably absent from the fields of the Bride Trade. The absence has caused a great deal of speculation.

Onward. On the continent of Strithia, in a human town named Halles just beyond the edge of Strithian territory, in a tall black tower already ancient beyond imagining, ghosts of the future illuminate the carved inner walls, moving restlessly in search of a secret from the past, a secret that the tower has hidden since a time before men walked the surface of the world. These ghosts become especially active in moments just before disasters, but they have never been so plentiful as they are at this instant. Inside the tower, their presence and frenzied movement give the illusion of sunlight pouring down from the ceiling. Outside in the streets of Halles, no one notices, because it is already daylight. Had it been nighttime on this side of the world, the people of Halles at least might have had some warning of what was to come. But they, like everyone else—or everyone else human, anyway—are oblivious.

Deep in the heart of true Strithia, however, where humans may enter but may never leave, the pending disaster is no surprise. The Ska-ols offer sacrifice after sacrifice, building the power that will shield the essential parts of their empire against the onslaught that they know comes.

And in the Dragon Council, back in Oel Artis, the Master of Research, sitting in on the emergency meeting that has been called by all the Masters, is recognized by the Landimyn of the Hars, who has demanded his place as true head of the Dragon Council for the first time in a hundred years—and the Master of Research rises to speak. She is closely watched by a man named Faregan, who has motives far removed from the good of the Empire.

Around the world in this instant, children are born, old folks die, people celebrate and mourn, dance and grovel, pray and swear. Around the world in this instant, frozen for eternity like a gnat in amber, the world still holds the shape it has held for tens of thousands of years. This is the last instant in which that will be true. All moments lead to the end of a world, but some lead there more decisively than others. The next moment holds an irrevocable act. A misjudgment, perhaps, a mistake— or perhaps the will of gods bored with playing a game where the rules remain the same and the pieces fit too well. Even from the vantage point of gods, it is sometimes hard to find the one true cause of disaster.

The well-known and once-beloved face of Gellas Tomersin filled the display. "Solander gave us the magic to end the evils of the Dragons, and the god Vodor Imrish has given us the power to do in one night what would have taken mortals with only magic to aid them days or weeks. But Vincalis the Agitator gave us the words by which we have gone forth to destroy that evil which has rotted the heart of the empire. Vincalis said:

> *Each of us is in part a god. We are each Masters of our souls. Others hold rights to the flesh of our bodies, others claim the effort of our backs, others own the fruits of our labors—but each man's soul is his birthright, his stake in immortality, his foothold to imminent godhood.*
>
> *Yet the Dragons above you claim flesh, bone, blood, will, and thought from men, women, children, babes in arms. And beyond, they claim their souls. They claim them, they burn them, they destroy that which they can never own—for convenience, for art, for their own power.*
>
> *No more.*

"There is no easy path to honor," Gellas Tomersin—Wraith the War-rener—said, and tears glistened like diamonds on his cheeks. "There is no soft path to freedom, no good road to what is right. No painless way to truth. What we have done will hurt innocent people even as it frees innocent people. The Dragons cannot continue burning the souls of the Warreners to give you flying cities, cities beneath the seas, aircars, star-yards. They have gone beyond the right of a government, have claimed more than they can own. We each have inalienable rights—the right to our own thoughts, the right to our own bodies, the right to our own souls. The Empire has claimed these rights as its own, has stolen them from its most helpless citizens. But we have taken the souls of the Warreners away from the Empire tonight—and, in the weeks of the next month, will take away all flesh and bone, all blood and will. By the end of this month, if the Dragons do not use new sources of power, all magic in the Empire of the Hars Ticlarim will die. The cities of the air will topple to the ground—even now, they are sinking lower. The cities beneath the sea will flood or be crushed—even now, pressure on them begins to increase. Aircars will not fly, ships on the sea will have to navigate by the stars and sail by the wind, for their engines will fall silent."

He bowed his head for a moment, and a small sob escaped him. Then, straightening his shoulders, taking a deep breath, he lifted his head and said, "We have made the end of magic gradual to give each of you time to evacuate. If you live beneath the sea, leave. If you live in the air, leave. If you live in a city beneath a city built on air, leave. You will need food, you will need clothing against weather that, without magic to temper it, may become harsh. You will need a way to protect yourself and your family—you should band together with people you trust for your own safety.

"I'm sorry," he said, and he sounded like he actually meant it. "If we had been able to find any other way, we would have taken it."

The Landimyn of the Hars crooked his index finger, and his servant switched the display unit off. "If you didn't see it live, now you've seen it." He leaned back and stared at them. "I want this fixed. I want it fixed now. I will not have this Empire destroyed by these fanatics. These lunatics. This will not happen on my watch. Tell me—how are we going to render these criminals and their spells impotent?"

The Master of Research, Zider Rost, tapped the table in front of her to signal that she had something to say. The Landimyn acknowledged her with a nod.

Zider rose and said, "Within five minutes of leaving here, I can launch the first twenty spell-birds that will turn the Warrens and everything in them into a liquid fuel that we will be able to use to power this Empire for the next generation. Within a day, if I push my people, we can have the hundred-plus others ready to go. We may have to cut corners to get them out the door in time, but any corners we cut won't be in effectiveness. I recommend, however, that we do this immediately, because the longer we tarry, the less power we'll have to deliver them to their targets."

The Landimyn looked pleased but startled. "I've heard nothing of this plan."

"I'm sure it was working its way up through your underlings to you—I sent you the complete information on it the day the Council voted to develop this weapons system."

The Landimyn nodded. "It's safe?"

"Not for the Warreners." Zider Rost grinned around the room at the other councilors, and a few managed appreciative if strained chuckles.

"It will eliminate the spell these . . . monsters . . . have cast?"

"It is the most powerful spell-set that has ever been developed by the use of Dragon magic. We have had to create an entire new system for *rewhah*-handling just to accommodate the power that this spell will generate. I promise you on my life and soul, there is nothing those petty bastards can have thrown around the Warrens, in the space of the few minutes they would have had to cast before our people spotted them, that will stand against what we have created." She waved her right hand over the band she wore on her left wrist, and in the air above it, the face of a young man appeared. "You have the information for me, Rohn?"

"I do." The young man smiled. "I can find no evidence of an actual shield around any of the Warrens, other than ours. And all of ours are still intact. We do show minimal energy loss, but we suspect some sort of leaching device implanted to make us think that these people have done what they said. Our teams have been able to enter test Warrens across the Empire without difficulty, and report no changes in the behavior of any of the units."

"They were lying?" The Landimyn looked relieved.

"Perhaps." Zider Rost held up a hand. "They use a system of magic foreign to us, and it is possible that they are telling the truth, but that we won't see the effects of what they've done for several days. I strongly, strongly recommend that we not give them the chance to bring the Empire to its knees. I advise we strike now, while we know we can end this."

Around the Council table, silence. Doubt on the faces of the Masters who had not had the chance to inspect the spell-set. Concern over taking such a drastic, irreversible step.

And then Grath Faregan rose.

"Two points," he said. "First, you cannot show weakness in the face of the threats of rebels. Doing so only encourages more rebellion. If the bastards have done what they say they have done, and if you don't act, the Empire and all that is good within it will die by your hand, and yours will be the names reviled in history for all time. And if they have not done what they claim, and you don't act, every Empire-hating lunatic from here to Strithia will swarm the Hars, and the Empire will die anyway.

"Second . . ." He paused and smiled. "Second, I've located the rebels' hiding place. By the time you've turned the Warrens into liquid, they should be back to their base. And when they return, you can drop a spell-bird on them."

The table erupted with demands that Faregan divulge the location, but he just shook his head. "First things first. Save the Empire's energy. Then we'll go after the rebels. I want to be on hand personally to watch their destruction."

The Masters looked at each other, and then, one by one, said, "Second . . ." "Second." "I second as well." "Second." No one abstained, no one disagreed.

The Landimyn looked from one councilor to the next. "These spell-birds have been checked by others at this table? You are all satisfied that they will do what they are supposed to do, that they will do it correctly?"

The Master of Energy said, "I vetted them myself. They'll work. They aren't pretty, but they'll work."

The Landimyn sat still, eyes closed, for just a moment. Then he nodded. "Master of Research. Go immediately. Launch every spell-bird that you have ready. Have your people prepare the rest to launch at the soonest available moment. Do what you have to do to make this happen."

Zider Rost, Master of Research, smiled coldly. She rose, bowed to the Landimyn and to his colleagues. And then she left the room at a run.

"We have to get back in the aircars now," Wraith said when he'd finished the transmission.

"Obviously we need to get out of here," Patr agreed.

"No. Not just out of here. We need to run. And we need to take the men here with us."

Patr blanched, but then smiled slightly. "You're talking about taking hostages? I didn't think you had it in you."

"Not going to be hostages. Going to be survivors. Something is wrong." Wraith pointed to the transmission operators and shouted, "Take them with us. Run! Back to the aircars!" Then he grabbed Jess and, with his hand clamped around her wrist, bolted for the exit. Behind him, he could hear the four employees protesting. But he heard the pounding of many feet behind him, too—and as he alone spoke for Vincalis, damnable Vincalis, they'd do what he told them. He didn't need to look back.

He jumped into the first aircar and dragged Jess in behind him; she smacked a shin going over a door he could have opened had he taken more time, and yelled, and he could feel her glaring at him. Patr, whom Wraith had heard running and swearing right behind him and Jess, had one of the employees in tow—and that man was in a frothing rage. Patr shoved the transmission operator into the aircar and jumped in with him, and instantly the vehicle lifted off the ground.

Patr was panting. "What's going on?"

"Something terrible. I'd no more than finished the transmission when I got the image of disaster. The collapse of the city, I think."

The employee glowered at the three of them and said, "You're *causing* the collapse of the city, you cretin—you amoral son-of-shit-weasels. You're going to murder the city in a month, and now you're having second thoughts."

"Not in a month," Wraith said. He stared down at the other aircars. The lights on the landing pad of the transmission building lit them well enough that he could make out what was going on. The aircars were filling and soaring into the air as fast as the one he was in. The sense of urgency, of terrible, oppressive, impending nightmare clogged the air.

Why? What would happen? He'd told the people of the Empire what they needed to know. Hadn't he? What more was there?

But the god Vodor Imrish was pulling them out faster than anything Wraith had ever seen—and the panic almost felt to him like it emanated from the god. But why would a god panic?

He watched the last of the aircars lift off of the landing pad. And then, from last to first, they began winking out like stars, simply vanishing from the sky. His mind had only an instant to register what it had seen, and then the colder-than-death cobwebs that moved him from his world into the darkness beyond brushed his face and his skin, and all of life and light fell away. He hung in the darkness, wondering what was at that moment befalling his world, his home, and the people he had left behind.

Luercas and Dafril made it out of their aircar and into the temple first, their frantic charge scattered the priests and set all within the temple into panic. But not so much as their instructions to the priests, given as the rest of the Dragon plotters began to arrive.

"We go to join the god, who has summoned us," Luercas told the head of the priests. "When our spirits have left our flesh, you must clear our bodies away from this place. Burn them or bury them, whichever is more convenient to you—they have no importance, and must not be permitted to become a source of disease for you or your priests."

The head priest nodded. "Will the god summon us to his side some-day?"

Luercas shrugged. "I cannot speak for the god. Perhaps. Perhaps you will serve until you are an old man—perhaps you will join us with the god soon. But never question; if the god summons you, you will have no doubt in your mind that you have been called. And if you are called, you must come immediately."

"I serve with joy and reverence," the priest told him. "We all do. Whatever the god may command of us, we will do." He looked some-what askance at the number of people filing into the temple chamber that housed the Mirror of Souls. "All of these have been called?"

Luercas said, "The god has need for servants in the beyond, as well as in this realm. We have been called to serve, and we do not question. And neither should you."

Chastened, the priest hung his head.

"Everyone who's coming is here, I think," Dafril whispered in Luer-cas's ear. "Or if not, we at least have enough to put together a full gov-ernment when we return."

"Is the Mirror ready?"

"Waiting only the final button combination."

Luercas felt an edge of dread. They knew the Mirror would take them in and hold them, but had only the promise of untried numbers and equations that it would release them when the time came. So many things remained untested. But the faction of Dragons in power was about to make itself hideously, hellishly unpopular. He and his people could wait no longer. They could not afford to be associated with the debacle of wizard war and wizard resistance that was about to ensue. He guessed that in five years, much of the Empire would be a shambles, and would be ripe for the arrival of heroes who could set things right—but if things became entrenched, ten years could pass.

"The priests must guard the gates of the temple now," Luercas said. "You are sworn upon threat of death never to touch the receptacle of the god; swear each of your priests to this same oath, or surely the god who summons us now will destroy you totally."

The priests were bound to the site by magic. And their fervor would bring new acolytes—new men and women who wished to serve a living,

present god. Luercas had to trust. In this moment, he had to have faith:
that the thing would work as he planned, that one day he would have a
body that truly belonged to him and only him, and that he would stand
at the head of his own Empire.

The priests left, closing the doors behind them. They would return
later and remove the bodies. He shuddered a little, thinking of leaving
his flesh behind in a cooling heap on the floor. Nevertheless, he acted for
the future.

"Ready," he said. "As ranking Dragon, I will operate the Mirror and
pass through last."

Dafril said, "It's set to take us all at once. With our concern for time,
I thought we did not dare a slower course of action."

Luercas felt ill. "Reset it, then."

"We would have to power it completely down and bring it back up
again, and then put in the new commands—that alone will take nearly
an hour. And the process of moving people through individually will
take more than a minute apiece."

Luercas backed away. He could still flee. He could change his
mind—and those who stayed behind would know his shame. But what
would that matter if, once they were inside the Mirror of Souls and he
alone remained outside, he destroyed the mechanism? They would never
be able to tell anyone of his cowardice, or his treachery.

But if he didn't go, he would lose his chance to be Master of the Empire. And that was not a chance he would throw away lightly.

Luercas stood before the Mirror of Souls. It was a thing of tremendous beauty—a column of glowing blue energy surrounded by a tripod
of the purest cithmerium, the best of all metals for magic work. The energy flowed upward into a basin of six curved cithmerium petals, and
swirled smoothly within the basin. Carved gemstone buttons, their
meanings carefully disguised by the use of wizard glyphs, looked more
part of art than of function. The Mirror of Souls looked like a huge metal
flower—half the height of a man—but a metal flower alive and alight
with power.

It was a thing of beauty, but, too, a thing of terror. Of death now, and
death to feed its power, and death in the future to give those within it
new life. If he used the Mirror, he would die. Die. How could he let himself embrace physical nonexistence, even for the promise of future
power? How? But how could he bypass potential ascent to virtual—or
even actual—godhood? Survival now? Greatness later?

He rested his fingers on the buttons that would transport everyone in the room into the realm of death. He looked into the eyes of those around him, and saw his own fear reflected a hundredfold.

No warning, he thought. No good-byes—no see-you-on-the-other-sides—no chances for second thoughts. He pressed the button, and radiance red as arterial blood rose from the column and billowed from the central pool like bread risen beyond its pan, and then the light embraced him and everyone with him.

He felt a sharp snap.

He felt a single moment of nightmarish pain, and fear that eclipsed anything he had ever experienced before, including taking the *rewhah* from Rone Artis's failed power spell.

He felt cold. With the horrible finality of death, darkness descended, and silence, and senselessness. If he could have, he would have wept, but all the functions of body were gone. He hung, abandoned and alone, in the infinity of nothingness, and he understood for the first time the absolute magnitude of the error he had made.

The spell-birds flew, or were flown, according to their nature. The first to land was the massive bird built for the Warren of Oel Artis—delivered personally by the Master of Research herself, who carried it through the gates of the Warren, which still permitted entrance to those with appropriate passes, and laid it in a stairwell out of clear view of the street. How unfortunate if some guard, doing rounds, discovered it, guessed its nature, and tried to disarm it or remove it from the Warrens. She checked its timer—the spell-set would activate at naught-and-one by Pale, the first minute of the first hour of new day.

Satisfied that the spell-bird would perform correctly and at the appropriate time, the Master of Research left the Warrens.

Liquid, she thought. They would all be liquid—and when they were liquid they would be no more trouble at all. She could hear them moving around, crying out as if they were lost, as if they were in pain—making sounds within their buildings for the first time. Animal noises. Horrible, sickening animal noises. Perhaps, then, the rebels had managed to free them from the blessing of numbness in which they had lived their lives, into the pain of captivity in their flesh, in these Warrens, in the vacant spaces of their lives. If so, they would not suffer long. Or at least they would not suffer in human form for long.

As liquid, she thought they might suffer for quite some time.

And she was fine with that.

In the ten nearest mainland cities, other members of the Department of Research placed their spell-birds by hand. They had no more difficulty than the Master of the department herself—and they, too, noticed that the Warrens were no longer silent places.

The spell-birds flew on their own to farther destinations, and neatly delivered themselves into the hearts of their respective Warrens. The spells the rebels claimed to have cast kept out not a single official, and not a single spell-bird.

All twenty-seven readied spell-birds reached their destinations—the biggest cities in the Empire, and the largest Warrens. The smaller Warrens would become liquid in the next day, or perhaps within two days. But, on land and undersea, the greatest Warrens, which supported the greatest cities, were the first and most essential targets. Their demise would be what broke the back of the resistance.

In the moments before spell detonation, the Master of Research—now returned to the department core where she could remotely monitor the integrity of the shields that would keep the spell-birds from damaging people or territory beyond their targets, and where, too, she could keep an eye on *rewhah* levels—declared the shields for each of the target Warrens intact. She told the men handling remote switching for those spell-birds that had switches to stand down.

"The birds will do what they're supposed to do, and nothing more," she said. "They're all on target, and they're all safe."

Her people watched the transmissions from mage-viewers placed at the closest of the Warrens—where nothing changed.

Zider Rost, Master of Research, listened to her people start counting down the last few seconds of the time remaining until the spell-birds detonated, and she smiled. Her name would stand in history for all time: the woman who delivered peace and energy to the Empire and eliminated the threat of the rebels in one master stroke. She would probably become head of the Dragon Council in a few years, and Landimyn of the Hars in only a few more. Who else had contributed so much? In the grand history of the entire Empire of the Hars Ticlarim, the Jewel of Time, who had contributed as much as she?

"Ten . . . nine . . . eight . . . seven . . . six . . ."

Twenty-seven spell-birds, tossed around the globe of Matrin into the glittering hearts of the twenty-seven greatest cities of the Empire, fluttered their wings in the last second of their existence, as if they knew what was about to happen and would have fled, had they the capability to do so.

The twenty-seven greatest cities of the Empire of the Hars Ticlarim, the Jewel of Time, the grandest and most glorious statement of the hand of man and the magic of gods ever known—or perhaps ever known within the written history of the Hars itself, but that is neither here nor there. History is all that humankind can hold and encompass and pin down, not all that is. History is neither truth nor completeness. It is simply the best story people can string together at the time, out of whatever facts and snippets they might have at hand.

The twenty-seven greatest cities of the Empire of the Hars Ticlarim, homes of art and artists, music and sport, great lovers, great killers, governments on both the small and the large scale. And of those twenty-seven cities, which held between them eighty-one thousand years of accumulated history, the correct names of only five would survive the fall of the spell-birds to resurface a thousand years later.

Twenty-seven spell-birds, each small enough for a child to pick it up, each lovely enough that, had it fallen where a child might find it, such a thing could have happened.

The spell-artificers in the Department of Research had been most thorough in their casting of the spell-sets for the first twenty-seven birds. None were duds—all detonated as they had been designed to. With one small exception.

The casting of spells can be compared to a form of martial art. A much smaller opponent with the correct focus and the correct leverage, who is in the right place at the right time, and with the right skills, can not only hold off, but utterly destroy a larger and more powerful opponent.

The Master of the Department of Research had been correct when she surmised that the spells cast by the rebels—the Falcons—were comparatively weak. She was not correct, however, in assuming that the power-heavy Dragon spells would blast through them, as would have happened had they been other Dragon-cast, *rewhah*-laden spells. Though it was entirely defensive, *rewhah*less magic had every advantage over magic that had to deal with a powerful backlash.

A shield cast using stolen energy—a Dragon-type shield—was a bubble of magic that surrounded the potential target. It had to be a bubble because the magic would do harm to anyone or anything it touched. But this meant that, if an attacker could penetrate the bubble, the target that lay beneath would find itself defenseless.

Falcon shields didn't work that way. They were drawn from clean magic—magic that could touch, could even penetrate, everything it was set to protect without doing any damage. The Falcon shields had no need to keep anyone out of the Warrens, because the shields penetrated and protected each object and each person within their sphere. Thus the Dragons carrying their spell-birds could enter freely. Their mere presence did not harm, so the shields did not expel them, or the quiescent spell-birds. Because of this, the Dragons thought no shields existed; after all, they only truly understood their own form of shield, and did not know they were not looking for thin, deadly bubbles that would fight their presence. It was an honest enough mistake, born of ignorance. It turned out, however, to be the single worst mistake made in the world of Matrin.

For when the spell-birds came to life within each chosen Warren, the living energy of the shields rose up from underneath each spell-bird and pushed. Gently, gently—but with irrevocable, unstoppable firmness.

The spell-birds seemed briefly to come to life. As their inner workings summoned the spells and set them in motion, and thus as the spell-birds became a danger, the Falcon shields moved them to a place where they would not pose a danger to Warrens or Warreners. The spell-birds rose into the air, wings fluttering, and soared in long, curving arcs—over Warren walls.

Out beyond the shields intended to contain the spell-birds' damage, out into the beautiful glittering white cities, the spellbirds toppled. They fell into cities beneath the sea. They landed outside the boundaries of the Warrens on each of Matrin's continents, and on the island of Glavia that was the cradle of civilization, home to the mother city of the Empire, Oel Artis.

A beautiful white glow radiated from each of the birds, but the glow could only be seen for an instant. Then the hard earth turned liquid and each spell-bird turned to liquid with it. This thick, crystal-clear fluid spread out and down, silently, absorbing and converting everything it touched into more of the same. Roads and buildings and people collapsed into each puddle, which became a pond, which became a lake. In perfect circles, the fluid expanded, devoured, expanded, always adding to the wave that forced the clear, viscous fluid not just downward, but outward. With each human devoured by the spell, the Dragon magic increased its strength and its speed.

The force of the magic as it pushed outward lifted mounds—and then mountains—of earth and debris before it, piling ground and masonry and scrambling people upward and outward in a roiling, churning, screaming mass. As the mountains built along the outer circle, they dissolved into the liquid on the inner circle. The roar of heaving, sliding earth—the grinding of the bones of Matrin—and the cries of the people trying desperately to get to safety, signaled the start of the next phase of the disaster.

The second phase of the nightmare spawned itself from the wash of the first. The *rewhah* birthed from the destruction of lives, the stealing and binding of flesh and bone, blood and will, and most of all soul—which was never meant to be bound by anything—built into storms than ran just behind the leading edges of the spreading, sprawling seas.

If the energy of the spreading seas was invisible, the effects of the *rewhah* could be seen by anyone. The *rewhah* storms rose like fiery clouds, upward in billowing, spiraling fury, outward with the crack of thunder and the flash of lightning, and they transformed all they touched. The cities in the air were no havens, nor were the aircars that floated above the ground, for the *rewhah* storms hit them, and tore through them, and left everyone within them twisted, transformed, transmuted . . . irrevocably Scarred. Those whom the *rewhah* storms did not devour and char into dust outright, they left monstrous. Anyone suspended above the maelstrom, thus changed, was not even then free—for the shields cast by the Falcons increased in intensity relative to the onslaught of the nightmare raging around them, and as they protected all those within the Warrens, they cut off all magical power to those outside the Warrens. The cities fell silent for an instant as every magical device ceased to function at once. So outward, in those portions of floating cities where the liquefaction spells had not yet hit, the screaming started as the cities dropped without grace to the ground below. And below, more screaming, as those who heard the whistling wind of the falling cities and looked up in time recognized the disaster that they could not escape.

No one suffered long in the flesh, however, for the wizard-cast seas grew at a pace far faster than a man could run—faster even than most aircars could fly. Mothers and fathers, daughters and sons, innocent and guilty, pure and evil, all became fodder that fed the swelling seas, the blazing storms.

From sea-birth to spell-stop, no spell-set ran for more than half of one hour. In that time, each expanded either to the predetermined maximum perimeter or to the point where it ran out of human life upon which to feed itself. But though each of the seas came to a shuddering, careening halt, nothing stopped the *rewhah* storms that the seas fed. Towering now up to the extreme edge of Matrin's atmosphere, blazing like infernos, these monster storms blasted outward across the surface of the world, wreaking havoc. In places two of them would intersect, and at the point where they intersected the storm would die out. In places, the expanding circle would thin out, and so some patches of the planet were spared. One massive storm tore up to the western coast of Strithia, and the magic of the Strithians diverted it southward; it met storms coming up from the southeastern coast of Strithia, and the whole blazing nightmare devoured itself.

Each of the greatest cities in the Empire of the Hars Ticlarim—as well as the Empire itself—died in that half-hour hell. Those cities and the surrounding areas had housed between them nearly three hundred fifty million free citizens. All but a few of those people, whether instantly dissolved into the mage-spawned seas, or first twisted by the *rewhah* and then tossed down into the crystalline depths, died within that first half hour.

Beyond the circles of first-spell destruction, the paths of the *rewhah* changed or killed every living thing within twenty-five leagues of the edge of any soul-sea. Beyond that, the *rewhah* storms thinned and took erratic paths, so that some places were spared entirely from the devastation, while the storms twisted others into nightmares beyond recognition.

More than a billion people died in the *rewhah* storms. And twice that many lived but had reason to wish they hadn't.

Even in the places spared from the touch of the *rewhah* storms, though, everything changed. Because of the massive and deadly rise of ambient magic, the Falcon shields in every Warren in Matrin shut the Warrens down tight. Dragon magic, which in the cities untouched by the spell-birds and the *rewhah* storms could have sustained those cities as they had always been, died suddenly and without warning. Cities built on air toppled, crushing everything that lay beneath them. Cities under the sea drowned, and with those undersea wonderlands, every free inhabitant. And even those places uncrushed and undrowned suffered, for all magical transportation, all magic-based water delivery and plumbing, all magic-augmented food services and farms—everything that depended on magic; in short, everything—stopped dead. In those parts of the world which lay in darkness, the sudden death of light felt absolute and terrifying. Everywhere, the abrupt cessation of industry, transportation, entertainment—civilization—held in its echoes the whispering death of the world as it had been.

In the Warrens themselves, the situation was, in most cases, better, at least for a while. The Dragon shields worked in reverse, protecting the Warrens that were supposed to be the focus of all the Dragons' destructive power. But those shields could not survive the universal shutdown of Dragon magic when the *rewhah* storms erupted, and they died. The Falcon spells protected the Warrens, but not the ground beneath them. So the mage-born seas burrowed under each Warren as well as encircling it, and those Warrens aboveground became in mere moments floating bubbles in the centers of hellish, outward-racing seas.

The Warrens in undersea cities destroyed by spell-birds floated upward, their Falcon magic protecting them, holding them together. Those in undersea cities not destroyed, however, stayed trapped beneath the surface of the sea, their inhabitants now awake, foodless, with dwindling air supplies and the utter, awful darkness of their final grave the last thing any of them ever saw.

Afterward, survivors whispered that half the world had died that day and that half had been changed. It was not so many, but the civilized peoples had forgotten how to live in hostile places, and of the many who survived the *rewhah* storms as true humans, only a few would live to see the end of the first year after the destruction of the Wizards' War.

Faregan left the meeting excited. He did not go to the observation of the Warrens' destruction with the Dragons of the Council—he didn't really care to watch what would, from the outside, be a lot of nothing. Instead he went home to his collection, to his pretty little girls and boys, some of whom he'd kept suspended in time for fifty years. He thought he would take them out and play with them while he waited for the news that the Warrens were no more.

The blank space in the center of his collection mocked him; he still didn't have Jess. He would never have Jess. But now no one else would have her, either. He felt . . . fulfilled, as if he had accomplished something both difficult and worthwhile. As if, in guaranteeing her destruction and the destruction of something that had been important to her, he'd won a long and difficult game.

And such a game demanded a reward, he thought.

Perhaps the destruction of his collection. He could start a new one afterward, and it would never be tainted by an empty space at the center.

Yes. He would break all of them, one at a time or maybe in pairs—at least for the small, weak ones.

He reached for sweet little Jherrie, who had been nine for nearly fifty years, whom he had healed of lethal wounds a hundred times, and whispered, "Today we finish our game, darling."

And then he heard a roar.

He waved a hand and murmured, "Windows clear," and his spell turned his walls to windows. In three directions he saw blue sky, and the perfection of the sea, and the Belows in the hazy distance, with a light scattering of clouds racing beneath him.

In the fourth . . .

He screamed at the pillar of fire that blocked out the earth and the sky, that exploded out from where he stood in all directions, that devoured the world. He had time only for that one scream and then the fire was upon him, and pain ate him and tore him and ripped him to pieces—deformed him and flung him to the ground even as the magic all around him died; and his toys, his dolls, his playthings, broke free from the prison in which he had held them. They fought toward him— but the *rewhah* that destroyed him destroyed them, too.

Bad became worse, as all magic-driven power in Oel Artis Travia died. With a screech of ripping whitestone, the city toppled into the soul-sea beneath, and the soul-sea consumed it and everyone in it. To the last atom, to the last soul.

Faregan became aware. Aware of who he was, of what he was, of his death, of the screaming horror of every other soul mingled with his. And in the instant that he became aware, the souls that had been his playthings for so long became aware of him.

But now each of them was his equal in size, in strength. And all of them together were more than his equal in rage.

People create their own hells. Faregan would have a very long time to regret all the effort he had put into building his.

Chapter 27

f Oel Artis, and of the glorious island Glavia, upon which the Jewel of Time had been set like a diamond in emerald, nothing remained. The circle that spun out from the heart of the island devoured it whole, and in its place left nothing but a pathetic Warren bobbing in the center of a sea of damned souls.

Magic birthed the seas in half an hour, and magic sent the *rewhah* storms tearing across the surface of the world and twisting along the floor of the sea for half a day. Such a little slice of time, such an insignificant percentage when weighed against the life of the whole of the world of Matrin. Matrin was one world when it started, and someplace else entirely when it heaved to its dying close.

In the shocked silence that followed the storms, twenty-seven seas of souls cried out to the gods for vengeance. But if the gods heard, they did not choose to answer. Or perhaps it was that they had worked so hard trying to save something beautiful of the world they had once loved, and their power was spent.

Do gods ever tire?

What had the gods been doing while their world and worshipers were run to ruin?

In the remains of Cachrim, in Ynjarval, not far from where the storm from the west and the storms from the east smashed into each other to their mutual destruction, creatures, sprawled on the ground as if dead, began to wake and to move through the unscathed streets. Furred, heavy-bodied, with flexible ears and mobile faces, they did not look like accidents of magic. They had a strange beauty, a solid grace that had nothing of the human about it, but that did not lack for that.

They tried to speak to each other in their remembered tongue, but their new mouths could not make the sounds their old mouths could. They looked for food, but discovered that their new stomachs did not hunger for the same things that their old stomachs had. They could communicate, but with difficulty.

No matter. They lived, they survived, and if they were distraught by their loss of humanity, still, these new bodies functioned. They had senses humans had never known. They offered . . . promise.

Far to the north, a mad and sobbing sea replaced both a beautiful city and a lovely lake. And in the steep, stark hills piled up around its perimeter, still smoking from the explosive power of the spell-blast that had created them, creatures with skin dark as midnight, skin that glistened with gemstone colors, with hair that floated like feathers around their faces, clung together in weeping clusters, and then, as they realized the nightmare had passed and that they had survived, pulled away, and began trying to determine who among those who survived were family, and who friends, and who enemies.

West, to the chain of islands spun like a necklace from Manarkas to Arim, where, rising out of the massed dead, the few survivors flexed taloned fingertips and admired sleek, striped fur, and felt dagger canines at the corners of their mouths. Still capable of running on two feet, but now also flexible enough to drop to all fours to pursue prey, they grinned at each other and coughed the words that they could still shape, and began to hunt those not lucky enough to have been made both beautiful and fast by the will of the gods.

Across the face of the world, in ten thousand different shapes, the living in their myriad forms moved away from the cities that could no longer be home to them, in search of prey, in search of mates, in search of companionship. By the hand of the gods, they found others like themselves. That was the clearest proof that the gods took an interest in the outcome, for *rewhah* on its own is a chaotic force, making changes at random that rarely leave a viable creature at the end, and that would never create breeding populations of viable creatures in territories that might support them.

In the madness of magic run wild, the gods tossed their dice. Millions died, millions changed forever, millions remained unchanged in a world suddenly hostile to them in every way.

The gods' dice landed. The new game began. And life went on.

A light spun through the void, gently brushed into another—two tiny sparks of consciousness that somehow found one another. Luercas, lost and terrified, with no idea of where he was or how he might hope to find his way back to the Mirror of Souls and the gate back to warmth and color and light, suddenly found himself no longer alone. And with this other soul—the soul of Mellayne, who had found a way to adapt to this horrific solitude—he discovered that he could reach out and locate other tiny sparks of thought. His people.

He summoned them—called the first meeting of the Star Council.

Five years, he thought, feeling them moving toward him. Five. Or maybe ten. I can survive this for ten years if I must. Surely I've been here for months already.

In the eternity of cold and dark, Wraith felt a tearing, searing pain, and a scream like a world in agony dug itself into his soul and would not let go. It started, but it did not stop, and it reverberated through him until he thought he would be torn apart by it.

In that scream he saw the face of Matrin as if he stood in the heart of the *rewhah* storms, as if he floated with the lost souls in each of the twenty-seven new seas that held not a drop of water between them, as if he were once again in a Warren among Warreners awake and lost, and now trapped with no way out unless someone came and rescued them. Vodor Imrish showed him everything, all at once, so that his soul experienced all the horrors of the world through the eyes and heart of a god. He was more than one of the tortured, the dying, the scarred, the trapped. He was, for a god's infinity and a single moment, all of them, and it was more than he could bear. In a place where he had no body and should feel no pain, the finger of Vodor Imrish marked him with a remembrance of the suffering of the world, and then, when Wraith was sure he would go mad from the anguish, pushed him away. Wraith spun through freezing, clinging strands of silk into light. Into dawn, above a sea that was as perfect a circle as if it had been drawn by a draftsman's compass.

Jess, beside him, wept.

Patr, across from him, wept.

And, he realized, he, too, wept.

"The death of the world," Patr was repeating between sobs. "The death of the world."

Jess turned her face away, but Wraith turned her around and pulled her close and held her. The two of them reached out to Patr and embraced him, too. Three survivors, adrift in the sky at the end of the world.

Wraith caught his breath after a while, and he and Jess and Patr
moved apart. The sun warmed Wraith's skin. The wind dried his tears.
"We are not done here," he said at last. "We are alive so that we can work.
So that we can gather up the people and take them home."

Patr looked up at him. "The world is dead," he said. "You saw it die.
You felt it die."

Wraith said, "Not all of it. This is what Solander meant when he gave
me the Prophecies, when he said:

*From the death throes of the Dragons the True People will be scat-
tered, and set upon by wolves and bears hungry for their blood, hungry for their destruction. The weak will fall, and the brave will falter,
but the Falcons will gather them, and guard them, strong and weak,
and take them home.*

*'For these are my people, the True People,' says the god Vodor Im-
rish, 'And I am not yet done with them.'"*

Patr's harsh laugh sounded like a slap in the face. "*You* wrote that. Do
you think you'll fool me with 'prophecies of Vincalis'?"

Wraith looked at him calmly and said, "Should we let them die?"

Patr, who seemed to have been expecting some other response, said,
"What?"

"Should we let them die? The people trapped in the Warren we're
hovering over right now, that's floating in this wizard circle? The ones in
the little towns surrounded by . . ." He shrugged. "Surrounded by the
lost and the damned? The Scarred? They will die, you know. Most of
them have no weapons, no skills. They aren't the Kaan, who will be able
to pick up their lives today as if nothing had happened. If any of the
Kaan are left. They aren't the Gyru-nalles. They're city dwellers, magic-
dependent." Wraith shrugged. "If I wrote the prophecies, what of it? You
felt the hand of a god. You know we act as servants to a will greater than
our own. It's not as if I pretend guidance from some false force to give
myself power."

He felt a tug in his mind, and without knowing why he did so,
Wraith turned away from Patr and looked down at the sea below them.
An aircar hovered over the floating bubble that held a Warren within it,
and Wraith could see that the bubble had started moving—in great
haste—toward solid ground. He could feel the spells that were being cast
to send that bubble—and twenty-six others like it—to safety. Move, he
thought, in unison with the soft pull of voices in his head. Move, by my

will, by my bones and blood, flesh and soul. *Move.* He realized he felt magic, that it now coursed in his veins as strongly as his own blood.

The touch of a god, he thought—and felt an instant of searing pain beneath his breastbone. He couldn't breathe, and, gasping, thinking that maybe he had presumed too much and Vodor Imrish was done with him after all, he clawed open his tunic.

The pain stopped. The shock, though, could have killed him. He found a glowing brand there: a mark no bigger than the print of a large thumb, an oval in which a falcon sat perched on a branch, looking outward.

Patr stared at Wraith's chest and said, "I thought you were immune to magic."

"I thought so, too," Wraith agreed. "But not, I imagine, to the touch of a god." He noted a glow beneath Patr's tunic and pointed. "Nor was I the only one touched."

Patr looked down, and opened his tunic, and touched the mark he found there—a secret mark of favor from a god. His finger pressed against it and tears started down his cheeks again.

"Me, too," Jess said.

"You feel it, don't you? Both of you? All of them—all of us—linked together by mind and will and spirit. We have become Falcons . . . and that is something more than I ever imagined it might be."

Jess and Patr nodded.

"Help them, then. Help us. Join your will to ours so that we can save the Warreners."

Together the Falcons, now truly united, mind to mind and soul to soul, brought the Warrens across the raging seas of souls to the havens of dry land.

And as the aircar in which they sat settled on the ground near the beached edge of the Warren they'd rescued, Wraith looked at the mark on his chest, now no longer glowing. The falcon looked toward the future, he thought. Toward the west, where he, in his guise as Vincalis, had been shown a place where humans might live safe from the bears and the wolves of this new age—new bears and new wolves and more, who in their twisted bodies carried the minds of angry, vengeful men.

Safe for a while, anyway. While they grew stronger. While they learned to live as part of the world again. Maybe someday the true men and the new men would find peace between them. Maybe all of Matrin would one day be a good place for everyone. But this was not that day.

They climbed out of the aircar. The other one that had circled with them now moved on—Wraith knew they were headed for another War-

ren. The Warreners would need someone to lead them south, where the
Falcons on this continent had agreed survivors would meet.

Wraith led Patr and Jess into the Warren, through Vincalis Gate, now
toothless following the death of Dragon wizardry. Wraith thought he
would find people panicked, mute, lost. But instead he found them already gathering up anything that would serve as weapons, standing in
lines facing the gate—men, women, and children. All pale, under-
dressed, hugely obese, but with awareness in their eyes, and fierce determination.

"Of course," he whispered. "All the ones who weren't born in
there—the outlanders, the political prisoners . . . the criminals . . ." He
winced and glanced sidelong at Patr. But outsiders in the Warren didn't
explain everything. It didn't explain the calm, the fact that everyone
looked ready to face what lay beyond. He knew some of these people
had to be native Warreners, and they should have been terrified and
helpless—but even they looked clear-eyed, confident, and somehow capable. How could that be?

A red-haired man marched along the lines, calling out, "You who
have names, stay on the far side of the line. You without names must
raise your hands and I will give them to you. No person steps through
those gates without a name. We Warreners deserve names. We are people, and we will live like people, and die like people."

He touched a girl's hand. "You're Brown." And a boy's hand. "You're
Tallboy." A man, weary and stooped. "You're Courage." He stopped by
the man, and touched him, and said, "We're both Warreners born, you
and I—but now we're free. Our souls and our flesh are our own again;
the monsters that devoured us are gone. You can feel it. Believe, man! Believe. We're people now, and all of eternity is ours." The weary man nodded and managed a small smile, and the leader moved on, again giving
names. "You're Hunter . . . you're Copper . . . you're . . ." He stopped in
front of a gawky, rail-thin boy who didn't fit with the others—who
looked lost and starved and broken in ways none of these others were.
"You have no name?" he asked the child. The boy shook his head. "You're
from the Warrens?" The boy nodded. And the red-haired man smiled
and said, "I have just the name for you. Your name is Wraith." He leaned
in close to the boy and said, "It's the best name of all. I was saving it for
someone special."

Wraith couldn't believe what he'd just heard. He stared at the mountain of human flesh who had just said that, and tried to equate the man

before him with the skinny red-haired boy he'd known so long ago. He couldn't believe it, but it couldn't be anyone else.

He pushed past the people crowding toward the gate and the promise of freedom, squeezed along the wall, and came up behind the red-haired man. He had a lump in his throat, and tears blurred his eyes so badly that for a moment he couldn't see at all. Wraith touched the man's arm, and when the Warren leader turned, said, "Smoke? Is it you?"

A long moment of silence. Then, "Oh, gods. Wraith!"

They hugged, and Smoke finally pushed him away and stood staring at his face, nodding. "You look the same."

"You don't," Wraith said, and laughed a little, and wiped the tears from his eyes with a quick swipe of the back of his hands.

"No," Smoke agreed.

They stood for a moment, lost for words to bridge the gap of years and nightmares.

Then Smoke said, "Even when I was Sleeping, I knew you'd come back." Smoke's eyes shifted left and down, and his smile turned disbelieving. "Jess? It can't be. You brought Jess with you, too?"

"It's me, Smoke." She rested her hand on Wraith's forearm and said, "Wraith moved a world to get here."

"I felt it move," Smoke said. And then he turned to Wraith. "Thank you. Thank you for not forgetting about me—about us."

"Never," Wraith said. He felt Jess's hand slide into his, and tightened his fingers around hers. When he looked down at her, she was smiling up at him; Wraith saw tear stains on her cheeks.

"You were right about the Warrens," she told him.

He nodded, and kissed her forehead. "I know."

Beyond Vincalis Gate, a new and frightening world waited. But the Warreners were still alive in spite of everything an entire civilization had thrown against them. Having conquered odds so terrible, Wraith had to think these people had a chance to win it all—the world and everything in it.

Jess whispered, "And what about you and me?"

"We have all the time in our lives to figure that out." He put an arm around her shoulder and pulled her close.

And the first Warreners stepped through Vincalis Gate and into the wilds beyond.

About the Author

Holly Lisle, born in 1960, has been writing fantasy and SF novels full-time since November 30, 1992. Prior to that, she worked as an advertising representative, a commercial artist, a guitar teacher, a restaurant singer, and for ten years as a registered nurse specializing in emergency and intensive care. Originally from Salem, Ohio, she has also lived in Alaska, Costa Rica, Guatemala, North Carolina, Georgia, and Florida. She and Matt are raising three children and several cats.

She maintains a large readers' and writers' Web site at www.hollylisle.com/ and offers a free irregularly published writers' newsletter, plus a readers' mailing list, active readers' and writers' communities, games and contests, sneak peeks at new work, and much, much more.

Holly's e-mail address is holly@hollylisle.com. She reads every letter and e-mail, though she cannot promise to answer all of them.